MEGA DEATH

TORY QUINN

WITH MARIE VIBBERT

The author of this book is solely responsible for the accuracy of all facts and statements contained in the book. This is a work of fiction. Names, characters, places, events, and incidents are either the product of the author's imagination or used in an entirely fictitious manner. Any resemblance to actual persons, living or dead, is entirely coincidental.

This book is printed on acid-free paper.

Published by:
Level 4 Press, Inc.
13518 Jamul Drive
Jamul, CA 91935
www.level4press.com

Library of Congress Control Number: 2019943896
ISBN: 978-1-64630-066-2
eBook ISBN: 978-1-64630-067-9

Printed in the United States of America

Other books by Tory Quinn

MINDBORG
TWILIGHT OF THE GODS
TRANQUILITY
FAILS
PERFECTION
ALTERED
KRUEGER

DEDICATION

To everyone who wanted to die when their team lost, and most especially to fans of the Cleveland Browns. WOOF.

1

Megan laughed as she plowed her elbow into a man's cheek. Teeth clacked like breaking ceramic but she was already pivoting, driving past him. He was nothing but a sweaty surface to spring off of as the ball came, almost in slow motion. She turned her hip at the last second. Nine pounds of solid rubber hit with bone-jarring pain. She left her opponent on the ground and charged up-court where the other players were already diving for the ball. Her bare toes dug into hard clay and grit. Vine-choked ruins crowded the court, and two giant gold numbers floated in the cloudless sky: a six and a seven. A tie would reset the score to zero, and her opponents were passing the ball back and forth over her useless teammate. Megan threw herself forward, sliding to get between them. The virtual ground was real enough, burning along her shin and elbow, but she got there. She pushed hard off the dirt with one powerful arm and hit the ball toward her own goal, where her teammate had gotten to his hands and knees.

"Score, damn you!" she shouted, and he reacted, moving in slow motion. The man she'd knocked down earlier was coming in for a tackle as the ball sailed; her teammate wasn't going to make it.

Megan's right knee complained as she rolled and pushed her body to its limits to get there. Sweat was streaming down her legs, spattering into the dirt as she lunged with a primal cry. Grime and flesh met, her arms bare on his legs, his muscles straining against hers as she hauled him against her chest. She heard the air leave his lungs as he hit hard, and then she heard the cheesy mariachi music. She looked up, panting heavily, at a sky darkened to night to show off the sparks of red and green fireworks around a giant 6–8.

Underneath it read a message: Upload Game Record to Central?

Megan returned to her body with the fatigue of climbing out of a swimming pool after a hundred laps. In front of her was the game menu, off perspective now as the neural link separated. In the game her sweat had smelled of jungle air and good, clean exertion. Here it had a sour, confined stink. She kicked her way out of the leg harness and pushed open the pod with angry force. The high never lasted.

"Damn, Mori, you are intense!" Her opponent, the last man she had tackled, was sitting on the edge of his pod, panting. The legs she had hugged to her chest now splayed in front of him. He worked in the university library. An English major, she thought. Like her, he was glistening with sweat. Everyone was, the men and women she had just played against, popping out of their pods at their own speeds, down the length of the gym. People she had thought of only as obstacles or assistance transformed back into the girl who led the intramural club, the guy from the dorm. Slowly the smell of jungle and sweat sharpened into rubberized flooring and industrial cleaner. The never-ending clang of weights from the next room grounded her in where she was, the campus gym. She was an education graduate student, not an Aztec warrior. Alas.

"After that bout, Central's giving us top odds for the season," the intramural girl said.

Megan made a noncommittal sound to get out of the conversation before it started.

She limped to the shower, feeling pain in her hip from those hard hits and the sting of abrasions on her shin. Did the pods really have to convey that much realism? She peeled her leggings off to reveal a long swath of sore, puffy, red skin.

The shower felt amazing though, and it was so good to feel the exertion in her limbs, the weakness that told the tale of strength. What had she been so angry about at the end of the game? She couldn't remember.

It was a bright fall day on campus, with a sky so blue the orange leaves seemed to vibrate against it, and the glittering lines of the wireless power grid were visible. Megan hitched her gym bag higher on her shoulder. It was one her grandma, Oba-chan, had brought her from Japan. She tried to remember where she was supposed to go now. Didn't she have class after her usual game? Or was it work? A campus tour guide walked by, backward, talking cheerily to a crowd of visitors who craned their necks at the faux-colonial architecture like they were in a museum. A few tennis-ball-sized camera drones hovered over the crowd like eager pests: distant families taking the campus tour via pod. Megan pushed her way past and into the throng of students bustling along the walkway.

Through a break in the crowd, she spied an arm raised, waving to her. First, she saw the warm brown eyes, the loving smile, then his broad shoulders in that sweater she loved to cuddle, and finally his other arm straining low . . . ah!

"Ciera!" Megan called to her daughter. She was so tiny! But doing so well keeping up with her father on the path, holding tightly to his hand like she ought to.

Ciera caught sight of Megan and wriggled out of her father's hold, running with full toddler speed, her tiny white Mary Janes pounding the pavement. "Mommy!"

Megan laughed, so relieved, so happy. How could she have

forgotten she was meeting her special girl for lunch? "That's my girl! That's my athlete!" She crouched and received the three-year-old missile, so perfect against her heart. Ciera smelled of strawberry shampoo and dress starch and that special, deep-down scent that was just her. Megan knew mothers loved to see genius in every test score, but wasn't Ciera's hug strong for her age?

A tweed trouser leg bumped her shoulder. The crowd was pressing in. Had a large class just let out? She looked up to see where Greg had gone to and was startled to see him stumble as hurrying students bumped into him left and right. Greg was strong, a powerful rower since undergrad, so it was strange to see him almost knocked forward off his feet as someone's shoulder hit him. He was trying to swim through the crowd toward Megan, but they were closing in, cutting off her view of him.

"Mommy? Mommy, that's too tight," Ciera said, and pushed against her with her sweet little hands.

Megan loosened her grip. Something was wrong. The crowd was milling. Angry voices were rising, and she saw people pushing each other on purpose. A knee knocked into her back, and Megan held her arms over Ciera, shouting, "Why don't you watch where you're going?"

A mousy girl with thick glasses punched a pimply boy in the face inches in front of Megan. The teen boy threw a stack of books, missing his opponent but clipping Megan's shoulder. The girl tackled the boy to the ground, her kicks causing her tweed skirt to hike high. Her glasses flew off and Megan saw them only a second before they were stepped on. All around her, fists and elbows were moving. The sky darkened.

"Mommy? Mommy!" Ciera's voice was muffled, but her panic was unmistakable.

Megan struggled to make room around herself, pushing legs and bodies. Ciera was gone! No, there she was, reaching toward Megan as the crowd closed in around her, pulling her away. "No!" Megan threw herself forward. Her fingertips grazed Ciera's and slipped free. "No!

Someone! Someone help! My baby!" A denim-clad knee pushed her down. She struggled to get up.

Ciera screamed.

Megan couldn't move forward, the heavy woven strap of her gym bag holding her tight. She tugged hard, but more than one pair of boots was on it. She slipped free from the strap and elbowed the body nearest her hard in the ribs. "Back off! Ciera! Ciera, baby! Stay still! Stay low and still. Mommy's coming."

Her thighs strained as she waded forward, pushing, kneeing, crawling under tussling figures. Wasn't this where Ciera had screamed? The weight of the crowd fell in on Megan, limbs like piles of rocks dumping endlessly, crushing her. Was that another scream?

"Ciera! Get off! Goddamnit! I'll kill you! Where the fuck is my daughter?!"

Megan woke like she was falling from a height, her limbs spasming, something heavy in one hand. She windmilled her arms, flailing against a clinging sheet, hitting a post, and finally stumbling to her feet. Where? How? What?

Slowly she became aware of her surroundings. A strange bedroom. Streetlights cast pale beams through blinds across a midnight scene. Two virtual home kits were tangled on the floor like discarded clothes. On the bed, a naked man was curled, one muscular arm over his head, his flank bare behind a pillow he clutched in front of him like a shield as she dragged the sheet from over him. "Jesus," he said.

Megan didn't recognize him. Her heart, racing like mad, started to slow. Under the tensed muscles, the fight-or-flight adrenaline, she felt the lassitude of sex. In her hand she held a smooth glass sphere, a paperweight. Imbedded in the swirling depths were the words "San Jose Monsters—Regional Champions 2110."

Shaking, she put it back on the bedside table. A smart-mirror on the wall caught her in its area and rotated her head, thinking she wanted to see how she looked. She turned away quickly, ashamed to see herself, but caught a glimpse anyway of her rendering, hollow on the back side. She kicked the sheet. The leg and arm sleeves from the home VR sets lay like a pile of shed snakeskins. She poked through them with her toes, looking for her panties.

As she stepped into her briefs, the man on the bed recovered. "Are you okay?" He pulled the sheet up off the floor and wrapped it around himself. "Do you need to talk?"

What was there to say? Another one-night stand she wouldn't see again. It was a shame, he was as fit as she was, all sculpted muscle. The nightmare faded, and she could remember where she was, how she'd gotten there, after a pick-up game, they'd done Ulama, too, but half the players had been garbage, too easy. She still had energy to burn and there he was, coming out of his pod with his shirt clinging to him, and she had invited herself home with him. He had been strong and sure in bed, driving the thoughts from her head just the way she wanted. Was his name Derek? Dirk?

Derek-maybe-Dirk stood. "I don't have coffee. . . I know, no one has coffee. Is tea okay? I'll get you a cup." He held his hands out to her like she might attack. "Take it easy, okay?"

Megan found her last piece of clothing and walked out without saying goodbye.

Megan slept maybe twenty minutes in her own bed, but the nightmare came back, so it was with the empty-headed blankness of insomnia that she pushed herself through her favorite running course, up and down the steepest hills in her small, rural California town. Central painted the course for her in holographic arrows only she could see, colored to reflect the time of day. All around the city, other joggers would have their own routes, personalized and optimized. Thanks to Central, half the city could be jogging and never cross paths.

The sun just started to streak hazily through the scrubby pines and eucalyptus. Bicycles and scooters rested in their attached garages, no one on the streets to bother her as she pounded the empty pavement. The world was there to be chewed up by her feet and turned into strength. Back around the long block, she passed a slacking jogger and turned sharp at the corner on a single foot-plant, just to do it. She felt her endurance sapping, the last of her strength, and that was the sign to push harder, to squeeze that extra bit of vitality from her quaking muscles. She turned up the steepest street at the end of the block and pumped her legs, punishing her body to feel the strength of chopping her way against gravity.

She had to be fast. Fast enough to catch . . . fast enough.

"Ugh. Wait up. Megan!" A thin voice, gasping, far behind her, coming from a slight, bent-over figure with sweat-damp metallic-purple hair and rounded, shuddering shoulders. "You're killing me."

Megan didn't wait up. If Lola took her training seriously, she'd push herself. Sure, the pods gently enhanced performance—they fixed physics so you could jump ten percent higher, throw ten percent farther—but every player had to play with their own muscles. Megan powered her way to the top of the street and only slowed when she reached the highest point in the town, where the street took a sharp turn before switchbacking its way down the other side of the hill. She jogged in place, the closest to rest she'd allow herself, and measured just how far behind Lola had lagged this time. She could barely see her little sister jogging desultorily way down at the start of Buenavista Street. Her ring display overlaid her eyesight, easily marking the distance, and provided a helpful link to Lola's fitness profile on Central. Just like her sister to share personal information with the world.

Running downhill with exhausted legs was a challenging exercise in control. For this reason, and no other, Megan turned her back on the gentle switchbacks and took the steep path back to her sister. Her knees quaked in a dangerous way. She imagined the last ounces of weakness draining from her like the sweat she left in drips behind her.

With a block left between them, Lola stopped pretending to run and shouted, "You suck!"

Megan breathed out with every other step, panting through her exhaustion. When she got within two strides of Lola, she said, "Beat me home or I won't let you run with me again."

"Hello, Central? I'd like to report child abuse," Lola retorted, but she also pivoted and followed Megan.

"You're seventeen; you're not a child."

"Try telling that to Mom and Dad."

Megan gritted her teeth, the best smile she could do without letting up her pace. She always knew she'd be good at motivating a . . . a younger person.

Lola hadn't done the full route, and had teenage energy on her side, but she wasn't a serious athlete. She didn't train, she played. Megan could beat her.

The whole point had been to give Lola an achievable goal, but now Megan didn't want to lose. She forced her exhausted legs into a sprint. She would humiliate her little sister. That was a completely normal thing to want to do.

But Megan hadn't slept, and she had run an extra mile on the warm-up before she lapped Lola on the long block and went up the hill. Her lungs burned. The sun came up over the hills and instantly the air lost its coolness, became harsher in her throat. The house was just another block downhill.

Lola panted at her heels, chanting in time with her footfalls, "Kill. My. Sister. Kill. My. Sister."

They were almost there. Megan found some energy deep inside herself and pushed the last half block at a full sprint. Lola roared behind her like an enraged warrior kitten.

They hit the last sidewalk slab almost in step, and Lola threw herself dramatically on the ground.

"Cool down. Don't stop cold." Megan paced the front of the house, feeling her pulse and checking her stats on her ring. Speed good, blood sugar good. She wasn't building muscle, though. Body fat was way too low. She'd forgotten to eat again. Who had time to eat enough?

Lola sat up, and after a theatrical sigh, got to her feet. "You don't *let* me run with you, by the way. You think it's a coincidence I'm always up when you are? I set a motion tracker on your bedroom door."

Megan gaped at her sweet little sister, with her pierced lip and her shock of metallic-purple hair glinting in the sun. The perfect old-fashioned girl. An amateur spy?

Lola gave her such a smirk, like Megan's face had betrayed her as the lamest old person ever to grow old. "If I didn't tag along, you'd forget what it's like to talk to human beings. I'm the only thing keeping you from full-on wandering hermit."

Megan didn't have to listen to this; she knew Lola had an ulterior motive. "So you aren't here because you want to be a pod player?"

Lola touched her toes with lazy ease. "Like you don't want me to be a pod player. So we're both here for that, and by coincidence I'm helping my sad older sister with actual in-person interaction. For a change."

Megan briefly considered telling her kid sister she'd had a one-night stand, but that felt like it would be too immature for even a teenager to take seriously.

The ring's heads-up told Megan that her heart rate was back in the "healthy active" zone. She was ready to work out again. Three hours of hard cardio already this week. She blinked to tell the eye-motion control not to upload the award badge to Central. "Twenty minutes for breakfast, and then we're going back out for cross-training."

Lola's arms hung limply by her sides. "This is why you have no friends."

When they went inside, Megan's father was in the kitchen, juicing oranges. "You girls are up early! Big plans?" He looked at Megan, specifically, with mixed worry and hope. She avoided his gaze and went to the fridge to get a pitcher of protein milk.

"Megan has the 'kill my sister with exercise' plan." Lola dropped onto a stool at the kitchen counter.

"You survived." Megan poured two tall glasses and slid one over to her sister.

Lola made a face at the drink and pushed it away. "Can't you take me to the gym sometime and let me plug in? Everyone I know trains in the pod, not killing themselves running up hills."

Megan pushed the drink back toward Lola. "Everyone you know is a teenager and not destined for the big leagues."

"Whoa, now." Dad turned off the juicer. "No one is playing in those dangerous games. Those electric shocks have killed people, and I'm not even talking about that horrible tournament where people die on purpose."

"It was a figure of speech," Megan quickly said. Her father didn't need to know she'd wagered worse than electric shocks on games. It was fine when she did it; she always won.

"It's just school league, Daddy," Lola said. "You know athletics looks great on college applications. You want me to go to college, don't you? Otherwise I'll be living on basic income. You'll never get rid of me." She was teasing, but the "like Megan" part went unspoken. She picked up the protein drink and took a sip, immediately grimacing at the taste.

Megan thought better of saying anything. Lola only called their father "Daddy" when she was asking for something.

Dad poured a glass of orange juice for each of them. "It's all well and good that you watch and root for your heroes, and I don't mind that you're keeping fit, but you should be preparing your mind for a rewarding life, not your body for games that demand the losing team be hurt."

“It isn’t always pain,” Megan said, quickly and calmly before Lola screwed this up. “People wager chores, possessions, even money. And it’s all monitored by Central. They wouldn’t let kids bet anything permanent.”

“Until you get to the ‘big leagues.’” Dad said it like it was a euphemism for something awful.

Megan’s watch beeped. “That’s twenty. Come on, we have weight training. Don’t want to waste a Saturday!”

As Megan and Lola ran out the door, their father called, “Just be safe!”

They both mimicked his voice, repeating the line as they jogged up the street. In the innocence of the moment, Megan’s heart squeezed. It felt like a betrayal. She sped up, leaving her sister behind.

2

Lola's big sister used to be the absolute best. Like a grown-up, but on her side, taking her out for ice cream and teaching her how to unlock cheat codes. Now Megan hardly left her room, and if she was unlocking anything, it was achievements in isolation. She always wore the same worn out exercise clothes, her greasy hair pulled back like she didn't want to be bothered with it.

And how could she keep running so fast? "Seriously, though," Lola gasped, catching up, "there are pods at the gym. We can skip those boring burpees and jump right into Ulama, or Javelins, or Swords Knight. I'm never going to make it to the pros lifting chunks of metal."

"No." Megan snapped the word out like a drill sergeant. "The best way to train is in the real world. A strong body can take the punishment, but all the virtual enhancements in the world can't train the brain of a flabby body to move like a fit one. You have to inhabit that strength to use it in the game. It has to be part of you."

Ugh. This was the Megan Mori channel, all day, every day. Work hard, have no life. Lola only put up with it because she remembered the old Megan, the girl with the snarky one-liners and hot boyfriends. She remembered Megan cheering like a maniac, embarrassing her at her first junior high varsity game. The good kind of embarrassed. The game had been something they could share, something they both cared about. Now it was the only thing, the only thread, Lola could use to pull her sister out of whatever it was she was in.

They slowed to a jog on Main Street because Megan finally had to or else risk banging into random people on the sidewalk. Soon after that, they turned into the community gym. It was a big brick building in the old federalist style. It had been a library once, which was why there were brass books for door handles.

A new banner for Team North America was being raised over the check-in desk. Lola hadn't seen this year's design yet. They wouldn't announce the roster until next month, so this was the preview design. Still important, though, as it would set the tone for the season. The message. As of yet, it was a holding pattern on the mesh as two tiny drones lifted it into place. There was the North American logo: an eagle on a cactus that was inside a maple leaf colored green, red, and blue. It always filled Lola with excitement.

Megan tugged Lola forward. "I can't believe you're even looking at that garbage. They put it up every four years."

The check-in clerk nodded in agreement. "It'd be different if they ever had a chance of winning."

"It's a rebuilding opportunity!" Lola couldn't believe this disloyalty. "Last time's team was unfairly handicapped. If India had been playing, they'd never have lost in the first round. It was fishy how quick they disqualified her for bronchitis. I've played with pneumonia!"

The clerk held up his hands. "Hey, I care. Go team. I want to be able to afford coffee again, or not have to apply to see my grandma in Colombia. I'm just being realistic. We lose, we suffer. And we will lose. You need pods?"

"Gym floor only," Megan said before Lola could seize the opening. She passed her ring over the sensor and led the way to the weight rack at the back of the gym. No one ever went back there. Another way Megan was weird. How could a hard-core pod gamer not care about the national team, the nation's place in the international order, the national pride? But then, Megan didn't seem to care about anything these days.

She didn't care that Lola was quietly checking Central to see if the odds for Team North America were any better today than yesterday. Ugh. They were worse. Another National League player had announced no plans to try for the World League. She closed her connection and waved for Megan's attention. "Okay, how are you ruining my life today?"

Megan picked up two enormous hand weights from the very end of the weight rack. "Pick a set of hand weights. Heavy as you can. We're doing One-Legged Romanian dead lifts."

"That's not even a real exercise! You made that up!"

"You want to play, you have to work." Megan started doing one-legged toe touches with her weights.

What the actual hell?

Lola picked the smallest weights on the rack and tried to copy her sister's motions. As she bent over, her back leg wavered, and she nearly toppled before she touched the weights to the ground. Okay, now she had to get back up. Easy. Wobble, almost fall, flail, stand. "One!"

Megan was going like a machine, and her weights were the size of her head. Both sides.

Lola tried her best. Her hamstrings and lower back burned, and she was sure she had only done one real, good dead lift, the rest all being floppy failures where she put her back leg down or didn't quite touch the ground. She did ten attempts on each side and looked up to find that Megan had already switched to a different exercise. Now she was bowing forward and straightening with both feet on the ground and the weights on her shoulders. Lola copied her, and her lower back started really aching.

Then Megan was doing upright rows. Lola couldn't keep up. She gave up on counting and just switched when Megan switched. Lola was drenched in sweat and her arms were quaking. She was turning into pudding.

Megan unceremoniously dropped her hand weights. "Come on, we're moving to the bench press."

It took a second for Lola to catch her breath enough to speak. "Megan, I . . . I need a second."

"Keep up or drop out," Megan said, already on her way to the bench.

Lola swallowed the hurt. She watched Megan load up the bench press with way more weight than Lola could ever dream of lifting. "Um . . . I can't do that."

"You're not going to. You're spotting for me," Megan said, and lay down.

Lola set her hands dutifully under the bar as her sister lifted it from the rest, not that her arms would do anything but bend like broken reeds should Megan drop it. She tried to see some emotion in her sister's concentrating scowl. "What are you even training for? You're not on a team anymore. You wouldn't even go to that tryout I told you about." If Megan would just join a team, she'd have friends to talk to.

Megan didn't answer, only huffed her numbers as she did her set. Lola knew the real answer, though. Her sister needed to be strong. She needed to know that the next time someone tried to take someone from her, she could stop them. Lola wished she could tell Megan she understood, but to do that she'd have to bring up Ciera, and that was not allowed.

Lola fell into her bed. Every part of her body hurt. Her hair follicles, somehow, hurt. She looked at the video poster on the opposite wall. One of her favorites, it replayed a killer ball steal from the 2100 MegaDeath Games. LaTonya Verbeuren slid right under this other guy, twisting with balletic grace and just powering the ball out of his hands. The last time North America made it all the way. It always filled her with hope and inspiration. Except right now. Now she hoped never to move again.

She wished LaTonya hadn't been sacrificed after the humiliating defeat in 2104. She wished that wasn't the last time the North American team made it to the semifinals. Everyone was scared they'd be eliminated again this year. If that happened . . . well, the country would barely survive! It wasn't fair that they had to start over with a new team every time they lost. At least Indía was playing again, and certified bronchitis-free.

The stats-makers didn't share Lola's faith in Indía. According to Central, easily accessed via her ring and displayed on her wall, Lola's high school team had a better shot at the championship.

She groaned and turned over to look at the one wall that didn't have a Team North America poster. That was because it was the wall with the window in it, but still. She wished she had a poster from when Megan played for the Kern County Crusaders. Then she'd see her sister smile. Megan used to smile when she even talked about playing. And when she played? It was the kind of smile that made everyone else join in, even the other team. It was like she couldn't believe how wonderful the world was and that she got to play in it.

That smile hadn't made an appearance in years. Megan used to gush about her job at the research center, but then she simply stopped going to it. She didn't even smile when their dad cooked spaghetti. She seemed to have forgotten that there was anything in the world but Ciera. But Ciera wasn't in the world.

Ciera's sweet, chubby hands, her innocent eyes, yearning for her, reaching for her, receding under a tide of disembodied arms. Megan reached into a sea of gnashing faces after her, alone, weak, so much flotsam rolling on flesh and bones.

She woke drenched in sweat, clutching the sheet to her chest. Another bad dream. She sat up and heard the rip. She'd torn the top of the sheet clean in half in her sleep, and now the tear extended to her knees.

That would need to be fed to the fabber return lines before Dad did the laundry. Otherwise he'd want to ask her what happened. She sighed and got up. She should take the sheet to the fabber and probably take a shower, but her hand was already reaching for her gym bag.

Judging by the darkness outside, there were hours left before the others got up. She stepped into her sneakers and pulled on a sports bra. She was reaching for the door when her mind caught up to her.

Lola set a motion detector?

Megan stepped back, then crept forward, listening. Something was humming in the kitchen, probably the fabber printing ingredients for breakfast. In the other direction, Dad and Mom were snoring in syncopated tandem, her higher wheeze and his deep bass. Megan inched toward the wall she shared with Lola's room, listening. Could a teenager actually be quiet? No, there it was, barely audible through the wall: the heavy breathing of sleep.

Not to take chances, Megan opened her window and lowered her gym bag onto the lawn outside, grateful that in a California ranch-style house, all rooms were on the first floor. She could almost step over the sill. Almost. Her toes kicked the top of the grass while her crotch pressed into the window frame.

She let her weight fall onto that foot and eased her other leg slowly over the ledge. She didn't look back as she jogged to the street.

Behind her, a small light turned on in Lola's room.

The arcade was the one place Megan could find sure relief. Local teams trained there during the day, but at night it was open for pick-ups and anyone wanting to play online. Megan mostly played online against anonymous strangers from as far away from home as she could find. You didn't have to interact with anyone in person at the arcade after hours. There was no clerk, no guard, just the discreet presence of automated security. She slipped into her suit in a dingy cubicle and grabbed the first free pod.

Her body vanished as her vision filled with solicitations to join games in progress or waiting to start. She liked Ulama, it was a classic, but tonight it looked like most people were playing some new game, StarCrush. She felt a knife-edge grin split her face. New meant challenging. She skimmed the stakes. Mostly "sentimental item." She had to skip those; she had thrown out everything when she moved home. One group was betting tattoos. Winners would pick what the losers got. Cute, but she didn't want to have to be creative. Megan liked high stakes. She needed the rush. Ah, there was a good one: a StarCrush game waiting for two more players. Stakes: Level-Four Prolonged Electric Shock. No heart conditions or medical implants allowed.

Game on.

3

Lola checked the weather on Central and scanned for any crime in the area, and then quietly told her device to disable all alarms in the house. Kiko had told her where to download all the best scripts. You couldn't stay on Central's network; it would babysit you to death. There were old maintenance servers out there where once you got in, nothing tried to anticipate your needs and select choices for you. If you knew the name of the program, you could find it. So easy! Now she could just walk out the front door and have the security alarms back in place before she was past the row of decorative rocks her mom liked so much.

Kiko met her at the corner, standing all casually like she was waiting to catch a cab. "Hey, operator."

Kiko called everyone that. She said it was from a movie, but Lola suspected it was just something she heard a cool kid say. Lola smiled in greeting. "You got it?"

Kiko snorted and lifted her jacket to show Lola . . . nothing. There was some paper crammed into an inner pocket, but that was all Lola saw before Kiko pressed the jacket back against herself. "Ye of little faith. Come on, Marty's waiting."

They were doing this at Marty's house because, while he was not the greatest friend on account of being a boy and also having once tried to get Kiko to date him, and when that failed, trying to get Lola to date him, he was worth the annoyance because his parents stayed out all night every Wednesday for "date night."

Also, it was actually a pretty cool house, just down the block, and she heard that they had a new home pod set.

Marty opened the front door grandly, like a butler. "Welcome, ladies. I have prepared a fine repast."

"You're such a dork." Lola smiled and slugged him in the arm.

Marty did her the courtesy of acting like she'd hurt him. "Jeez, okay. Let us retire to the game room." He led the way. The game room was the coolest room in the Ellefson's house. It was as big as the living room in Lola's house and built on the same plan. All their houses had been built at a time when fabrication was, like, really slow, so you couldn't customize things much. You built a house in one shape, and that was it.

Like Lola's living room, Marty's game room had a peaked ceiling and a triangle of windows under it on either side where the wall stopped and was topped with glass. Unlike Lola's living room, there were two game pods, black and sleek and almost as nice as the ones you could rent in the arcade. They sat in front of a stone fireplace that took up the whole back wall. What she thought was the backup to a wireless power and wireless network wasn't; there was a fat, multi-headed cable connected to the pods, the kind that fed directly into the fabber utility lines so you could have organics pumped in to create smells and tastes. You could eat, drink, and—even though it was kinda gross—even relieve yourself when the system was switched on. 24/7 gaming. Woohoo. Gross, Lola thought, but infinitely cool. The lines ran along the wall inside a row of fake stones.

Kiko went straight to the table laid with cheese and cookies. High-quality, not fabbed. So Marty wasn't so bad. Lola went straight to the nearest pod.

"I have also secured . . . libations." Marty produced an old-fashioned domed serving tray that was spidery with tarnish. He whisked the cover off a little clumsily, getting it caught on what was on the tray, causing him to dance sideways and slap the lid back on to prevent whatever was inside from rolling off.

He shrugged. "It's real beer. Like, not the fabber stuff." He set the tray down and lifted the cover more carefully. Four green bottles lay on their sides, perspiring.

"Those are going to fuzz all over when you open them." Lola bent to check the interior of the pod. Interesting. It had a faux leather look to it, but then, you didn't need to sanitize a home pod every time. She ran her hand over the surface. It even felt like leather, but she knew, embedded in the surface were those wonderful hapzils, the nanobots of which represented a single point of sensation—temperature, pressure, texture. This smooth seat could become beach grass or a gentle breeze, springy parquet or a wrestling mat.

Then Lola heard the sound of beer spraying everywhere and Kiko laughing hard. She sighed. "Come on, guys. Let's do what we came here to do! Let's hack into the game!"

Marty held a beer far from himself, foam dripping over his knuckles. "You know, we could get caught."

"People do it all the time." Lola wasn't sure that was true, but it was something she'd heard people say.

Kiko brushed a hand down her jacket. "I have log-in codes to piggyback on two players, Jerry Myers and . . . Indía Thomas!" She looked smugly at Lola, relishing her squeal. This was too good. Too much. Lola could hardly stand it. Her favorite player!

Marty sipped foam from the top of his beer. "Not that I'm saying we're really doing this or anything, but how did you get that? It costs a fortune to watch from inside a top player."

Kiko casually tucked a lock of black hair behind her ear as she leaned against a wall, playing this up like she was a super spy. "If you know where to look, there are lots of people willing to sell part of their ticket. They don't mind sharing, but I guess it's not strictly legal. They even advertise for it on Central, but they have to call it 'time shares.'"

Lola felt a twinge of fear. If they did this, she'd be alone, in India's head, with someone with so little respect for the supreme honor of being there that he'd sell part of it.

Marty fiddled with the paper label on his bottle. "How'd you pay for that, though?"

Kiko rolled her eyes. "Did I say we were buying? We're hacking. We're taking the spot the buyer paid for, and since the ticket owner is expecting someone, they won't know anything is wrong. And since the person we're replacing is doing something illegal, they aren't likely to complain when they can't get in." She spread her hands. "The perfect crime."

Lola took one of the beers and opened it carefully; it bubbled all over anyway, and she had to put her mouth over it while Kiko laughed. She didn't like beer, but her friends did, so she relaxed and tried to stay cool.

Kiko cracked a bottle, and unfairly it did not foam all over her. She looked so smug.

Lola shook her head at the unfamiliar grassy flavor of a real, not fabbed, beer. "Come on, let's do this thing."

"How do we get out?" Marty asked. "I mean, what if the ticket holder's a pervert or something?"

Lola knew the answer to that one. "You're ghosting onto their feed. You don't get the log-in and log-off screen."

Kiko looked annoyed that Lola had answered before she could, but she took a slurp of beer and grinned. "I know you're irresistible, Marty, but you'll just have to let whoever it is chase you around until the game is over. You should be more worried about what happens if we get caught." She strafed them with her gaze, building suspense. "We could all go to jail."

"Or be banned from competing," Marty said. "I know I'm not the best on C-team, but I'm hoping, in college, I'll hit my stride."

"What stride?" Kiko asked, but she nudged Marty to take some of the sting off. Kiko wasn't that great at the games either.

Lola had a more pressing question than what might happen if they got caught. "There are only two pods."

"Of course, it should be ladies first." Kiko unfolded the paper from her coat, revealing a data chip. "Marty can be our lookout."

Marty scowled. "It's my house."

"And I'm the genius who got this working, so I have to go," Kiko said.

They both had a strong claim to going first. Lola felt her chance slipping. "I'll ask my host to log off at halftime? Then we can trade places?" She pleaded with her eyes.

Kiko met her gaze and then looked at Marty. "There's always a halftime." She shrugged. "And maybe we'll want to switch up, anyway. I hear it gets intense!"

Lola didn't wait for more arguments. She pulled open the pod and pushed her legs into the sleeves.

Megan skated on a surface of pure light, having to keep half an eye on all five other players in this free-for-all. Any shadow created a void that you could fall into, hurting yourself against the sharp edge at the least, or plummeting into the abyss below for an automatic forfeit. She caught the edge of her own shadow when she turned too sharply. If that weren't enough drama, big, pulsing star shapes passed slowly overhead, pulling the shadows left and right. The game had started with eight players.

While keeping herself on the light surface, which slid underfoot like wet ice, Megan had to tag other players for points, and the player with the fewest points had seconds to tie with someone or be ejected via a stomach-hurtling fall.

Megan pivoted to avoid a tag and hit the other woman on the calf for a point, but her momentum careened her toward the edge. She scrambled with her hands and feet, her core muscles clenched tight. Still she slid. She flattened her hands against the slick surface. It screamed like glass, heating her palms, and she slowed but didn't stop. She tried to grab the light with her teeth, but they passed right through. Her right foot and then leg slid off over nothing, but she swung hard left and got her knee on what felt like a sheet of ice. She crawled forward and left, her shadow shifting right, and laughed, seeing another player fumble and fall. Someone else had dropped out; she didn't see how. And now there were four of them, watching each other, crouched, hands out. No one wanted to move while the stars spun overhead, pulsing rainbow colors in time to the game's cheerful electronic soundtrack.

The muscular man to Megan's left straightened. "Oi, look at the time. The big game's startin' in ten. How do you all feel about calling it quits here, eh? No forfeit?"

"No forfeit for me, anyway." A rangy woman with rough, sun-damaged skin dove at him, checking him into the void with her shoulder as she reached for Megan, clearly planning on using her to stop her momentum. Megan slid easily out of the way, letting her scramble and scream to her doom.

The last man held up his hands and seemed about to say something, but Megan had already moved so that her shadow cut the ground out from under him. The field was hers, and the sky rained golden coins as her opponents received prolonged electric shocks.

Heaviness returned to her body. Megan sighed. It had gone too fast, and the "big game" was to blame. As if any game were bigger than any other. If people really wanted to watch other people play, there were opportunities in every local gym.

Megan scanned for other pick-up games. Damn. The scene was dead, everyone gone to watch the first pre-tournament qualifier match for North America's MegaDeath team. What a waste of time. It was a glorified tryout, and they'd all rather watch it than play themselves. What was wrong with people?

She felt like a fire that had only been one-quarter doused. She kicked out of the pod and picked up her gym bag on her way out, prepared to jog home rather than waste the rest of her night.

Lola's heart jumped like a fish caught on a hook as she lowered herself into Marty's pod; she was going to learn so much more in an hour being Indía than she would doing a thousand Romanian dead lifts. This was a chance to *be* Indía during the first qualifier match of the season.

Marty hovered. "You know how to put everything on?"

"I'm not a baby!" Lola pulled the sensor lines up her legs and slid her arms into the sleeves.

Marty looked over at the other pod. Kiko was already pulling its lid shut. "Don't hog it all night. I'll be waiting. I'm your host, remember?"

"I know, I know."

Lola put the helmet on and pulled the pod closed. Instantly, she felt she was floating, only without the gross stink of the pods they used for games at school.

With a blink, she opened the file Kiko had loaded and felt herself rush forward, like being pulled by a water slide, and *bam*.

She breathed. She blinked heavily lashed eyes. She was in a stadium, colorful flags flying overhead. Her hand was still on her heart as the stands roared and the last notes of the National Anthem faded. Her strong legs were shoulder-width apart, relaxed but ready, like a weapon at parade rest.

She was Indía.

"Hey."

She was also in a room. It was like she could will herself forward and see out of Indía's eyes, or she could fall back, and there was this space with vinyl-covered lounge chairs and a buffet table and a big window-wall looking out at a stadium. Like an expensive stadium loge. They used to have those when people played and watched sports in person. Like a mini living room with food and drink. People with dumb old pods like she had at home would mime drinking and pretend, but now with those fancy fabber lines like Marty had, she could . . . she grabbed a cup of soda that was sitting there and experimentally raised it to her lips. Sweet, bubbly pop slid into her mouth. It was so real! The texture of the liquid, the plastic rim of the cup. She got distracted thinking about the pod feed lines pressing against her mouth and sputtered and almost spilled the cup.

In this mini living room there was this guy. Maybe thirty? He had a scraggly beard and was wearing a purple shirt, unbuttoned, which was weird. You could program your clothes in environments like this, which was why Lola was wearing the latest designer hiking shorts and a cool ironic tank top, so why would you program your clothes falling off?

"Uh, hey. Thanks for sharing the game," Lola said, and willed herself forward again. Presumably, the dude would be watching too.

Oh! Something strange was happening. Indía was poised, her legs bent and tensed, waiting. She kept her eyes on a woman opposite her on the green field, but her focus was half on Jerry Myers, the team captain, standing several yards behind and to the left of her. A whistle sounded, up, down, up, and Jerry ran forward. Indía started running the second she heard the hard *thunk* of Jerry kicking the ball. She ran into and pushed aside the woman she'd been eyeing, a violent shoulder-shove as her strong legs sprinted forward. Only a second's impact and it was passed. Indía was looking far ahead, where a man crouched, arms open, watching the sky for the ball. She bent low into her run, arms pumping, intent on getting to him.

Lola quickly checked the sport description. Oh, it was a historical. They did this sometimes, drawing games from the different team's pasts. This was called "American Football." She'd heard of it.

But by the time Lola turned her attention back to Indía, everything was tumbling, hard, violent bodies impacting bodies, and that whistle hard and sharp in the air.

This was an odd game. It had a lot of stopping and starting. A woman dressed in black and white stripes picked the oblong leather ball off the grass and walked a few feet to the side and set it down there. Everyone just let her and lined up on either side of it. This game had to have, like, pages of rules. Indía was again in her dancer's stance, tensed and waiting, the tension clear throughout her body as she pressed her foot into the turf, prepared to spring forward with breathtaking suddenness, and then she did, slipping like a fish through a crush of bodies to grab one player and throw him to the ground. How had she even known where he was?

Lola whirled. She could never learn this. It was like magic. Indía was watching twenty people at once, jogging backward then diving forward, always hitting her target, grabbing men twice her size around the knees and flinging them to the grass. The strength, the feeling of power, of imposing her will on another body . . . it was intoxicating.

A glittering figure bounded into view, making punching gestures as Indía got to her feet again. "That's the way to make a quarterback pancake!"

Indía saluted the figure. Oh, gosh, was that Mitzi, the head cheerleader? She was even more beautiful from this perspective, wearing a bodysuit of metallic red and green, and glowing with the non-combatant marker, like sparkles all over her. Wow, Lola had never seen that. They filtered it out for the audience so the cheerleaders looked the same as anyone, but the players needed to know that these people were not touchable. Mitzi was cheering right at Indía. At Lola. "Get it, girl! You're powerful, you're beautiful, you're unstoppable!"

Mitzi jogged backward, off the field. Lola wanted to follow her, but of course, Indía was in control. She turned her back on the cheerleader and ducked into a tight huddle of teammates. Jerry barked some numbers and words that made no sense. "Pistol strong, twenty-three power, on two. Break."

A diagram flashed over Indía's vision, X's and O's and arrows. Something changed. The team lined up differently, and now Indía was behind Jerry. He was really handsome, his soft brown hair blowing in the virtual breeze as he bent over and shouted numbers. Numbers Indía, presumably, understood. He was wearing these incredibly tight, shiny pants. Well, everyone was, but on him, they mattered.

Abruptly, his beautiful behind swiveled out of view. Jerry handed her the odd-shaped ball and her foot dug into the ground, tearing it and turning her sharply, a shoulder lowered as she grazed between two teammates and two opponents. Leaping gazelle-like to the side to avoid a flying tackle, she danced over fallen bodies and her thighs labored, so much power, so much muscle straining every ounce to push, to vault, to dig deep . . .

All to fall in a collapse of bodies.

Lola pulled back, breathing hard. Damn. She was going to have to do more squats. A lot more squats. She hated that her sister was right.

"So . . . really into sports?" An arm dropped around Lola's shoulders. It was the guy with the purple shirt.

Lola quickly sidestepped out of that. "I'm a real fan."

"It's fun and all, but don't get attached. This team's going to die before the quarters." He rubbed his chest, super weird, opening up his shirt more. He had a lot of hair there, maybe he liked petting it. "I think the real reason you came in here is you like to have a good time. Right?"

"Yeah, it's fun to be in the game." Lola cringed away from him. Could she sink back into Indía with this guy so close? "Do you mind backing up?"

"How does it feel to be inside another woman?" His mouth hung open. "Do you like that? Her firm, tight body? The sweat trickling between her breasts?"

"Uh . . . not so much. I mean, I'm thinking about playing." She turned her mind back to the game. She did feel sweat between Indía's breasts, itchy and unpleasant. Indía couldn't rub it away because of the heavy pads laced across her chest. Her teeth sank into something firm, her breaths coming hard through her nose as she lowered her shoulder into another body, shoving the opponent to the ground and stumbling over their rolling limbs into clear grass ahead. Her goal was near, just four more yards, her legs opening up, no sign of an opponent . . .

Lola was pulled out unwillingly by the sensation of a hand on her back. She shuddered, and this time she physically pushed the man in the purple shirt away. "I'm trying to watch."

"Hey, I paid a lot for this ticket." He put his arm in front of her when she tried to step back into the game. "I thought I made it clear I only wanted someone interested in a good time."

Lola backed up, but there wasn't far to go. This was a pocket universe, closed to the ticket. She thought about Kiko's words to Marty about getting chased until the end of the game. "Um, you're nice and all, and thanks for letting me tap in. But . . . didn't you buy this ticket to experience the game? To be Indía?"

"Yeah, but that was before I knew you'd be such a babe." He finally gave her a little breathing room, but it was only so he could do this creepy up-down look over her. "You're what, twenty-one?"

Lola knew she shouldn't feel flattered. Older people were always guessing her age way too high. Normally she played along with it, but she figured it was better to shut this guy down with the truth. "I'm seventeen."

He didn't back off as expected. He didn't even pause. He put his hand on her back again and she sidestepped out of it. This was turning into a run-in-circles thing. "I could teach you so much. You know, in virtual spaces . . . it doesn't count." He ran his hand down her arm and she shuddered.

"Central?" Lola called. She reached like she normally would to find the exit controls. She blinked at the edge hotspot . . . no control panel, no alerts. "Call Central."

He tilted his head, following as she retreated. "Why would you want to call Central? I mean, if you need to call someone, just tell me. I have the controls." And he was touching her again. "But I don't think you really want to call."

Somewhere, dimly, in the back of her head, Indía fell, wrapped in strong arms, against the hard, green turf.

4

Lola felt herself ripped from the world, falling into stifling darkness. What? Her skin crawled. Was that man still touching her? Had he done this? She was in a seat, on her back. Her hands raised in front of her and she saw them dimly through a clear visor. They were wrapped in smooth black material. She was in the pod. She blinked for the interface, but it didn't come up. Everything was off. Slowly, she pushed open the hood of the pod. Megan was standing right in front of her, holding a handful of cables in one hand. Marty was trying to peek around her, his hands clasped under his chin.

Megan threw down the cords. "How long has this been going on?"

Kiko crawled halfway out of the other pod. "We weren't—"

Megan silenced her by holding one finger up. "When I want to hear an excuse, I'll ask for one. Lola, you want to explain to me what you're doing up at this hour, hacked into a professional game? Do you have any idea the kind of shit that could have happened to you?"

"Ki—"

She barely had the syllable out when Megan whirled that finger in front of her. "And the one thing I do *not* want to hear from your mouth is someone else's name."

"Hey—you asked me to explain. And I don't know why I have to explain to you. I'm old enough to make my own choices, and you're not my parent."

Megan's face drained. That was a blow; Megan wasn't anybody's parent anymore.

Lola immediately wanted to take it back, to try a new tack . . . she felt herself shake as she peeled off the pod sleeves. "You're right. It was getting ugly, Megan. Th-thank you, you saved me." She went to put her arms around her sister but was stopped dead by her cold look.

"We're going home," Megan said. "Now."

She turned on her heel and marched out.

Marty stepped from foot to foot. He mumbled to the ground, "You don't have to listen to her, you know, you're almost an adult."

"Shut up," Lola said and jogged after her sister.

Megan was marching purposefully down the center of the street toward their house when Lola caught up. "I know it was dangerous."

"Ha."

"But it was worth it! Megan, this was a chance to feel what it's like to play at that level. The team! The precision! It's what you've been trying to tell me, about how your body has to know how to move."

Megan strode on, eyes forward. "You are so lucky someone else didn't see your obvious hack job. If I hadn't been scanning the local network to check on you—"

"You were checking on me?" Lola couldn't believe her sister would violate her privacy like that. Wait, why was she checking at all? "You saw me leave, is that it? Was it the door? Did it make too much noise and wake you up? God, could you not watch me every minute? I'm not ten years old!"

"No, you left your light on, genius, and when I got home, I saw it and thought you'd followed me to the arcade." She smacked her forehead. "What am I doing? I am not going to help you improve your rule-breaking techniques."

"Oh, jeez, stop being so self-righteous. You never noticed when I snuck out before."

Megan turned to look back at her but didn't break her stride. "You did this—" She stopped herself and resumed looking resolutely forward. "I don't care."

"That I broke rules? Or that I was in danger today? Because it looked like you finally cared a little bit about me, for a second there." Lola jogged to catch up. Megan's face was regaining its blank look. How weird was it that she wanted her sister to stay mad? "I was only doing it for you. I mean . . . to be like you, the way you want me to be."

"I don't care if you're like me or not. You can stop trying."

Lola slowed. They were almost home. "But you keep pushing me. I thought you wanted me to get better."

"I'd do that for anyone, and anyone else would respond better. I don't need you tagging along on my workouts. I want to be left alone."

Lola stopped in the middle of the street. Her sister didn't notice, didn't turn around. She wanted her to take note, without having to make her, but Megan was jogging up the drive now, not even slowing. Lola shouted, "All you care about is yourself!"

Megan stopped, at last. She stage-whispered, "You're going to wake up Mom and Dad!"

Well, good. At least Megan cared about that. "Why did you come rescue me? You don't love me. You barely even see me!"

Megan trotted back to her, gesturing down, like she was patting a dog, still trying to shout quietly, "You risked yourself for a game. No, not even a game, a qualifying match. I can't begin to imagine a more frivolous reason to break the law and terrify me."

"How can you call the first MegaDeath qualifier frivolous?"

"Because it is. I enjoy playing pod games, but I know they're not important. They're just . . ."

Just all she ever thought about, all she was ever doing. Lola wished she was smart enough to say the exact right thing to get her to see that she was being selfish and hypocritical. "MegaDeath determines the voting order in the World Court," she said, which was stupid, a line from a schoolbook, repeated so often it didn't mean anything anymore.

But it was true. The tournament did do that. It was important and had real consequences, like how no one could get coffee since last year's loss because South America was a dick about it and imposed a quota on shipments to North America. The countries got to vote in the World Senate in the order in which they finished the tournament, so if you were eliminated in the first round like North America had been, you never got your way on anything.

Megan shook her head. "It's a stupid game, and you are eating up what they teach you. The whole world is sick. Risks, odds, the betting… it's addiction, and they sell it like it's the end of all war."

Lola knew that maybe the world wasn't as perfect as her teachers said it was, but she also knew it was a lot better than it had been back when people starved and stuff. And how had they even gotten on this subject? "All you ever think about is your pain. You're so wrapped up in it you can't even see anyone else."

"I'm selfish? Have you even thought what this will do to Mom and Dad?"

It wouldn't do anything to them. Lola was the one who would get some risk factor added to her personal scores and get turned down for jobs or school programs. "Why should I? You've never once thought about them, or you wouldn't act the way you do!"

Megan reeled back at that, and her face shut down, became a mask. "I'm not arguing in the street. I'm going in and going to bed. You can stay out here for all I care." And she turned and walked up to the front door.

Lola hated that she had no choice but to follow. "You can't see anything bigger than yourself. You can't see that there's a bigger story going on all around you!"

"What bigger story? Six psychotic jocks feed their gambling

addiction so one section of the world can get cheaper coffee?" Megan opened the screen and pressed her thumb to the front door lock, mumbling the family password when it beeped. "You need to stop looking up to people with more muscles than brains."

"Indía is a hero. She's putting her life on the line for her country! For the greater good!"

Megan glared at her, one foot in the door. "They killed my daughter for the greater good. Don't you dare use those words with me." She slammed the door behind her, leaving Lola out in the cold.

Lola wasn't locked out, of course; she knew the family password, and the door knew her thumbprint. She waited, though, imagining Megan's passage through the house to Mom and Dad's room to wake them up and get them started on grounding her for life.

It was chilly out, and Lola's sweat from the pod, the fright, and the jog had turned into ice water. She opened the door and went to face the music.

Except there was no music. All the bedroom doors were shut, and she heard only the soft night sounds of snoring and the nibbling of the self-cleaning floor returning small organics and discarded items to the fabber lines. Her shed skin cells were heading back into the community grid to be made into someone else's breakfast.

Lola crept into her room, surprised that she was more disappointed than relieved. She'd really thought the anger meant that Megan cared.

Megan's little sister stopped bothering her. She could slip out of the house in the early hours to run without a purple-haired shadow. Lola's door would close when she opened hers. For days it was like they lived in separate, parallel worlds. Well, good. That was what Megan wanted, wasn't it? To be left alone?

She lay in bed. She hadn't checked the clock or the calendar, but she knew that today was Ciera's seventh birthday. She'd seen the date looming and stopped looking, but some masochistic grain inside her had counted the days like a rosary.

Today, she'd be seven. Megan imagined a taller Ciera, grown into all the wonderful complexity of a child who wanted to do the bedtime reading instead of being read to, who had a social circle, a schoolroom world she could talk about with elaborate depth and condescension: "No, Mom, I'm not friends with Erica anymore. Alex doesn't like her because she was mean to Jess on the playground."

Ciera would rush into her parents' bedroom at the crack of dawn, excited to start her special day. Megan would have bought an ice cream cake with rainbow frosting. Or maybe Ciera's tastes would have changed and she would stubbornly insist on chocolate with fat red flowers from the grocery counter. She would have a new dress, and the house would be full of balloons. She would have to be chased away from the pile of presents as she tried to peel the wrapping back to peek.

None of these things were happening. Today, the same as yesterday and the day before, Megan woke in her old bedroom in her parents' house. No one rushed in to wake her. No one asked her what she was going to do today.

Through the window, she heard Greg arrive, the soft whine of the electric cab, the opening and closing of doors. Her mother greeting him like a son. "You look so good! Growing a beard. I like it. Very woodsman."

He laughed. It was unfair how familiar his laugh was. "This? Just too lazy to shave."

Her mother had been off on an entomology trip all week, like she was every other week, traipsing through the desert, checking the little robots that counted bugs for her study. Megan found it disloyal how eagerly she cut her trip short to see her ex son-in-law.

Her father's softer voice didn't carry, but she knew he was saying something nice, flattering, or sympathetic. Then Greg again, so loud he could be in the room, "Hey, Lola-bola. I hear you're playing in the all-city!"

"Youth division," Lola said with obvious false humility. "It won't be anything like how you and Megan used to play."

Where was the greater good in this? The stupid games. Send volunteers to risk their lives instead of having wars. So much better. Certain death for the losers so the World Congress could put everyone in the pecking order for all decisions for the next four years. After all, there were resources that couldn't be fabbed. Rare organics, minerals. Not everyone could have them, so someone had to decide who went without. Losing countries put up with it because they might win next time and be on top. Was it really more humane? By the end of the year, Lola's hero, Indía, would be dead, and Lola would sob for her worse than she did over her own niece.

Not that Megan remembered how Lola cried, or if she had cried. She didn't remember anyone else's face, either, from that entire year.

"Is she coming?"

Whispered like she couldn't hear.

"Dude, she hasn't been out of her room all week."

Her mom's gasp was fake. "Lola! That's not true."

"Someone should actually ask. Would it help if I talked to her?"

Dad's mumble was worried. Her mother sounded like she was re-broadcasting him. "Oh. Oh, no, Greg. No, you know how she feels."

"Do I? Look, if anyone could . . . but it's not the same. I've been mourning her, too, for the past four years."

More whispers, hushed, moving away from the window. Megan wanted to scream at them. *Just say it. Say it all out loud. Megan has lost her mind. She can't go to a cemetery and lay flowers on a grave with her ex and her parents.*

"Hey, do I have to go?" Lola, not bothering to whisper. "My team has practice." A quiet answer. "It's an extra practice. The game's on Saturday."

The little shit. Megan covered her face with her pillow so she wouldn't have to hear Lola trying to wheedle out.

Then there was a knock on her door. "Megan?" It was Lola.

Megan stayed as she was, with the pillow on her face. Another knock. Greg's voice this time. "I know it's . . . there's about twenty minutes before the next cab comes. We're in the kitchen."

Quiet, kitchen sounds. Forks on plates, cupboards opening. The sound of domestic intimacy, an alien planet she had come from but could never return to.

Finally, Megan heard the soft whine of a car decelerating in front of the house, and four doors opening and closing. They were gone, and the house was silent again.

She couldn't sleep, doubted she could ever sleep again, and there was nothing in her room but her bad-smelling laundry and her gym bag. She got up and went to get a glass of water.

"Central-Sponsored Local Youth Tournament" read a flyer on the fridge. The date was circled in an animated pink ribbon. Another flyer announced, "Community Spirit Day. Wear Your Green and Red on Fridays for MegaDeath 2112."

Megan took a glass from the cupboard, and it slipped through her fingers, shattering on the tile counter. She spent a long time staring at the shards, wondering what it would feel like to take one and slit her wrist with it. She picked one up and it sliced the meat at the base of her thumb. It didn't hurt. It didn't feel like anything.

She dropped it and started shaking, because a thought, unbidden, crept into her mind. *How could I explain it to Ciera?*

Ciera wouldn't understand. Ciera wanted more birthday parties. More friends. More days at the beach. She would hate her mother throwing away something she wanted and could never have.

But I'd be joining you, baby. Ciera wasn't there, couldn't hear her thoughts, and she couldn't pretend she was, not even to imagine what she would say. She was a crazy woman, talking to herself.

Still, she swept the pieces of glass up and tossed them in the fabber. *Happy Birthday.*

Back in her bed, hours later, having stared at the ceiling slowly growing dark, she heard four car doors open and the voices of her family. "I always feel better—" that was Lola "—after I see her. Like, most of the time I don't even remember her that well, but when I do, I'm sad, and I get real sad right when I see her name, but getting sad makes me feel better after. Is that weird?"

"I think it's her spirit." Greg. A soft sound, and Megan just knew he was mussing Lola's hair. "She was a cheerful girl, and she's still spreading joy." His voice was warm, sweet, and sad. She felt a wealth of love, pain, and kindness in that voice.

She didn't remember his face at the funeral. What he said, or did, or if he held her.

"Thank you for coming, Greg," her mother said, and there was the sound of a kiss on a cheek.

Megan rubbed a tear from her own cheek, and half-unwilling got up and went to the window.

Greg's arm was around a strange woman. Her arm was around his waist. Megan's father was shaking her hand. "It was so good to meet you. Take care of our Greg."

The strange woman ducked her head against Greg's strong shoulder. They walked together, hand in hand, to a waiting car. She kissed Greg and brushed a hand over the back of his head, a habitual gesture, comforting, intimate.

Then she turned to look at the house, and Megan had to jump back to avoid being seen.

She heard Lola and her mother in the kitchen, her father saying, "I really hoped this year we could bring her with. It's not healthy how she hides from her grief from us."

"Shh. Bert, she can hear you."

Megan fell belly-first on the bed and screamed into her pillow.

Then she grabbed her gym bag. She didn't look up or acknowledge anyone as she marched through the hall, kitchen, and front room. Someone tried to touch her arm, someone called her name; she didn't care. She started running the second she was outside.

At the arcade, she scanned the wagers for something awful, something permanent. The best she found was "cut off your right pinky toe."

She had forgotten her personal haptic suit, so she was in the dirty, often-used sleeves. She was crying as she slipped into the hood, and the opening screen blurred. Her avatar, stepping into a forest clearing, cried dutifully with her. A man dressed in the traditional Ulama loincloth tilted his head at her. "Are you all right?"

Megan answered by walking to the center of the court. "Forearm or hip?"

The other players were there, looking uneasily at her. Good.

"Forearm," a woman said. Her avatar had cloth wrapped around the right forearm, ready to hit the ball.

"Let's get started, then." Megan crouched. The tears streamed down her cheeks, but her eyes were only on the timer and the ball. The cheap haptics made the world feel greasy, like everything was covered in plastic film.

Just start, she demanded, glaring at the countdown.

A horn sounded, and the ball was served. Megan charged it with single-minded focus. She didn't share the ball, didn't pass, didn't block. She scored. She powered through her own team members to score. In seventeen minutes, she'd made the eight points, and the game was over. Cheesy mariachi music, her teammates cursing at her for ruining the fun.

She wasn't satisfied. She hadn't escaped herself. She joined the first game she found that was waiting for players and stormed through that one too. The sky flickered with showers of sparks, spelling out something about a world top score.

She didn't notice or care.

Megan woke up to the sound of incessant knocking on her bedroom door. She felt like she'd been beaten like a bowl full of eggs. Hungover without the benefit of drinking, she had no recollection of coming home. She threw her pillow at the door. "Go away."

Something snicked in her door lock, and the door swung wide. Lola picked up the pillow from her feet and threw it at Megan. "You gotta hide me. There's these people here who look like fucking government agents." She dove onto the bed and tried to crawl behind Megan. "I think it's because of the G-A-M-E. The thing. You remember? At Marty's?"

Megan's head was still reeling, and she had a near-adult trying to cower behind her in a single bed. "Who the hell is Marty?"

Lola said, "You were there, that makes you complicit. Save me or we both go down."

Megan's mother appeared in the doorway. "Megan? There's someone here to see you." She frowned. "They're in the living room. Do you want me to buy you some time to put yourself together?"

Wearily, Megan got up. She smelled bad, so she threw off her shirt and put on a clean one. Lola dogged her to the bathroom. "They're wearing dark glasses and it's still morning. Don't tell me they aren't secret agents."

Ugh. The woman in the mirror over the sink looked like she'd rolled home as a spare wheel. Megan splashed water on her face, but it didn't improve anything. More water, and she smoothed her hair back. "They're here to talk to me. They're probably . . ." Her mind blanked. There was no reason for anyone to want to talk to her. What? For her research on the benefits of non-predictive gamification in pre-K pedagogy? She nudged Lola out of the way.

"You aren't going out there!" Lola whisper-shouted, pulling at Megan's arm. She gave up when Megan got within four steps of the living room, letting go and hiding rather than risking being seen.

A man and a woman, alike in dark suits and immaculate hair, sat on the living room sofa like they had never done such a domestic thing before and didn't like the feel of it. Damn, they did look like secret agents. As Megan entered the room, they stood together.

"Megan Mori?" The woman held out her hand. "I'm Officer Phelps, this is Officer Greenlee."

"Is this about my kid sister hacking into a pro game?"

Phelps and Greenlee looked at each other. Greenlee winked like they were in a badly-acted comedy and he wanted the audience to know they shared a secret. "We are aware of that, but there's no call for action at this time."

"We're from Central." Officer Phelps dropped her outstretched hand, which had waited patiently for a handshake Megan wasn't giving.

Officer? "Central doesn't have police. It's a communications company. Is this about how I keep turning off stats?"

Officer Phelps clearly had to work to keep her smile. "We're from the Professional Pod Gaming Division. Ms. Mori, we're here to offer you the chance of a lifetime. We want you to play for Team North America in the 2112 MegaDeath Games."

5

"This isn't a guaranteed spot," Greenlee quickly added. "We're not representatives of the team or the government of North America, but Central is impressed with your talent and authorized us to step in and arrange an opportunity for you to try out. We're confident you have what it takes to represent North America in the MegaDeath Games."

"And make the games more popular in the North American viewing market," Phelps added, her smile finally genuine, as though this were the real prize.

Megan clenched her fist and felt the puckered cut below her thumb open and bleed sluggishly. "I don't follow the World League."

Phelps waved this away. "We know. We also know you're the best player we've seen in a long time, and the team needs fresh talent."

Greenlee turned on a holo-display over his ring. "Last night you completed a five-on-five forearm-rules Ulama Game in seventeen minutes, thirty-one seconds. Do you understand how incredible that is? It takes an average of one minute, forty seconds for a healthy athlete to make a hoop shot starting from the center line, unopposed."

"Because of the angle and the need to rebound," Phelps said.

"Yes, the rebound. And you didn't rest. You came off that win and immediately wrecked the global high score in SailRacer." As he spoke, he pulled charts and graphs out, turned them, and gestured at them emphatically. "Then you scored a hat trick against a semipro soccer team that just happened to be slumming on the open net. What were the odds?"

Phelps yanked a graph out of the muddle. "Given that team's habits and the time of day, the odds were as good as one in three she'd play them, but leading a group of individuals who hadn't trained together to victory *and* the hat trick? Look at that number. Just look at it."

The two officers of commercial sports excitedly pointed things out, talking over each other. About her? The incomprehension was only matched by her terror that this might mean actually interacting with people. Phelps noticed first that they'd forgotten Megan and addressed her directly. "You have the speed, the agility, and the flexibility needed in this level of play."

Greenlee nodded. "We have the numbers, and they look good. You fit in nicely with the rest of the team on statistical models. Your strengths and weaknesses."

Megan's head spun, unable to look away from the graphs and charts they'd left floating in the air between them. How had they gotten all this information? She hated data collection and had thwarted it every chance she could since she was little. No one was going to tell her what she should do or eat or play based on her past behaviors. "I didn't upload my scores. I logged in anonymously. I turned off tracking."

Phelps tilted her head like that was cute. "We're Central. Anyway, relax, we abide by all data privacy rules as stated in the end user license agreements available via the system codex."

Greenlee stepped around the coffee table to block the graphs, which dutifully hung in place. "Forget that stuff. All we have left is to see the 'human factor.' How you actually play with the others. We can predict a lot, but, well, you know human nature. There's always unpredictability."

This made Megan more interested in the numbers. She pressed Greenlee's shoulder, and he let her move him aside. There were records of every game she had ever played. Games she hadn't remembered playing. Her college games, her high school games! "How is this legal?"

"Central has considerable leeway to access in-house data if we believe it will help our client nations with national defense." Greenlee looked apologetic.

"And national offense." Phelps nudged him with a wink.

This was too much. They had invaded her privacy. They were trying to press-gang her into what amounted to military service. Megan backed away into the hallway, where she bumped into Lola, who was crouched low. She latched on to Megan's arm with both hands. "You have to do this. Oh. My. God."

Megan could see her parents at the kitchen counter, pretending not to listen. Her father looked like he might faint. Her mother poured wine into his half-empty glass. Seeing Megan staring, she said, "It's an honor just to be asked."

Which meant: *You don't have to do this.* Her expression, however, was as excited as Lola's.

The Central people followed Megan into the hall between the kitchen and living room. They looked strange surrounded by her mother's Japanese fan collection. They saw the excitement and horror mixed in her parents' faces and spoke more to them than Megan. "This could be your only chance to make a real difference, to be a national hero, change the course of history." Greenlee patted the charts back down into his ring. "You have twenty-four hours to decide. The window is closing to add new players."

Phelps clasped her hands. "Really, we can't make any roster changes after the last qualifier, and we'd rather have you on board before that. Wouldn't make sense for your first live playing to be a death match!"

Megan was starting to hate this woman's sense of humor. "I'm not interested."

Greenlee eased Phelps back. "We've already sent the papers to your account. Look them over. Think about it. You could be a national hero."

"A hero to girls like Lola!" Phelps added with saccharine sweetness.

"And your family, of course, will be richly compensated," Greenlee said.

They were looking at her like she was a rapidly expiring paycheck. Megan's father set down his wineglass too hard, and red splashed over his hand. He went to the sink, then fiddled with the organics utility line, which was always coming loose from the fabber and spilling proto-meat. The silence stretched awkwardly as he reset the hose and wiped the already-clean counter.

"Let's leave them to talk about it," Phelps said, waving her partner toward the door. "You have twenty-four hours to decide. Don't waste them!"

The family sat, shell-shocked, around the kitchen island as the two Central agents showed themselves out.

The door clicked shut and Lola jumped, jazz hands out, toward her sister. "If you don't do this, I'm going to eat my own brain."

"Lola!" Dad threw his rag in the fabber. "It's dangerous!"

Mom put a hand on Dad's shoulder. "Maybe . . . she could just try out? Of course, sweetie—" she looked at Megan with mild fear "—it's your decision, and we'll support you either way, but don't you think it would be good, for a change of pace, to get out? To be part of something?"

"I'm not a part of anything." Megan went back to her room. The anger at Central was relaxing into her usual state of just not caring. Her next day and the next lay before her, unchanged. She didn't like it, but she didn't like any other option, either.

Megan came home (from where? What day was it? Why couldn't she remember?). She opened the door to her parents' ranch house, which was where she'd lived since the divorce, but as she stepped through, she was in her condo near the university. She missed this place, with its high ceilings and redwood panels. She missed the bright toys lying against the walls like colorful pebbles lining a stream. The plush carpet was mussed by toddler footsteps and the tiny tire tracks of a fleet of play cars. "Ciera? Ciera, baby?" As she ran eagerly down the hall, she grew anxious. It was too silent. She should have heard laughter, playing. She started searching the living room, the bedrooms, throwing toys and pillows and shoes.

Greg was at the kitchen table, holding a mug in both hands.

She wanted to strangle him for how calm he looked. "Where's our baby?"

He stood up. "Megan, you knew this would happen. It was time."

"Where's our baby?!"

"It's better this way. Better to know. I'm so tired, Megan. Tired of waiting, of wondering every night if I'm going to wake up and find her gone." Weak, still, unmoving man. She threw what she had in her hand at him. The door fob. It hit his chest and dropped ineffectually to the ground. His eyes were red-rimmed. "Megan." He started toward her, arms opening.

She didn't want any of that. She stormed back the way she had come, back to the street, waving frantically for a car.

The hospice center wasn't hard to find. They'd sent her the address a thousand times, all those invitations to visit, to see how *pleasant* it was. That was the word they used. "Pleasant." Like murder was a picnic in the country.

The center had a brick garden wall, crenellated, with baskets of flowers hung at each dip. The buildings were all Victorian, small cottages and a chapel-like main building, like a furniture store painting come to life. All that beauty to hide the horror.

Megan ran down corridor after corridor. Terra-cotta tile, Gothic windows, potted rubber trees. They decorated the place with carousel horses and Dolls of All Nations. Warm, friendly, cheerful. She hated it.

"Ma'am? Ma'am?" Orderlies raced after her as she passed desks without checking in. She threw open doors. Cozy rooms, fireplaces. Children and adults playing games looked up at her in surprise. Where was Ciera?

It was a blood disease. Incurable. But there had been a chance she would have lived years and years with the silent killer inside her. She could have lived a long time. But the state decided that in order to save money, to save resources, she would be brought here, at three years old, to enjoy her last weeks and be humanely put down. Some damned formula that weighed how much Ciera would suffer while sick, how much her illness would be an "emotional burden," like there was any burden too heavy to carry for Ciera. Like Megan wouldn't choose to suffer every day to make another day for her baby girl. Like the tiniest percent of a chance wasn't one she was willing to take.

But the computers didn't believe in miracles, and when their math showed Ciera's chances weren't chances at all, that was it. Better to schedule an end than wait on fate. The greater good. Less spent on impossible odds. Less hope.

Less Ciera.

Megan was not going to accept that. She was going to find her daughter and take her back. Another room, another group of people staring at her in shock over board games and trays of cheese. Over movies and novels. Over romantic hugs.

Another room, another.

There were drones following her, now, as well as orderlies. "Please, ma'am, please. Stop. Remain calm. Ma'am."

She wouldn't remain calm. She'd tear the building apart until she found her daughter.

They tackled her, but she fought them off; three bodies, but she was strong, she trained to fight. She made it to the next door and kicked it open. An old woman blinked at her over a checkerboard. Four bodies tackled her this time. She pushed, twisted. She used all the skills she had honed to win points and games to tear her body apart from theirs, to make it another foot down the corridor. She would find Ciera. She would take her home. She made it another foot, and something hit her from behind. Heavy, inexorable, an avalanche of limbs in loose cotton scrubs. She splayed facedown on green checkered linoleum. She felt the needle enter her arm, the coldness, spreading, the darkness.

The dream abruptly ended. Megan flailed, kicking and twisting, but nothing was holding her down. She was on her bed, kneeling now, the sheet and pillows flung around the room. She was alone. Slowly, she lay back down. Alone, forever, in this room. Every time she opened her eyes, this ceiling was in front of her, these plain gray walls cutting off the world.

She was never going to get out of this room, out of this endless spiral of grief.

She threw her legs over the side of the bed and kicked her gym bag, which was waiting, as always, for her to pick it up and head out. Well, that escape was out of the question now that she knew people were watching her, recording every move. What would she do without pod games? While she played, she was in the moment. She wasn't fighting to save her Ciera. Uselessly fighting, endlessly losing.

She could give in. Join their team. It was tempting, to sign up, to risk her life. The thought sparked something almost like interest. Almost fear. Risking her life—she could do it, just to feel something. She'd have her escape. But for those people? The people who took her Ciera?

Intellectually, she knew the games weren't the government. The decisions that caused MegaDeath to come into existence were separate from public health debates and population controls. But it was one society, and right then, she hated all of it, from presidential elections down to the most banal safety video.

She put on her running shoes and went to the kitchen for some water. To her surprise, Lola was there, slumped at the counter, and when Megan approached, Lola jerked upright. Her eyes were red-rimmed, and her cheeks were flushed and wet.

For a second, Megan wondered if she was dreaming. Was this the house she was supposed to be in? The seconds passed. Megan forced herself to walk to the sink without looking at Lola again. "Go to bed. Mom and Dad are going to be pissed if you've been up all night."

"What does it matter? What does *anything* matter?"

Overdramatic teen. Megan filled her water bottle and reached for her ring to check the time, but she'd left it on the bedside table. Her finger was bare. She glanced at the clock on the kitchen stove. 4:29 a.m. Okay, she'd check her lap time assuming it would be 4:30 by the time she started running. She jogged toward the front door.

Lola threw herself into Megan's path, arms wide. "All my life I've watched you get things I wanted, and not even like them. Oba-chan's hoverboard. Your own apartment. A wedding!"

Megan felt a headache starting. "I'm nine years older than you. Get out of my way, or come with." She shouldn't have offered: Lola would go back to dogging her all the time. Also, she was wearing a lacy nightdress. She'd freeze and look ridiculous, possibly glowing under the moonlight.

Thankfully, Lola didn't acknowledge the offer. "Why are you passing up a huge opportunity other women would shank their boyfriends for?"

Shank? What was Lola watching on her feed? "You're really this upset about that game offer? It's my decision. When have I ever shown the least bit of interest in MegaDeath?"

Lola sobbed between words. "Because you're so selfish! You don't care about our country!"

"I'm being selfish? You're asking me to sign up to kill other people and probably die so you can, what? Live vicariously through me?"

"Oh, come *on*, Megan. You aren't going to die and you know it! You're literally the best. You might as well be cheating."

Megan didn't dignify that with a response. "Or is it the trips, the gifts, and all the attention you know *you* will get as a part of a player's family?"

"It's not about that!" Lola curled her fingers in front of her like she wanted to strangle her sister.

Megan stepped back and glanced at the time on the stove. She might as well go back to her room for her ring at this point. She turned.

Lola scrambled, ducking under Megan's arm to take a position blocking the hallway. She planted her feet to each side and held out her hands like she expected to have to catch Megan running at her. "I want this for you. Don't you get it? I want you to have something." She pressed her palms forward like she was pushing that invisible something into Megan. "Even if I don't have it. I want you to have something and enjoy it. Anything. If you were into music and a band showed up looking for a drummer, Megan, I'd be begging you the same. You're into pod games. It's your thing. You should be doing something you enjoy."

Megan saw how earnest her sister was. She felt the start of tears coming, to match the ones she saw.

Lola sniffled and straightened. "Instead you're stuck here like a creepy guy in some horror movie, living with his parents and only talking to taxidermy otters until he goes on a killing spree."

Megan felt suddenly exhausted. "Okay. I promise not to talk to any otters. Can I go on my run now?"

"Your run *is* the otter! It's a metaphor. Don't you see yourself?" Lola rubbed her eyes with the back of an arm. "Every time anyone tries to talk to you, you go running. You go to the gym. You go play pod games. And you're not even *enjoying it*."

Megan put her hand on her sister's shoulder and easily pushed her out of the way. Lola let her go to her room and get her ring. She stayed put, slumped against the wall in the hallway as Megan returned. She looked older when she was quiet and tired. Megan jogged out the front door and left it open in case Lola was coming.

It was cold and sharp on the road, the moon as bright and close as she had expected, but menacing, a disk of light that threatened to swallow the whole sky. She focused on the road, on the way the streetlights made tiny sand grains glint and shine in the concrete. She felt her thighs shudder, weak from spending the day in bed, and pushed herself just a little faster.

It didn't work. Her mind didn't turn off. She was there, on the street she had ridden her first bike down, with its concrete curbs and identical houses. She heard her breaths and each thud of feet against the pavement.

She wasn't enjoying the run. She hadn't enjoyed anything in a long, long time. Her footfalls faltered.

No. With an effort of will that felt like beating the world open with her forehead, she got her rhythm back. She turned down Soledad Street, the steepest downhill in the area. It dove down the mountain all the way to Main. With her juddering thighs, she staggered, she tripped, she barely kept her feet. Her heart pumped, feeling the risk. If she didn't keep running, keep her legs going faster than her torso, she'd hit the pavement face-first, teeth breaking, maybe snapping her neck, but most likely not; most likely she'd live to feel every foot of grit tear at her skin, bones breaking as she rolled all the way to the bottom. A wrist, maybe a shoulder.

She was so enthralled with her imaginary fall that, when her right foot hit the ground sideways, it seemed another hypothetical. The ground rose toward her in slow motion. Then everything sped up. She barely got her arms in front of her face. Her legs flew up behind her. Her chin hit, and she slid to a stop.

She had been at the bottom of the hill. The flattening angle of the pavement might even have been what tripped her. She lay in a heap near the corner of Soledad and Main, the neon sign for the town arcade painting her and the empty storefronts blue. *That was stupid*, she thought. She tried to get up. Her arms and legs quivered, exhausted, and she gave up, letting herself rest on the sandy concrete.

"Hey, you all right?" A thin, toothless man shuffled toward her from the 24-hour grocery, raising his loaf of bread like it might help. She recognized him, a pitiable figure at the fringes of her life, haunting the park and other public areas he couldn't be barred from. He probably lived on the minimum guaranteed income, living with some relative, dealing with some mental or physical problem that made him spend so much time wandering the streets, unwashed. He was, in short, damaged, but not damaged enough for society to euthanize. Someone society thought a better monetary risk than Ciera. She hated him.

And his shaking, papery-skinned hands were gently lifting her arm, helping her to her feet. "It'll be okay," he said.

He was too gentle, soft like a dead thing. Megan shivered all over. She pulled her arm from him. The hurt on his face was raw, too real and too close.

She turned her back on him and jogged, very slowly, back uphill. Her right ankle was sore, but in a way she recognized would get better in a day or two with some ice.

The house was dark and silent when she got home. She paused near Lola's door until she heard a gentle snore.

She couldn't stop thinking about that harmless old man who had helped her up. For a moment, she had wanted to kill him.

She sat on her bed and opened her ring interface. The number was there, in her received messages queue. She hit it and didn't wait for the voice on the other end. "I'm in. Send me the details."

6

Megan's grandmother, Oba-chan, came from a long line of professors and teachers, and had been expected to fulfill her destiny in Japan, preserving history in the capital of Pacific Rim. Instead, she'd come to North America to reintroduce beef to the cuisine of the continent. Her passion was hamburgers, long forgotten and easily vat-grown. After the food riots, even artificial meat had been taboo in North America, but Oba-chan had been in love with historical depictions of food, and classical American epics of comings of age always included, for some reason, hamburgers.

Oba-chan had taught her to never let someone else tell her what she was going to be. So maybe that was why, after all, Megan gave in. No one expected her to.

The final MegaDeath tryouts for Team North America were in Los Angeles, an hour's drive from Megan's parents' house. Megan wasn't sure if that was always the plan or if Central had changed everything to accommodate her. Was that paranoid?

Lola bounced in her seat, palms plastered to the window of the auto-cab. She always got this way on special days, playing up the youngest role. "My team is going to be so pissed at me for bailing on the local youth tournament, but, oh, my god, the Junior Nationals Champions! I can't believe they invited me."

Megan believed it. Central's agents could probably get anyone they wanted on the Junior team, and had done it knowing Lola would turn into a drama-warhead if Megan backed out and cost her the spot. They would find, if she decided this wasn't for her, that her tolerance for drama was high enough to drag Lola back to her small-town game.

Their cab swerved gracefully into a line of vehicles mag-chained together to save energy, like a string of clear plastic bubbles. "It's just a tryout," Dad said from the front seat. Megan saw that he was holding her mom's hand tightly, low where he probably thought she couldn't see. "You don't have to agree to anything."

"Bert, be happy for our daughters. This is an amazing opportunity."

Lola leaned between her parents. "Dad, Megan has to make the team. She's the best."

Dad let go of Mom's hand. "Sweetie, stay in your seat and put a seat belt on."

Mom said, "No matter what happens in the tryouts, we will have a wonderful weekend in the city as a family. This is an adventure we'll be able to talk about for years to come."

Megan felt something unsaid pass between her parents. Her mother's mouth pressed flat, her father looked for something to justifiably distract him outside. They were thinking it was a chance to knock her out of her depression, whether she joined the team or not, and Mom wanted her husband to be the one to say it.

Outside the cab, the tidy suburbs gave way to larger buildings that peeked over the freeway sound walls. There had been a lot of ugly warehouses and office parks built around there in the old days, and some of them were still there, converted into arcades, betting parlors, or restaurants. The first building more than four stories tall they passed had a giant banner with a picture of an athletic woman with sharp eyebrows and voluminous brown curls.

"Oh, my god, it's Mitzi!" Lola threw herself at the window on that side. "I love what she's done with her hair. It wasn't like that in the game." She glanced back and cleared her throat. "The game that I watched . . . a long time ago." It was a good thing Lola didn't want to be an actor.

Strange how her little sister hacking into a professional sporting event had so quickly become something cute. Megan doubted Mom and Dad would even say anything if they figured it out.

To stop her sister from further embarrassing attempts to cover up, Megan asked, "Do you like Mitzi?" For the first time, she had a reason to care about the people on this team. She might have to beat them. "How does she play? She's a favorite?"

"Megan! She's the head cheerleader! I can't believe you get to be on this team and you know nothing."

"Oh." Megan sat back, enjoying the success of her tactic. Lola was wholly absorbed in talking about cheerleaders past and present, their careers and duties.

Lola hardly ever got to go near the big city. Now it was rising around them, and banners and flags for the upcoming tournament fluttered from every building and post, like the city was a present wrapped for her. There was India, unfairly far from the highway. There was Jerry, and Hasan, and . . .

Mom gaped at a poster lashed to a highway bridge of Kendall in skimpy Ulama gear. "Are those her real arms, or do you think they altered the image?"

"They wouldn't dream of that," Lola told her with authority. "The league is very serious about authentic depictions. The pro players don't even get to add on cool scars or tats. Everyone has to look exactly how they are."

Dad gave her a sappy look. "Remember when you got those purple stars on your cheeks for your fifth-grade final bout? You were so proud."

"That was a thousand years ago. Megan, tell them how serious these rules are!"

Megan ignored her, leaving Lola to wonder. How could she not be enjoying this? They were coming into the city, not as spectators, but as athletes!

Lola started filming a video. They came out from under an overpass, and it was like the city blossomed around them, glittering man-made canyons festooned with color breaking free from the dull brown outskirts. "I'm finally here. It's real. My future starts today."

"It's a car ride, Lola, not a moon landing," Megan said, not looking up.

They left the highway to slide through streets that felt narrow and dark from the skyscrapers around them. People walked by in the latest fashions, colored ribbons flying from their wrists and throats, all looking unhurried and happy. "There's Central Tower!" It was a fixture of the skyline, but Lola had never seen it close up. Passing the base of the building, it was smaller than expected, a filigree egg stretched to the sky, ringed by a lush garden with bushes pruned into loopy shapes, *Hello, Central! Your one stop for information!* scrawled cheerfully around every fat flowerpot.

"Look at that, Megan, they're cut into binary codes," Mom said, but it was about as effective as an echo. Megan didn't look at anything.

Then they turned a corner, and Central Plaza vanished behind less famous buildings. Plain silver things from two hundred years ago and spiky neo-deco pagodas from the turn of the century. Ahead of them sprawled Champion's Village. Lola felt her heart in her throat as they passed under the archway. Now everything was in team colors. The buildings changed too. Here were things like hotels and stadiums, and running tracks and pools, utilitarian structures of corrugated concrete, and fancier places with swoops of machine-printed lace. "Oh, my god, that's the team captain in person walking down the sidewalk like a normal person!" Lola grabbed Megan's arm, but Megan just shook her off.

Lola had seen Jerry Myers up close in the game, had been a few feet from him, in Indía's eyes, but it was so, so much different to be there, to know that the same air was touching her and his beautiful bronze skin. He was just walking there! Talking with a statuesque woman . . . skin too dark to be Indía . . . Kendell? Well, now they had passed and she couldn't see.

The car stopped in front of an elegant hotel. It had a big awning over the road and a mannequin wearing white gloves waiting to open the door for guests. Mom and Dad held each other's hands, not getting out for the longest time. "Well," said Dad.

"Well," said Mom. She patted Dad's hand. "This is where we leave you girls. The car will take you on to the housing for athletes, and we'll see you later for dinner."

Finally.

"Bye," Lola said, ready for their departure.

"Call us the second you get to the dormitory," Dad said.

"We'll meet up for a wonderful dinner to celebrate once you're all checked in," Mom promised. "Tomorrow's the big day for you, Lola."

Lola wanted to scream. Would they get out of the car, already?

Megan snapped out of her daze and opened her door. Like that was what they were waiting for, Mom and Dad got out too. Megan got their bag for them and gave them each a robot-stiff hug, except robots could probably hug better than that.

Lola submitted herself to the necessity of hugging too. First Mom, then Dad. Dad's hug was stronger, and she misted up. This was it. She was going to a real, national tournament, and she was going to spend the night away from her parents, not at a friend's house, but in a dormitory like a college student. "I won't let you down."

"You can't," Dad said, and kissed her forehead.

"Look at us, a bunch of dramatics." Mom pulled Dad gently away. "We'll see you girls at dinner! Break a leg."

A group jogged by, four strong, handsome players in matching golden tracksuits. "That . . . that's Team Europe! Megan, it's Team Europe! There's Francois Aleman!" The magazines always talked about how strong he was. His shoulders looked like bowling balls threatening to burst out of his suit. He almost maybe looked their way! What if this was the start of her first romance? A whirlwind affair, two athletes, distracted by the heavy burden of representing their homelands, hungry for physical touch . . .

Megan closed the trunk of the car and got back in without even trying to look at this hunk of male beauty rapidly getting away from them. Not only was she all messed up emotionally, but apparently she'd lost her eyesight too.

Lola slumped back into the car, and Megan hit the button to tell it they were ready to go to the next destination. Mom and Dad stood in front of their hotel, waving as the car pulled away.

Megan picked at a callus on her thumb. "Maybe we should turn the car around. I don't know why I'm doing this."

Lola felt her stomach drop. If Megan flipped out and took her from this huge opportunity, well, that was it. She'd never have another chance like this. She knew she wasn't really good enough to get recruited for the Nationals. She tried to breathe calmly. "You're doing it because you love playing. For the love of the sport." She thought those were the best points to lead with, but Megan didn't say anything, so she had to dig deeper. "To make our parents proud? For your country? To inspire little girls?"

Megan really looked tired. Was this too much? Lola had hoped for some way to break her sister out of her funk, but was all this excitement too over-the-top to work?

The car slowed. Megan shook her head. "We're here."

The car parked itself under an awning in front of a tan building.

It had a long balcony dotted with doors painted orange, like a motel. Lola got out slowly, wanting to enjoy every second of entering this new world, like entering a hot tub. "This is where we're staying?"

Megan had gone around to the luggage compartment and pulled it open. "No." She dropped Lola's bag on the ground. "This is where *you're* staying. I have to report to the professionals' dormitory. Don't forget that you said you'd call Dad when you got in."

And just like that, Megan was back in the car, and it was gliding away with a soft electric whir. Again, her sister just left her.

But Lola practically crowed with delight. She was on her own! Finally treated like the adult she was! Alone and free in a city. Anything might happen . . .

A guy jogging by in a Team Australia jersey slowed and stared at her. She flipped him off. Then she picked up her bag and went into the building, looking for registration.

The Junior League Champions' dorm was plain, every surface painted beige or tan, but Lola loved every inch of it. She loved finding out there was an actual "House Mother" to greet her and swipe her ID. She loved the room, which combined sterile and austere with the rough edges of having been lived in by many people: nicks in the corners of the walls, mostly, and stains on the chic, modern hassocks.

She was only staying the weekend, so her clothes would all fit in one corner of one drawer, but she separated her shirts from her shorts and her socks, just to use the whole dresser. She got a map, a chat server invite, and an orientation video sent to her ring, but there was hardly time to look at them with all the other athletes arriving and looking so sophisticated.

Megan picked Lola up for dinner at 1800—everything listed the time in 24-hour increments, just like when countries fought actual wars with soldiers instead of athletes. Lola tumbled into the car almost before it stopped, so full of exciting things to report that she didn't know where to begin. "I have a roommate! She's from Ohio! I checked her stats on Central. She has a sprint of—"

Megan held up a hand. "Can we please not talk about sports? I just spent two hours being lectured about statistics and nutrition."

"Not talk about the main reason we're here?"

Megan pinched the top of her nose. "It's bad luck. Talking about the game too much on the night before."

Was that true, or a lie to get her to go along? Lola thought her face would cave in. "Sure, yeah. Um . . . how was the dorm?"

"It's a building."

This was going to be the worst conversation ever.

Mom and Dad ran to meet the car, all dressed up. "I made reservations at a fun place." Mom flicked the address from her ring to the car. "This is going to be a night for us to remember."

"Does this place have VR hookups? There's a qualifier match between South America and North Asia." Oops. Lola was not going to keep not talking about sports. Megan didn't say anything, though; she was pinching the bridge of her nose again, eyes closed.

"Sweetie, no electronics," Dad said. "We want to have this night to remember as a family."

What torture was this, that she was finally in the big time, and she had to completely ignore the entire sport? "I'm not a kid anymore. I can check now and then and pay attention. I'm not going to ignore you guys."

"If Megan goes through with joining the team, we won't see her again for . . . until . . ."

She saw her father struggling to finish his sentence without the word "if." This was bad territory. Parents were always way too worried about danger. It wasn't like Megan was going to join the team just to lose. "Megan's tryout isn't until Sunday, so we're going to have at least two family dinners, guaranteed."

Mom, who was the last resort, the best chance to get a yes when Dad said no, turned all the way around in her seat and put her hands on Lola's. "Do this for your father, sweetie."

The car dropped them at a place called 2020. The front of the restaurant was formed out of these big, blocky red letters spelling . . . Netflix? And the door was flanked by two rows of statues, one side wearing all this black armor and carrying clear plastic shields, the other wearing bandannas over their mouths and carrying what looked like cardboard signs with random things written on them. "Lives Matter!" and "MAGA."

Oh, she'd seen stuff like this in VR programs at school. What did they call them? A *historical diorama*. Lola followed her parents in over a tiger-skin rug with Megan trailing. There were these clunky rectangular screens hung all over, showing something called the Super Bowl. Some people in orange helmets and brown shirts were running around against people in blue helmets and white shirts. "Oh! I know that sport!" She let it slip before thinking. Mom looked surprised at her. Right, she couldn't exactly say where she knew it from. It was pure luck Megan hadn't ratted her out. "I . . . I mean, I think I remember it? Wasn't it big before pod games?"

A man with purple lipstick bowed and held a white plastic rectangle toward Mom. "Welcome to 2020, please take a mask. Your iPhone will tell you what table to go to."

There were four bins of masks to choose from: plain white ones, colorful ones, floral-printed ones, and plaid ones. They were all paper with string ties. Other patrons were wearing them around their necks like bibs or on their heads like hats. Kids were coloring on them. "What are these for?" Lola asked, picking a colorful one.

"Oh, everyone had them in the early 2020s," Dad said.

Mom tied a floral-printed one around her neck. "My grandparents talked about how no one could go anywhere without one, there was a disease, but also there was something political about it? Like different masks meant different things?"

"It's a Japanese thing?" Megan frowned.

"No, no, this was Grandma and Grandpa Louis in Seattle."

"Oh! Remember those!" Dad pointed at a row of silver kettles with black lids and buttons and clocks on their fronts. "Instant Pots! My great-uncle had one."

Lola had a feeling this restaurant was way more fun for grown-ups.

And they did have VR hookups, dang it, close enough to touch and yet forbidden. There were jacks at every table, built into a sort of funky touch screen with thick plastic edges like they had in old movies. The display wanted her to answer trivia questions about cows. All around, everyone at the other tables had at least one person hooked in. Everyone was watching the game! And she was stuck, unable to even talk about what she wanted to, with nothing to distract her but the Cleveland Browns and some mannequin asking a plastic box, "Can you hear me now?" every few seconds.

If only she could talk about what she'd learned about that sport, that the guy in orange there was playing the role Jerry had, handing the ball to that person who was doing what Indía had done. How there had been all those weird numbers and it was more complicated than it looked. Lola sank dejectedly into their booth. At least she could get herself a nice, greasy burger. Thank you, Oba-chan, for reading those historical novels about "The Baby-Sitter's Club" that made you want to print meat patties.

"Don't get anything too greasy," Dad said. "You're playing tomorrow."

There went her only consolation.

"Let them live a little." Mom winked, picking up her menu. "I'm getting the Bacon-Bacon Cheese Explosion Burger."

Around the room, people connected to VR grew quiet, breathing in unison. Lola saw a boy at the table behind theirs straighten, stiff and tense behind his VR headset. Then he jerked and relaxed, laughing.

His action was echoed by a tumult of excited cheers, cries of horror, more cheers. Something was happening. Something intense. North Asia was playing South America, and the rumors had it they were both trying out some amazing new players. Lola stared at the hookup sitting there by her elbow, unused.

Then she realized everyone at the table was looking at her. Someone had asked her a question? "There's nothing on this menu that I want that isn't greasy," she said.

"You like risotto. They have one that looks good." Her father started pointing out the healthiest things on the menu while her mom appended tastier suggestions. It was all fabber-printed anyway, what did it matter if it was shaped like a salad?

The boy at the table behind them jumped out of his seat, arms in the air, as a cheer went up all around the restaurant. But which side? The winner of this match would determine who North America faced in the first round of the tournament, and Lola was desperate to be privy to this information.

Megan put her hand on Lola's. "You're killing me with those puppy eyes. Plug in."

Megan? Megan was saving her?

Dad put down his menu. "Don't encourage her. You should share this moment as sisters."

"Dad, all we're sharing is knowing she's unhappy. You can't force family memories." She looked at Lola, really looked at her. "There's never enough of them, no matter what."

"I suppose it wouldn't hurt, for a few minutes," Mom said.

Lola didn't have to be told twice. She distantly heard Dad admonishing Megan, but Megan said, "It's research. She's playing tomorrow."

Wow. Megan was being nice. Maybe, just maybe, this trip to the big leagues wasn't too much. Maybe it was just right.

7

Megan's dormitory room was clean and new, with dark gray rubberized flooring should she decide to exercise, and a giant shower stall with trailing plastic flower-vines and stone walls. The massive showerhead created natural-feeling rain as she watched the fake flowers nod against the real, darkening stone. She felt . . . lighter.

There was nothing in the suite to remind Megan of her life, of her past. These weren't her towels. She had eaten a good burger and drunk a beer. Her parents were safely ensconced somewhere they couldn't bother her. Lola was no doubt asleep in her own dorm room.

Megan lay down. She couldn't smell herself against the brand-new bedsheets. There was nothing to worry about.

Except Ciera.

Was this a betrayal? Was she doing this just to have a chance to die without suicide? Did that make it suicide? What would Ciera think if she saw this place? That her mother was living it up without her?

Megan couldn't remember how a person got to sleep.

With a sigh, she got up and threw on some sweats. There was a tourist bar outside the residence. Perhaps a few shots of whiskey would shut her mind up.

The corridors were designed with sleek lines, bright against dark, a décor that made you want to jog. She took the stairs down and felt good for the blood pumping in her chest. It was a warm, comfortable night. She heard laughter as she approached the bar. It sounded like a bunch of fraternity boys at a convention. She opened the door expecting to see a group of raucous fans. It didn't occur to her that other athletes might be in the bar.

The whole of Team South America was there, celebrating their victory in the test match earlier in the day. They were wearing gaudy satin jackets, red and yellow with a blue globe on the breast pocket. She didn't recognize the heraldry, though she saw the name "South America" stitched across everyone's shoulders. The people next to them at the bar were just as fit and athletic looking. With nervous energy and staring smiles, they had the edge of people risking their lives. They could have been any team, or from a group of teams, as they weren't wearing regalia. They seemed part of the celebration, though.

None of these people were mourning tonight. Megan wondered where North Asia was drowning their sorrows. That would be more her speed. She headed to the far side of the bar, where no one was sitting, and gestured to the bartender. She would have two drinks and avoid eye contact. She could make it out of there alive.

No sooner had she sat down than one of the gaudy-jacket wearers slid down the bar to the stool next to hers. "Join us! No one should be alone on a wonderful night like this."

He had chiseled features and sparkling eyes. Something in them, though, something brittle under the smooth surface, made her wonder if he was a psychopath, or a criminal measuring her for a con job. She waved past him to the bartender and ordered a double shot of cheap scotch.

"I'm fine," Megan said.

"I'm Jax." He held out a hand with long, tanned fingers, a strong hand. It looked like it could juggle cannonballs. "You have, of course, heard of me?"

The bartender was mercifully quick with the scotch. Seeing this Jax fellow was still waiting for her to respond, she frowned. "I haven't heard of you. How about you go away and give me a chance to?"

His brows rose, his shock comically exaggerated. He adjusted his jacket, set his elbow on the bar, and said, "Let me start over, then. How do you do? I'm Juan Pollard, captain of Team South America. My friends and fans call me Jax. You sound local. Californian. Do I guess right? Are you a player or staff?"

"I am drinking alone," she said pointedly. His talented hands and jacket-straining muscles said "one-night stand potential," but no, there was definitely a vibe about him that was putting her off. Like a pretty bottle of poison.

"Staff, then." Jax winked. "A player never refuses a chance to brag. Let me buy you another. What are you having?"

This guy was not getting the hint. She leaned all the way away from him. He reached for her glass, and she put her hand over it. "What I'm having is a bad time."

An equally beefy and overconfident man pointed at her, striding purposefully over. "There you are!"

Megan narrowed her eyes. He had the sort of bland good looks casting directors fawned over, dark brown skin that made his light brown eyes pop, coiffed hair of the deepest black, and the look of someone who never doubted he was wanted.

"Excuse me?" He pushed his shoulder between her and Jax. "We were waiting for you." He faced her, winking, so Jax couldn't see. "Remember? Over at our table." He jerked his head toward the back of the room.

Ah, this guy thought he was "rescuing" her.

Jax, for his part, reared back like a cobra. "The lady was talking to me, Myers."

The said Myers smiled his movie-poster smile. "That may be, but we had a previous engagement. You can't cheat your way to that."

At the word "cheat," Jax jumped to his feet. "You are calling me a cheat? That's rich."

The hate between these two men was visible, burning the air between them. "So that wasn't you in Barcelona?"

"You talk a lot of shit for a man whose team isn't expected to make it past the first round."

Myers pressed close until their chests were almost touching. "Spoken like a man who owes his neck to a technicality."

Jax tilted his head and licked his lips. "If you're alive next year, *I'll* be able to say the same."

Megan picked up her scotch. "I'll leave you two lovebirds alone." She retreated to the one empty table in the bar, in a far corner.

A woman at the next table leaned back from her chair as Megan approached. "They are lovebirds! Good one!"

Megan hadn't said it for anyone else's appreciation. She knocked her double shot back. It burned nicely, but she felt no effect from the alcohol yet.

"Let me," the strange woman said, and improved Megan's opinion of her by already having a tumbler of whiskey at hand, which she passed to Megan. "I was doing a flight." She listed drunkenly, so that was certainly true. In front of her were three empty glasses and another full one.

Megan sipped the whiskey. It was smooth and smoky.

"I'm Mitzi!" the woman said, bouncing as she said it, which such a name almost required. She held out a bronzed hand with candy-pink nails.

Megan squinted. The voluminous brown curls and surgically precise eyebrows rang a distant bell. She was wearing athletic wear, a zipped hoodie, and a silver whistle on a chain. A coach? Megan imagined her posed contrapposto on a giant banner. "You're . . . a cheerleader?"

"Got it in one!" Mitzi slapped the table, spilling some of her remaining drink. "It's probably the drinks, but I love you."

"It's the drinks."

Mitzi laughed like that was the best joke she'd ever heard.

Megan curled over her glass and tried to drink fast. The whiskey was too fine to gulp, but she sipped quickly.

Myers the movie star came over. "I'd like to apologize for that." He tilted his chin back toward the bar.

Hrm. There was nothing dangerous in his eyes, just arrogance. This Megan could work with. There was nothing quite like a guy you didn't like for a one-night stand. You didn't feel bad leaving him in the morning. She leaned back. "No need to apologize. I enjoy watching two muscular men rub against each other."

"Touché." He dropped uninvited into the seat next to her. "Jax and I have . . . issues. He thinks he's God's gift to the sport."

"Whereas you think you aren't?"

His bright, even smile flashed. "I didn't say I *wasn't*. But Jax was just lucky. Four years ago, if North America's two best starters hadn't been sidelined by injury, well, we wouldn't have to deal with his witty repartee."

Megan remembered enough of Lola's constant chatter to know one of those sidelined players was the renowned India. "I notice a lot of people like to rewrite history in this sport. I'd have thought you'd be more consigned to fate."

"Fate is what we make it," he said with a settling of his shoulders that implied he made his own fate with his fists.

"I think it sounds like Jax is right. You talk like a man who hasn't been tested."

He raised an eyebrow. "*I've* never been tested?" He said that like she was supposed to know something about him.

Megan nodded. The good whiskey was warming her up. "Fate makes fools of us all."

"So you have never seen me, specifically, be tested? Seen me single-handedly drag victory kicking and screaming from the jaws of defeat?"

"That is a lot of mix in that metaphor." Megan tapped Mitzi and waved for her to hand over her last drink. Mitzi was talking animatedly with another woman and seemed surprised she still had it, so she passed it, only spilling a little.

Myers shook his head. "You seriously have no idea who I am."

"That was Jax's line too."

He addressed the ceiling. "I love this."

"I doubt it."

He bit his lower lip, studying her now. "I'm Jerry."

"I'm really not interested in who you are."

"No?"

She let her eyes drop down his body. "I just care what you can do."

He licked his lips. "I can outscore the entire Eastern Seaboard at Javelins."

She shoots, she misses. How unsubtle did she have to be? Megan got up. "I am not talking about sports, and I need another drink."

He was in her way. "You can't be here, in Champion's Village, and not want to talk about sports."

"What's to talk about? It's a game. You play, someone wins, someone dies."

He gaped at her. "It isn't just a game."

"Yeah, it is." She let her body brush thoroughly over his as she stepped around him. The firm bumps of his arms and thighs felt nice indeed.

He followed her. "What about the deaths caused by wars? The inhumanity? Armed gangs going from country to country to brutalize and force their leaders' agendas? That doesn't happen anymore. Because of the game."

His eyes were intent. This was a true believer. His potential as a one-night stand was vanishing. True believers never shut up. "That's what you see. I see a state-subsidized gambling addiction." She was going to have to get very drunk to get through this night. She waved for service.

Jerry wasn't finished, however. He blocked her view of the bartender. "You say it's addiction, but it's human nature. The id is part of us, and without a healthy outlet, we'd have anarchy. We'd have holocausts."

"Yeah, whatever." She finally got the bartender's attention. He disentangled himself from a needy group and headed her way.

"We are putting our lives on the line for the good of humanity." Jerry gestured over her head. "I'm defending our country with my skill. Because I care. I could have stayed in the National League, saved my life, lived comfortably. Any team would be glad to have me."

She gave him a frank look. "That so? If you're too slow to pick up on a pass, I'm not sure you're any kind of player."

He clearly didn't get the hint. "I'm the best player there is," he said, eyes flashing heat.

Was he serious? "Not better than me, Mr. Jerry Myers."

His smirk was pure condescension. "You just got here. What are you? Some team's nutritionist? A high school coach? Aspiring wannabe reporter?"

Megan felt a snap in her spine as she straightened to her full height. "You don't know what I am. Put your muscle where your mouth is. There are plenty of practice pods. I'll beat you at your favorite game."

He backed up. "That is . . . adorable. But, look, we're in the pre-trials. I can't go playing a random pick-up in a bar. Central would not be happy with me."

"Wow, that's a new excuse."

"I'm sure you're very good for your level, but I could hurt you." He held up his hands. "Save your ego for your local tryouts. I have nothing to prove smashing some poor amateur."

Amateur? He was probably some local semipro who hadn't played anyone outside of the city limits, here to try for the big leagues. Like her, but not as good. "I think you're all talk."

Megan's order of four shots of Jack had arrived. Jerry picked up one of them and downed it. He breathed out hard through his nose. "What the hell. No risk, no reward."

Megan snatched the next shot with a proprietary glare. "I'm not risking anything."

"I mean—" He lowered his face to within an inch of hers "—what do we wager?"

"Prolonged electric shock."

He raised both eyebrows. "It's not fun if it isn't anything personal."

Too bad she'd lost interest in banging him; she had a number of very personal bets she had made in the past with men in bars that they had always ended up delivering on. As it was, the risk factor never motivated her directly. "What do you want, my class ring?"

He looked her up and down. "A kiss."

8

Megan blinked. "A kiss?" The man who had missed two very competently executed passes threw this at her? As much as she would have enjoyed extorting a kiss herself from the right guy, being asked to give one up rankled her. It made her less than a competitor. It made her the prize.

She didn't want to think too hard about the hypocrisy in that. "That's not happening. Dream on." Any interest she had had in him was fully gone. He'd probably missed her flirting because he couldn't handle a woman with a mind of her own.

He shrugged one shoulder, smiling like he'd already won. "It's only a problem if you think you're going to lose."

She wasn't going to lose, but that didn't mean she couldn't do what she could to make him regret his chosen stakes. "If I win, you'll be kissing *where* I want you to kiss."

"Is that so?" He looked intrigued, and Megan almost cackled, already imagining having him kiss Jax on the lips. Two handsome men, equally pissed off, kissing each other because she'd beaten them. Yes, that would be a good end to the evening.

Mitzi stumbled up to them. "Oh, gosh. You guys are going to play? One-on-one? Jerry . . . Jerry, Central won't like this." She tottered and pointed slightly to his right. "You're drunk. You could get injured. Think of the team."

Jerry offered the tipping cheerleader a hand. "Relax, Mitzi. I've got this one in the bag."

One more over-the-top statement of his confidence and Megan was going to make that a French kiss between him and Jax.

People around the room were rushing to plug in to the table hookups to watch. A dark man with a shaved head hurried into the booth nearest her. "A one-on-one! With Jerry Myers! I'm posting odds."

His companion said, "Sweet! Bar fight!"

Megan overheard a woman behind her whispering into her device, "No, man, if Herman Rivera gets wind of this, it'll be all over the news. We'll all be in trouble."

"I can't believe I get to see this," someone else gushed.

Megan herself couldn't believe all those people were talking about it like it was a big deal. This was her usual Thursday night, with one exception. She checked that Jax was still at the bar. Her beautiful bet wouldn't work if he left. Excellent, Jax was plugging in to watch the match. He caught her glance and smiled. He pointed at her and raised a thumb like he was betting on her. *Pucker up, asshole, you're about to kiss a true believer.*

The bar had pods specifically for one-on-one games like these, initiated over drunken bravado. Megan felt tipsy, but on the good side of it, no dizziness, just that warm sense of invulnerability and her own cleverness. She strapped into the public pod with practiced ease. It was faux wood grain with thick, indestructible plastic, but still a good model for a bar, no doubt owing to the neighborhood. The sleeves that replaced a personal hap-suit were clean and had self-adjusting nanites that trimmed them to her size as she slipped them on.

The game loaded before she had time to read the whole menu. Javelins. Ah, of course, the one he'd bragged about. Megan found herself on a grassy plain, a lone baobab tree in the distance. The sky smoldered with orange and red. Fourteen javelins with pink ribbons were staked point-first into the ground before her. She was wearing a suede tank top and bikini bottom, both edged with feathers and beads.

Jerry appeared opposite her. The game had put him in a sexy little loincloth. His legs were as muscular as his torso. Feathers on leather thongs adorned his calves. Definitely worth the view. He had fourteen of his own javelins, each with purple ribbons fluttering from the shaft. He stalked back and forth, hefting one in his hand. "Do you know how to play?"

"It's been a while." She yanked the nearest spear from the dirt. "I prefer to have my hands on people when I beat them."

"Ah, a barbarian. Too bad you said I can pick the game. I prefer elegance and skill." He balanced his javelin gracefully and waved his hand through the glowing "Ready to Start" sphere.

Javelins was a timed game, so you had to agree to start. Megan adjusted her stance and grip, then waved through her own soft, glowing orb.

The ground shook underfoot, and a chasm tore open between them. He'd selected the highest starting level, with randomized terrain hazards. Animals started coming, screaming in panic, their earthquake steadier, pulsing. When the game first came out, people objected to virtually killing wild animals, so now the object was to not hit the fleeing ibex, cheetahs, and zebras. Scrambling between them were alien monsters, purple whirls of claws and tentacles snarling and snapping at the varied creatures of Africa. (She knew these animals were not all from the same area, but what were virtual realities for if not to bend the rules?)

Megan didn't spare any attention for Jerry after seeing his first graceful, expert throw. She ran forward and threw just as her feet planted; it took her full body to get a straight throw hard enough to pierce alien chiton. She didn't look to see if her shot made it, yanking the next spear as a soft chime alerted her to the score.

The ground tore in front of her, and she had to leap backward. The earthquake made her stumble. She was tipsy, and it had been a long time since she'd played this, and never on a level with so much chaos. A series of chimes announced Jerry was racking up points. She pivoted, planted, and threw. A pillar of stone burst from the ground next to her, just to be difficult, and then, as she plucked her next spear, it toppled toward her. She had to roll to safety. Falling rocks? On the African savanna? There was no time to get mad. Megan shook the dirt from her face and focused. She felt the warmth, smelled the dry grass and the torn earth. She plucked another shaft without looking and leapt onto the stone pillar for the height advantage.

Jerry threw two quick shots at the start so he could relax and enjoy the view of his opponent. She was a lynx of a woman, and that kiss was going to taste sweet. Her small breasts really looked beautiful in that top, just a mouthful each. She was strong too. She was probably a coach or fitness adviser. Her legs were all muscle. Look at her leap!

Jerry assumed she was secretly flattered he'd picked the kiss wager and was playing it cool. Win or lose, she was going to have a chance to kiss North America's most eligible bachelor. What she wouldn't know was how much this meant for him. A real kiss, from someone who didn't know who he was. It would be nice to be with a woman who wasn't a groupie, didn't have all these preconceived ideas about him. He could remind himself he was still able to capture hearts just by being himself.

It was lonelier than he had imagined, being a top athlete. Even his teammates didn't really know him, the guy inside the muscles.

So, Jerry had a plan. He would pick the easy throws and score just above this woman, make it feel fairer than it was. Make her feel she'd earned it. Even if, let's be real, this wasn't even going to be exercise for him.

It was two scores to one, and there was an alien coming close. He dodged a warthog. Dangerous, the pod could beat you up with those hooves, but he had time. He slew his alien and checked the social chatter. It would be great if some of his fans caught wind of this. Beautiful publicity. Ah, there were a few watching, and the team. Wait . . . what was Mitzi talking to Indía about? He couldn't bring himself to ignore their comments.

Whoever this girl is, we need her on our team.

It's not over yet. He's buttering her up.

Maybe we should trade him for her.

Cute. Trade him for a woman who wasn't even going to play on a pro—

Jerry tossed an easy shot and happened to glance toward his opponent. She was jumping every terrain obstacle like they were chalk lines for four square. She ran straight up a stone pillar, and at the top she threw two spears at once, hitting both targets!

The ground tilted under him, and Jerry had to leap backward, narrowly missing a stone trap of his own. An ibex bounded over him, hooves breezing centimeters from his head, and he found himself in the dirt, away from his spears, and the sky overhead read 6–4, Pink.

She was better than he had expected. He shook his head and started to play for real. The random earthquakes and the charging of the animals picked up as the timer counted down. He had ground to catch up. With a shot clear and no choice where to run if he wanted to take it, he almost collided with a lion. He could smell the stink of its hide and fear-sweat as the animal pushed away from him, claws mercifully digging up dirt, not his chest. Mitzi was going to give him a lecture for that risk.

Perspiration poured from his brow into his eyes, and his hands slipped on the familiar wood shafts. He grunted, kept running, jumped a chasm, and took two more points quickly.

When he had done so, he looked up, ready to feel smug. No! It was tied, 7–7. And the random amateur lady was in the air, like a Valkyrie descending, her glossy black hair behind her and her javelin soaring from her hand straight toward a snarling, extra-point, giant alien.

The glowing letters now read 8–7.

How was she keeping up? No one threw javelins like he did. His shoulders were the size of her whole torso! He needed to take this seriously, or he was about to be publicly humiliated by some chick he just met in a bar. He felt the spectators, knew they were there, like chittering bugs in the background.

His social feed was lighting up. He had the publicity, all right. Hero defeated by a random schoolteacher. The obstacles were coming hard and fast now, and it was all he could do to stay upright and find an opening. He scored. She scored. He scored. She scored.

It was tied at ten apiece, and the clock was running out. He would not be able to live it down if, by some fluke, by some crazy accident, she beat him. He plucked up two javelins and ran toward her. He threw them at her feet. Not technically against the rules. She was running forward, and her ankles tangled with the wood, sending her sprawling into a chasm. Hitting any living thing that wasn't an alien was a negative point, but by the time she recovered he could easily score twice. Five seconds to go, the animals were pressing all around, the aliens themselves leaping over him, tentacles reaching, two easy hits at close range! He won! 11–10.

He howled his victory to the skies, fists raised as the sunset faded to black and the alien mothership descended, engulfing everything with doom, darkness, and the screams of animals.

Jerry popped the top of his pod and threw his hands up again in re-al-space. "Woo!" His teammates pressed forward to congratulate him. Kendell hoisted him in her strong arms. "That's my captain!"

Mitzi, looking much less drunk behind the throng, shook her head at him. "You are so lucky you didn't get hurt. I'd hurt you myself if we didn't need you."

There was his prize, yanking off the leads from her own pod and looking at him with obvious heat. He imagined her heart was racing, the adrenaline of the game rushing through her with no place to go, hitting up on the flattery of him wanting her, and also the beauty of seeing him perform. This was going to be so hot.

She was coming right for him. He raked his fingers through his sweaty curls. "You see? When you care, when it's personal, you play your heart out to win." He puckered his lips.

She shoved him, two hands flat to the chest, and he toppled back-ward over someone else's legs. "You almost broke my neck." She glared down at him, fury in every line of her features. "Never come near me again, asshole."

She stomped off.

Jerry sat on the floor. India helped him to his feet and gave his hip a squeeze. "Her loss."

Jerry felt like he'd missed something.

9

Megan covered her eyes against the bright lights as she entered the auditorium for the Junior Nationals tryouts. Fury and whiskey had sent her to a quick, deep sleep, but it had been way too late, and she was definitely dehydrated. Dad, thankfully, took one look at her and handed her a bottle of orange juice. "Up training, sweet pea?"

She made a sound that might have been mistaken for yes. Everyone should have a father who assumed the best of them. She could feel the headache bleeding out of her body as she drank the life-giving orange juice.

"Your mother said she was holding seats for us . . . ah! There she is."

Megan risked a wincing glance. This place was so white. White ceiling, white chairs, white floor. What sadist had designed this? Someone who hated the cleaning staff?

Mom was standing and waving for them, Lola beside her in a new Team North America (Junior Division) bodysuit. Lola looked terrified. Well, it was a pretty big deal, this junior match. She wasn't ready for this level. She hadn't trained enough. Maybe this would show her that.

The auditorium floor held sixteen pods—eight each for the two teams, arrayed in fans facing each other like giant sunflower seeds setting up to tip-off at basketball. Behind this were diaphanous screens waiting to be filled with real-time views of the game during play for those who didn't bring a device to jack in or who didn't want to lose the feeling of being in an audience.

Lola fidgeted nervously. She scooted over to Megan as she took her seat. "I did squats all night. My butt is killing me."

That was dumb. Megan only just stopped herself from saying so. Mom and Dad wouldn't approve. She scanned the bleachers now that her head was feeling better. She stopped, shocked. The jerk who had cheated at Javelins was sitting in some high-class box off to their right. "I can't believe it, that asshole. He must have a younger sibling or something playing. I feel sorry for that kid."

Lola followed her gaze. "What ass—" She cut her eyes quickly to Mom and Dad and amended "—butthole?"

Megan pointed. "I met that idiot last night. He cheated me at a game of Javelins. For a kiss. Creep, right?"

Lola's eyes got big. She grabbed Megan's shoulders. "You got kissed by Jerry Myers?!"

"Ew, no. He cheated. I'm not paying on that wager. Anyway, who is Jerry Myers that you care?"

Lola, with eyes like a crazy person, dragged Megan from her chair, down the length of the bleachers, and out to the street entrance to the auditorium. She pointed up at one of the huge banners adorning the light posts all along Champion's Village. "That is Jerry Myers!"

Sure enough, there he was, smug movie-star grin and all, with a goddamned javelin in hand, re-created in twenty feet of glistening muscle and shining fabric.

Lola said, "He's only the most famous person on the planet! He was on the last championship team! He had a clash with the coach and had to work his way back after dominating every city and state team and oh, my god! He's the best player ever!"

Megan snorted. "He ain't that good. I should have beat him."

She turned on her heel and went back into the auditorium with Lola's "Oh, my gaaaaawd!" echoing behind her.

The Junior Nationals were playing Ulama with full safety rules. They were sloppy and tentative in a way you didn't see in the pros, and yet had flashes of brilliance you didn't see in a school game. Megan expected to suffer through watching, but from the first hit, she was on the edge of her seat. Her kid sister had fire. How had she missed it? That drive, that quick plant-and-pivot: that was her work, forcing Lola through those ladder drills. It was hard not to get caught up between her own pride, Mom cheering at every point, and Dad wincing at every hit.

But it was maddening to watch a game and not be able to affect its outcome. Megan twitched every time Lola went left when she should have gone right. Then Lola completely missed an opportunity to block. Megan held her head, more upset than she thought she would be. Her dad blinked cluelessly.

"What's wrong? That was good. She got away from that big girl before she hurt her."

Situational awareness. Megan hadn't taught Lola anything about keeping her head on a swivel. "She's not going to make the team, that's it," she said.

They let the other team tie things, which put it back at zero-all. Megan felt like she was going to pass out before the game was over. "Left! Your other left!"

Lola planted and pivoted, turning her right to a left, surprising the entire other team, who'd left her an open shot at the hoop.

That . . . that was pretty good. Megan felt her heart racing.

The game ended in a tie after two hours of regulation play—junior rules.

Lola joined a mob of her teammates on the field, all laughing, and hugging, and talking. Their coach talked to them too. Megan and her parents were part of a general throng held just off the play area.

"They aren't announcing the team," Mom observed, craning her neck to study the overhead screens.

At last, Lola came up to them, all drenched in sweat. "I think I did pretty good!"

Megan tried to get her to calm down to listen. "You need to remember to check out-court. They come up behind you when you're charging the wall. And when you rebound—"

Suddenly, everyone in the room was cheering. Mom jumped up and down, clapping her hands. Lola broke free from Megan to run back into the play area.

The team roster had just been posted. Lola Mori was one of the six who would go on to represent the national team after this elimination bout.

Megan felt her dad's arm on her shoulder, hugging her. It was too loud to hear his words, but he repeated them a few minutes later: "She knows you're proud of her. Come on, it's pizza time."

Megan found herself alone in the bedroom of her parents' hotel suite, checking over her gear for tomorrow. She'd packed it all ahead of time. Her suit, her powder, her athletic tape. Her head ached. She shouldn't have drunk so much the night before. She was at a deficit on hydration. She pulled open a liquid-gel pack and sucked it down. In the other room, the rest of the family was eating pizza and drinking sodas, watching the news to see if there would be any mention of the Junior Nationals Team.

The bedroom door banged open. Lola grabbed her arm. "You have to come! Hurry!" She looked panicked. "Come on!"

Confused, Megan let her little sister draw her into the front room. Mom and Dad looked back at her with shell-shocked expressions from the room's sofa. The media front man for the games, Herbert Rivera (she knew who he was: a hell of a lot more famous than Jerry-kiss-me-javelin-man), filled the screen. He was an uncle type, softly handsome in an aged, comfortable way. He was talking excitedly, so excitedly that sweat shone over his expressive dark eyebrows. "This is not a drill. This is an exclusive, straight from Central. Team North America just got an upgrade!"

The camera cut to a motley crowd in a bar. A mean-looking woman pushed a man to the ground. Oh, no. That was her. That was her pushing Jerry. They didn't include sound, so people couldn't hear her parting words. What would they assume, out of context? That she attacked random men in bars? She thought she looked good, though, stomping away through the crowd.

What were they doing filming her in a bar and putting it on national news feeds? Would they be showing footage if she had actually kissed the asshole? That was a horrifying thought. "He cheated," Megan said, voice weak.

Lola shushed her. Dad tried to wave her back. "You don't need to see this, honey."

Herbert Rivera gushed, "She's a fiery one! Jerry Myers can't defend himself from her charms! That's right, you just saw the newest edition to the team, Megan Mori, showing Jerry Myers what she thinks of anyone doubting North America can go all the way!"

"That's not why I pushed him," Megan said uselessly.

"I'm sure he deserved it." Her father tried to gently turn her away.

"Bert, she needs to see this!" her mother snapped.

Now the screen showed her struggling over a moving plinth, glistening with sweat under a tangerine sunset as she hurled a javelin. She recognized that shot, it was toward the beginning of the game. Her form was excellent. "Double M has her sights set on the world! Minutes after narrowly losing to the incredible, incomparable Jerry Myers, Central has declared this secret weapon is out of the bag. Signed to the team two weeks ago—"

Megan backed up. "That's not true."

"Your bout was all over the chat feeds." Mom jumped to her feet, hands clasped, looking like Megan had just been named Player of the Year. "Why didn't you tell us you played one-on-one with Jerry Myers!"

Her father sighed, stepping to the side to block her mother. "I can't believe you were so reckless. Playing strange men in bars. He's a killer. All these people are, and you don't belong with them."

"I was fine. I'd have beaten him if he hadn't cheated."

This wasn't the thing to say to her father. He threw up his hands. "It doesn't matter who won the stupid match! You almost defeated their star player in public. If they didn't hire you, they look foolish. So they lie. They act like you already signed on. It isn't right." Dad paused his angry rant and lowered his voice, looking pleadingly at her. "You have to say no. You can still say no. People quit all the time. Say it was personal differences."

"I'm not saying that. They haven't really offered me the job yet." Surely she still had to try out, right? There would be a contract, something she would have to read?

"Don't listen to your father. Every year, other families risk their children to serve our country. It's a privilege to be asked." Mom wiped tears from her eyes. She wrapped her arms around Megan. "I know you haven't been happy in a long time, and if this makes you happy . . . well, whatever you decide, I'm so, so proud."

Megan felt drained of emotion. There was too much to feel, in too many directions. "I guess I'm on the team."

Her dad went into the bedroom without another word. Lola did a splits-jump, cheering at the top of her lungs.

Megan had a message on her ring confirming that she was on the team and didn't need to report, but there was no message saying she couldn't report to the tryout, and it felt wrong not to.

Never do what they expect.

The World League elimination bout was in a larger, open-air stadium with twelve pods per side to determine who the final six players on each team would be. It was easy to find; she'd walked past it the day before.

Megan didn't know how to feel, still. She'd had strange, mixed-up dreams where she was teaching Ciera to play Javelins but her little legs and arms were not powerful enough, she was too slow. As Ciera was torn to pieces by wild dogs, Megan yelled at her baby daughter to fight harder.

She woke up terrified, reaching into a maelstrom of teeth and fur, disgusted with her own subconscious. She was supposed to meet her parents and Lola for breakfast. Worldwide House of Pancakes. Instead she went for a run.

Mom and Dad were supposed to head home tonight, after the tryout, back when it was going to be a tryout. Mom had to catch up on her bug counts. Dad had meetings with Lola's teachers to cover the work she'd miss while competing. Megan hoped they kept their plans, but she had a bad feeling they would linger nearby as long as she was in danger, as long as Lola was competing.

When it was close enough to the tryout start time that the venue would be open, Megan headed there. A woman in a staff T-shirt frowned in confusion when she scanned her ring, but showed her to a luxurious locker room, as yet empty. The lockers were wide cabinets in cherrywood, the floor thick carpet. Megan showered off from her run in a twelve-head shower room tiled in twinkling glass mosaics. There was something meditative about using such a large room alone.

As she packed her street clothes in a corner locker, a man with spiky blond hair, pale skin, and electric blue eyes stomped up to her. "That's my locker."

Megan looked at the cabinet, and around the large, empty room full of spacious, unclaimed lockers. "There wasn't a sign on it."

He strained like an attack dog on a leash. "I always take the locker in the corner. I need to be in the corner." His pale skin was flushing an alarming red. Veins stood out on his neck.

"Oh . . . kaaay." Megan gathered up her things and moved to a locker on the other side of the room.

The man opened the locker door violently and tore his bag open. He slammed one shoe and then another into the floor like he was trying to bury them.

"I see you've met Chet." A tall, graceful man walked in. His shaved head and goatee had hints of gray that stood out against his caramel skin, but he looked youthful. He held out a hand. "Hasan. You won't remember me, but I saw you push our captain onto his ass."

Megan hesitated, but took his hand. His fingers were cool and dry. "How do you feel about that?"

Hasan squeezed and let go. "You don't play at this level without learning to forgive eccentricities. Me, I have to have a locker with an even number." He opened the locker next to the one she'd just moved to. "You don't mind?"

Megan glanced back at Chet, who seemed to be having an argument with his bag. "Is that your only eccentricity?"

"Hm." Hasan sat down and set about removing his shoes. "You might not want to look too deep. Chet over there? He's a pure-born psychopath. He's in this for the pleasure of knowing he might kill a man."

A woman walked in, head upright like she had a crown balanced on it. Her raven hair hung in a heavy ponytail down her back. She gave Hasan and Megan an imperious glare, like she'd expected this to be an empty room, and went straight back to the shower area. Hasan tilted his head after her. "India? She's one of those who simply can't imagine losing. This is all a pageant to her greatness, far as she can tell."

Megan stretched, half her attention on Hasan's warm voice as he described each player who came in. "Ah, Rucker. She's here for the pure love of the game. I think she'd play against herself, wagers and all, if she were the last living person on the Earth. And that's Rex. Don't mess with him. Just don't. He has a rage in him. This is the only place he can exist."

Megan wasn't sure how useful any of this information was. It wouldn't help her hit a person at the right moment to know he was angry. "Half of these people won't be back tomorrow," she said.

Hasan was still and quiet at that, like he wanted to say something and was stopping himself.

Megan brushed her hair and bound her ponytail tight for the pod. "How does this tryout work if you are already on the team?"

Hasan gave her a quizzical look. "Just a second." He got up and met the next woman, who had breathtaking musculature and very dark skin, at the door. She could have been a model, a weight lifter, or both. Hasan gave her a half hug and back pat that she returned with an extra squeeze and a touch to the back of his head.

"Kendell, you're an ease to this old man's heart."

"You're too good for this," she said.

Were they a couple? No, it was mere friendliness. Kendell went and gave a similar hug to the next man. She even bumped fists with Chet, who put his fight against the universe on hold to grin, wrap his other hand around her wrist, and nod. That might have been as close to a hug as he went.

Megan felt uneasy. The room was filling up. These people . . . this was their lives. They had pursued professional pod gaming to the highest levels, and they knew they shared that, whatever their personal reasons. They'd played together in lower leagues or in previous tryouts.

They were a part of a community. She was just looking to fill the emptiness. Suddenly, she didn't want to be around Hasan anymore.

He brushed his elbow against hers. "Here comes Indía. First thing you should know about her—"

"Is she a prattling gossip? Because that would suck." Megan picked up her wristbands and moved away. The last thing she needed was the guy everyone liked. He could keep his commentary and the secret in his sad eyes he was so obviously eager to let slip.

She was dressed. There was no reason to hang around. She hurried to the exit.

And ran right into Jerry. He looked down at her, eyes smoldering with heat. He had probably seen the news too.

She felt a flush of embarrassment, but also anger. "So, they let cheaters in this tryout?"

"Let's get one thing straight." He pushed her, hard, and she stumbled backward, barely keeping her feet. "You don't belong here. A public relations manager somewhere decided to give you what you didn't earn."

Megan was really glad she hadn't slept with him. "I really don't care what you think."

"You should. I'm team captain."

"Which means what, exactly? You get the big drink cup?"

"I don't like troublemakers on my team. I don't like people who don't care about the greater good, who aren't willing to sacrifice themselves for North America."

Megan couldn't believe this garbage. "So just you and Chet, then?" She jerked her thumb back at the crazy white guy who was doing push-ups with punishing ferocity in front of his locker.

Jerry's jaw clenched tight. "Central sees something in you. Better make sure it shows in the game." He hit her with his shoulder as he stalked past.

Megan shook her head and left the locker room. The open space of the stadium was better. There was sky, and wind, and sun. And fake grass. She looked at the insane number of seats. There were already people in some of them, tiny figures camping out, making the stadium look even larger.

She started a light jog around the perimeter. Was this any different than running around her neighborhood? Did she feel any different?

"Mori! Hey, MM!" A figure turned away from a conversation to wave at her.

Were people going to be bothering her now? Was she a celebrity? Megan scowled and sped up her jog to a full run.

"Wait!" the voice called, and then faded.

She made it around the track where a stout white man stepped in her way, waving his hands, a ball cap in one fist. "Mori! Talk to you a second."

She swerved around him. He followed. "I'm your coach, goddamnit. Coach Mustaine."

A coach? She really didn't sign up for this. She hadn't had a coach since the Kern County Crusaders, and she'd been a different person then. She'd . . .

She couldn't imagine being that woman again. Getting up at dawn for practice, joking with her teammates, caring if they beat San Bernardino.

He was a heavy man, muscular and thick, like a wrestler, but he kept pace with her. "I got questions. They say you're in no matter what."

He was huffing hard between words. Megan took pity on him and slowed to a walk. "I'm not so sure about that."

The coach wiped his forehead with the back of the hand that held his hat. "Everyone playing at this level has a bigger chance of dying than making it to the final game, and in that final game you still have a fifty percent chance of dying, do you understand that?" He stepped in front of her, making her stop. "A lot of people, they come in thinking they're the exception, like they can't lose. They've never lost a pick-up or a school game. Is that you?"

"I lost last night, or didn't you hear?"

Coach Mustaine knit his brow at her. "I don't think you understand what I'm getting at. You're about to be one of six, and every one of them has either a god complex or a death wish or both. You're some rookie foisted on them at the last second. If they think you're hurting their odds of winning, they will find a way to remove you."

"I'm not afraid to die. Are we done?"

He huffed and looked back at the tunnel to the changing room. "Every person in that locker room is not afraid of death. That's a requirement to get past signing up. Dying's easy."

"Well, I don't see what else they can do to me."

"Believe me, they'll find something. They'll hurt you in a way you have to live with." He stared hard at her, and then shook his head and flapped his hat like he hadn't liked what he saw and was giving her up as a lost cause. He jogged back toward the locker room entrance, where other players were emerging.

10

Megan was in no mood to listen to a pep talk after that, but Coach Mustaine called everyone together. Twelve rivals, fighting her for a chance to risk their lives, and they were supposed to form a circle around Coach like they were just another sports team.

Mustaine slapped his cap against his thigh to silence the last muttering. "After tonight, our team roster is final. You've all checked your stats and scores and think you know where you stand, but we're not leaving everything up to the eggheads with spreadsheets and predictive models. I'll be watching, too, and our staff of veteran players. We're looking for more than raw ability." He pointed his cap at Indía, who rolled her eyes. "We need to see heart and teamwork." He pointed with the cap at Hasan and then Kendell. He turned in a slow circle, looking each of them in the eye. "People have been talking shit about our chances. They say too many losses have sapped all the talent out of our nation, that we'll never have another LaTonya, another McKee, another Caprita Bell. I disagree. Six of you are the men and women who can restore our national pride. Defend our freedoms. Put North America back on top of the World Order. Is that you? Do you believe it?" He finally affixed his battered cap on his head, like screwing the top on a jar. "You'd better."

The gathered men and women were riveted to this drivel. Megan glanced up and saw Lola and her parents waving frantically from the front of the stands. She imagined waving back wasn't appropriate. God, would they stop talking and just play already?

Mustaine called a moment of silence for the fallen players from the last games. It crawled interminably on until he finally lifted his head and slapped his hands. "That's it. Ten minutes to suit in. No fancy outfits, no tattoos, no personal mods of any kind. Stay in standby until you see green, and then I want you all to come out hard. Good luck."

Finally.

Megan jogged to the nearest pod and strapped in. It felt like it had never been touched. The seat was supple, conforming to every curve of her back. Cool air blew in through the seat. Nice. She hoped that wouldn't interfere with her immersion.

She closed the lid and waited for the neural link. Her vision flickered with the fastest loading screen she'd ever seen, and she sank into the standby area, which was dressed as a colonial palace, a vast dome overhead and statues in niches around the distant circumference. The terrazzo floor was cut into rays of colors and stars.

The others materialized around her. Jerry gave her a dirty look, then shouted to the center of the room, "Play fair, everyone, but play like your lives depend on it. That's the only way to play from here on out."

Good. That was the only way Megan ever played.

Indía tossed her head and rolled her shoulders. She glanced at Megan. "Don't get in my way, rookie."

"For North America!" Kendell shouted, and most of the players echoed this.

Then the dome became fully infused with green light and fell away around them like a curtain cut free from its ropes. The world was now rainbow-colored. Fat, saturated spotlights roved against a darkness that felt close. The warmth and pressure implied they were in an enclosed room. The floor was shining wood, bent and curved into hillocks and twists that the spotlights glided over.

"It's Roller Madness!" Herbert Rivera called from who-knows-where. He sounded like he was all around her. "What an unorthodox pick for the final team qualifier! Possibly chosen to highlight India Thomas's days in Junior League roller derby."

Megan picked up one foot to start running, and her other foot flew out from under her. She hit the floor with her ass. Her feet were heavy and slippery. Skates. They were all wearing skates. The air was filled with the rumble of wheels on wooden tracking. This wasn't a sport she had played before, and she was flailing badly, trying to get a feel for her feet, while others sailed easily by. She saw them going up and down the hills. Was it one track, or several?

Text scrolled at the bottom of her vision. Comments from people watching, odds calculations. She heard screaming, a group chanting, "In-dee-ya! In-dee-ya!" How was she supposed to concentrate to move herself in all this noise?

Megan craned her neck up. Up among the swimming spotlights, the darkness thinned to show the stands, a virtual representation of the people really watching the match. It was hard to see any individual, but their presence was heavy, like a council of gods.

She got one foot under herself, and then the other, and slowly raised back to standing. Of all the things, why had she never learned to skate? She made tiny motions, scooting forward. She was doing it. She was moving. She tried to see someone else's feet. Okay, so she could drag one foot back and to the side . . . yes, she was rolling. She did it again.

The track dipped sharply and she screamed, an airless moment, windmilling her arms, and she was back on her ass.

"Get up! You can do it!" A startlingly handsome young man suddenly appeared, crouched in front of her, reaching out as if to help her up. He glistened oddly, like a firefly light was dancing over his skin, and he was in sneakers. Sweet, wonderful sneakers. She reached for his arm and passed through it.

He curled the hand back with an apologetic look. "Cheerleader, sorry. I'm David. But come on! You got this! This is it, this is the day you leave it all on the field. There's no second chance on today."

Megan crawled to the top of the next hill and got her feet under her, if only to shut him up. He vanished as she started moving steadily forward. She was getting the hang of it, shuffling forward. She crouched as she rolled downhill without falling. The speed carried her part of the way up the next hill, and she kept the momentum. Yes, she could do this.

An elbow slammed into her, hard, from behind, sending her sprawling. "Oops, sorry, rookie," India said, swaying as she skated backward to wave mockingly. The sound of coins falling accompanied the glowing letters "India +1" that rose out of the ground and faded as they reached eye height.

Mitzi appeared, glittering the same as David had. She still had her silver whistle, swaying as she bent over. "You have to pass people for points."

Wow was that information she didn't need. "I can't move four inches without falling! How do I pass people?"

Mitzi gave her a sad look. "You knock them down, sugar."

Megan dug the rubber toe stops on her skates into the floor and launched herself after India with an inchoate roar. Skittering, pushing, she got going fast, but India was faster, crouched forward, a hand behind her back as she skated in an effortless rhythm up the next hill and around a bend, out of view.

"You got it!" Mitzi cheered and stepped sideways, melting into a low wall that separated the next section of track from this one. Her insubstantial ass was off to bother someone else.

Megan's knee squeaked against the floor, a painful sound

accompanied by the heat of friction, but she got around the bend mostly on her feet. Someone was coming up behind her. She could hear their wheels shushing.

She was going to be passed again, giving someone else a point. She looked behind. It was Kendell, staring her down, coming like a freight train. Megan grabbed the top of the low wall Mitzi had vanished into and got herself almost standing. There was a smug grin on Kendell's face.

Megan pushed off the wall. She sailed without control, flailing, but she'd timed it right. She collided with Kendell, sending them both sprawling.

Megan dug deep for the strength to move her heavy, skate-bound feet, scrambling as fast as she could over legs and arms, forward, around the bend, where she hit a sudden, very steep drop. She got into a deep squat and let herself be a wheeled cart, a prisoner of gravity. Like a bowling ball, she crashed into a tangle of ankles.

The sound of coins falling and pink letters rose up around her. "Megan +2."

Megan alternated using gravity and bear-crawling for the rest of the game and swung her skates out to trip people as they started to pass her. It was dirty, ugly, and inexpert. There was no time to look at the scores, but the screaming from the crowds seemed to coincide with her doing something right.

A timer counted down, the fans chanting along with it, and then there was a loud buzzer. Megan stood, panting, able at last to glide forward on her own two feet as the world faded away around her.

She fell out of her pod feeling like she'd been tumbled in a barrel of rocks. She had friction burns on her knees, shins, and the heels of her hands. She blinked in confusion at the sunny day. The crowds were farther, their roar tinny with distance now. She cradled her arms and limped away from the pod so she could see the hanging screens. Around her, everyone else was getting out, not nearly as cringing and sore.

The screens flashed, and the standings came up. The audience roared its delight, like the results were unexpected but wonderful. First place, Indía, second place, third . . . fourth place Megan Mori. She'd done it. She had earned her place. She raised her chin and straightened her spine, though it hurt.

Unlike the Junior Nationals, there was no allowing the spectators onto the field to congratulate the athletes. Most of the other competitors jogged up to the edge of the stands to squeeze hands and exchange well-wishes over the fence. Lola and her parents were in the throng there, reaching their fingers toward her. Megan turned and made her way to the locker room, counting the steps until she could sit down.

Coach was standing near the entrance. He didn't look up from a screen he was projecting. "Exhibition game in one week. Better ice your everything. If you kill yourself, that's gonna give me paperwork."

Asshole. She limped into the locker room, thankful she was hidden enough from sight. But she wasn't the only one heading straight in. One of the losers was crying, slumped against a corner of the wall, sobbing like he'd lost everything.

Hasan sat next to her locker. He looked like he'd given up all hope in life.

He'd come in second.

Megan found herself moved to a new floor in the residence, with six luxurious suites for the six players on Team North America. It had the same dark gray rubberized flooring and bright red and black accents, but it was larger, with a white leather couch and a minibar. A contract waited in her inbox, waiting for her to record her assent. She knew, because six giant banners with their names on them now flew from the front of the building, that the full team was herself, Jerry, Indía, Hasan,

Kendell, and Chet. An arrogant pretty boy, a drama queen, a gossip, a fanatic, and whatever Chet was. There was something wrong with each of them. She wasn't like them, was she?

Was this a luxury hotel or a madhouse? She was glad the door had a chain lock.

There were anxious messages from her family. Directions to another restaurant for dinner. Weirdly, that Mitzi person had sent her a welcome message. It was a brief looping video of Mitzi standing with another, darker woman and two men, one of whom was the Asian hottie who had utterly failed to help her roller skate. "Welcome to the team from your cheer squad: Mitzi, David, Kirk, and Mtume. We're here to help you succeed!" They all waved, and then the video looped. She deleted it.

She kept to her suite. There were little bottles of whiskey in the minibar. She drank herself to dreamlessness.

Her ring buzzed her awake in the middle of the night with a reminder that she hadn't signed the contract and that the facilities were for team members only. She should have taken it off. Her head felt large, cottony. She rolled over and scrolled to the bottom of the contract, blinking and making the gesture to sign.

She would tell her dad she thought about not doing it.

Assuming no one would bother her for keeping whatever hours she wished, she got up and went for a run. Champion's Village felt like a stage set after dark. No lights on, no dogs or cats making noise. No one really lived there. The roads were smooth, though, good for running.

She turned a corner and stopped. The building in front of her had a giant poster of her covering its entire side. She was turning into a high kick, a snarl on her face. Whatever she had been kicking was whited out, like she'd touched off an explosion with her foot.

What had she gotten herself into?

11

Megan kept to herself. Her parents and sister called every day and left rambling messages. She ignored them. She'd successfully made a move, gotten out of her parents' house. Shouldn't that make them happy? There were messages from the team, too, long documents on strategy and practices.

She knew she should go to the practices. The idea of facing those people, though. A couple times someone came and knocked on her door. "I have ice cream!" Mitzi called. That almost worked.

Every day felt a thousand years long. She counted the seconds until she could get into a pod again. At least it was only a week until their first game. She endured it like a prison sentence.

Saturday morning, they flew to Yakutsk, Russia, in a private ion drive plane. It cut the air silently, the long wings glowing. You could hear the occasional call of a bird outside. Jerry walked down the lane of couches, handing out personal information sheets on the North Asian team. "They finalized their roster yesterday. Nergui is out, much to no one's surprise after that loss to South America. Their strong arm is now Davydov. Study him, Kendell."

He stopped next to Megan. "I'm probably wasting my breath,

seeing how much effort you put in to coming to practices, but I want you to concentrate on Gimhae. She's a flanker, and now you are too."

Megan didn't raise her ring finger to take the file Jerry offered, so it bounced back to hang in front of him. He dropped his hand to his side. The file projection cut into her knee. "What is this, you made the team, now you want us all to die?"

Megan returned her gaze to the window. "It's an exhibition match."

"You play how you practice. I need you to play this match like your life depends on it. Next week is too late to get your head in the game."

She waved him away. "I always play like my life depends on it."

Jerry picked up her hand and forced the file into her ring. He then stomped away as loudly as he could in the narrow, carpeted plane.

Kendell leaned over the back of her seat. "Hey, North America is dead last in the World Congress right now. Our country is depending on us to get at least up to halfway. Then we'll have the voting power to rebalance trade, bring coffee back to where we can afford it, fix the border with South America."

Megan tried to understand caring that much about such external things. "You'll be happy dying for halfway up the World Congress?"

Kendell raised her chin. "I love my country." Her expression was pure suicide bomber.

Indía kicked her long legs up across the aisle to rest on the back of Kendell's chair. "We should win this one, anyway. Starting us against North Asia is an insult. Central has it in for us. They're hoping we get soft."

"Central is neutral," Coach Mustaine said, not looking up from the screens he was shuffling in his lap. "All they care about is healthy betting activity. Trust me, pushing the low teams down doesn't stir up excitement."

"We aren't a low team, though." Indía sounded like she'd had this argument a thousand times before. She looked to Jerry for support, but he held up a hand, not willing to go in against Mustaine. Her eyes flashed reproach. “We’re underrated. They want us to be more underrated so it’s dramatic when we win. That’s why they had our first match be that offensive American Football.”

Hasan turned in his seat. “I like American Football. It lets us use all the potential players at once. It tests mental quickness too. We had to react to twenty different play charts.”

“No one outside of North America ever played it.” Indía gestured like she was serving the argument on a tray. “They made it look like we were starting out on easy mode, so even when we won, it didn’t improve our odds.”

“We only barely won,” Kendell muttered, studying her graphs with furious concentration. “We needed more defense.”

A lively debate broke out on the subject of the importance of defense.

Megan moved to the seat next to Chet. He was turning a knife over and over against his knee, but at least he wasn’t talking.

The Yakutsk stadium was a massive brutalist structure, an inverted Mayan pyramid. The impressive architecture was undone, however, by the pervasive smell of mold in the locker room. North Asia had been in the bottom rungs for longer than North America, and it showed.

Megan picked a locker this time that wasn’t near anyone.

“Good news,” Jerry said, walking in. “We won the toss to pick the game, so it’s Ulama, hip rules, minimal fouls. With my aim, Indía’s speed—” here he exchanged a choreographed hand-slap with Indía “—and Kendell clearing the way, we should have no trouble against this team.”

Megan felt the stress of the flight slough from her. Ulama was her best game. “Put me in front. I have the top score, worldwide.”

Jerry blinked at her like he couldn’t believe she’d talked. “Indía and I are the best shooters. You’re on flank defense with Hasan. Chet, you're on back-court like always. Get ready, everyone. Let's show this team they don't deserve to be in the same grid as us."

They logged in to a sweeping mountain steppe circled with flags. Other than the fancy starting room, it was just like logging in to a game at the local arcade. Megan saw the overlay: "Ulama—Hip Variation. Stakes: Level-Five Prolonged Electric Shock."

It was disappointingly familiar. She'd played this and won it a hundred times. Next time, the stakes would say "Life." That would be something. She felt a small thrill, anticipating it.

The proudly fluttering flags faded, and the Ulama court took their place, long and narrow, with the stone rings set high for serious competition. The crowd was replicated above, images of the highest-paying fans. More were present as voices and words slipped along the chat ticker at the bottom of Megan's vision.

There were odds, too, and statistics on bets placed. The projected words were like a soup of alphabet noodles swirling a foot off the ground wherever she looked.

The North Asian team wore blue loincloths and hip pads, the women sporting plain breast bands. Megan found herself similarly kitted out in red. The two teams formed a circle around the half-court line for the opening ceremony. Megan ground her bare toes into the clay, preparing to push off hard the second play began.

The other team served the ball into play. Megan leaped forward and . . . something went wrong. Instead of hitting a scrum of uncoordinated individuals, Megan was side-tackled before she got there. She scrambled to her feet, and the play was away from her, the North Asians forming a wedge to protect two players who passed the ball between them on their way to the hoop.

Suddenly, Herbert Rivera was standing on the foul line, gasping in over-sold shock. "What an unexpected break, early in this match, for North Asia!"

He glittered all over like the cheerleaders, a nonplay entity. What fresh hell was this? She was going to be risking her life with live color commentary? She tried to hip-check him in passing and passed through him like he was made of air. "Megan Mori was the darling of the betting sites this morning, but she doesn't seem to have what it takes in live competition. Can she recover from this humiliating mistake?"

"Flank!" Jerry shouted at her, running the other way.

Megan tore her focus from the sports reporter. North Asia was going to score, and soon. She didn't bother finding an opening. She headed straight to the hoop, at her top run. She would throw herself in the way. It was going to work, the other team was taking an oblique angle, avoiding Indía. Megan turned her back to the hoop . . .

And collided with Kendell.

"Watch where you're going!" Megan shouted, pushing her teammate down to get up to the hoop . . . too late.

"What an incredible shot!" Herbert Rivera floated in the air by the hoop. "Unbelievable. Very few Ulama games are decided by successful hoop shots. Most of the points come from fouls . . . like that one! Looks like Mori has gone out of bounds."

Megan had climbed the wall to get in the way again. Okay, it was a little against the rules. But they'd hit the hoop!

Worse than the orgasmic joy of Herbert Rivera's play-calling was the odds ticker Central kept running at the bottom of everyone's eyesight. There was no way to turn it off. North America now stood at an 85% chance of losing, and new calls to bet against them weren't being answered.

But Jerry had the ball. He'd managed to get between the North Asian players and knock it toward her. Megan scooped it from the ground with her forearm. She hip-checked a North Asian player who was trying to take it from her. Indía was open and gesturing to her to pass. Megan waved her off. She could hit the hoop from there. She was good at this. She bounced the ball from the wall to herself and lined up.

The shot hit the edge of the ring and bounced wildly. Megan dove to intercept it and collided with Jerry this time, but she was able to get up again and drive the ball in front of her.

Chet, of all people, that maniac, threw her to the ground and took possession of the ball.

Furious, Megan forgot they were a team and tackled him. He was all bone and sinew, twisting under her like gristle. It was all she could do to get separated from him again. Where had the ball gone?

"Get it together!" Kendell charged past. "I'm point, you're flank!"

Again with the flank business. Didn't they see they were losing? Now wasn't the time to stick with failed plans. This team wasn't trying.

David, the cheerleader, appeared in front of her, tight muscles glistening, wearing a tiny loincloth, jogging backward to stay on her as she caught back up to the scrum. "I will make sweet, sweet love to you if you just please follow the game plan."

Megan tore through his insubstantial form. Kendell was almost to the ball, now being passed between two North Asian players. Chet was hanging back by their goal. Indía and Jerry were staying near Kendell but letting her stay in front. They were blocking passing lanes. Okay, this made sense.

"Please." David popped in front of her. "Guard the flank, drive the play toward Indía, and I will do things to you with my tongue that will melt your brain."

Megan snarled, and he vanished on his own, hands held up in surrender. 4–0, North Asia. If she got four points, it would tie to zero. She could do this on her own, without their help. This was her game.

Megan charged forward.

Agony. Every joint locked against itself, every nerve a line of fire, her body wracked against the walls of her pod like a fish on the line, and she was helpless to do anything but scream through clenched teeth as it went on and on and on.

Chat boards ran with: "I knew they'd suck. They always suck. Why do I get my hopes up every year? Being a North American during MegaDeath every four years is like repeatedly hitting yourself in the balls."

Coach Mustaine sat at the back of the plane, conversing intently with Central. "Yes, of course, recruiting starts now. We gotta assume we're losing everyone game one."

Chet stared intently at Megan, rotating his knife, never blinking, and she thought again about ways she could be hurt that wouldn't kill her, that she would have to live with.

And on. Her throat burned down to her lungs, her br
it was boiling. She'd never felt this kind of torture. Why di
and end it?

And then the electric shock stopped. She hit the back
like gravity had just reinstated itself. She smelled urine a
sweat of fear. Tears were streaming out of the corners of he
this what she'd been subjecting her opponents to all this ti

So many times.

Had winning for so long turned her into a monster?

The pod lid wrenched open above her. Mustaine sho
"Well, get your ass up, loser. Lying there isn't going to make i

A reporter pushed a microphone in her face the secon
her feet. "How does it feel to have lost so thoroughly in yo
test as a competitor?"

"How do you think?" Megan lowered her head and push
a pressing crowd.

"That Megan Mori! She's still a firecracker. We'll be sa
go after next week."

No one looked at her in the locker room, or during th
pressed trip back to the plane.

No one said much of anything, the sound of various
describing how terribly they'd done. "Humiliated by Dav
North Asia have a new secret weapon?"

"North America's last-second personnel changes are ba
there any boneheaded mistake this coaching staff can't mal

"Let's watch the footage again, as our own Leah Ga
views a surly Mori coming out of her pod."

"North American political leaders from all four parties h
no knowledge nor involvement in the decision to bring tl
ruptive player on board."

12

A curtain opened in the rear wall of the plane compartment. Mitzi waved Megan over. "Come here a second."

The tail section of the plane held a small triangular room, half given over to the storage of hospitality items and a kitchenette. The rest of the area was bounded by low-cushioned seats, holding the cheerleading squad: David and another exquisitely handsome man, this one Caucasian, and the ebony-dark woman Mtume. A triangular table between them was set with drinks. Well, that was something Megan could use. She picked up a glass and poured clear liquid from a decanter. The bright scent of gin hit her senses like a welcome breeze.

Mitzi plucked the drink from her hand. "We need to talk about today."

Megan stubbornly got herself another. "Do we? The team sucks, and we're all going to die. That's what MegaDeath is all about."

Mitzi put her fists on her hips. "You want Hasan to die? You want Kendell to die?"

Those were, Megan supposed, the least hateable members of the team. "You're a cheerleader. I won't expect you to understand. They knew what they were signing up for."

Something dark fell over Mitzi's features. The three cheerleaders on the couches leaned back as one, like an invisible wave had knocked them over. Mtume topped off her drink with a long, slow whistle.

Mitzi held a hand out toward her team as if to stop a horde of responses. "I was on the team in '00 and '04."

The last year North America won, and the first year it lost. By rights, everyone on the '04 team was dead. Something must have happened to Mitzi before the end. "I thought you were all just groupies." Megan looked at David. She didn't mean to, it was rude, but he was definitely her concept of a groupie.

He lowered his martini to say, "And we could be having a much better conversation right now."

Mitzi folded her arms. "We're people who care about our country, using what we have to help. Same as you."

It was not the same. Cheerleaders didn't die. But Megan wasn't here to argue about it. She drank a long pull of gin. "The MegaDeath games can go to hell for all I care. It doesn't mean anything."

Mtume set down her empty glass, hard. "I don't have to listen to this."

Mitzi swore under her breath and drew Megan closer to the cabinets. "You need to decide right now if you want to die."

Megan shifted uncomfortably under her knowing gaze. "Is that why you don't play anymore?"

Mitzi looked insulted that a fear of death could have motivated her. "I was injured in '04. One game before the loss. I had to watch from the hospital. Josh, Coates, LaTonya, Martina, and Boom. The six of us had won the World Championships together, and four of us had survived the 2100 MegaDeath. You have no idea what kind of bond that is. You have killed, you've seen terrible things, and only these five people got you through it. No one shares that experience but your teammates. Your parents, your lover—they only know it by metaphor. I watched them almost make it, almost win it all, my friends and one scared rookie taking my place, and I watched them die."

Megan awkwardly mumbled, "Sorry for your loss," looking back toward the drinks. Could she get out of this conversation?

Mitzi snapped her fingers in Megan's face. "Yeah. I was twenty-four years old, and everyone I cared about most in the world died while I was getting my knee rebuilt. No visits in the hospital, and a room full of strangers when I came back to practice. So, yeah, I burned out. Like you."

"You're nothing like me."

Mitzi's gaze was intense, focused, forcing her to pay attention. "There's something broken in you, I can see it, a pain you're clinging to, hard, like a knife in your chest you're afraid to pull out because then everything will come out with it. That was me after my teammates died."

Megan had thought of Mitzi as a stereotypical bubblehead. There was more to her than met the eye. Almost afraid, she asked, "How did you get over it?"

"I didn't. I decided to keep living anyway. Do you intend to keep living, Megan Mori?"

Megan didn't know what to say. Did she? She thought she heard Ciera, soft, as if at a great distance, asking her to live.

Mitzi nodded as though Megan had answered. "Every person here is fighting for something. Glory, wealth, their country. An ideal, a belief. You have to look deep inside and ask yourself, what are you fighting for?"

Megan felt empty, helpless. "It's something to do."

Mitzi gripped her shoulder. "Find something you want. It can be as simple as not dying, but there has to be something. You'll play the way you need to if you have something at stake."

Megan felt the idea bouncing about inside her, looking for its place in her personality like a missing piece. She nodded. Mitzi let go of her shoulder and went back to her team, and Megan went back to the main cabin. She kept her eyes down. She wasn't prepared to look at anyone.

Back in LA, Megan found her schedule all planned for her again, with practices, workouts, and team-doctor-approved meals. This time, she obeyed the schedule. The constant motion and routine helped distract her from seeing her face on every billboard and newscast. There were insulting cartoons of her now. Every screen showed her falling on her ass the second the game started. Or some commentator angrily demanding to know why she wasn't cut from the team. Well, that would make her father happy, wouldn't it?

She walked into the weight room, and Kendell and Hasan, laughing and joking, fell silent. She did her sets as prescribed by the fitness coordinator and heard sighs of relief when she left.

She walked into the training room and multiple conversations stopped. The same happened in the private dining room they shared for meals. She took her food and went back to her room quickly.

It wasn't like she cared what they thought of her. She hadn't asked to be on this team. But all she could think about as she choked down the food without tasting it was exactly that. Did they think she was wasting their lives? What would Oba-chan say if she were alive to see this?

On Wednesday, there was a full team practice. Megan heard the muted gabble of conversation as she approached the warehouse-like practice gym. The big doors were open to let in the cool evening breeze.

Again, silence spread as Megan jogged into the room. Even the cheerleaders, stretching together near the back, dropped their smiles and bent to their work. Mtume managed to give her the side-eye while doing the splits.

Everyone looked at her like she had the plague.

Mustaine didn't look at her at all. He stood in the center of the room, gesturing wide at the scattered, stretching players. "Come on, we have a whole new game we gotta get ready for. You all need to work on your teamwork if you're going to survive the month. No time to waste. First drill's here in meat-space. Pair up."

Megan was too old to be offended when everyone scrambled to

pair up without her. Chet was the odd man out, so she started toward him. He backed up and gestured toward the cheerleaders. "How about Mitzi joins in for one?"

Mitzi barely glanced his way. "You're not getting me back in that easy."

"He's got a point." Coach cackled and pointed at her with his clipboard. "You never were cut from the official roster. You're still IR, Eliot."

Mitzi laughed. "Remind me to fix that." She moved her squad farther away, where they started doing a drill of their own.

Mustaine shrugged this off and turned back to the players. "All right now, here's the rules. You each get two cones. Set them ten paces apart. Don't get measuring about it, Hasan, it don't gotta be perfect." Mustaine dropped two cones on the floor in front of himself. "This here's a mirroring drill. Reaction. Take turns. One of you moves, the other tries to mirror. Mover wins if you can trick your way out of step. Mirror wins if they can't."

Coach called an assistant over, and they demonstrated, but the other players got it quickly enough. Everyone got moving except Megan and Chet. She held her hands up. "You don't have to like me. I don't like you."

He turned in a circle, looking for some escape.

Jerry and India were laughing, feeding off the joy of competition between them. Hasan and Kendell were huffing, moving hard, really pushing each other. Mustaine stood there, arms crossed, frowning, offering no help. Megan shrugged and did a little half-step side to side. "There, I beat you."

Chet turned red in the face. She thought he'd smack her, then she thought he'd run for it. Instead, he crouched low, fists at his side, shaking, and stutter-stepped left. Megan had to hurry to catch up. He moved right, left, left, right. Chet was fast and unpredictable. "Got you!" he shouted, stutter-stepping twice and catching her into a rhythm.

Megan gave herself one slow breath and clenched her anger tightly. He wouldn't get her again. "My turn to lead."

Left, right, stutter, right, stutter, left, left, right. She could mix it up by thinking in numbers. Left for odd, right for even. Her birthdate. Ciera's birthdate. Lola's. Megan tracked Chet's eyes, and he moved with her, intently, neither of them looking at their feet now.

Her address. Her log-in PIN. Her wedding anniversary. "Got you!"

"Fuck." Chet shook away sweat droplets. "My turn."

They barely paused. Left, left, right, left, right, right, left, right. No, don't get into the rhythm. She locked eyes, felt the minute movements of his face, the way he would tense just before changing direction. Left, right, left, stutter, left, right, right.

"Okay, break it up, lovebirds!" Mustaine shouted.

Chet blanched and backed away, comically fast. Megan laughed genuinely for the first time since Yakutsk.

Coach Mustaine waved everyone into a circle and walked around, handing out three balls: a soccer ball, a tennis ball, and a medicine ball. "This is supposed to get you all listening and reacting to each other. Jerry is one, India is two, Kendell is three." When they'd all been assigned a number, he pointed around. "If you have a ball, call out a number and throw the ball to that person. Simple, right? Three balls, six people. You should be able to do the math and not throw to the same person. Keep your eyes open because each ball has to be caught differently."

Megan guessed that no one would throw her a ball the first time, even though someone had to eventually. Sure enough, two people threw to India, and she caught the tennis ball and medicine ball.

"Come on, people," Mustaine sighed. "This ain't a popularity contest."

"One." India tossed the tennis ball lightly to Jerry and shouted, "Six!" which was Megan's number. She hurled the heavy ball hard at her head.

Megan barely caught it. "Hey."

Mustaine said, "Come on. I need you all alive next week. Don't aim for the head."

India shrugged. "It's hard to miss; it's so big."

After that, everyone was throwing their balls at Megan. Fine. More practice for her. Too bad dodgeball wasn't on the list of official MegaDeath games.

It was all she could do to catch and throw. "Wrong number again, Mori!" Coach shouted as she just shouted numbers at random.

So she went in order. Jerry, then India, then the others in number order, no matter who threw to her. She kept up with all of them.

Jokes stopped. Smiles stopped. Megan thought she was winning, but every face around her grew more hostile with every catch and throw.

Megan limped to lunch feeling pummeled. No one was in the room. She blinked wearily at the options over the serving counter. The man behind it waved his ladle. "The pasta Bolognese is good."

"Yeah, whatever." Megan picked up a tray.

"Take as much as you want. The others went to the taco place." He bit his lip after saying that, as though afraid he'd scared off his only customer.

"Pile it up," Megan said.

She sat alone in the empty room and told herself it was better than being off to the side, alone in a full room.

For just a second, it had felt like she wasn't alone during the drills, like she was part of something like she had been in college. It made her wonder if the camaraderie on the Kern County Crusaders had been an illusion too.

After eating, they were supposed to go into the pods to play Ulama. Megan didn't doubt the coach chose that as their next drill on purpose. She had to prove herself. She nibbled the pasta, then left it to hit the medical vending machine, sticking her finger in to get her pulse and blood levels. It printed her a painkiller and an anti-inflammatory.

The practice Ulama field was low-res. A plastic world, all in grays, so that they wouldn't be distracted by it. Coach sat alone atop one wall, dangling his feet. "Okay, Mori, guard Myers's flank."

Jerry looked coldly at her. "I'm not comfortable with that. I need someone I can trust on my left."

Mustaine threw up a hand. "I only got six of you, and there's only so many spots. What do you want me to do?"

Megan stared hard at Jerry. "I can guard a flank."

"You proved you can't."

"It was one game. I haven't played with a team since college."

He walked away from her, up to Chet. "Take flank, have Megan be safety."

"No! I like my spot," Chet said.

Megan pushed her way between the two men. "I said I'll do it. Coach Mustaine is in charge, and I'll do what he says."

"Will you?" Jerry raised his eyebrows.

"Damn it, you're a bunch of assholes, but I don't want you to die, all right?" Megan's outburst was followed by an awkward silence, thick as jelly. "Either we all have a death wish or none of us do. I don't care. I'm here to play."

An electric shock ran through them all. Mustaine held up a red card. "Are we done scratching each other's balls so we can get some work done?"

Jerry took his position without complaint. Megan shivered in the aftermath of the shock. "Does he do that a lot?"

No one answered her.

Megan returned to her private room for the night and immediately itched to go out. If she were home, she could slip down to the arcade and join a game. She could go back to where she could be the best player on the field without trying.

There were the pods down in the bar. They were encouraged to use the practice pods against AI opponents, but no more logging in to the greater network and playing at random. How crazy was it that she'd signed up to play pod games, and the cost was she couldn't play pod games? Physically exhausted but dreading sleep, she checked the media feeds. The news was full of her picture, of people talking about her "dangerous instability."

It was odd, after hating herself alone for so long, to have the entire world hating her.

She saw a message from Lola, a short video, only seventeen seconds. Megan gave in and hit play.

Lola sat in her bedroom, surrounded by posters of athletes of the past that glittered and shimmered with motion, a still face in a maelstrom. She had her hair in a severe ponytail, the purple streak lost in the black. Her face was screwed up like she'd been thinking hard or preparing herself for this. She took a breath. "People are talking trash about you, but I wanted you to know, Ciera would be so proud."

Lola's eyes moved to the right, her ponytail swinging left in response, and the video jumped back to start. It auto-replayed twice. Before the third time, Megan slapped the screen down like it was about to bite her. Tears gushed out of her like she'd been holding them in forever.

Ciera wouldn't be proud. Ciera would barely recognize her mother.

Opening Ceremonies were set to take place in South America, in La Paz. It felt too soon, but Megan had missed the first round of exhibition games and all the pre-season events.

It felt strange to land in a city filled with banners of other players. The advertising artists used the same poses, the same lighting, but instead of Jerry with his javelin, there was Jax Pollard with a sword. The blue background became yellow. The streets of La Paz were decked in the same density of ribbons, flags, and animated soft-screens. There was a Champion's Village–like area with residences and playing fields. It felt like the same city in a different dress. The climate, at least, was its own.

Megan jogged onto a track with snowcapped mountains in the distance, the air crisp and dry as though she could taste how high they were. She was grateful to have the time alone after the stifling plane ride.

She didn't make it half a lap before Jerry showed up. He did very few stretches and started jogging behind her. Megan gritted her teeth. Too soon, they would start another passive-aggressive practice. She would keep her head down and keep working.

Something fell right in front of her on the track. She barely had time to vault it and land, stumbling. She looked back. An equipment bag. India stood nearby, just about throw-an-equipment-bag distance, her hands clasped over her head, innocently stretching.

Jerry jogged over. "Hey, keep the track clear."

"Just messing with Rookie." India bent to touch her toes. "Be a shame if she tore a knee and couldn't play."

Jerry shook his head. "That rookie showed up on time. You could do the same."

Megan slowed her steps, turned to see if she'd heard right. Was that a compliment? But Jerry and India were already running the other way.

She wouldn't read too much into that. By the time she finished another lap, everyone else had arrived.

As a team, serious and silent, they warmed up, showered, and changed into their gaudy patriotic tracksuits for the big celebration. Megan dreaded Opening Ceremonies. It was going to be dull and long.

Who even watched these things? She never understood why anyone would watch sports when they could play them. Would you watch other people read books?

But there was no way out of it. They were marching in a parade, the North American team and their four cheerleaders, with a healthy empty space before and after them. Pairs of local teens held balloon arches in their flag colors. Then there was a double rank of team staff, including Coach and three alternates. Ahead of them were more balloon arches, more teams and coaches. All the competition a decent distance away. The people she'd have to kill if she wanted to survive.

They walked out of Champion's Village, the streets crowded with families sitting on curbs and waving flags. They turned downtown, and there were more people waving from windows in buildings. Finally, they walked onto a four-lane highway as millions of spectators screamed their delight from stands as tall as skyscrapers.

Megan gasped for breath. All of humanity joined in a moment of hope and joy. A human canyon that vibrated the air with their screams. The sky was painted with flashes of light, acrobatic drones tracing neon lines, all the flags of every nation that had ever come up with one, together, at peace.

How humbling to be the focus of all that, to be walking in soft-soled shoes on a street that had been meticulously cleaned so millions could toss confetti at them. Megan felt, all of a sudden, that she was walking into a vast cathedral.

"Welcome! Welcome, everyone!" The sky drones reconfigured, forming enormous images of the speaking podium still far ahead of the parade, with Herbert Rivera himself, smiling that "come hug me" smile. "Welcome to the MegaDeath Tournament! I'm the lucky fellow who gets to start things off by thanking Central, our information partner, for making all of this possible!"

The voice carried distinctly. State-of-the-art sound systems canceled reverb and echo from tiny flying speakers that carefully preserved the oceanic surge of crowd noise. Here was humanity itself, or at least a very large chunk of it.

"Today—" Herbert Rivera seemed to have trouble controlling himself, eyes glittering with tears "—is not about death. It's about life. Today we celebrate these lives, willingly risked for their countries, for the world, for peace and prosperity." His giant hand gestured down at the parade walkers, massive fingertips vanishing as they dipped out of the frame of his camera. He looked like he wanted to pick them up, tiny figures in the palm of his hand. "Where once there were tiny nations shooting and killing each other over rising waters and dwindling resources, today we are a united world culture, celebrating and resolving our differences through the exalted sphere of sport!"

Ahead of the walkers was a cluster of buildings, the end of the parade route. The stands encroached, narrowing the road with lower-level dignitaries and celebrities. Megan could see the actual stage ahead, the tiny figure of Rivera at his podium, his silver hair gleaming. She glanced up at the crowd, and there, waving frantically, bent almost double over the safety rail, was Lola. One tiny person in a sea of people, but once she saw her, Megan couldn't imagine missing her.

Lola saw Megan noticing her, and she jumped up and down, then pointed at the sky, clasped her hands over her chest like she was holding her heart in, and then pointed at Megan. She did it twice. Sky, heart, Megan. And then they had moved on, and Lola was too small to pick out in the throng. It was a message. Up, proud, you. Or not "up." The sky could symbolize heaven, if you believed in that. Megan stopped walking. Of course. "Ciera would be proud of you." A reminder. It hurt, but not as much as the first time Lola had said it. More like cracking a rib than burning alive.

Jerry glanced back at her. She'd slowed out of formation. She jogged a step to catch up.

They reached the plaza at the base of the stage. All the teams together, intermingling and shaking hands, while explosions rocked the sky and camera drones whizzing like fireflies captured the moment. Three-dimensional holograms were being prepared and sent out, archived to flood the news feeds when one or the other of a pair of hand-shakers did something memorable in the games or died tragically. Megan was aware she was posing for her own epitaph.

She wasn't worthy of Ciera's pride, but she could look like she was. She smiled and tried to feel the smile down to her bones so it would look genuine. She reached for the next hand and squeezed it firmly.

The man on the other side of the handshake didn't let go but drew her hand up to his lips. "Querida. I saw your crazy moves last week. They worked better against Jerry than North Asia."

Jax, from South America. He was wearing the same satin jacket. Megan slid her hand from his. "You're still prettier when you don't talk."

His smile was as smooth as a dagger in the kidneys. "Such passion. I'd love to play against you. Too bad you'll be eliminated before I get the chance." He backed away with a hand on his heart. "I'll remember you fondly."

Asshole. Jerry muscled between them. "Still scaring off every woman on the planet?"

Jax sneered, "Ask your mother."

So much for friendly greetings. Megan put some distance between herself and Jax and put him out of her thoughts. The handshakes and fireworks were winding down, and already some in the viewing stands were packing up their blankets and coolers. For them, this was the event, the thing they would write about in their diaries and tell their kids about, the time the MegaDeath Games came to their town, how they got their tickets, how far they flew.

For the players, this was the last moment they would appear in public and be sure to survive. The camera-smiles turned grim around Megan, and the handshakes got longer, leaning into hugs.

Tomorrow, the games began.

13

As the final seed, North America didn't get any home games for the first half of the season. If they made it that far. They flew straight from Bolivia to New Zealand to face Team Oceania in Christchurch. Mustaine hoped traveling quickly would give them more time to acclimate and relax before the game.

Megan found it hard to sightsee when she had a humiliating defeat fresh in her memory and another game in five days. She wanted to check in to the hotel and stay there, but the team had required appearances, and she didn't need any more bad blood. So she put on a flowered shirt and suffered through a boat ride on a wide, lush river and then a tram through downtown. Media camera bots zoomed around them like flies.

"Mori! Stop looking at the cameras," Mustaine barked. She felt like a rube.

The others were better at pretending they weren't there, answering dumb questions like, "How does it feel coming off a big loss like that?" Jerry in particular could answer as if the camera drone were a good friend, and he'd decided to bare his soul. It was surreal.

"Odds of you lot making it through regular play are one-to-twenty," a little old lady selling waffle cones told Megan. "So, I put a wee wager on you. Nothing to lose, eh? Here, I need a snap of this." She waved for her security camera to capture them. "It'll sell nice when you're dead. Oh, no offense."

Megan wasn't offended, but she saw Kendell throw her waffle cone in the trash.

They gathered in the city stadium, which was a wide and low structure open to the cloudy sky. A man and woman approached the team carrying a long tray covered in black velvet. On it were six unadorned chrome collars like Megan had seen on pictures of players in past years. The others each took one, and the tray-bearers held it closer to Megan.

"No, thanks," she said. "I'd rather not."

"It's required." Jerry slid his on with a practiced motion. It clicked, and he rolled his shoulders. "From game one until all done."

"For our country," Kendell said, raising her collar up in salute before slipping it on.

India flicked her beautiful hair back after fastening hers. "What's the matter, Mori? Afraid it won't go with your outfit?"

It wasn't heavy, but it was cold metal. Megan wondered if it would affect her play. The hinge was hard to see, and the clasp impossible. Yet, when she closed it around her neck, it tightened with an audible click. She felt a moment of claustrophobia and pushed it down. She'd never liked wearing chokers or shirts with high collars. "They always wear these. Is it symbolic?"

Chet found that so funny he danced backward, pointing at her.

"It's how they kill you if you lose," Hasan muttered, slipping his own on. "Lethal injection. The dose is already in there, and the needle." He tapped the side and smiled like that was a good thing.

Jerry held his hand up. "We put our own collars on because we aren't afraid, because we are here willingly, and we know fate is on our side." His casting-call smile almost made Megan believe him. "This is it. Today we prove ourselves. Prove that our country, our families, and our loved ones were right to depend on us."

She thought she would be more excited. More thrilled by the risk. Perhaps once she was in the pod it would hit her.

As a team, they jogged onto the field. The stands were packed, screaming, though there were very few North American flags to be seen among the endless star-spangled blue of Oceania. Megan could see how the Oceania team took the field with their chests raised, buoyed by the support.

She was glad to close the lid of her pod on that fanatic, screaming crowd.

They had been given the game the night before: soccer. They knew this sport and how to play it. They had their positions and their assignments. Megan wasn't going to be blindsided again. She was going to be a team player.

If she failed, well, the stakes were printed across the stone grotto that was this team's loading screen. She had imagined the words, and now she read them. Stakes: Life. She felt like she had to imagine being in the situation she was in to react to it. Before she felt ready, the sky turned green, and the playing field grew around them.

The virtual arena was a larger, more glamorous version of the real one, with virtual avatars for all the fans in the stands. The sky was a breathtaking blue, almost purple at the edges. They were going to receive the kickoff, that was good luck. Megan flexed her knees, watching an Oceania player charge the ball at the halfway line.

Megan ran forward, keeping to her zone, letting Indía field the ball. Indía had the strongest legs on the team, Mustaine said. Megan kept her pace, kept her head on a swivel, tracking the other team, her team, and the ball. It would be easy to lose track and fall behind in a sport that moved so quickly over space as soccer did.

The ground shifted under her, but Megan kept her balance and her pace. It was one of the advanced difficulty options—the ground would move randomly, strips of grass sliding past each other as easily as conveyor belts, ruffling and settling again without a sign where they would move again.

"Mori seems unsure of the footing," Herbert Rivera gushed unhelpfully from a neon podium.

Indía closed in on the goal, but Oceania players were crowding her. She struggled to get free. Megan waved an arm to show she was open. Jerry was open too. Indía ignored them both and tried to juke her way free. An aggressive, pale striker stripped the ball, and Megan moved quickly to defense, tracking the ball, its possible trajectories. The grass slid sideways under her. Kendell stumbled with it. This left a gap in the left field where Kendell wasn't quite caught up. Megan felt her feet move instinctively toward it, but she corrected herself. She had to trust the plan and her place in it. Trust Chet back in the goal. She knew firsthand how insanely quick he could be.

A scrappy little Oceania player kicked, and the ball sailed beautifully just past Kendell's diving form, hooking slightly in the air like a ballistic missile with perfect aim, over Chet's outstretched fingers and into the top corner of the net.

"Goal!"

Megan stopped mid-run, gasping for breath, as Chet fished the ball out of the netting.

A goal in the first possession. Not a great sign. But it was okay. They had a lot of game time to make it up in.

"Shake it off!" Mitzi dashed across the field, shining with nonplay sparkles and her bright silver cheer outfit. "Here comes the ball. You got this. Play your game!"

It was hard not to notice the scrolling numbers cutting across her ankles. That single goal had dropped their odds of winning from one in twenty to one in fifty.

Chet lobbed the ball to Indía, who was immediately swarmed. The other team wasn't even trying to block Megan. It was like they knew no one trusted her. Jerry came to Indía's aid and slipped free with the ball. He charged to midfield and made a daring kick for the goal. The Oceania defenders were caught out of place, running desperately to get in the way. It was a clear shot.

The Oceania goalie made a spectacular leap and caught the ball with one hand. It was such a beautiful play Megan couldn't even be mad about it.

And that made her mad about it.

For the next forty minutes, Megan never stopped running, stumbling four times as the ground shifted underfoot. The teams vied and struggled over the ball, up and down the field, falling to trip traps the game created and flipping sod, but the ball didn't make it in either goal until seconds before halftime when, after all that frustration and effort, it sailed past Chet's reaching fingers to score a second goal for the home team.

The problem with being disheartened was that Megan hung her head low, which put all the swimming words floating off the ground more in focus. The odds were at one in a hundred that they could tie the game, one in a thousand that they could win. Betting slacked off, and Central hucksters pleaded with North American fans to show more patriotism.

The halftime bell rang, and Megan found herself instantly transported to a locker room set with the other players and cheerleaders. In the real world, their pods were cooling them, massaging them, getting them ready to keep playing. India limped back and forth, keeping her legs warm. "I can't do another forty minutes of that."

"They've played this game all their lives." Hasan stared into the middle distance. "It's as natural to them as breathing."

"Well, they're all over me." India gestured. "I can't see open grass to save my life. They aren't covering zones, they're just covering me."

"They know you're our strongest kicker," Kendell said. "Give me the ball."

It wasn't strategy. Megan wanted to scream at them. This team was simply better. They should be enjoying this respite. It was the last one they'd ever have.

Jerry paced furiously. "What are you all looking so sad for? It's 2–0.

So? That's just two scores! We're in this. India, when you get the ball, pass it right away, then get open and downfield. We'll get you the ball where you can do something with it."

Mitzi jumped up. "My team will do a better job of scouting for holes in the defense. Watch for us. We'll split the field evenly. We'll get in their faces more too. Create distractions."

Jerry started drawing diagrams on the wall. David was sitting on the bench near Megan, so she leaned over to ask him, "Why isn't Coach doing this part?"

The cheerleader looked grim. "You think Coach cares about you guys at this point? He's already planning his next team."

Megan moved away from David. She felt the distance between her collared throat and his bare one too keenly.

All too soon, the locker room pixelated down to reveal the stadium again. Megan jogged to her place, not as confident in their second-half plan as she had been in the first-half one. Indía charged forward and got the ball right away, then got rid of it fast, and just like Jerry had promised, the other team chased it, swarming Kendell, who powered her way ahead to pass to Megan, who passed the ball to Jerry before the defense got near her. Jerry got Indía the ball deep in the other team's territory, and she made a kick so hard Megan felt the thump of the ball from across the field.

But their goalie was still incredible. She seemed to float in the air, grunting as the powerful ball hit her chest.

Megan shouldn't have been gawking. She hurried back to her starting position and tripped, running backward. She felt the grass pulling in two directions under her, and she rolled to her knees. Shit, was it shifting more now in the second half? The ground disappeared under her hand as she tried to get to her feet, and she wobbled, airless for a moment. There was a one-foot-square bottomless pit in front of her.

She jumped over it and tried to track the ball, keeping part of her attention on the treacherous terrain.

She'd missed another quick series of kicks; the ball was in Hasan's control now, and he was having trouble getting sufficiently open to kick it away, but India came close enough that the defense assumed she'd get it next and pulled toward her. Megan got open; Hasan saw her.

And her stomach flew into her ribs as the ground vanished under her. She only barely caught the crumbling sod at the edge of the pit, gasping as she smacked the wall, her breath pushed out of her. The fear and scrambling left her shaking, and for what? The play was miles away from her. She jogged toward the action, only to be sidelined by another pit.

Why was she even on this field? The ball never came near her. With one less player to worry about, the Oceania team had an easy job shutting down their frantic offense.

There were only fifteen minutes left, and they were still down 2–0. Megan considered that these were the last moments of her life. Going out not with a bang, but with a sprint that came up just a little short each time.

If she died, she'd no longer have to miss Ciera. No longer have to feel that she'd failed to protect her daughter. She wouldn't feel anything. She'd be gone. The idea was comforting. She slowed, stopped running.

"What are you doing?" Mitzi screamed at her, gesturing frantically. "You could have had that! Hurry! Play coming this way again!"

Everyone on the team, she saw, was playing like they were already dead. Maybe they knew it all along. Why had they wasted all that time practicing?

"Come on!" Mitzi was almost in tears. She batted at the odds swarming her shins like she could bury them. "Don't look at that. No, not the clock, either. You are still alive. You still matter. Remember why you're here. You have a reason to be here!"

The ball was heading toward their goal, no one between it and the enemy players, Chet standing despondently, making no move to prepare to block. This score would be the death knell of the game.

Jerry flew out of nowhere and caught the ball hard on his chest. He landed forcefully but scrambled up from the dirt with a determined cry and ran after it. He was really giving his all, even when it was so obviously the end.

"Yes!" Mitzi danced and cartwheeled down the field with him, cheering with all the joy of a child.

Megan looked across at Indía, holding her sides and gasping, and Kendell looking confused, Hasan on his knees. That wasn't the way to make Ciera proud. Ciera would be dancing with Mitzi, her every movement a pure expression of the joy of living.

If Megan was going to die, she was going to die playing her hardest. She took off after Jerry. He caught a glance, fast, as a defender crowded him, and passed her the ball. She fielded it easily. The defenders crowded her, and just before they got too close, she passed back to Jerry.

Suddenly they had a rhythm, the two of them, back and forth, up the field. The other team would get the ball, they would take it back. She took a shot at the goal and missed, but Jerry recovered the ball and got it back to her. The defense was ready, swarming her, blocking her view in every direction. She scanned for Jerry. He was running forward, an easy angle. She saw the shot she'd need to get the ball to him. He had a clean shot to the goal. She toed the ball back to give it a firm kick, and a pit opened under Jerry. He fell sideways, arms pinwheeling. He was gone. Her distraction almost cost her the ball. She was alone, scrambling against three players, the ball slipping and regaining under her feet. There was no way . . .

"I'm open!" It was Indía. She suddenly looked like she'd had a full night's rest. Megan passed to her, kicking as hard as she wanted to kick the Oceania goalie in her face.

There was that tremendous thump and a sound Megan hadn't heard all game—the silence of the crowd as the ball hit the back of the home team's net.

It was like a shot of fresh adrenaline. Or hope. Jerry was hanging by his elbows in the sod. He crawled out of the pit and straight into a jump, whooping. Megan met his eyes and Indía's. They nodded.

The game was finally starting. Five minutes to go. No, like Mitzi said, stop looking at the clock.

That ball was hers, and she was getting it back.

Megan charged. Rules, terrain—nothing mattered but that ball. She wouldn't have seen a volcano if it had erupted. She slid to kick the ball between an opponent's legs, and Indía was there to collect it, hooking it over to Jerry, who kicked to Hasan, who kicked to Kendell.

Everyone was awake again. They were a team, responding to each other, single-minded, determined. Indía made another incredible kick, but it met an equally incredible block. Megan dove to steal the ball as it was pitched out; she kneed it, stuttered over some shifting grass, and knocked it toward the goal.

Megan watched, breathless. The terrain shifted again, but this time in her favor as it changed the ball's trajectory just under the goalie's reach. The game was tied! Two minutes to go.

The field rumbled. Spouts of fire joined the bottomless pits. The crowd was on its feet, delirious, screaming. Mitzi and the other cheerleaders were cartwheeling and hugging each other. The odds feed had paused, the computers baffled by the surprise in the action, numbers decaying like confetti in the grass.

Megan got the ball to Jerry, Jerry to Indía . . . back and forth, around the opposition and through, Mitzi cartwheeling and doing flips, half to distract the other team, half in pure joy.

Oceania had a clear shot. Chet blocked but fell in his exhaustion. Megan was there this time to make the save when they attempted to rebound.

She fell, and a jet of flame nearly got her hand as she pushed off the grass. An Oceania team member shoved her from behind, and she hit the ground again.

Jerry picked her up by the arm. "These are going to be the dirtiest minutes of your life."

He wasn't wrong. Oceania was fighting for their lives too. Megan couldn't see across the field for all the flame and smoke and gouts of soil raining upward. She ran as fast as she dared on ground that felt like a waterbed in an earthquake.

Jerry got the ball and passed it to her over a sudden pit. She kicked without looking, the ground giving way under her as she did. She lunged desperately for turf. Where had it gone? Which way was the goal? She was in a war zone.

She got to her feet only to be lifted off them. The sky was filled with fireworks.

She hadn't seen her kick land the winning goal.

The scene blanked. Megan fell back in her pod, gasping, heart still pounding, shocked by the strange darkness, the sudden change from arms around her, fire in the skies. She was shaking, but it was with euphoria. She'd never expected to feel so much emotion all at once again. She fumbled with the straps and harness, weak as a newborn. Outside, the crowd, the real crowd, was dispersing in silent bitterness while a small group of North American fans tried to fill the stadium with their screams of joy. They'd spilled out of their seats to the bottom of the stands, a bigger group now that they were all together, united in their colors, waving flags and singing a victory song.

Jerry ran up to her, sweaty, grinning a thousand-watt smile more genuine than she'd ever seen from him. She held out a hand to shake.

He slapped it wide, grabbed her waist, and swung her around, planting a firm kiss on her mouth.

Startled, she pushed him away.

He winked. "There, all paid up."

She'd almost forgotten he was an asshole. She made sure he saw her wipe her mouth vigorously on the back of her arm.

But then India was there, holding out a hand. "We have to go to the podium. Come on. This is your first win. You're not a rookie anymore."

Six small, square platforms rose out of the ground, waiting for them. Chet stepped on one, and it flew into the air. Hasan next, then Kendell. They each got one. Megan stepped on hers, and it rose more gently than she expected. She had her arms out, prepared to lose her balance, but it adjusted with her every motion, like a kind giant lifting her in its hand.

They settled into a hover ten meters up. Megan could see the Oceania team standing on their own platforms, but they didn't rise. They looked stunned. Megan locked eyes with a young man with full lips and long, curly hair. He gazed up, throat long. He was beautiful. His brow quirked in confusion. He looked away, toward a podium where an official was speaking. Megan didn't catch the words as they were distorted by being so perfectly delivered. The official dropped his hand. The beautiful man gasped and fell like a doll whose strings had been cut.

Team Oceania lay sprawled over their six platforms, as still as if they had never breathed. The crowd, which had silenced somewhat for the speech, went wild.

The politicians took to the field and shook hands with the crowd, each other, and the coaches. Probably the same ones who had distanced themselves from her hiring decision in the news.

Megan felt nauseated. She'd hated the other players during the game. She'd wanted to stomp on them when they beat her. Minutes ago, she would have shoved any one of them into a bottomless pit.

Now the wind ruffled their hair as a cleaning crew straightened the bodies to carry them away, and they looked like somebody's children.

The platform she was on sank to the ground. Strangers were patting her back and shaking her hand. She couldn't keep her hands away from them. Dimly, she realized questions were being asked, flashes of light recording images and videos.

"How does it feel to have beaten the odds?"

"My readers want to know, what changed the momentum?"

"Here comes Jerry Myers! Jerry, what did you tell the team in the locker room at halftime to affect such a sweeping change in strategy?"

Jerry put his arm around Megan. "I didn't say anything. My team knew what to do." He raised a hand to wave, conveniently blocking another reporter, and steered Megan to safety, toward a gauntlet of guards and groundskeepers leading back to the locker room. "Stay with me, Mori. We're wheels up in an hour. Our job isn't done."

14

In a haze, Megan showered and dressed. What did he mean, their work wasn't over? She left the locker room, and suddenly there were people everywhere, a human conveyor guiding her from a tram to the airport. More people, urging them out of the tram, grabbing their bags from their shoulders. She asked one of them, "What's the rush?"

The attendant tossed her equipment bag to someone else, who tossed it into the plane. "They like the scourging to start as soon as possible after the end of the match. Enjoy your flight."

The scourging. Megan had forgotten that part. It was something to skip past on the news feeds when she had more important things to do. The winning team would be set loose to rampage, exempt from any laws, in the wealthiest city of the losing team, all so rubberneckers in both regions could ooh and aah over the destruction like it was a competitive sport of its own.

Jerry paced the airplane aisle. "Off your feet, everyone. Get as much rest as you can. This is the real endurance workout right here, and I want everyone at the top of their game."

Megan was glad enough to get off her feet but held up a hand. "Yeah, I'm not doing the scourging. All I want is a scotch and a bubble bath."

Jerry looked at her like she'd insulted his mother or the flag. "This isn't voluntary. This is our duty to our country."

"Acting like drunken hoodlums is our duty? To what? The tabloids?"

Jerry breathed hard out his nose, and she thought for a moment he might hit her. He took a few steps away and turned, strafing the compartment with his gaze. "Someone want to fill in the rookie?" When no one answered, he turned back to face her. "This is our most solemn duty. Without the violence, without damage, there is no catharsis, no release, no reminder that something was always at stake. Not just for us, but for the fans. We are the avatars of an entire nation's bloodlust, and the world is watching." He paused, broke the grand speech character. His next words were softer, from one friend to another. "Think about how countries used to settle their disagreements. Buildings were flattened, cities decimated. Hospitals and schools were blown up with people inside them. Doing it this way only works if we give them catharsis. It's not about you and your feelings, it's about doing what must be done."

He really believed this. His perfect eyes bugged out, his face glistened with sweat. Megan wanted to say more, but if you argue with a fanatic, all you do is create a stronger fanatic. A flight steward came through and brought her a scotch and soda. She toasted him and leaned back to stare out the window.

She'd always thought the free-for-alls were optional, something the players did because they lacked discipline, hopped up on the thrill of nearly losing their lives, but this man set his jaw with a firm resolve to cause mayhem. For the greater good. How little she understood about an event that had been at the periphery of her entire life!

They touched down in Sydney and were rushed through the airport and onto a maglev that brought them downtown, where they were pounced on by hair and makeup people in a tent. Before she knew what was happening, she was staring up at the temporary ceiling while a woman attacked her face with tweezers, snapping orders like a trauma surgeon. "No time to wax. Get the vibra-gel. Move. We're a centimeter from unibrow here."

I'm being sent to commit atrocities, and they care about the shape of my eyebrows.

Twenty minutes later, feeling freshly peeled, Megan stumbled into the open air and onto a red carpet. She hadn't expected that to be a real thing. Nor the honor guard of the North American military. She couldn't remember the last time she'd seen soldiers. Probably a Unification Day parade. This felt oddly like one, with the flags and the colors. Though now, instead of Canada, Mexico, and the United States flags, there were North America's and Oceania's, like they were being unified.

Megan and her team walked the red carpet across a town square where small, old buildings stood in front of larger, newer ones. A bronze statue of a portly woman looked down at her like she owed her something. All around, tiny camera drones buzzed and flickered. There was another stage, more banners, but the crowd was . . . weird.

It wasn't a crowd. There were people, yes, but they were standing in rows like soldiers, wearing jumpsuits and chrome collars, bulkier than the ones the team wore. India leaned into her view. "Don't stare at the prisoners." She tossed her perfectly-styled mane. "It's rude."

Prisoners. Megan had always wondered why people were even in the scourged cities, since they'd know ahead of time it was coming. They had no choice. Megan watched the prisoners as she alighted the stage, as the politicians spoke and shook hands. A representative of Oceania handed a folded flag to a representative of North America, and everyone had to shake hands. Megan felt the same helpless boredom as the prisoners, watching under guard.

Sydney's mayor was the last to speak. She turned toward the team afterward, bowing slightly. "It is now my duty, and honor, to surrender our city to its victors. As promised in the international compact that has kept the peace since the first tournament, the city is populated and unarmed. Ladies and Gentlemen of North America, at the sound of the bell, for the next twenty-four hours, Sydney is yours."

Megan expected reluctance or an "I hope you choke on it" expression, but the mayor was all smiles, and then the dignitaries were leaving. The guards around the prisoners backed away, the armed drones following them. The soldiers that had marched out with the team moved to ring the stage, protecting them in the prison guards' absence.

It was quiet enough to hear the retreating footsteps. The team stood, waiting. Chet bounced on his toes. Indía grasped first one foot behind her, then the other, stretching her legs. "I'm getting a painting," she said. "The museum's just a few blocks over."

A shutter rattled down, covering a church window. The politicians left.

The prisoners stirred. One of them, near the back of the crowd, stepped backward out of rank, then stepped again. Like a signal, this sent them all scattering out of the square, into the alleys between the buildings. Megan shook her head. "What are they afraid of?"

Chet grinned. "Us."

And then the church bell tolled.

The honor guard let up a yell, wild, almost inhuman, and took off. Chet bounded like a gazelle off the stage after them.

Jerry said solemnly, "Time to go to work." He strode forward, then picked it up to a jog, a man on a mission. The rest of the team joined him, a wedge of athletes chasing a melee. Megan followed. She didn't know what else to do.

Chet had someone by the arm, a skinny figure in a baggy jumpsuit, and was ramming his head into a wall over and over with the blank, joyless rage of a child breaking his toys.

Herbert Rivera was there, of course. Wasn't he always? His face on countless surfaces, eyes wide. "Indía Thomas is off to an early lead! I can barely watch. Remember, this is a team that has years of frustration behind them. No one thought they'd survive even the first round."

A knot of soldiers formed ahead, and there was a heavy, wet sound of fists and boots hitting flesh. They looked like a swarm of ants on a speck of jelly. Megan felt sick. She backed away, then turned and ran.

There should be plenty of places to hide in a city for twenty-four hours. She wasn't taking part in this farce.

She made it half a block before armed guards surrounded her. One of them addressed her. "Ma'am? Where are you going?"

They wouldn't shoot her for not being an asshole, would they? "The, uh . . . museum."

He nodded behind her. "That way, ma'am, two blocks west, one north. Do you require assistance?" There was something pushy in the way he said it, advancing with his gun across his chest, like if she didn't get with the program, he'd make her.

She turned her back on the soldiers and jogged west. She heard screams. Individual screams. A higher voice and a lower. Someone begging, and those sickening, wet thumps.

This was a nightmare.

"Come on, Double M! The cameras are rolling!" a tiny voice from a camera bot shouted at her. Fuck their cameras. She ran. Running down a city street. Wasn't that something she did all the time?

The neighborhood was posh, filled with glass-fronted shops and soaring buildings, museums and art galleries. A camera drone buzzed her cheek. Another thumped into her back like an oversized fly. Would they do worse if she didn't respond to their impatience?

Glass shattered ahead of her, a sudden, enormous violence, and then the pieces skittered like ice across the road. Kendell walked out of the vacant display window of a jewelry store in the clattering alarm, admiring the bright diamond chains all up and down her dark arms. She waved at Megan.

Ahead was the museum. Something was smoking beyond its vast entrance. Reproductions of silk Japanese banners fluttered in the wind, the window in front of them broken away. At least Megan hoped they were reproductions.

It felt like a war. Wasn't that what they were trying to prevent? This wasn't civilized, token violence. It was a Viking raid, screaming people running in fear. The soldiers who accompanied the team swung their guns as clubs, poked them like bayonets. Ahead, a group of prisoners had banded together, carrying boards and throwing garbage at the advancing, well-armed troops.

Megan dodged smoke and running people, past alarms and debris and explosions of glass. She had to get away from the main thoroughfares. She turned at a corner, sought out blandness in the buildings, a way toward residential streets, fewer signs, more plants. She turned again, a narrow alley, empty, tall brick walls blocking the worst of the noise. She slowed, her breaths coming deeper. She'd made it out.

Something slammed into her, between her shoulder blades, driving the air from her lungs and sending her sprawling. The alley floor was sticky with something acrid smelling. She scrambled to get her hands under her, but there was a body on her, grabbing her hair, reaching for her throat. "How's that feel, eh? How's it feel when we fight back?"

His fingers dug into her neck, squeezing the breath from her while he grunted insults against the back of her skull. "You expected us all to be sheep, didn't you, bitch? We're supposed to be sheep. Fucking sheep." Black spots formed in her eyes, like the hovering cameras that zoomed hungrily around them, capturing her assault, the knee digging hard into the small of her back, the sweating, shaking intimacy, the filth grinding into her chest.

Megan thrust her hands against the pavement and threw her head back, cracking it into her attacker's nose. His fingers loosened, and she rolled hard to the left, kicking blindly until she was free.

Her attacker grabbed around her legs, trying to pull her back down. After everything, all her grief, all the violence of the game, not knowing if she'd live, not knowing if Ciera would hate what she'd become, all she'd wanted was rest. He wouldn't let her go. Something snapped in her. She grabbed a handful of his gray coveralls and pulled him closer, jabbing her fist into whatever landed in front of it. He swung wildly. She caught his punch with her forearm, curled around his arm, and smacked it down against her knee. Something crunched inside. He screamed.

Every hurt, every injury, she felt anew. The insulting interview questions. The roller rink. The terrifying bottomless pits. She beat the thing that had attacked her, the thing in her hands. She punched and kicked and broke and twisted and shoved until the punches that came at her turned into blocks, and the blocks turned into stillness.

She shivered, coming back to her senses, standing over the unconscious body. Her fists were slick with blood, and she couldn't tell how much was hers. She stumbled back. The camera drones followed her. She had a sudden feeling they wanted to lick the blood from her split knuckles.

She turned and ran. This time, she didn't stop.

Megan woke, stiff and sore, on a slick-painted park bench facing some playground equipment. A bird twittered somewhere out of sight. The blood on her hands, on her jacket, and on her pants was dried brown and flaking. The night before felt impossible. The day before. Her head was empty. Everything ached as she got to her feet. She limped a few steps, then started walking in a random direction.

A fist-sized camera drone lowered to hover in front of her face. "Ms. Mori, so glad to find you! A breakfast is being served at the Park Forest Manor Dining Room."

Megan coughed and felt the echo of the bench seat in her ribs. "Well, lead the way."

It bobbed, which might have been meant as a nod, and flitted ahead. The deserted streets showed little evidence of the rampage the night before. Broken windows, tossed trash cans. The messes felt petty in the golden light of dawn. Intact displays on second floors counted down the remaining hours of their twenty-four. Megan supposed the night before could now be forgotten, like a particularly bad bender, and they would relax, robbing the swank hotel of its services until their time ran out.

Then she turned a corner and saw herself.

An intact news screen was playing, on repeat and in high-definition color, a close-up view of Megan's snarl as her fist pummeled a scrawny, red-haired man. His hands were up, weakly struggling to hold her off.

"Savage in Sydney" read the headline.

It wasn't her. She wasn't that cold, that violent. She wasn't.

Megan forced her feet to keep moving forward. The bots were swarming, recording her self-loathing for the entertainment of the masses. Buzzing voices came from their tiny speakers. "Ms. Mori, did you know your performance last night has the world calling you the breakout star of this year's games?"

She didn't know if they meant her performance in the actual game. She tried to bat the drone away.

"Ms. Mori! What are your plans for the rest of your stay in Sydney?"

She pushed her exhausted body into a jog, and then a run. The cameras trailed her. "Would you like directions to the nearest target? Turn here. No?"

"The prisoners are all radio-tracked. Would you like one on his own, or a group? Oh! There's an injured prisoner very close. He's moving slowly. You should catch him easily at the next intersection."

Megan fled down an alleyway. Her chest was tight. She wanted to sob. She didn't even care if she got to the hotel anymore. The drones followed. She burst onto another street, her hands over her head. "Leave me alone!"

Mitzi jogged up to her. "Oh, hon." She pointed a remote at the bots. They dropped to the ground, buzzed, and died.

Megan sobbed. She let herself fall onto a low curb. Mitzi settled next to her, rubbing her back. Slowly, Megan became aware of the scent of the ocean. A seagull cried.

"Let's go in, hon," Mitzi said. "Get some breakfast in you."

Megan hugged her knees to her chest. "They'll . . . they'll be talking about what I did."

"Not the team. And if any screens pop up, I have this." She waggled her remote. It was a strange, boxy thing with exposed wires.

"Where did you get that?"

"We all have our secrets." Mitzi led her up some steps and into the hotel she had stopped in front of.

15

Lola sprawled in the living room, hooked into the crappy home VR system, catching what she could of the post-Oceania highlights with no haptics, no smells! They were going to get a new set delivered soon from the Team Family Benefits package, but so far all they'd gotten was a smart couch. What was pressure-sensitive massage compared to full immersion? It was so unfair that Mom and Dad got to pick what gifts they got first.

She'd been too involved to enjoy the game the first time, when the family had watched together at the local arcade. Her whole body had twitched with wanting to influence the outcome, and she'd been so focused on Megan, she'd missed all the coolest moves by India.

Something tugged on her head, and the world of Sydney dropped away, replaced by the darkened living room and her annoyed mother, holding the headset. "What are you doing up this late, young lady?"

Lola rubbed her eyes, then stopped because that might make her look sleepy. "I'm checking up on Megan."

Mom's stern look got anxious. "Oh. Uh . . . okay." She fidgeted with the headset in her hands, like she didn't know what to do with it. "You know, it's . . . freedom . . . has a price. We hope we won't pay it, but all these other people have paid it and . . ."

Oh, yeah, the "freedom" talk. Lola noticed her mom said all this with the gently purring smart couch behind her. She handed the headset back and backed away. "Well, don't stay up too late, it's a school night."

Lola watched her mom retreat, hardly able to move lest she disrupt this miracle. Her mom was letting her stay up on a school night to watch sports! Lola checked over the odds boards, though, before going to bed. Ugh, they still thought South America was going all the way. Just because they had for the past two tournaments. The oddsmakers were obviously blinded by the so-called "survivor advantage." Like agility ROI and speed stats didn't exist. Amateurs.

The betting board was going gangbusters, of course. You could see the raw feed if you wanted, all these posts so fast you couldn't follow them, but Lola had a filter already in place to look only at her team and just the bets and challenges from her age-mates.

Her eye fell on a video update from a hot boy. She blinked at it to start the video playing, but what he had to say was anything but attractive. "Team North America has been lucky. Everyone knows they suck and have sucked through three sets of athletes. If they even make it to round three, I'll trash my dad's antique Gibson guitar."

Lola felt a hot flash. How dare he? "I'll take that bet. My sister's going to sweep round three, and if she doesn't, I'll . . ." She faltered. "I'll burn my mother's collection of silk fans."

Oh, no. What was she thinking? Her mom's fans had been brought from Japan by Oba-chan and were probably way more irreplaceable than some stupid guitar, but the pretty boy had already flagged an agreement to the bet.

Lola signed out and took off the VR hood. Was she making too many bets? There'd been the week of math homework, her new sneakers . . . she couldn't quite remember all the ones she'd made.

She put it out of mind. It was only a problem if Megan didn't win, and she was so going to. She had to . . .

Megan's team sprawled like drunken potentates around a single long table in the lavish penthouse dining room. All the other tables had been pushed haphazardly aside, leaving them with the best place, centered in front of the expansive picture windows. The Sydney Opera House dominated the view, as well as the bay and boardwalk area nearby. A thin column of smoke was the only visible sign of yesterday's carnage. That and the piles of stolen loot on the floor. Chet had a personal jetpack lying next to his feet, and India had her desired art collection, paintings and vases laid out on a table near at hand.

When Megan entered, accompanied by Mitzi, she was cold and aching from her night on the park bench. There was the heady scent of coffee, and the table was heaped with trays of bacon, eggs, pancakes, fruit, potatoes, and foods that Megan had to admit she didn't even recognize. She took a seat and piled a plate. There was only one news display in the dining room, and it was loudly gushing, "Madness and violence unprecedented . . ." Mitzi winked and used her remote to turn it off.

Jerry leaned toward Megan. "How are you doing?" He looked like he actually cared.

"I flipped out and beat a man, and now it's international news. How do you think I'm doing?"

He chewed his lower lip, concentrating on her, the full impact of his dark eyes disconcerting, like he was looking deep into her. "It's hard. What we do. No one is judging you."

The bacon turned tasteless in her mouth. She washed it down. At least there was coffee. "I'm judging me."

"That's because you're a good person." His smile was genuine, none of the asshole confidence she'd seen before, and that intense stare was softer now. "Good people sometimes do bad things. It's the situation, not you."

She felt herself wanting to give in to the comfort. She didn't trust it. "You don't know me like that. Why do you even care?"

"Because you're going to have to do it again if we survive the next match." He reached over and squeezed her forearm, a quick, brotherly gesture.

Something cracked inside her. Long after he removed his hand and went back to joking with Kendell and Hasan, Megan stared at the place his fingers had imparted a moment of warmth and understanding. An intolerable intrusion into the insulation she'd built around herself, that touch, still burning, still demanding she reach back. She'd smack him, but Coach would shock her for in-team fighting. Again.

The room's news screen flickered back to life of its own accord and displayed the very large, leering face of Jax Pollard. "Hello, future losers! I heard you somehow made it through a game!" He backed away from the camera enough to show he was on a city street, fireworks, or perhaps just fire, painting the night sky, a weather-stained bronze statue behind him. He raised an arm, and a woman fell against him and blew a kiss at the camera. Jax laughed. "I wanted you to know, Jerry the mouse, I just looted a ton of brandy here in Bucharest, and I'm betting it all against your next game. Thanks for making the odds a little more competitive." He raised an elaborate bottle in his fist. "Here's to the fallen Balkan Conglomerate and to not having the indignity of tripping over your inept ass on my way to—"

The screen winked out. Mitzi set down her remote. "Sorry that was slow. I had to put down my drink."

"I hate that asshole," Kendell said.

Mitzi peeled the screen away from the wall, inspecting its back. "He had to have gotten the feed address from someone local, but I bet it was Tulio who did the hacking. Jax isn't that smart."

Indía came around the table and draped herself in Jerry's lap. "I wish I had a man as obsessed with me as he is with you."

"I used to think it had to be a woman between them. Never saw two straight guys so hung up on each other." Hasan flicked a toothpick at Jerry.

Jerry retaliated with a potato from his plate. "There was at least one woman, I'll have you know, and he only dated her because I did."

Mitzi dropped the screen. "Oh, no, you do not tell this story straight. Listen, there wasn't a woman, and it was in Chicago—"

Soon everyone was talking over one another, telling stories of pranks played by Jax and Jerry on each other. Just like that, Megan was on the outside again, looking in. She picked up her plate of bacon and moved to a place she could sit alone and watch the fire rise over the bay.

What would Ciera think of her mother now?

Megan felt hungover as they boarded their plane that evening. A long nap on the hotel bed had left her just as sore as the park bench. She couldn't wait to never see Sydney again. She didn't think to ask where they were going. She assumed it was back home, right up until their silent craft glided onto a snowy runway, far too soon after lifting off.

Coach Mustaine clapped his hands. "What do you all have to look so tired for? Shake it off! We have a publicity tour of Theil City in ten minutes, and then you'd better get a good night's sleep because there's practice in the morning. I am not letting you lazy, sloppy idiots cut it that close again! Let's go!"

Megan wasn't the only one groaning and dragging her feet, at least. Jerry threw her a sympathetic glance. Maybe, just maybe, having won together, she was part of the team at last?

Once more she was forced to endure eyebrow waxing. It didn't feel like it had been long enough for them to grow back. There wasn't much time for testing the team's feelings as they were hustled into their makeup tent and out again, then marched from location to location. The others seemed to be able to smile convincingly, as if they enjoyed eating snow cones on a glacier or having their pictures taken with penguins. Penguins were a lot taller than Megan expected, and surly.

A full day of bustling activity, and she felt as if she had touched no one, said nothing. The hotel had comforters a good foot thick, and massive pillows. Megan felt like she was drowning in goose down all night, which made her too anxious to sleep, even with the smart glass windows blocking out the midnight sun.

Her ring showed messages from her parents and Lola. Just seeing Lola's name brought back her last message and made Megan's veins turn to ice.

She deleted all of them unread.

Megan cranked the steering wheel hard, and her body slammed into the padded side of her go-cart as the tires spun helplessly, kicking up sand on a virtual beach. Along the roadway, behind short barriers, people jumped up and down, waving flags for North America and the ice-blue-and-white flags of Antarctica.

This didn't feel like Antarctica. Palm trees and cobblestones, a picturesque faux-European village with steep hills and sudden turns. Megan shoved her weight right, and the wheels on that side caught, jerking her forward and back onto the road.

She felt sand under her butt and tasted sickly-sweet exhaust whenever she pushed the tiny, exposed engine. Hot, black clouds of un-combusted fossil fuels erupted with every slam of the pedal against the floor. In her rearview, she caught a glimpse of a flying bomb heading her way and zagged violently, letting it sail past to hit the person in front of her, then steered frantically to get the poorly responding cart through the smoke and debris.

Only the team from the coldest country on earth would have picked Death Kart: Beach as their game. Sweat from the simulated summer day poured down her face and made her thighs slip on the tiny, hard seat.

Far ahead of her, Indía was in the lead, her purple cart barely visible, but a green Antarctica cart was gaining. Megan remembered the layout of the track from the previous lap and knew she could take a shortcut there. She yanked the wheel while braking, skidded sharp left, then sharp right, and ended up in front of the green cart. She could keep going, come in second, but she knew that wasn't the move that would most benefit her team. She had been last in the first lap, and the green cart had been in second place. It had the most points.

She slammed the brake again and jerked the wheel left, spinning out to block the green player, letting Jerry and Hasan sail past. She heard the Antarctica player cursing her as she pumped the useless gas pedal. Megan's cart sputtered and jerked into motion, almost free. She saw the finish line ahead, but another Antarctica car was coming fast. Megan turned into it, jamming it back into the green car as the sky exploded with fireworks, announcing that someone had crossed the finish line. She hoped it was Indía.

She was still struggling to get her cart free from the jam she'd created when the world faded, leaving her in her pod, hands still clenched on a steering wheel that wasn't there.

Darkness. Shit, she hadn't looked at the ticker. Why did she keep not doing that? She opened her pod slowly, afraid of what she might see.

Jerry's strong hands grabbed her wrists and pulled her free, his face beaming. "That ending! What a move!" He lifted her. She stiffened, putting her hands on his. He set her down. "Okay, Mori. I promise, no more victory kisses."

Megan was not as relieved as she expected to be. She squeezed his hand and let him pull her toward the platforms for their victory ceremony. He smiled at her as he let go, and that made her feel she'd been right to hold him off. He got it.

This time she avoided looking at the Antarctica team. She didn't want to remember any of them as individuals, only the impression of six bodies on the ground, below the Queen Maud Mountains, so white against a painfully blue sky.

The air was blissfully cool and gentle after the sweaty, gritty race. Theil City clustered around them, concocted of soaring glass and white limestone to blend in with the dramatic glacier-topped mountains dominating the view. The red carpet was blue. There was no crowd of prisoners under guard. Antarctica didn't keep prisons. Instead, they'd brought out volunteers, mostly the elderly and tough-looking teens, exactly the percentage of the city's population required by treaty. It looked like less than half the number they'd seen in Sydney. But Theil was a small city. The volunteers milled about and clustered, talking with each other, not kept in line by drones with guns. Somehow that was worse.

Jerry met her gaze and nodded slowly. She felt his support like a much-needed brace but feared that connection. She had to stand on her own. Didn't she?

The siren went off, and the team rushed forward. Once again, Megan hesitated. Jerry turned back and waved for her to come with him. What did that mean? She looked at the cameras; a few had stayed hovering nearby. Jerry gestured again.

After a pause, she relented and jogged to him. He turned, and she matched him as in the game. They had an easy rhythm running across the square. Jerry led the way down the main avenue, avoiding the scattering locals. She was grateful for that. He stopped in front of a store, frowned at it, then ran to the next one. Megan asked, "Don't we have to . . . I mean . . ."

"This is just the thing." He flashed her his golden smile and picked up a rock from a flowerbed. He hurled it through the window, then kicked the remaining shards away. He turned and held his hand to her like he was asking her to join him on an elegant dance floor. No, she couldn't. She shouldn't. He flexed his fingers, waiting. A camera drone came close, bleeping a warning about their stillness. Megan bit her lip and took his hand.

It was a hardware store. The alarm rang endlessly, lights flashing from the ceiling as Jerry walked coolly down an aisle. "Here we are." He held up a cylinder. Spray paint. He tossed it, and she caught it automatically. White.

He picked another and shook it. "Vandalism time!"

Megan was relieved. She ran after Jerry as he sprayed a line of blue over the shop wall and out onto the sidewalk. Megan wrote her name, badly, on the side of the building, and caught up to Jerry putting the finishing touches on "North America Rules" on the middle of the street.

This was the perfect choice. They were doing their part, inflicting damage, and no one was getting hurt. The locals had long since run away from the main streets. Megan perfected her name on trash cans, park benches, and any other available surface. She tried spraying her teammates' names onto the snow in a vacant lot. The snow melted on impact, but that only embossed the letters.

When their cans of paint ran out, they wrecked some more stores. "Hey, beer." Jerry pulled a few bottles straight from a restaurant bar.

"Is this . . . penguin jerky?" Megan frowned at a package from a gift shop. She tossed it to Jerry.

"I think it's just penguin brand. Not going to try it, though."

They circled back to Central Square as the sky filled with the glorious floating ribbons of the aurora australis, the southern lights. Jerry had a snowshoe he'd taken off the wall of a bar and was holding on his shoulder like a flag. "The team always converges on the biggest hotel in town for dinner and sleep—if you want to sleep." Jerry flung the snowshoe end-over-end down the street. It clattered to rest against an information kiosk. He threw his hands up. "Goal!"

There was something childlike in him. Megan packed a snowball and sent it after the snowshoe. "Mori scores again!" He held up a hand, waiting for a high five.

Megan sauntered past. "You're not such an asshole, when you try."

He dropped the hand. "Thanks. I think."

They shared a quiet, comfortable silence that was more intimate than any conversation. Megan couldn't believe she'd gotten away with this. The hotel was just ahead, shaped like a glacier, rising like a mountain to a curtain wall of angled glass. She'd made it through without hurting anyone, and without having to sleep on a park bench, either.

And this handsome man, this surprisingly kind man, liked her. She closed the distance between them and started to reach for his hand.

A high, feminine whoop cut through the air. India bounded up to them and threw her arms around Jerry, kissing him full on the lips. There was blood on her cheek, and Jerry, after a moment's hesitation, wrapped his arms low around India's hips and lifted her against him. "Have fun, you minx?"

"Not as much as I'm going to have," she replied.

"Hey," Megan said, but she didn't know what she planned on saying after it. Jerry was carrying India into the building without a look back.

16

Lola entered the lunchroom at her high school feeling eyes on her from all corners. Admiring eyes, even though she had on last year's jeans and a boring T-shirt. She wore an invisible cloak of celebrity. Lola felt her best, prettiest, quietest self. She smiled and nodded to less-fortunate kids who didn't have a sister on the national team. Even super-popular boys noticed her. Seniors. The student council secretary. The hot college-student teacher's assistant from gym class.

Lola set her tray down like a queen, generously staying with her original friends now that she was popular. Kiko picked at her food and looked at her with awe. She was taking it well that she was no longer the bad girl of the group. "I saw the news say your sister was so unpredictable the oddsmakers just gave up."

Marty jumped on this like he'd been waiting for the conversation to start. "Did you see that surprise sacrifice move in Antarctica?"

"Of course! I haven't missed seeing any games live, no matter what the time zone." Lola saw Marty's face fall and realized she was bragging. Not everyone was getting a free pass from their parents. "I mean, the replay was almost as good."

Marty didn't look mollified. "Aren't you scared, though? For your sister?"

"No way. Megan is going to go all the way." The question itself had raised a frisson in her gut. It was her sister. A real person. She could die. Lola covered her fear with a gulp of chocolate milk. "Can we watch at your place? In the pods?"

That did it. Marty straightened proudly. "My parents use them during the matches, but they won't be as interested in tonight's coverage."

"This is so intense," Kiko said, and they all sighed in happy agreement.

Laurel Coden, the most popular boy in school and captain of the pod team, walked up to their table then, with Kay, the most popular girl in school, and her best friend who was always standing around repeating her. All three of them wore the most authentic Team North America jackets, complete with silver death collars!

"Hey," Laurel said, lifting his chin. "I'm your sister's biggest fan."

Lola freaked out. Inside. She barely shrugged outside. You couldn't let people know you were into them. "I beg to differ, but she is my sister."

Kay and her friend tittered. What fake laughs. "You can't be the biggest fan. Look at your neck."

"Yeah, look at your neck!"

Lola wasn't sure what that was about.

Laurel leaned close. His eyes almost vibrated with excitement. "What if I were to tell you there's a way to be the Ultimate Fan?"

"But I am an ultimate fan." Lola's voice was weak, breathy.

Kay tugged Laurel's arm. "Not here. Teachers."

"Yeah," said the tagalong. "Not here."

"We'll talk," Laurel said, and the cool kids drifted away in an air of mystery.

"That was barely adequate." Coach Mustaine paced in front of a holo-screen that had just played through the end of their Death Kart race.

He paused and pointed at the video with a laser, drawing a circle around Jerry's car as it swerved too far to avoid a collision. "That's the kind of pussy behavior that made this race be decided by just nine points!"

Megan slumped in a wooden school desk, wondering how Mustaine had found a room exactly as uncomfortable and cold as his film review room back at Champion's Village in every city so far. That took dedication.

Jerry raised his hand. "Coach, we didn't prepare for this. There are very few racing games on the official list."

"Exactly! The name of the game in MegaDeath is versatility. You gotta prepare for the unexpected. We're in Paris tomorrow, and who knows what they'll throw at us. You could be swimming through mazes or shooting the moon." Mustaine kicked the wall, and his holoscreen faded away. "Push these chairs back. We're going to play a game right now."

"I got a headache." Chet rubbed the back of his neck. "Think those carts gave me whiplash."

"I'll give you whiplash." Coach started kicking chairs and legs until the whole team got up and obligingly moved the chairs to the edges of the room. "Before we play Europe this week and you all die, having lived just long enough to cost me three weeks of prime recruiting time for the next team, I'm going to teach you a game that's about skill and cunning and thinking on your feet."

Everyone grumbled. They were in Madrid! After grueling photos ops in the Plaza Mayor and the Royal Palace, after miserably reliving every second of the last game, they were looking forward to a night off. The last photo session had been redolent of spicy meat from a food cart, and Megan wanted to eat something badly. Kendell sighed about the Prado Museum; they had only seen the exterior. "C'mon, Coach, museum closes in an hour. Can't we come back to this after dinner?"

"You guys don't care if you live, say so now and I'll replace you." He held up his red card.

That got everyone moving. Megan shifted to a position on the tacky, thin carpet and caught herself worrying about who would sit beside her like she was still a kid in school. Jerry, fortunately, settled down cross-legged to her right before she fully panicked.

Coach put his card away. "I'll walk around and tap you on the head. If I say 'duck' you stay put. If I say 'goose' you have to catch me before I run around the circle clockwise back to your spot."

Indía straightened her legs. "You have got to be joking."

"Nope. Come on, you know the game. Let's see if you can compete at it without practicing. And pay attention, I'll change the rules."

Coach patted Megan on the head. "Duck."

This was absurd. Chet's face was red, his fists shaking on his knees. They were adults, elite athletes, and they were leaving this crappy conference room to sleep in the best hotel in town and dine on whatever they wanted.

Kendell was the goose and reached Coach almost immediately, but he blew his whistle and said, "New rule, run the other way." She breathed heavily from her nose and pivoted. Even at her better speed, she couldn't get all the way around the circle and back to the space they were aiming for before Coach dropped into it. "Now I'm out. I ain't doing that twice."

Kendell picked Jerry, who picked Hasan. Coach made them hop on one leg when running, changed the direction again. Hasan rebelled by taking forever. He went twice around the circle, three times, four times.

The electric shock buzzed down Megan's back. "Do I have your attention now?" Coach spoke with his teeth around his whistle. He spat it out. "New rule: one point for catching the goose. Negative one point for going around the circle twice. The top three scores in ten minutes get to leave early."

Megan felt the air draw out of the room. A tremulous moment and all hell broke loose. Hasan smacked her head hard and took off, full speed, and was halfway around the circle before the word "goose" ended.

There followed the most intense, violent, and cutthroat ten minutes of Duck, Duck, Goose Megan had ever witnessed. She burned her knee and the heel of her hand on the carpet, collided with Chet and India. When the coach blew his whistle to announce the time was up, everyone was soaked with sweat and panting.

"Well, look at how it is when you have something on the line." Coach shook his head slowly.

"Just tell us who won," Chet hissed.

More head shaking. "Who can tell me the lesson here?"

Megan raised her hand. "You're a sadistic bastard?"

He pointed at her. "Wrong. The game is a sadistic bastard. We play again on Friday, and if we lose the toss, Europe is picking the scenario. So I want all of you to get in the official games list and make damn sure you know the rules for every single one of them." He mimed crumpling something up and throwing it away. "Get out of here. You disgust me."

Well, he didn't have to tell Megan twice. She bolted for the door faster than she'd bolted after India when she was the goose. Her hot, grimy forearm brushed against Jerry's as they both reached for the door. He laughed. "Yeah, no waiting to see if he changes his mind." He stepped back and gestured for her to open it.

Megan felt a warm flush like when he'd invited her into the hardware store in Antarctica. She jerked the door open and rushed into the cool night air. "I'm starving," she announced to the city street. An old man walking a dog turned to frown at her.

Jerry cupped her elbow. "Me too. There's a place down the block I noticed when we got in, and it's all I could think about for the past hour."

Megan grabbed his hand before he could be too gentlemanly about it and broke into a run. He let her pull him along, falling into step.

Neither of them noticed India Thomas standing in the doorway behind them, arms crossed.

As they ate, Jerry talked about playing for the city leagues, and Megan shared her stories from the Kern County Crusaders, and everything felt so much less important, less dire. Megan fell asleep that night calm, at peace. Whatever game they were playing on Friday, there was no way it would be as ridiculous as the one they'd played that afternoon.

Megan sat astride a horse. Its chest expanded between her legs as it panted for breath. Lightning bolts cracked across a purple and black sky. The bolts were impossibly long and formed spiderwebs that mimicked the vine-choked walls of a nearby castle. The horse shifted and tossed its head, pawed the stone.

And she'd thought Death Kart was an odd choice.

Europe had won the toss and chosen Swords Knight, a game Megan didn't care for and never chose to play. For one thing, you had to stay on a horse. A massive beast that twitched and had an AI of its own, and Megan had a feeling this one kept trying to shrug her off. If you fell off your horse, you were disqualified. The rules of this game were one point for each person who made it to a chamber at the top of the castle, through rooms that moved and had secret doors. There were puzzles to solve, and, of course, other players trying to stop you. It would be a thousand times easier without a ton of herbivore between your legs.

Megan's horse tossed its head and stamped impatiently, as if aware of her thoughts. It very well could be programmed to respond to her neural transmissions, though this beast would only do that to be as obstinate as possible. Megan tugged on the reins and drove her knees against the massive body, but it only huffed at her.

"We're lost, stupid horse!" It had bolted early on when a trap door nearly opened under her, and had taken her up to this stupid balcony, a long gallery that wound around the exterior wall and didn't have anything in it, like a way back to the game's central maze.

A crack of thunder and flash of lightning arrived together, close enough she felt the heat, and the horse bucked and reared. Megan clung with knees, hands, and arms, and begged the horse to not drop her as she felt her ass hanging out of the saddle.

Disappointed at not dislodging her, it bolted back into the castle, which was where she wanted to go anyway, but now she was clinging to the stallion to keep from hitting her head on a chandelier.

It slowed to a walk in a hallway lined with sculpted figures. "Twelve statues!" Megan called out, hoping someone on the team could hear her. You weren't supposed to get separated. The statues were almost certainly another dumb puzzle. Knights with different weapons in different poses. Ugh, what did it mean? Arm up, axe raised, sword at side . . . was it an old-style game cheat code? Up, up, down, down, left, right, left, right . . . no. Well, maybe. Whoever'd designed this game liked cheap gags like that. The first room had had a door with an awl on it and one with a nun on it. Very old-school graphics, so maybe an old-school cheat code.

She memorized the statue order in case something came up that required a sequence, and nudged the horse forward. This time it obeyed. "Jerry? India? Chet?"

Herbert Rivera appeared in a sumptuous medieval robe, velvet trimmed in fur. "Alas, Fair Megan hath wandered down a treacherous path!" He took a bite from a turkey leg and disappeared.

She was starting to hate how much that man loved his job.

The corridor ended at a T, and Megan's horse screamed, pawing the air again. There wasn't even a loud noise! Megan wrestled the reins and—oh. Another horse charged toward her, nostrils flared, the man on its back in full armor, sword high. Megan barely got her sword up in time to parry the blow. She slid in her seat, one hand on the reins, one hand trying to push this man away as he recovered and swung again and again.

This stupid game. Swords were terrible against another opponent on horseback. You could barely reach unless you were a monkey-armed giant like this Frenchman. When Megan was finally able to throw a blow instead of just blocking, her sword point sailed centimeters from her opponent's chest. The horse struggled against her, twisting her away. She hastily wrapped her blade behind her to deflect a blow as the horse pulled her out of range and started to flee.

Which wouldn't have been bad if another knight in armor weren't already blocking that direction. The whole game, Europe had been playing like they had the castle mapped out.

Megan ducked this man's first swing by dodging behind the horse's head. She felt a blow hit the armor on her back. It stung through the metal. She twisted, side to side, block left, block right. She couldn't even think of striking back. Her sword shoulder was burning with exhaustion, and there was no way out.

17

Megan had just managed to get her horse to turn in a circle, helping her block the relentless onslaught, when there was a deep rumble of stone against stone. The top half of the wall in front of Megan fell away. Jerry cantered in place on a higher corridor. "Jump up here!"

Horses didn't have buttons labeled "jump." Megan tugged and lunged in her saddle. She had to stop to elbow her opponent as he tried to pull her from her perch. She kicked her heels into soft flanks. "Jump, idiot!"

A sword smacked her flat on the leg, and her opponent cursed in French, but Idiot Horse finally got the idea and lurched onto the higher platform with a clatter of slipping hooves and crumbling stone.

Jerry clasped her wrist briefly, and that more than anything felt like a rescue. He spurred his horse around and led the way. Walls lowered and fell around them, creating a shifting maze. She kept her focus on Jerry and gently nudged the horse forward.

In the swarm of audience comments sliding at the bottom of her vision were a lot of instructions on how to ride a horse, with exasperated capital letters. "JESUS, lady, squeezing your horse is going to make him RUN and jerking on the reins like that will make him STOP!"

That would have been useful at the beginning of the game. Maybe there should be a loading screen? No big deal, just that her life depended on it.

The corridor opened into a chasm, a huge interior court of the castle, with hallways and windows opening into it from all directions. The team was almost all there, on different levels. They were trapped, no way forward from where they were on narrow ledges and in corridor-mouths. Portcullises slammed down behind them, preventing backtracking.

"I know this level," Jerry said. He waved his sword overhead, catching Hasan's attention. "I think the switch near me will help you. Be ready to move forward." He and his horse moved along the ledge. There was a slightly raised square of stone on the floor. When Jerry's horse stood on it, it sank. At the same time, a wall rose between Megan and Jerry, and a drawbridge swung down to connect Hasan to the corridor across the chasm from him.

"I think I have Chet," Kendell said, and the sound of her horse moving filled the space with echoing clops. A bridge swung down, connecting Chet to another corridor across the way. Of course, they could each help one other person. Now Chet was in a position where he could hit a switch that freed Jerry. Megan waved to India, who was above to her right. They were the last pair not to have made the first crossing. India must have the button for Megan. Megan had to admit, begrudgingly, it was good game design.

India looked right at her, their eyes locked, and . . . nothing. India turned her horse and attacked the portcullis.

That was when the arrows started flying. Clockwork archers had appeared along the battlements overhead. Hasan found the switch for Kendell to cross, and then all four of them were on the far side. "India!" Jerry shouted, looking regal as he stood in his stirrups in his suit of armor. "Hit the switch!"

But India had wedged her sword in the portcullis, and it raised.

"I'll meet you in the ballroom!" she called. Her horse reared, and she disappeared back into the hallway she'd come from.

India had abandoned her! The game gave a point for each team member who made it to the final room. They could win without everyone, but only if the other team came up short too.

Jerry's horse cantered in place. He looked as nervous as the horse. "Everyone, keep going, I'll catch up." He drew his sword and waved for emphasis. "Go! Get to the ballroom!"

Megan looked helplessly across the chasm at Jerry. Her horse shifted uneasily, making her feel precarious. "There's nothing you can do to help me."

Jerry paced his horse back and forth on the ledge twice. He looked unsure. "I think you can jump to where India was."

"Jump?"

"The horse. Get the horse to jump to India's ledge." He pointed with his sword. It was a good six feet away, and higher.

"No way. I'll miss, fall, and the pod will break my legs."

"I believe you can make it," Jerry said. "Jump up there and activate your bridge. That's all you have to do. The jump back will be easier, lower."

Easy! She backed the horse up to the wall. It pawed the stone impatiently. This would never work. "Jerry, just go! Get to the final room. We need every point. Maybe I can circle back and stall someone from Europe."

Jerry sheathed his sword. "I'm not budging until you make that jump."

Bastard. They couldn't win with both of them behind. She had no choice. Megan gripped the reins firmly, leaned forward, and shouted, "Yah!"

The horse ran pell-mell to the edge of the platform. Megan had to squeeze her fear deep down into her gut to keep from reacting. A flinch could end everything. Powerful muscles gathered under her and sprang into the air. They sailed effortlessly, magically, and then hooves were clattering again on stone.

Her horse tossed its head as if to say, "Told you so."

"Ha ha!" Jerry called, every inch the medieval hero. "We ride!"

It was no less scary leaping back, but the bridge was there, and she was motivated by wanting to catch up to Jerry and kiss that smirk off his face.

Lightning cut the sky overhead as they clattered up and up. What a surprise, there was a row of statues all holding their weapons in the air, and Megan got to dictate, "Up, down, left, kick, left, right, up," while Kendell smacked the statues to get them into position. When the last one was set, they fell away, revealing a ramp. The top chamber was ahead, and India stood in it, imperious on her horse, her sword dripping with blood.

The sun was rising sullenly over Paris, an egg yolk in cloudy cream. Megan pressed her sweaty forehead to the glass of her hotel window. The Champs-Élysées glittered below, spread with broken glass and discarded weapons. "We could all be dead now. I got to the end point just three and a half seconds before their last player. If I hadn't made it, we would all be dead. Doesn't India realize that?"

Bare feet padded up behind her. "Do you really need me to spell it out to you?" His hands reached for her waist.

"Don't touch me!" Megan snapped.

David huffed. "You really have no human emotions." He snatched a piece of clothing from the floor.

Megan felt a stab of conscience. The cheerleader had already forgiven a lot from her to be here tonight, and he was beautiful, his body as sculpted as the art deco lamps that covered him with dappled light. He built up a bouquet of garments and paused, having finally located his underwear. She should apologize. What came out of her mouth was, “I have emotions.”

“Yes, we’ve all noticed.” He angrily stepped into his shorts. “You have angry and sad and angry-sad. But if you ever thought about other people for a second, you’d understand that India and Jerry led Chicago to the National League Championship last year. Together. They have history. And now there’s someone who can play with Jerry the way only India did before.” He raised his eyebrows.

“There’s nothing special about the way I play with Jerry. India should be jealous of herself, then! Or Hasan or Kendell!”

David pulled on his shorts, somehow making the act sensual, a reverse striptease. “I am wasting my talents on you.” He stretched his arms behind his head. “You’re in love with him. It was obvious the moment you threw yourself at me.”

How dare he look at her so knowingly! Megan turned her back on him and studied the sunrise. “You don’t know what you’re talking about.”

“And you’re lying to yourself.”

Megan had thought Jerry would stay with her again, as he had in Theil City, but when they were set loose in Paris, he’d gone straight into a heated battle with the prisoners. The convicts fought hard and fiercely here. Europe gave out pardons for those who defended the city with appropriate zealousness.

Megan hadn’t wanted to fight, but she’d seen a man coming at Jerry with a pipe wrench and had rushed to his aid. She’d hit the assailant’s forearm with her own, knocking his swing wide. The impact had driven her into Jerry. He’d given her a heated look, and then run off . . . with India.

She wasn’t jealous. If she felt betrayed, it was because she’d barely made it out of the Place de la Concorde alive.

She’d crawled like a rat in the shadows while prisoners with makeshift weapons had stormed the streets in search of glory. Explosions had popped and flared, lighting up the night, and all Megan had seen were running figures and stark flares. Rocks had flown at her. Figures on rooftops had flung missiles at every moving shadow. One had hit her back and left a soft, pained spot. She'd been confused and desperate by the time she'd found the hotel, bleeding from minor wounds.

David had been sitting on the front steps, admiring the chaos like it was a calm night. He'd looked especially beautiful in the firelight, peaceful. She'd wanted to disturb him. She'd grabbed him forcefully, but he'd been languid as a river. He'd expected her. He'd responded and given way, and that was why she felt so sure he'd had all the control.

Now, he fastened his shirt behind her, his image reflected in the window. "I see your wheels turning. You know I'm right. Something happened in Antarctica. You look at Jerry now like you need him, and you have made a career out of not needing anyone. Her Majesty Queen India isn't blind. She sees it. And she does not like to share."

"I'm here to compete," Megan said, and almost believed it. "I don't care about Jerry or India."

David slumped as if she'd disappointed him all over again. "Take it from someone who's had a good view: teams that don't care about each other don't make it." He picked up his shoes and walked to the door. "Next time, if you want meaningless sex, ask one of your fans. I'm sure they'd be happy to oblige."

Megan stared at the door after he closed it behind him. Who was he to leave her?

Her disloyal inner monologue answered her. A handsome, sensible young man who knows what he wants. Someone not nearly as messed up as you.

Teams that didn't care about each other didn't make it. Hadn't their every win been by the narrowest of margins? They didn't deserve to still be alive. The oddsmakers were certain of that. Three seconds of luck wouldn't cut it against South America.

She should forget it all and enjoy the hedonism of the moment. Wasn't that why she'd asked David to come back to her room? Their hotel for the night was over three hundred years old. The first floor was a palace glittering with real gold and painted plaster in colors so deep they glowed. She could go down to the restaurant and have something amazing, drowning in sauce. This next week they had a bye and would be engaging in a victory tour of their own country before the semifinals. She should be enjoying the moment, relaxing. She didn't care that Jerry would rather be with Indía. She didn't care about Jerry. She didn't.

Keep protesting too much, self. You might actually start believing it.

Megan slipped off her silk hotel bathrobe and started to get dressed. Her pants were on top of a Tibetan rug she'd forgotten she had.

Jax had sent them all mocking presents, items looted from his victory over Tibet. "Pray to get resurrected. Then you might actually get to play against me!" He had hidden depths of psychotic organization. The news feed showed him kicking over market stalls in Lhasa, yet he'd found time to pick up a few trinkets and pen notes to go with them. Megan could barely multitask checking her messages and breathing after the elation-fear-elation roller-coaster of a MegaDeath game.

She buttoned her pants and pulled on a sweater, and laid the Tibetan weaving over the rumpled bed. She wished she could laugh with Jerry about it. Megan was going to have nightmares tonight, and there was nothing she could do to hold them off, no one to hold her and keep her in the present.

Numbly, she put on her shoes. When she headed down, she heard happy voices coming from the banquet room, so she continued past, down, and out the front of the hotel. She broke into a jog. Eighteen opponents dead, three cities scourged, and she still found herself running alone in the early morning. All that had changed was the city.

18

Megan didn't know how to act around India and Jerry. On the plane, Jerry was all business, talking about what they could do better in the next round. He didn't mention India purposefully leaving Megan behind in the castle, and Megan didn't bring it up.

"Enough business. Let's have a round." India waved the attendant over. "Shots of Patrón for my team. Let's toast a week off!"

The waiter brought a tray of glasses, and India played hostess, handing them around. She paused slightly before handing Megan hers. "All for one and one for all."

Kendell repeated this toast with significantly more emotion, her deep voice buoying Megan out of her seat to clink glasses. Even India didn't do anything to make her feel excluded for that second. Well, she was part of the team. They had risked their lives together three times. It counted for something.

Jerry gasped after downing the shot and pointed over his glass. "It's not a week off, though. This bye-week tour is going to be the hardest work you've done all season."

"Never a silver lining you can't see a cloud in." India sat on the arm of a seat to be near him. There was something proprietary in how she nudged him. "Get my boy here another shot."

Jerry laughed uncomfortably, gently urging Indía away. "Thanks, but I'm not sure I want to get drunk before a public appearance."

Indía's expression turned heated, as though he'd turned down more than a drink.

Megan broke into the awkward silence. "I've been meaning to ask—" Now Indía was glaring at her, and Jerry looked irritated. Megan hadn't been meaning to ask anything. She saw one of the stupid Tibetan souvenirs, a colorful cloth Hasan was smoothing between his fingers. "Jax." She congratulated herself. Everyone's expression froze at that name. She turned to Jerry. "What is it with you and him? Why does he care so much about putting you down?"

Jerry shook his head. "Oh, man, where to begin?"

Indía acted like she'd vacated her seat on purpose to hold court and raised her shot glass. "Like you don't know! We all know where it began. Junior World Championships, three years running, Jax and Jerry faced off against each other, and to hear him tell it—" she laid a hand on Jerry's arm "—Jax cheated."

Jerry scowled. "He did cheat. Twice. But he says—"

"Jerry, man." Hasan waved his scrap of fabric. "You know you played him dirty."

"That was one time, and it wasn't illegal. Well, it was against the rules, but sometimes you take a penalty if the—"

"Always a dirty player," Indía laughed, and she pushed a drink into Jerry's hand. This time, he took it. Jerry, Indía, Hasan, Kendell, and even Chet were talking over each other, reliving youthful competitions and transgressions together. Like Megan, they had competed in high school for low-level electric shocks and then went on to college betting grade points. They had opinions about what level was the truest, most honest level of play. Small local teams, Hasan said, those just playing for community recyclers and water rights, like the Kern County Crusaders.

Megan returned to her seat and stared out the window, feeling alone in the tight compartment full of bodies.

They landed in New York for a parade and speeches, then flew to Toronto for dinner with the president. Then it was Mexico City and the vice president, then San Salvador. They slept on the plane. Megan was losing track of what city they were in and how far into the week "off" they had gotten. It felt like one long day.

She didn't remember falling asleep when Mitzi shook her awake. The beige lounge didn't look familiar. She vaguely recalled stumbling away from some assembly, muttering apologies so she could be alone a moment and close her burning eyes. The nightmares and sleeplessness were catching up to her.

"Come on, we're grabbing dinner."

There was a spot of drool on the couch arm. Megan wiped her face. "Uh . . . is this the governor dinner or the youth sports council?"

"Neither. We actually have a whole, complete night off. Come on, we're going out to a real restaurant, just the team. We're going to eat, drink, and not talk about how much we love each other to strangers for one damn night."

That had been the worst. All the interview appearances where Jerry would flash his brilliant smile, and India would toss her perfect hair, and they would lie about "cohesion" and "feeling like a family." Weirdly, the idea of spending a night socializing with that same "family" felt like a break from the act. Megan also realized she was starving. "Lead the way."

"That's the spirit." Mitzi draped an arm over her shoulders. "And you're welcome. I turned off a buttload of screens and displays in that room. I could tell you needed some rest."

That reminded her. "How do you do that, anyway? I asked other people about turning off screens, and no one could."

Mitzi waved dismissively. "It's not hard if you know how the tech works. Oh, not to put anyone down. You wouldn't believe the security most screens have, just to keep them on. Sometimes it's easier to break into the local power grid." She gestured at a blank screen as they passed it. "You're lucky I'm an old hand at bypassing security systems."

Megan felt lucky. Mitzi led her down a back set of stairs, then had her wait as she checked for reporters and camera drones outside. Megan hadn't done anything to earn this protection, this friendship. Mitzi yanked the door open. "Coast is clear. Come on, I have an auto-drive cab waiting, and you know how squirrelly those are if you take too long."

They ran together. The auto-cab started to power up, and Mitzi said, "Oh, no, you don't!" and pointed her remote at it.

As they fell into the cab, laughing, Megan asked, "Is overriding electronics a common skill for cheerleaders?"

Mitzi beamed, tucking her remote away in a sequined purse. "I wasn't always a cheerleader. I was getting a degree in network security when I started making a name for myself on the college pod team. If I hadn't hit the big time, well, I'd be the one making the screens hard to turn off."

Megan couldn't remember her last close friend. Had it been Jacque Martin, from the research group? Jacque had left messages long after the rest of her coworkers had stopped. Megan didn't remember why she last saw her in person. To invite her to a graduation? A wedding? Megan had said something short and possibly nasty, and Jackie had backed away with her hands up. "Have a nice life," she had said. And that had been it.

Megan had pushed everyone away after Ciera. What had she done to herself? She leaned against Mitzi. "I misjudged you when we met."

Mitzi threw an arm around her and squeezed. "Everyone does.

Now, me, I didn't misjudge you. Though I'm still waiting for you to catch up and recognize yourself for who you really are."

The restaurant was a steak house high over the city, upscale enough that the other patrons controlled their glee at seeing the team and the cheerleaders. They were probably not the only celebrities dining there, although Megan wouldn't recognize any of the others. She did not want or need to look at the astronomical prices. "Just bring me a steak and whiskey."

The waiter vanished without another word.

At the head of the table, Jerry flipped through displays emanating from his ring, the images projecting above the table, his own drink untouched. "I don't like the odds for North Africa versus The Subcontinent. I think it's going to be Subcontinent versus South America, and Jax knows Natarajan's moves. They were in the men's singles finals last year."

Kendell shook her head and gestured eagerly. "Don't count North Africa out. When India and Pakistan agreed to buy that failing, impoverished island . . . what was it called? It's on the tip of my tongue. It's, like, where Shakespeare came from?"

Jerry grimaced. "Britain."

"Yeah, they bought Britain, and Britain made them put one of their guys on the team, and that guy has been terrible all season. I don't know why they haven't cut him. I say North Africa takes advantage of that weakness, if they win the toss, and pick a game that needs all players—"

Indía put her hand over Jerry's ring to interrupt the projection. "Stop it. Not another word about odds or player stats. We hardly ever get a night off!"

"We should be talking about Central Africa. That's who we have to defeat to even see another opponent." Hasan nudged Indía's hand off

Jerry's, ignoring her dirty look, to point at a graph. "Look at the strategic complexity scores. South America has the raw talent, but Central Africa is the smartest team in the league. Did you see the highlights from the Oslo game? They flat-out out-strategized. They played Ulama like it was chess."

"I'm with India," Megan said. "No odds talk. Not until I've had my steak."

India gave her a tight grimace that was probably meant to be a smile. "Exactly. Kendell, you have to agree. Let's have all the women on the same side."

"I want to talk about Central Africa," Kendell said. "But I can wait. Tonight, I get to see my girlfriend. She's taking the train down from Oregon." Kendell pulled a photo out of her ring, and everyone admired the handsome couple mugging for the camera. Kendell wore a sharp tailored suit. Her girlfriend was in a peach chiffon dress, the sort no one wore except bridesmaids. The disco ball behind them confirmed the setting as a wedding.

A commotion at the front of the restaurant drew Megan's attention. A strangely familiar voice squeaked, "No, it's fine. We have reservations!"

A gaggle of teens wearing Team North America jackets, jogging suits, even silver collars, pushed past the maître d' and went to their table. "Uh-oh." Kendell put away her photo and stretched. "Fans."

Megan tried to look anywhere else than at the approaching half-dozen teens, hoping they would fawn over Jerry and India and leave her alone. Then one of them said, "Megan!" in a definitely familiar voice.

Lola bounced on her toes. "Why didn't you tell me you'd be here? Kiko had to hack into your itinerary." The girl next to Lola waved shyly. She had a round face and long black hair.

Megan stared at her sister, who stood slightly at the front of the pack, like she was their leader or spokesperson. "Lola, what are you doing here?"

Lola swayed, gesturing exaggeratedly. "Uh . . . we live here? I mean, not far from LA, anyway."

They were in LA? Wait, there was something more important to ask. "Are you drunk?"

Lola's loose-limbed shrug was definitely the move of a drunk person. "Are you super stuffy? C'mon, we spent all night trying to find you." Lola threw back her hair and made a weird pose, one arm up, like a store mannequin gesturing at a sign. "What do you think?"

When Megan didn't respond, Lola waved her hand at her neck. Oh, the collar. Like the jacket, it was an excellent forgery of the real thing, though this one had the Team NA logo and colors worked along the edge instead of being plain silver. "It's . . . very nice," Megan finally said.

"Nice?" one of the boys behind Lola exclaimed, insulted.

Lola waved him down, giggling. "I don't think she knows what they are!"

Jerry stood up and held out his hand. "You're Megan's sister? Thank you for supporting the team."

Lola melted, literally dropping a foot as her knees buckled. Her friends laughed and supported her as she shook Jerry's hand. "This is, like, the biggest honor."

"The honor is mine." Jerry somehow managed to sound and look sincere, shaking the hand of a drunken teen while the waitstaff gave him horrified glances.

Indía hurried over. "Aren't you the sweetest? Why, look, Jerry, it's our future. Team North America 2120."

If Jerry's handshake had made Lola almost fall, Indía's attention nearly killed her. She pushed Jerry out of the way to lay hands on Indía. "I'm your biggest fan! Like, since you were playing for Princeton! I had you on my fantasy team before the draft!"

Megan could see Indía was eating this up. Okay, she cared. She wished she didn't. It would be petty to compete for a teenager's attention, especially her own sister's. "I think our food is coming. Why don't you head home, Lola? Tell Mom and Dad I'll call later."

Lola fell drunkenly between Jerry and Indía, an arm around each. "Megan! Take a picture for me! I heard a rumor that Jerry and Indía were an item. Is it true? Tell me it's true." Her eyes all but glittered with hearts and stars as she gazed up at Jerry and Indía.

Megan bit her lip and tasted blood in her mouth, but she took the picture. She hoped when Lola sobered up she'd see the smug smirk on Indía's face and realize she was not worth idolizing.

Indía hugged Lola and tapped her collar with one elegant finger. "These are so cute."

"You've got the look down, all right," Jerry told her.

The teens laughed as a whole, delighted at how dumb the adults were. One of the girls burst out, "Wow, how are you guys so out of touch?"

Lola shushed her friends. She patted Jerry's arm. "Look up 'Ultimate Fan.' You'll see."

Megan transferred the photo files (and a short video so Lola could see tomorrow how drunk she was behaving) to Lola's ring. "You should really let your friends take you home. Can we get back to dinner now?" Obsequious waiters slipped dishes onto the table, hardly ruffling a sleeve as they darted in and out efficiently. The steaks smelled heavenly. They were all different, too, meaning this restaurant had an artist designing on the fly for their meat printer, or maybe just for the winners the rarest of the rare—real meat?

Lola threw her arms around Megan and gave her a sloppy kiss on the cheek. "I love you!"

Lola was pliant and warm in her arms. Did it take a world tournament and too much alcohol to make a hug between them feel so loving and natural again? She pressed her lips to Lola's smooth, bubblegum-scented hair. "Yeah. You too. Go home. Be safe."

Lola snorted. "You too!" She let go with a squeeze, and she and her flock of teens staggered off, singing the team fight song off-key. Exeunt, pursued by the maître d'.

After dinner, Megan returned to her rooms at Champion's Village and was startled by how short the cab ride was. She really had lost all sense of place on their publicity tour. She set her bag down and fell on the big soft bed. The room smelled the same, slightly like a gym from the rubberized flooring. It felt like a homecoming. Had it really only been a month since she'd first set foot in this building? A month since she'd been in the same time zone as her family?

Megan sat up. She hadn't seen the Junior Championship. Lola hadn't even mentioned it. Her sister had moved back home, with a trophy or with an electric-shock headache, and wasn't even mad that the focus was on Megan. What else had she missed about her little sister while she had been so concentrated on her own pain? She opened her ring display and asked for the Junior Nationals results.

Someone knocked at the door. Megan was too tired to answer. It didn't matter because Mitzi charged in anyway. "Sit down, Megan. Oh, you already are. I'm not sure that's better." Mitzi paced the room, messing up her already disarrayed curls. "Let me find a point to start telling you what I just found out."

Megan closed her ring display. "Just spit it out, and we can both get some sleep."

"Ha. Sleep. After this?" Mitzi finally stopped pacing and took a deep breath. "I looked up that 'ultimate fan' thing those kids were talking about. Your sister and her friends. Megan . . . they're betting their lives." Mitzi froze, hands open, waiting for her to react.

Megan had heard the words, but her tired brain couldn't process them. "What? Like . . . how?"

"How do you think?" Mitzi grasped her throat. "Those collars aren't reproductions. They're the real deal, lethal injection and all. They bet another fan that if the team dies, they die. In some other country, there's another idiot for each of those teens wearing a collar for their team."

Megan was at the door before she knew it, Mitzi calling after her. Megan ignored her, running down the stairs in her socks. She checked her ring as she hit the ground floor. "Ultimate Fan." There was a whole section of eBet dedicated to it. Contracts like any other bet, promises of the "speedy delivery" of the locking collar in their team's colors. They had samples on display for South America, Central Africa, all four of the final teams.

Megan stumbled on a curb, trying to read and run at the same time. She was heading to the nearest bus stop, but it was too late for service. Still running, she contacted a cab service and gave them a corner two blocks away. Standing still to wait felt impossible.

Megan barreled into her parents' house. Dad stepped into the hall, blinking sleepily and blocking her way. "Megan? What is it? What are you—"

She pushed him out of the way and grabbed the doorknob to Lola's room. Locked, of course. She pounded on the door. "Lola Demora Mori, I know you are in there!"

Her father tried to grab her arm. "Megan! Sweetheart, people are sleeping. Your mother—"

"What's the racket?" her mom provided, coming into the hallway while wrapping a robe around herself.

Megan hit the door again so hard it jolted in its frame. "Your daughter is gambling with her life, that's what."

Her parents held on to each other like they were afraid. Of her? Her father cleared his throat. "It was your choice, of course, but if this means you've changed your mind about competing . . ."

"Not me. Your other daughter. Lola!"

A lock slid back, and Lola opened her door, scowling. "Are you trying to wake the neighborhood?" She was wearing sleep pants and a tank top, and the silver collar.

Megan grabbed the collar.

"Ow! Hey! Watch it."

Megan easily thwarted her sister's struggles. "There's got to be a way to take this off." She found a seam and pried at it, breaking her fingernails.

Lola twisted out of her grip and fled to the far wall of her room, both hands on her throat. "Are you psycho? If you break the lock it'll blow my head off."

Megan froze, her fingers reaching. She hadn't thought of that. Her own collar had anti-tampering safeties built in. "Take it back. Cancel the bet."

"There is no taking it back. That's the whole point." Lola's expression softened. "Look, when you win the final game, it'll unlock and that's the end of it. I'll get to keep the collar forever as a memento. Pretty cool, right?"

Megan felt her father and mother behind her, holding her shoulders. Her mother asked, "Is she saying what I think she's saying?"

Her father spoke louder, and with an edge of panic. "Talk your sister out of this."

Megan advanced a step. "Lola, please. I can't play while I'm worrying about your life!"

Lola raised her chin and dropped her hands to her sides. "What, so you're good enough to risk everything and I'm not?"

"This isn't about being good enough! No one should risk their life for a sport!"

"No one but you, you mean. Anyway, it's not even a risk. We both know you're going to win, so why not win some bets while we're at it?"

Megan stared at her little sister, so calmly talking about the death of some other team's fan like it was a poker chip. Her father was in full panic, but his words washed over her unheard. Her ring buzzed. She was in trouble for leaving the team dorm without permission. She had an hour to get back.

Lola crossed her arms and shouted over the din, "I told you, it's done and it can't be undone!"

Her father bent low, pleading with Lola, but all Megan heard was Lola's reply, "I am the Ultimate Fan. I'm sorry you guys don't agree."

Her mother shook Megan. "Do something."

Megan gawked at her stricken parents, her defiant little sister. The only thing she could do now was win.

19

Megan's punishment for going AWOL was running laps. She almost made a joke about it, but Mustaine's face had been red with fury. Well, it was his fault he chose to punish her with her favorite exercise.

She tore into the fake grass of the practice field, feeling an unfamiliar panic. She had to be the strongest, she had to be the fastest, or a girl would be taken away, again. Two games to go. Two chances to die. It hadn't seemed so terrible, so dangerous, when it was only her own life.

Kendell ran up beside her and then fell into pace, sweat pouring down her face. "Central Africa is coming here," she huffed between strides. "Smartest team in the league."

So Kendell had said last night. "Yeah, so?"

"Good to . . . have a home game at last."

Megan thought about robbed museums, broken windows, beaten bodies. She thought about the people of Los Angeles who would survive to live with her failure. She didn't want to make small talk. She pushed herself to run harder. Kendell fell behind.

Megan punished the fake grass and pumped her arms, trying to outrace her own fear. She lapped Kendell, who had slowed to a jog.

When she had exhausted herself, she stumbled into a shaky walk, knowing if she sat down, her muscles would cramp. Kendell stood in her path. The larger woman looked away from her as she spoke, her expression stoic. "Okay, you don't want to talk. I get it. The Ultimate Fan collars, they're catching on. Especially with people who know us personally. Like my girlfriend. Thought you'd want to know. Because of your sister."

Megan's knees wobbled. She put her arms around the other woman, who was stiff at first, then returned the hug with strength. It felt like not being alone.

Megan came into the private team dining room that evening to find everyone silent, all watching a news broadcast like the president had died or something. She slid into the seat next to Jerry and whispered, "What is it?"

"Shh. Watch. They're about to replay."

Herbert Rivera appeared on-screen with that gleam in his eye like he knew a dirty secret about every person watching, but would never, ever tell. "We're back with our top story, the only story, a world exclusive! One of the world's top teams is calling out another with the bet everyone is talking about!"

Herbert pointed his chin to the side like he was about to lead the audience to a peephole. "Let's take a look," he whispered.

The screen changed to a talk show stage. Seated on a sofa together were the handsome and sinister Jax, from Team South America, and a gorgeous woman with extremely long tawny-brown legs. The show's host, a woman with arched brows and a feline look, leaned close to her. "Tell us about yourself, Angela. You're the head cheerleader for South America?"

The woman ducked her head modestly. "And I'm dating this hunk too." She squeezed Jax's hand in hers.

"That must be difficult, balancing your official and romantic roles?" Angela blushed, and the host licked her lips. "All right, tell us what you came here to tell the world tonight."

The camera swooped in close. Angela faced it full-on, sliding her head subtly with smug confidence. "I'm calling out my counterpart, Miriam 'Mitzi' Eliot from North America. I believe in my team, do you? Put your faith in your man where your neck is." The camera panned out again to show a silver collar balanced on her elegant, manicured hands.

Mitzi jumped up from the table. "Which man exactly is she talking about? I never dated any of you drama queens."

Jerry placed his hands on her shoulders. "It's a dig at me. Jax has always had it out for me and can't imagine a team captain not messing around with the head cheerleader. Because he's a pig."

Megan felt uncomfortable watching this model-pretty woman hold a death collar up to her slender throat. She got up and turned off the screen. "Why are you letting her upset you? Ignore her stupid bet."

Mitzi sighed and clenched her fists. "It's in the spotlight. People are going to expect me to respond, and she's framed it so if I say no, I'm saying I don't believe in our team."

Megan gave her waist a reassuring hug. "It's in the spotlight today. Saturday we play again, and the headlines will be about how we slaughtered Central Africa."

Mitzi looked, if not convinced, willing to pretend she was, and that made Megan feel better.

Central Africa had trounced Scandinavia and Southeast Asia so thoroughly that the betting boards were still talking about it. This would be Team North America's hardest opponent yet, a team favored against everyone except South America. Herbert Rivera's giant face grinned down from every surface as Megan jogged the short distance from the team quarters to the competition field. "This will be the game to watch! With the similar strengths between the two Americas, we'll get a taste of how Central Africa will approach the championship, and whether their strategy can best South America's speed and strength. I for one can't wait to see Kwame Ilunga head-to-head against Juan 'Jax' Pollard in the finals! Jerry Myers is an adequate approximation."

"Now, Herbert," a female co-anchor cooed, "don't count North America out. They do have home field advantage."

That didn't feel like a lot as Megan jogged onto the track and saw the early crowds hanging on the guardrails at the front of the stands. As she passed, onlookers stretched their arms out eagerly as though they could touch her, a full three meters below. Almost every one of these early-comers was wearing a silver collar that glinted in the sun.

Mitzi was doing a hurdler's stretch near the middle of the field. Megan jogged up to her. "Did you see? The collars."

Mitzi switched legs without looking up. "I'm trying not to."

"I can't believe there are that many fanatics willing to risk their lives. Who even are these people? I don't love us that much. If I could do this without the collar, I would."

Mitzi stretched her arms overhead. "There's something to be said for mob mentality. We do the unreasonable when the people around us do. The more people who do an unreasonable thing, the more it begins to look reasonable."

Megan considered the evidence in the stands and did some grim math: each collar represented two people, both sides of the bet. Hundreds of people were going to die this way, regardless of who won. More if the other bracket was experiencing the same thing. "It has to fade out." She was aware she was trying to convince herself. "After this game, after some of these bets are paid, they'll stop. They'll have to when they see this is real."

Chet came onto the field then with a little old lady. She came up to his chest, and he had his arm around her. He waved to them and pointed, grinning proudly. "My mom!" he shouted.

She was wearing a silver collar too.

Central Africa won the toss and chose Laser Panic as the game to play. Megan would spend the next two hours in a confining space suit, realistically too hot and too cold at the same time, her breath occasionally fogging her view. Why did the attention to detail have to be that attentive? They could have skipped the breath moisture meter and maybe programmed a thermostat.

The playing field was a derelict spaceship, blown apart by some past space battle. There was a backstory, but Megan hadn't read it. In the arcade version, there was a cinematic to explain it, but she always skipped past, watching the ship explode in fast-forward and the space pirates or aliens or whatever zip away into space.

All she needed to know was that a point was scored every time you hit an opponent in the chest or head with your laser. Blue lights signaled a hit, but not a score; red lights let you know you had a kill. She could generate a temporary shield by holding her laser rifle in both hands and pressing a button on the stock and the barrel. This was designed so that blocking came at a significant price in firing time. Megan figured she simply wouldn't block. Spray and pray was her usual tactic.

She materialized in an open space near the edge of the playing field where the ship's outer hull blossomed outward in eerily still fragments against a deep-black star field. Flashes of light through the maze-like debris told her where the others might be. These would be her last moments free from inertia, hovering in the wreck. She took as long as she felt comfortable, just looking.

Heavy firing was happening far off and to the left. Nothing in the immediate area moved. She activated her jet to move forward. Exposed corridors and nets of wires provided avenues of attack and cover. It was tempting to swim into the intact-looking corridor overhead, but it could lead her right into an ambush.

She maneuvered into shadow, her back protected against a jagged spire. She looked carefully up at the opening. Empty. She let herself drift slowly toward it, checking for anyone hiding in that clump of debris to her left—

Her chest-plate vibrated, alerting her that she'd been tagged. Shit. She fumbled with the rifle, but the other team tagged her twice before she got the shield up. Where were they even coming from? She kicked off the spire and flew for the cover of the corridor. Her finger faltered on the forward shield button, and another tag landed on her head. She spun and fired, only catching a foot trailing out a doorway. Shots to limbs didn't count.

Shit. Eight minutes in, and the score was already thirty-seven to nine in favor of Central Africa. The odds ticker was in free fall. Megan's panicked breaths were amplified in the confines of her helmet, growing higher in pitch. Lola's life was on the line. Lola had trusted her, put her life in her hands as surely as if Megan were holding her heart instead of a pretend laser rifle, and she had let herself get ambushed three different ways.

Mitzi floated in front of her, her space suit impossibly form-fitting, a purple, glittering jumpsuit, with a helmet like a pure crystal bubble, exposing her wide, made-up eyes. "Hey. Forget it. You are here now. Do what you can do here, now."

The steady voice grounded her. Megan held her breath and let it out slowly.

Mitzi nodded as if she'd said something, then mimed pushing her. "Go get those bastards."

Megan had played this game before. She knew this ship. She had to trust herself. She glided through the coral-like structures of circuits and pipes, head on a swivel, moving, not hanging back, but checking every approach.

Hasan was braced in a narrow niche. When she came into view, he raised his rifle to greet her. She gestured that she could cover his advance. There was a crossroads of sorts ahead where many corridors came together. That had to be where Central America was attacking from, striking and retreating. If she and Hasan could get behind their line, then they could be the ones racking up points.

Megan waved Hasan forward. He kicked off, found a new secure position, and propped himself up, nodding back to her that he'd cover her advance. A Central Africa player swooped out of a jagged hole above him before she could move. The hits flared in blue rings, painting the edge of Hasan's shield. Good. Megan fired at the attacker, knowing their shield couldn't be up if they were firing, and her hits flashed red against the enemy space suit, marking a kill even as they pinwheeled their arms and fled.

Thirty-nine to fourteen now. No, don't watch the score. "Your turn," she radioed Hasan. "I'll go ahead, be the bait." He nodded.

No taking chances with Lola's life. Megan put her shield up before sailing through a zigzag-shaped space. There was an opponent lying in wait for her, but as the shots flared bright on her shield, Hasan followed on the attack.

Forty to seventeen. "Let's find the rest of the team," Megan said. She could radio everyone, she saw, but she didn't know if that would give away some hidden locations with sound.

Slowly, methodically, they inched through the wreck. They came to a great cylindrical space with an elaborate tower in the center, glowing eerily: some imaginary engine. Indía zoomed back and forth, kicking with her powerful legs from one wall to the next, spraying fire and roaring her rage.

"Backup here," Megan radioed. "Down and left."

Indía settled into a defensible position above Megan. Her response was heavy with gasps and static. "Three of them, up-left, down-right, opposite me."

"I'm bait," Megan said, and pushed herself off toward the center column. Immediately, a shot hit her shield. Just one. The Central Africa team was on to the bait gambit. They were waiting to see who followed.

Megan flipped her rifle around and sprayed fire at them while she was exposed. Hasan sailed over her with his shield on to provide cover.

Indía seamlessly joined the pattern Megan and Hasan had set, but it was hard, moving deliberately, not taking chances. They hardly dared message each other when they could gesture, for fear of being overheard. Megan glanced at the score ticker and stiffened with panic. She wished she could turn it off.

One bulkhead, one panel, one free-floating floor at a time, they hunted deeper into the wreck.

It felt like they fought for days. Weeks. A year. Their score inched up, but so did Central Africa's, until it was 43–40 and sirens flashed, announcing that time would soon be up.

"I hate that sound works in space," Kendell complained. "It's not accurate."

They were pinned down in the engine room. Central Africa had someone at every exit. For the past five minutes, the score had stayed static.

Jerry floated up to the top of the engine, his weapon loose in one hand. "This is it. One minute left. One minute to die as heroes or live forever in history. I don't intend to spend it cowering. Who's with me?"

"Yeah!" Chet pumped his rifle and threw himself toward an entrance.

"Charge!" Jerry shouted. "Charge, everyone! It's now or never!"

With a strange, mad joy, they rushed, each of them picking a direction and just firing. Megan ended up in a narrow tube, firing through the red flashes of someone hitting her.

She didn't have time to see the score, to see who she was hitting, to see anything. She only fired, fired, fired. The sirens got louder, lights flashing everywhere, and a bored female voice saying, "Ten seconds to reach minimum safe distance. Nine seconds to reach—"

Megan ran right into the Central Africa player. She grabbed his suit with one hand and kicked his rifle wide. She held her weapon upward and screamed as she pressed fire again and again into his face.

She was still screaming and firing when her vision was whited out by the simulated explosion of the derelict, and everything fell silent.

When gravity returned to her limbs in the pod, Megan felt crushed by it, confused by the massive stability of the ground under her and the air pressing down on her. Her legs wobbled as she climbed out into their home stadium, unsure still if she was going to her death until she heard the uproarious applause. Fireworks lit up the sky brighter than day, and the announcer was repeating, "North America wins! North America wins!'

Only then did she glance at the scoreboard. 57–58. One point's difference! The Central Africa team hugged each other. Indía whooped and leaped into Jerry's arms.

He put her back down and walked to the winners' stands with a glazed expression, zombie-like.

Indía huffed. "Does he think we lost?"

Megan had a feeling what he was thinking. She watched a Central Africa player reach around the person he was hugging to grip another's hand. It was his last action. As the visiting team fell, someone standing at the very front of the stands toppled, his body landing half over the railing. How many others had fallen that she couldn't see?

Megan did not feel euphoric this time. She felt ill.

20

"Like gasoline on a flame!" Herbert Rivera gushed. Behind him was a solid wall of frolicking fans, all wearing collars in the colors of North America as well as South America. "Every day, more fans are making the ultimate pledge. Some even say that the lack of Ultimate Fans is what cost The Subcontinent its game against South America. Would they have played harder if they knew their country was completely behind them? We'll never know. Perhaps it is for the best because The Battle of the Americas has taken the world by storm! This will be a game unlike any in the history of sports! The whole world is getting involved! Fans from Europe and Oceania are betting against the team that beat theirs, as are fans in Tibet and the Balkan Confederation!"

Jerry hit the armrests on his seat as he jumped up. "Mitzi! Turn this thing off."

Mitzi ran in from the back of the plane. "Sorry." She pointed her box at the screen, killing the feed.

"What's your problem?" India crossed her arms. "I was watching that."

Jerry held up a hand as if to ward off Mitzi from turning the screen back on. "Fans died. Fans. And instead of being scared off, more people are putting their lives on the line. I don't want to know about it. The guilt is already crushing me."

India tossed her head. "Well, I, for one, am strong enough to be glad to see the country proving they're behind us, believing in us."

Jerry stood. He stared at India, his expression pleading. "We're supposed to be preventing deaths. We allow small-scale violence. Small-scale death. Like an inoculation. That's the whole point of MegaDeath. This . . ." He gestured at the silent screen. "We might as well be at war."

India scowled. "It's not indiscriminate. These people are choosing to risk their lives, freely."

"Millions of people. Millions. Entire cities. That is indiscriminate."

India got up then and met Jerry eye to eye. "So you're going to take away every person's free will? Say they can't decide what to do with their lives?"

Mitzi had backed away but was still close to the two tall, powerful athletes, their faces scant inches apart. Softly she said, "There's the mob mentality. It's . . . it's a decision they may already regret and can't take back."

India snorted. "Like the way you took it back?"

Mitzi reached for her empty throat. "You know I didn't—"

"Didn't what? Didn't stop risking your neck?" India advanced on Mitzi. "No, tell us again how you're still on the roster when I don't see a collar around your neck."

Mitzi's voice was weak. "I'm giving my all for this team."

That was when Mustaine dropped his screens, quit making calculations, and stood up. "No," he said. "You haven't. Not this year. I don't want to hear more from you while the news says our cheerleaders don't care."

Mitzi turned and ran from the compartment.

No one said anything. Megan stood up. "Mitzi's been there for us the whole way."

Mustaine resumed his seat. "This is the way the world is now, Mori."

"No, it isn't. We're making it that way. This is a choice, and we can back away from it."

"You have a job to do for your country." Mustaine pierced her with a glare. "No more lip. You're good, but you're not so good I won't petition to have your collar activated and pull someone new from the backup list."

Megan could not believe what she was hearing. She staggered a step back. "You're threatening my life? For standing up for my colleague?"

Indía stepped in front of Coach Mustaine. "If you're not with us, you're against us. Even Mitzi."

"That's right." Kendell raised a fist. "One for all."

Megan looked to Jerry, but he'd slumped, defeated, back in his seat. Megan went back to her seat and stared out the window. In two hours, they would land in Kinshasa to inflict their patriotically demanded violence. Another pointless, brutal farce. She didn't want to keep going. She didn't want to have to see the same destruction in Rio if they went all the way. If it weren't for Lola, she'd tell the coach off and jump out of the plane.

Kinshasa was a city of new wealth and sprawling parks. They were set loose in a market square with quaint old stalls and broke off down the wide main avenue. Megan saw the prisoners ahead, forming a line with spears and clubs. Indía and the others charged for them, shouting about flanks.

Megan quietly slipped out another way. A camera drone buzzed close. She swatted it. "Ms. Mori—the majority of combatants are to the north."

"How dumb for them," Megan snapped. She grabbed the camera drone. Tiny servos on its surface tickled her palm as she wound up and threw it like a baseball into the nearest stone wall.

She ran. A block away, and then north. The hotel would be the best in town. She saw where the buildings were tallest. She headed there, pausing only to attack camera drones and throw them into things.

Let them replay that footage.

The Hotel Kinshasa gleamed with chrome details and elaborate stained-glass panels. Megan hid behind one. It depicted a waterfall in exquisite detail, water pouring in depths of blue and teal.

She paced behind it impatiently until she saw Jerry arrive. Seeing him come back early felt like the answer to a prayer she hadn't made. She stepped out of hiding. "We need to talk."

Jerry flinched, then relaxed. "Yeah. Not here." He waved for her to follow him.

They hurried down a corridor, ducking away from the windows. They found a lounge area tucked under the grand staircase. Mitzi was already there and jumped up from a small sofa, spilling a lap full of electronics.

"I didn't think cheerleaders got in on the looting." Megan picked a circuit board up and handed it back to her.

"We don't, not usually. I needed some things." Mitzi hugged her electronics against her stomach. "What are you two doing back already?"

"Shh." Jerry crouched to peer around potted plants. "We have to be very careful and hope the others are making enough drama for the cameras. Central could steer fights toward us or blow something up just to get us back into it."

Megan started to ask if they would do such a thing but stopped herself. Of course they would. "Well, let's not waste time. We need to talk. Quietly. Whole cities are reporting their entire populations are now 'Ultimate Fans.' Are we the crazy ones? How is this happening?"

"I don't know." Mitzi shuffled her gadgets. "I've been trying to trace the origin of these collars. Where did the idea start? The manufacturer is almost too clean. They didn't advertise. Just let eBet know they could provide the devices if requested. And they even had a lawyer and a psychologist sign off before they asked Central for the design. I thought maybe . . . maybe someone orchestrated this. A crime boss. A madman. Some villain. But it's all on the up-and-up so far. Spontaneous decisions by a few crazed fans that others copied, and it caught on."

Megan sat next to her on the little sofa. "I get how you'd want there to be a bad guy, but there's an easier explanation. People just . . . get blinded by the thrill of gambling, by the idea of patriotism, by being part of the crowd."

Jerry settled back on his heels. "If the numbers they're talking about are true, we could be facing worse casualties than the great floods of '97."

Mitzi stared at her hands, looking helpless. "Sometimes we say things . . . like calling South America 'the enemy' . . . I know I did that once or twice. Or we say we're going to crush them or destroy them . . ."

Megan took her hands. "It's not your fault. Don't think that way. It's none of our faults."

Jerry pressed his knuckles to his lips. "What's the point anymore? Why make violence for the cameras when this is so much worse? I've done terrible things because I thought—" His voice raised with each word until it cut off. He stood up. "Why am I here?"

The silence was awkward. Megan wanted to comfort Jerry but wasn't sure if they were close enough, or even how to do it. Mitzi was the first to speak. "They're threatening my job. I'll have to step down if I don't take the bet."

Megan scooted back to get a good look at her. "Who is 'they'? That's obscene."

"Central. They can do it. They have veto power if they think any team member is a detriment to ticket sales and betting receipts." She sat up and looked guiltily at Megan and Jerry. "I . . . it's not that I don't believe you can win."

Megan didn't know how to tell her how insane it was that she was even thinking about the stupid winning odds. "No one is asking you to risk your life for us."

Mitzi fidgeted with her pile of loose electronics, fitting parts together with the same nervous energy someone else might use to pluck petals from a daisy. "I don't know what I'd do without MegaDeath. When I was injured, when I . . . yes, I burned out, and part of it was not wanting to risk my life anymore. Everyone says it, well, fine, it's true. I saw my team die, and it was real, and I had to mourn them. The thought of putting that collar on again terrified me. I couldn't do it." She fitted a series of tiny wires to two circuits and snapped them together into a housing. She paused and touched her bare throat with a shiver. "But cheering gave me a chance to still be a part of the sport I spent my life training for. Without it, who am I?"

Jerry put his hands over Mitzi's. "You're a brave woman. I don't know if I'd have the strength to walk away."

"It wasn't strength," Mitzi said bitterly.

Megan stood. "You're both talking like there's no way out. We'll get the team together. If all of us fight this, they'll listen. They can't have a final match without two teams. We'll refuse to play."

Mitzi and Jerry flinched away from her. Mitzi looked too afraid to speak. Jerry cleared his throat. "Megan, they'd just activate our collars and promote the second string. You were at the final tryout; there are people to take our places."

Megan looked from one to the other of them. "Would they do that? Kill the whole team? There are posters of you, Jerry! Of all of us! Kids are wearing your face on their novelty socks."

Jerry raised his hands in surrender, shaking his head. Mitzi bit her lip. "Maybe if we got everyone. But it would have to be the whole team. They'd go forward with just Chet. Trust me."

Megan took that for a ray of hope. She marched out of the protective cover. A camera drone immediately zoomed up to her and honked some warning about getting out into the fray. She waved it off and ran to the front of the hotel.

The scourge always concentrated on wealthy districts. They not only provided better footage of beautiful things to destroy, they were better able to recover afterward. Fires glowed in the distance, outlining the shapes of running men. All the storefronts on the square were broken open, a curse of too much glass.

Megan jogged toward the action. It was hard, now, to be looking for trouble instead of running from it. The trouble was more elusive. A knot of figures struggled in front of an impressive organic-tech building. Megan pushed through hanging vines to pull bodies apart, but there was no teammate at the heart of the struggle. They'd only been gathering up a spilled cargo of jewels.

She ran down the street. There! Kendell was shifting a bag onto her shoulder and dropping more jewelry as she did so.

Megan picked up a golden goblet she'd let slip. "Hey, you look like you've got enough."

Kendell smiled. "Hey, Megan. Gorgeous night, isn't it? The museum was incredible. I could have stayed in there all week."

"Ready to come back? Mitzi, Jerry, and I were getting an early start on supper."

Kendell's girlfriend had taken the collar. Kendell would easily come to their side, and then Mitzi and Jerry would see. They'd be strong enough to approach the others.

"Yeah, I'm beat," Kendell agreed and handed Megan more of her loot to carry.

Back at the hotel, Mitzi and Jerry met them at the doors.

Kendell reared back in shock when Megan explained the plan. "No, I mean, I get why you're freaking out. I freaked out at first, but don't you see? It's the ultimate patriotism. There is no us and them . . . we are all on the team. We are one. From the many, one." She clutched a hand to her heart and looked earnestly at them. "Come on, enough of that. Are we getting dinner or not?"

Megan felt her plan fall to tatters.

At dinner and on the plane ride home, it quickly became clear that Chet absolutely loved the death collars, and Hasan wouldn't say anything against the company line, even if Coach was not near. India had already made her allegiance clear.

Megan sat with the cheerleaders, draining their pitchers of margaritas. "You tried," Mitzi said, squeezing her shoulder.

"You'll come up with a great plan at the last second," David added, raising his glass as if in a toast. "You always do."

Megan didn't feel like the sort of person who came up with plans.

Landing back home in Los Angeles offered no rest. Instantly they were whisked into another makeup and costume prep tent. Megan was given a slinky evening gown of green silk and no explanation. She felt naked in the clinging, lightweight fabric.

Then they were put on a shuttle bus and dropped outside the warehouse-like building that held their main training field.

"Come on," Jerry sighed, taking her arm. "It only gets scarier if you wait."

The indoor practice field was decked with cocktail tables and hovering champagne fountains and was filled with men and women in formalwear. A wall of suits and gowns blocked her path, flashes going off. Megan ducked and ran, only to discover there was no safe corner in the room. Dignitaries and celebrities casually mobbed every member of the team, begging for photos and autographs.

Megan had never expected to meet the president. She had certainly never expected her to ask, "Where is that charming Mitzi? I wanted to meet her tonight! I've always had a soft spot for cheerleaders."

Megan didn't know where Mitzi had gone. She didn't know where anyone was. She had to search the sea of people to find a face she recognized. India was in a knot of admirers; Hasan was trying desperately to get to the edge of the room.

Megan smiled, said something bland, and let herself be passed from handshake to handshake until she was near enough to a wall to make her escape. She ran with no regard for dignity and crawled through a side door. Hasan was there, back against the outside wall, panting for breath. He grinned and gave her a thumbs-up.

Parties and press junkets were definitely Mitzi's thing. It was weird that she'd been absent, but Megan didn't think about it until she sat down for lunch in the private dining room the next day. She was the first one there, but the wall screen was on, playing to the empty table. Mitzi was on the news feed, smiling her megawatt smile for the cameras.

"Recorded last night at Central's LA headquarters," Herbert Rivera narrated, "a proud moment for North America, and for me." Mitzi held her hair up as Rivera himself snapped the silver collar around her neck. A crowd cheered lustily. A standing ovation. Mitzi threw her arms up in victory, but Megan could see the tears in her eyes.

21

Megan didn't look away from the screen until a shadow fell to her left. It was Jerry. He set his tray next to hers. "So you saw." He gestured at the screen. "That's where she was while we were at that welcome-home party."

Megan had watched numbly through the entire repeating news cycle. Her food had gone cold. She pushed the tray away. "Do you want this? I'm not really hungry."

"Me either. I wish Mitzi were here to turn this thing off." He took a step back. "I have a bottle of scotch in my room. That's your poison of choice, isn't it?"

Megan blushed to think of that night they met, when she had been trying so hard to get drunk and thought Jerry was a disposable jerk. "I'm more into rum, actually."

"Oh. Um, we can stop by the bar, or the commissary if it's open."

Megan pushed away from the table. "Kidding. It's scotch, all the way. I'm just trying to seem unknowable. Please, yes, let's get away from the news feeds."

Jerry's room felt much more lived-in than Megan's, though it was an almost exact mirror of it. Posters and memorabilia from Jerry's career with the Chicago Force and his college team decorated every surface, and a reasonable bar was set up on the counter by the room's sink, bottles in a neat line with a shaker and decanters of soda and syrup.

Megan sank into the room's armchair while Jerry pulled a distinguished bottle from the back of the lineup. "I have Laphroaig, and I have Glenmorangie, or I could make you a Manhattan with the cheap stuff?"

"Laphroaig is fine." He opened the bottle, but she could tell he was a little disappointed, which was cute. "You can show off your bartending skills on the next drink."

His smile was boyish as he poured. "I've spent my whole life showing off. Learning skills to show them off . . . and for what?" He handed her a glass and tapped it with his own. "I should have been a bartender. Then I could be making people happy and still have a life expectancy over two weeks."

"That's how you got into this? To make people happy?"

"Mostly. I came from a big family. If you weren't showing off, well, you didn't get noticed, and I liked being noticed." He sat on the bed, smiling at himself, his knees on his elbows.

There was something disarming about Jerry right then, as he looked down, his lashes against his cheeks. Megan said, "I play because while I'm moving, I'm not thinking." She was alarmed at herself. The words had slipped out, as natural as breathing. She took the first sip of her drink and held it on her tongue, the scotch burning pleasantly. "I've never said that to anyone before."

Jerry shrugged. "If there was ever a time for telling secrets, it's now. One game to go, everything on the line, and there's nothing we can do about it." He clasped his drink like a prayer and looked up at her. "I'm terrified, every game. Even the ones where the forfeit is trivial, like money. I'm afraid they'll see I'm just putting on an act, and behind the act, there's nothing but a scared boy with four stronger, smarter older brothers."

"I've never been afraid until now." Megan grimaced. It sounded like bragging. "I don't mean that. I mean . . . I feel the weight of their lives. Risking myself, that's nothing. I haven't much wanted to live in years."

Jerry set his untouched glass on the floor between his feet. He looked at her, earnest, searching. "Do you still not want to live?"

Megan felt the wounds in her psyche, like sticking your tongue against a sore tooth. It had been years since she had had the strength to willfully think about Ciera. To picture her sweet face, her chubby little legs. Her howl when she was really upset. Ugly and perfect. Megan swallowed and set her glass down next to Jerry's. "I had a baby girl. Ciera. She was three. When she died, I lost it. I attacked people. I had to do some jail time, some counseling. It was four years ago, but up until—" she blinked, realizing how recent it had been "—up until Antarctica, when you showed me we could have fun together with some paint. Up until that night, it felt like my baby died last week. My life rotted at the seams. This game gave me something to live for, and I think I've gotten used to it, to living, again. But now . . ."

Jerry closed the distance between them, wrapping his arms around her. His hair smelled like fresh green things, mint and basil. His arms were gentle despite the swell of muscles. Megan squeezed him tightly, and her tears fell onto his cotton shirt. He held her so kindly, without hurrying her, without words. He just held her. It seemed the most natural thing in the world to kiss the tender curve of his neck.

He pulled back, marveling at her. She brushed his cheek with her hand. "What? Didn't I owe you a kiss?"

"You overpaid." He picked up her hand and lightly kissed her fingers. "Have some change." Then he held her hand, thoughtful. "I know it's not the same, but my best friend, my mentor, really . . . she was called up in '04 to take Mitzi's place."

And died when the team lost in the finals. Megan felt a cringe inside herself. It wasn't the same. It couldn't be.

Jerry caught her pulling away, and wrapped his hug around her again. "I'm sorry for mentioning it. Stupid thing. It's just . . . I wanted you to know. I've been fighting a long time to take the place that should have been mine back then. She would be a better team captain. I still wish she were here instead of me."

Megan took his hand then and returned each peck with interest. She understood that feeling exactly. If she could have traded every cell of her blood for Ciera's, if she could have died in her place . . .

They were silent for some time. It was comfortable. Then she looked up, and their lips were inches apart. She paused. "I like you, Jerry. You're kind, and fun. I like what's under the performance. I don't want this to be just . . . just a fling."

His smile deepened. "We're one week from the championship game. There's even odds we're spending the rest of our lives together."

"Meaning we only have this week."

He smirked and kissed her. "Meaning, I can easily commit to a long-term relationship right now."

Megan's lips buzzed from the kiss, and she hardly heard his words, but she got the gist that he was being a smart-mouth. "You are such a jerk," she said lovingly, and then tackled him onto the bed.

In the still of the night, Mitzi snuck into the residence and up to her room, afraid to face the others, trying to ignore the unpleasant weight of the collar on her neck.

Now that she'd put her life on the line, she should stop worrying about the whole setup and focus on helping her team win, but she couldn't. If anything, her need to know burned like hot pepper oil all over her fingers. She logged into eBet and did a simple search for all "Ultimate Fan" bets on the finals.

Wow. The number was huge. Almost fifty-nine percent of the population of North America now, and sixty-two percent of South America. Wait a minute. The population of The United States of North America was five times that of The Republic of South America. Who was taking four-fifths of the North Americans' bets? She quickly dumped the data locally so she could run a database query on it, filtering out all addresses in the Americas. Only a few thousand scattered zealots were willing to risk their lives for a game between countries they didn't live in. There were millions of unaccounted-for bets! The betting site was supposed to be sacrosanct, unimpeachable. They wouldn't be doubling bets, would they?

Mitzi was running a worm, trying to get into the manufacturer's private network. It pinged to say it had something. She glanced at the output, then froze. She closed everything else. Ice ran down her back. She had to tell someone. She quickly dumped everything onto an offline storage drive and scrubbed her history.

She stopped at the door, feeling the cold collar, still new at her throat. She didn't want to see Megan. She was her best bet for an ally, but she was dead set against the collars. She'd be angry at Mitzi for giving in, or worse, she'd pity her.

No, the time was over for such selfish considerations. This wasn't just the games. The entire world was in jeopardy.

She ran to Megan's room and found it empty and cold, the bed made and unslept in. Her heart clenched. She'd noticed Megan suffered from insomnia and bad dreams. Poor thing was probably out on another penitential midnight run. Who knew where she'd have gone? Mitzi paced. Who did she trust second-most? Jerry! Of course.

Jerry's room was just two floors up, and Mitzi found the door unlocked. "Jerry! Wake up!" she shouted, storming in.

It was Megan she saw first, staring at her in shock, clutching the blanket to her bare chest. Jerry peeked over the blanket's edge a little slower, all tousled and dazed.

Mitzi couldn't help it; she bounced onto one leg and did a Herkie jump and victory swing. "Mori scores!" Now both her friends were wide awake and clutching the sheets. Ah, priceless. "No time for that, kids, I've got news. Something big."

Megan was all business, of course. She dropped the sheet and went looking for her clothes. Jerry sat up, still blushing, and said, "Well, this was kinda big too."

"Oh, shush." Mitzi picked a bra off the minibar and handed it to Megan, assuming it was hers. "Listen, something is really fishy with these Ultimate Fan collars. The manufacturer? I traced ownership back to Central itself."

"That's not surprising." Megan shrugged into her bra. "Central owns a piece of all the game industries. They're in viewers and players and scenery development."

"But I haven't found a human owner. No board of directors. Nothing."

Jerry looked up from trying to fish his pants out from under the bed without getting out from under the blanket. "Mitzi, do we have to do this now? Whoever owns it wants to remain anonymous. Maybe they have a conflict of interest, or it's a celebrity."

"I'm not so sure." Mitzi sighed. She didn't want to give voice to her theory. It was too outlandish. "Do you have something I can display this data on?" She held up her non-net drive.

"Yeah," Jerry said. He hurriedly got his undershorts on and pulled his pants off of what turned out to be a media console.

Mitzi gave him a saucy wink, because Jerry was adorable undressed and disheveled, and set to work. "Okay, now you'll both forgive me for getting you up at this hour when you see." She pulled the files and turned on the largest projection the tiny system allowed.

Megan and Jerry frowned uncomprehendingly. Megan said, "I'm seeing . . . numbers."

Oh, come on! It wasn't even all numbers. There were letters and operator signs! Mitzi pulled up a heuristic generator and got things nice and pretty. "Here are the number of bets placed for North America, and the number for South America. See the disparity?" A child couldn't miss it. There was a big pie chart of the two populations, and the North American pie chart was five times the size. Then there was the chart of the betting population, just as skewed. "This isn't percentages, it's numbers." Mitzi drew a circle around the larger North American pie slice to drive it home.

Megan got it. "My god . . . who are they betting against?"

"Right? Now, look at this." Mitzi quickly reformatted the info as it displayed. She hadn't expected to have to give a darn presentation. Collar shipment figures. North American addresses, South American addresses, other addresses . . . not remotely equal.

Jerry squinted at a file she hadn't meant to open. "No one works at the factory that makes these collars?"

Actually, that was an important point. "Fully automated. Not even a security guard or receptionist. All proceeds go to Central. All commands come from Central." Here was the theory. She was just going to have to say it. "What if Central isn't a company? No one running it, no one behind it. What if Central is, itself, an entity?"

Jerry scowled, paused in the act of pulling his shirt on. "What, like a rogue computer out to control us?"

Mitzi groaned. "It sounds stupid when you say it like that. But look at this." She had to kneel on the floor to type into the media console. "Hang on—jeez, this is hardly an operating system. There. I got looking, see, for the start of it. Tracing the bets back. As the numbers prove, a lot of the people who cosigned the bets aren't real. They're names and accounts and avatars, but there's no real person traceable from them. And the further back I went, the more avatars. Until I got to the first three people to place Ultimate Fan bets." Dang, she fumbled the command. She backspaced and hit it again: call up data lines 1–4, display normal. "There."

The screen exhibited three reasonable-looking user accounts. Joe Dada, Allene Nicole, Musharaf Jan. Bland user photos. Allene was fishing, white ball cap, sun bleeding the colors from her grin. Joe was standing on a golf course. Musharaf stood in a park with his arm around a woman half cut out of frame. "Tax IDs, health care accounts check out. You have to look deeper," Mitzi said. "None of their jobs are real. Like Allene says she's an engineer at Piro Technical in Des Moines, Iowa. Piro Technical has no record of her. Neither does the University of Iowa recall her master's degree. They all have profiles that look real, details you'd expect, but if you follow any of them up, anything that doesn't come from Central or a government, it's all empty."

Mitzi stood and faced Megan and Jerry, who had managed to achieve a state of half-dress in the meantime. "None of these people exist. People are betting their lives against imaginary opponents, using a technology owned by no one." She spread her hands wide. "Am I mad, or are we sacrificing ourselves to ghosts?"

22

Megan shouldered her way past Mitzi to sit in front of the console and page back through the data. There were parts she didn't quite understand, but it all looked legitimate. Someone had made millions of fake accounts just to tempt real people into Ultimate Fan bets. For all she knew, the person who had wagered their life against Lola's didn't exist.

It was Jerry who broke the silence. "We have to tell someone. Alert the authorities."

It sounded reasonable. Megan even reached for her ring and called up a directory, but she stopped cold, staring at the services she could call. Police? Ambulance? Voter registration? She turned to Mitzi. "What authorities can we trust?"

Mitzi pointed at her like this was the correct guess at a puzzling problem. "The corporation is international. North America can only rule over a part of it. The World Congress is the only authority that could do anything, and would they believe us? We're in the middle of a competition they have ostensible authority over. We'd be like plaintiffs in a court case asking the judge to rule on whether our case continues before the next witness speaks. We'd have to have a hell of an argument, and assuming we do, and assuming that my illegally obtained information is enough, would they even be able to make a ruling? They're set up to settle disputes between countries. No one has ever had to set up an office of Corporate Threats to Humanity. We have no one we can call."

Jerry threw up his hands. "There has to be something we can do. Tell the media! Call Herbert Rivera, promise him an exclusive interview, the three of us naked. He'd break the sound barrier getting here."

"That will just panic people." Megan imagined Lola learning about this from a media report. Maybe in school, in front of her peers. If Lola listened, if she believed the story, it left her wearing a collar she couldn't take off. Megan touched the metal at her throat. "We need to find a way to remove the collars."

Mitzi dropped heavily onto the bed. "You think that wasn't the first thing I checked? It's not hard to find the details on that. The full collar design is online, in its registered patent diagrams." She picked up the silver whistle she wore on a chain around her neck and rolled it between her fingers. "There's a molecular trigger in the metal lattice. No matter where you cut it, any centimeter of it, you cut deep enough, it explodes. The explosive is built into the metal too. It doesn't sit in any one spot, so you can't remove it, either. Oh, you think you'll just cut out the poison reservoir? We know where it is. Assuming you manage to cut all the way around it without triggering the explosive metal, the needle can detect if it moves away from the base layer, and that triggers the injection. I made some models on the specifications. The injection is faster than any cutting method that leaves the neck intact. You'll be cutting a collar off a corpse."

This was the thing Lola had put on herself. Voluntarily. Megan's fingers dropped, nerveless, from her collar.

Jerry answered her unasked question. "It's the same design we're wearing."

Megan felt dirty, complicit. She sat down on the bed next to Mitzi and realized she hadn't put her pants back on. "There's nothing we can do."

Jerry turned off the media display. "There's one thing we can do. We can win."

Mitzi threw her hands up. "That only saves the North Americans!"

Jerry pointed to where the display had been. "You said it yourself, North America has five times the people betting. We save the largest group of people. If it were the other way around, I'd say we throw the match and die to protect the larger group."

Megan clutched her stomach, suddenly queasy. She was glad she didn't have to choose that option. She wasn't sure she was strong enough to sacrifice Lola, no matter how many more people would be saved. "We're reducing people to numbers, to cold equations." This was, she didn't say out loud, exactly the logic that killed Ciera.

The bed bounced as Mitzi got up to pace. "There has to be something else. Something I'm missing. If we only had more time!"

"We have to win," Jerry repeated. "Millions of people die if we don't. That's priority number one."

Mitzi went to the bar and started picking up bottles to read them. "Of course it comes back to winning for you."

"This isn't about my ego." Jerry spoke in the tired, flat voice of an argument being rehashed. "I just said, if things were different—"

"They aren't different, though, and admit it, you were always going to find a way to shoehorn winning into the plan. No." Mitzi held up a hand to forestall Jerry. "Listen. It's why I had to get out. You get so that all you think about is winning. The next win and the next, and it's never enough. It's set up to never be enough. You don't even enjoy playing the games anymore."

"It's not a game," Jerry said softly.

Mitzi's mouth set into a firm line. "That's the problem."

Megan got up, still holding her stomach. Mitzi turned to look at her with a bottle of gin poised in one hand. Megan ran past her, out into the hallway. This wasn't who she wanted to be. She didn't want to still be the woman who ran out on guys before morning, but she couldn't stop thinking about Lola and about how easily they had all let these collars snap shut. About Ciera, and how easily it became an equation of many lives versus one life.

"Hey."

She turned to see Jerry. He ruffled his hair with one hand. "Sorry about that. Mitzi and me, we got into our old arguments. Didn't mean to shut you out."

"You didn't. I just . . ." Megan wanted to cry. She wanted to throw herself at this man. He didn't blame her. Someone didn't blame her. It terrified her, the power that gave him.

He stepped close, kissed her forehead, and whispered, "Also, you forgot your pants."

He pressed a bundle of cloth into her hands. He stepped back, gave her a slow once-over, and winked his approval.

"You asshole." She meant it, and punched his arm. "One life is not worth less than two lives. One million lives are not worth less than two million. Every one of us has only one life. Every life, individually, matters."

He fell back, and she could tell she'd hurt him, but he took the hit, and then he took her fist and kissed it. "We'll talk," he said, "and maybe . . . maybe, yeah, we don't have to win. We'll figure something out."

She let him pull her back into the room and collapsed against him, feeling less alone than she had in years. Maybe, yeah, maybe, they could do this together.

Indía lived for moments like this. Before the final game, Central sponsored a special banquet just for Team North America in Panama City. The soaring skyscrapers of the new city filled the windows on one side of the banquet hall, and on the other side, the picturesque red roofs of the old city stretched into the blue Pacific, painful to look at in the glory of the evening sun.

Even better was the view at the back of the banquet hall. Arrayed over the heads of dignitaries, swarms of micro-drone projectors filled the air with crowds in Toronto, Los Angeles, Mexico City, and San Salvador. Thousands of people filled each panning shot, holding signs with, among other things, her face. More scenes showed the people crowded just outside this building, and the arena where the final contest would take place in Rio. Fans were losing their minds like a New Year's Eve in Times Square, times six. Times eight. So many people watching, and her in the middle of it, recognized, adored. Indía shifted her legs and noticed a camera bot swooping low to catch the casual grace of muscle revealed by her high-slit skirt. She was glad she'd worn white with carnelian and lapis accessories. Panama City matched her.

The president of the United States of North America beamed at the audience from a podium in the center of the table, also wearing white. "We gather traditionally," she said, "on this night of celebration and triumph to recognize our team's hard work thus far, and to name our most valuable player of the year. We like to honor this person when the other team is around to see it." She paused for laughter. That was the way to put it, though it was just as true they wanted to honor the MVP while they were still alive. Not that Indía had any intention of dying.

MVP. Indía felt a tension in her stomach and told herself to relax. Hadn't she scored the very first winning point? Hadn't her kick beaten Oceania? She checked the crowds again, and sure enough, there were more signs with her face than Jerry's. There were a few of Megan, but she didn't think that signified anything. They were both brunettes. Maybe people had gotten them confused?

The president leaned forward. "One person has done the most to restore the honor of our country and bring us to this precipice of victory. With her inspired game play, athleticism, and ferocious after-game revelry, one name has stood out this season."

Indía started smiling at the first use of the "her" pronoun. When she heard "after-game revelry," she knew they had to be talking about that melee in Paris. She'd held her own against five brutes trying to defend some painting, and she'd come away with it, intact too. India smoothed her skirts to stand. She was half out of her chair, looking right at the president when the politician extended her hand and said, "Megan Mori, would you please come take a bow?"

Indía froze in place, unsure how many people saw her rise, unsure if sinking down would draw more attention. Her thighs ached with the awkward position. Megan? The Rookie? Megan had never even played National League! Indía carefully lowered herself and tried to see if Jerry found this as preposterous as she did, but no, he was looking raptly at Megan, that dowdy grouch. That mouse, stumbling and fumbling her way up to take the golden trophy that should have been Indía's.

Indía had to hold the table to stay upright. She felt a stab down her throat. That look also, by right, was hers.

Megan felt self-conscious sitting at a table on a stage. How were you supposed to eat with that many people staring at you? Then she had to get up, and the tablecloth dragged with her, and her palms were sweaty when she shook the president's hand, and she didn't want a stupid trophy. It was awkward and top-heavy in her hands. She nodded and mouthed her thanks. The crowd glittered with photo flashes. Was anyone there really as happy as they were pretending to be? Their smiles were stretched almost to grimaces, even the lovely Indía. Everyone looked like piranhas, waiting for the right moment to devour her.

That was when Megan had a terrible thought. It popped into her head, pushing everything else out. Everyone was looking at her, expecting something. A speech? She leaned forward. "Thank you." Her words echoed flatly. She stopped at her seat to set the trophy down, on its side because it really was top-heavy, then continued along the dais, past the waiters and guards, and kept walking, until someone tried to stop her, at which point she broke into a run.

Mitzi glanced at Jerry, and they jumped to their feet together. She didn't make it four feet before someone was in her way. A panicked intern from the media. He caught her attention long enough for a waiter, a politician, and two security guards to completely block her path. "What is it? Where did Mori go?"

Mitzi smiled for the camera drone she saw swooping in. "We'll bring her back." She put on her full airhead smile. "Jitters! We'll get her right back. Enjoy the soup!"

Had there been soup? Mitzi juked left and right to get around the thick press of bodies. She saw Jerry ahead, already at the exit. He didn't care as much as Mitzi did about appearances. He didn't have to.

Mitzi caught up to him at the back stairs, and together they raced down. They both knew Megan well enough to know where she'd head, to street level. She had a pathological love of running the streets. They'd have to split up. She could have gone in any direction.

But they didn't have to go that far. Megan was at the base of the stairwell, pacing back and forth from a security door to the stairs. She looked up at them as they slowed their runs to meet her. "Can't go outside," she shrugged. "Crowds."

Oh, yeah. People would be all around the hotel, watching any entrance for a chance sighting. Mitzi put an arm out so Jerry would let her descend first. "Are you okay?"

Megan didn't look okay. She pressed her fist to her mouth, stared at the exterior door, then paced back and forth again. "What if they don't honor it?"

Mitzi assumed this was a non sequitur, random words, but Jerry asked the obvious question, "Honor what?"

"What if they don't honor the bets? I know, it's crazy. They hand me this trophy, and I look up at the projections, all these fans mobbing the streets, and this is what pops into my head. Millions of fans are wearing a lethal injection, and we're just trusting that the sick bastards who came up with this bet will honor it? Even if we win, who's to say Central won't activate all the collars?"

Mitzi hadn't thought of that. Their "save the most" plan, always dissatisfying, crumbled like yesterday's sandcastle. "No. It's . . . eBet guarantees all bets. They always have."

It wasn't a good argument. Megan pointed angrily. "My sister has a gun to her head. You have a gun to your head. And no one knows whose hand is on the trigger."

Mitzi tried to cover the collar with her hands. "I'm doing what I can."

Jerry took the last step down to stand by Mitzi. "We have to trust that something we do matters. The game has to matter."

Mitzi wasn't sure he was still talking about the death collars. She took Megan's hands, forced her to hold still a moment and look at her. "I promise, I'll find out. I won't sleep. I won't train. I won't go upstairs and finish my dessert. I will break every law and use every dirty trick I know until I find out who is behind Ultimate Fans."

Megan squeezed her hands and nodded once, but she said, "It's not enough." She turned to Jerry. "We need to assume the worst: everyone in both countries wearing a collar dies at the end of the game. What we have to do is talk to Team South America."

Jerry looked pained. "Not that arrogant asshole."

"Arrogant assholes don't deserve to die either. Jax will want to save his own skin. We need the other team's cooperation. We need to keep this game from ending. We need to buy time for Mitzi to find the truth."

Jerry raised his hands over his head. "And all we have to do is convince an egomaniac to give up on winning the game he's dedicated his life to so that he can help the team he hates most of all."

"It's his life too. He'll listen. He has to." Megan put her hands on Jerry's chest, and he softened, looking at her. They really were a sweet couple. Then Megan said, "We just need to stall until Mitzi saves us all."

Mitzi really wished she knew how she was going to do that, or at least trusted in herself as much as these two did.

She clutched her silver whistle. No pressure.

23

Jax stepped out of his residence and took a deep breath of brisk morning air. Game day air. He had to admit it; he wouldn't have wanted the season to end any other way. There was something so sweet and poetic about facing Jerry in the finals. That smug pretty boy who still wouldn't accept that he'd ever been wrong.

All the pumped-up underdog drama North America was generating made it seem like it would be an even fight on the surface. Jax knew better. North America had barely squeaked by every single game. They didn't deserve to be in the finals. Which was fine by him. He didn't like to work more than he had to. Being a top athlete was about efficiency. No wasted motion, hitting the target exactly. Beating this team was going to be almost relaxing.

He kissed his fingers at Angela, who waved from their balcony, leaning over the rail like she would leap into the air if he got close enough. They never had sex the night before a game, to keep the passions hot. Her sacrifice to the greater glory. He would make it up to her after the victory.

The coin toss yesterday had left the choice of the final game to South America, and Jax had not had to consult with his teammates. They knew what he would pick and approved. It was a traditional choice, the Grand Melee. A fight to the last man standing, winner take all. If God above loved drama, as He seemed to, it would end with Jerry and Jax, man to man, a final reckoning long overdue. Jax had been so naïve, such a believer in fair play, when Jerry had cost him his very first international tournament as a lad of sixteen, making a foul, a known foul! On purpose, because it wouldn't cost him the victory. The rules were ever feckless, creatures of pure logic, neither good nor evil.

The Rio de Janeiro arena was packed to the fences. Illegal viewers crawled and snuck in every corner. A solid wall of humanity screaming, thrilling, yearning to touch the glory of the games. Jax crawled into his pod, uncomfortable in his suit, so full of passion as he was. The crowds were cheering his name and waving banners in the most beautiful colors in the world, the colors of South America. Pale blue, dark blue, green, and yellow. From diversity, strength. With reluctance, he pulled the hood closed and fell into the cool darkness of virtual space.

The game world unfolded before him, a misty forest with giant trees that stretched to the sky and a soft carpet of dry needles underfoot. Yellow dirt showed here and there. Dry. He brushed the ground with his foot, leaving little trace. Tracks would be hard to perceive.

Herbert Rivera, that Brazilian ham, even hammier in his own territory, grinned down like a false saint plastered across the sky. "Grand Melee is the purest form of gladiatorial combat. Very few choose the Grand Melee because it introduces a lot of chance. The winner is not the team that scores the most, but the team that survives the other." Ah, but chance was only a problem to those who were not right with God. Jax said his prayers, gave his tithe, and, having been born to the country with the most World Championships, proved he was living cleanly.

Rivera finally got to the rules. "Scattered around the play area are exactly twelve weapons. Our players won't know where they are, or if they'll be the first to the crossbow or the dagger. They'll have to use their wits and the natural cover of our simulated wilderness. An opponent is out of the game when they accrue enough damage that, if this were not a game, they would die." Rivera oversold the word "die," and his eyes flashed. "The symbolism is too real, isn't it? Because after all, this is MegaDeath, and only winners survive!"

Bloated sack of air, that one. Jax kept his eyes low on the terrain as the game got underway. As an added stroke of realism, there would be no team communications, no radios or texts, in Grand Melee. Jax saw a massive canyon off to his left, impassable, probably a map edge. Enemies could be between him and his crew. The game would have, indeed, scattered weapons about, and the sooner he found one, the better. Was that a bow and arrows under that bush or just more twigs? He crouched, checking every direction before he crossed a clear path.

With a shower of sparks, a cheerleader appeared next to him. Not even one of his own. That northern bimbo, Mitzi. She snapped her fingers and pointed at him. "Right. Good. Stay there." And vanished.

Jax shook his head. Like hell was he staying put. Cheerleaders sometimes tried to rattle the other team by getting in their way. He was above such problems. He hurried quickly away from the canyon and into cover by the suspected arrows and was rewarded. Yes, it was a bow and quiver, set cunningly in the angles of an ironwood. He quickly strung the bow and straightened. He needed to find high ground. The canyon edge marched relentlessly behind him, but otherwise the terrain was level here. There were mountains in the distance—but in every direction, and this world didn't need to conform to geological science. Perhaps he would stay near the edge and head west. There was a ridge of stone that way, blocking some of the view.

The sounds of breaking branches and running footsteps coming up behind him interrupted his thoughts. Jax drew an arrow and nocked it, turning in time to see his nemesis, Jerry, running right at him. What was this? Was Jerry going to give himself up like a Christmas goose in the first minute of combat? That wasn't the drama Jax wanted.

Jerry had his hands up. "Wait! Wait! Don't shoot!"

Mitzi reappeared. "Bing! You've found each other. Okay, are we good? Jax, listen to him. Just this once."

Jax lowered his bow, frowning. "What is this?"

Jerry approached, hands raised. "Sorry, I didn't know how else to meet you. Mitzi tracked you down." Said cheerleader saluted and vanished. "There's something wrong with the game. Really wrong. We need your help."

"I can help you lose." Jax re-nocked his arrow. "It's not sporting, you giving me this easy shot, but I'll take it." He shrugged. "Little glory in this, but there's no glory for the dead."

"Look at me. I didn't have to come to you, unarmed. I want to beat you as much as you want to beat me, but there's more at stake. You've heard of the 'Ultimate Fan' challenge?"

What was this, some psychological ploy? "Everyone has heard of it. Even my lover wears a collar for me."

Jerry took a small step forward. He lowered his chin. "What if I told you there are dummy accounts making the challenge? Your lover is betting against a ghost."

He sounded sure, but he was a liar, and Angela was too smart for that. "No. Not possible. She would know."

"It's not just her. Millions of people are betting against ghosts. Look in your profile. Mitzi has proof, mathematical proof. The file's called 'popcorn.' She uploaded it as a default file. You should be able to access it just like you'd call up a note sheet."

Jax was not about to avert his gaze to pull up a file. For all he knew, this was a ruse. Get him distracted and take him out. Jax kept his eyes steady on Jerry. "Not even waiting for the second minute to cheat?"

"Fine, don't look at it now. You can look later. It's in everyone's profile, so your team has it too. It is proof that there are more bets than people betting. And that's not the worst." Jerry lowered his arms a bit, even though he still had a deadly weapon aimed at his face. He stood there, hands out, like he was begging. "We have no way of knowing the bet will be made good on. There's a chance, Juan. There's a chance they'll kill everyone with a collar."

Jax didn't believe that. Yet he was stepping back, lowering his arrow. Something in him was cautious enough to listen. "No, Angela would know. She's smarter than me. That's why I love her."

Jerry nodded, lowering his hands farther. "They're fooling all of us. Central is masquerading, running up the bets. Is that so hard to believe? Haven't they done ridiculous things, year after year, to convince more people to bet?"

This was true. Jax had suspected more than once that a game was rigged, a coincidental injury here or there.

Jerry pressed his point. "You know that's all they care about. Someone behind Central wants lots of people to die. Your country or mine, does it matter?"

"Of course it matters! We are—you are—" Jax shook his head and planted his feet in position to fire. But his arm wouldn't pull back. "Why should I believe you?"

Jerry smiled like it was the question he was waiting for. "Because I'll tell you exactly where my team is."

No. He wouldn't. Unless he really believed this was more important than winning.

Jerry nodded like Jax had asked a question. "It'll be easy to check if I'm telling the truth, on your own time and with all the backup you want. Here's the deal: we'll play it soft. Exchange fire back and forth. We'll keep the audience watching but not kill anyone. We drag things out. I have a friend trying to hack in. The more time we give her, the more lives we save in both of our countries."

It was tempting. It was noble. Jax felt his muscles relax and fought against it. "God damn it! I'm here to win. You're asking me to betray the trust given to me by the people of South America! Three hundred million people!"

Jerry took another step closer. "I'm asking you to save them. I won't kill you, and I'll save those three hundred million. Don't kill me, and don't risk the fifteen hundred million in North America."

One and a half billion? Jax had never thought about the fans on the other side. Were there really that many more of them? He looked down at the feed from Central, but all he got were odds, betting percentages. He blinked through options to get raw numbers.

Jerry hadn't lied. There were so many lives in the balance.

"You see it, don't you?" Jerry stepped almost-touching close. "Over two billion lives are currently wagered on this game. This is bigger than you and me. If it helps . . . yes, I was a bastard that first game. I stretched the rules to win. You were right."

Jax didn't know how to process that. He had never imagined hearing those words. His bow lay slack against his thigh, the arrow in the other hand, loose.

Jerry gathered up his hand, with the arrow notched between the fingers, and held it between his. "We'll stay clustered near map grid G3. I'll send two people out sporadically, starting northwest, and moving through each eighth of the compass. I promise this. All I ask is that you meet us with like force and keep everyone alive. Keep it a draw. No one loses. If my friend finds the proof and we can change the plan, I'll come myself to tell you."

Jax felt a surge of feeling. It was unprecedented. It was not the way contests were decided. He had the advantage! Surely this was a trick to steal the victory. Yet the warm pressure on his palm felt genuine. Vulnerable. "How would I know? If you're lying?"

Jerry squeezed his hand and grinned. "Would I ever admit I was wrong for any other reason?"

Jax had to admit to that. He carefully extracted his hand. "I'll keep it to a draw for an hour. No more."

Jerry bit his lip, looked like he would say more, but then nodded. "That's fair. Thank you, Jax. See you in an hour, brother."

And he turned his back. Turned it fully and jogged away. Jax nocked his arrow again and drew it back, centering his aim on that broad back. It would be so easy.

Ah, that was why he couldn't do it. He un-nocked the arrow and let his shoulders relax. Damn that fool. It was hard to be untrustworthy when trusted. Jax shouldered the quiver and turned left. The ground seemed to rise slightly in that direction. The team had agreed, wherever they materialized, they'd seek the high ground.

He had hiked barely the length of a city block when a figure slid around a tree trunk in front of him: India Thomas, the most beautiful woman in the games. Her long legs were shown to advantage in the leather minidress the game had concocted for the forest scene. She held up a hand toward him. "Jerry is full of shit."

Jax had been climbing the hillside and was not prepared for combat, so he was relieved she wasn't leading an assault. He put one leg high and relaxed, his weapon at his side. "What makes you think I've been talking to Jerry?"

"Boy, please." She tossed her impressive mane and stalked across the path, fists on her hips. "You think he didn't tell us his bullshit conspiracy theory? Jerry has all of us holed up in a lousy glen, no strategic advantage, and he says he told you where it is, even."

"Ah, *querida*, what can I say? Men will talk. We're silly like that."

Indía crossed her arms. "I didn't bust my ass to make it to the finals so that my captain could sell us out on some namby-pamby gentleman's agreement. I want to win or die with honor."

Jax admired the fire in her, the taut muscles. He bit his lip. "But what can we do? It takes two sides to have an argument or to play a game. Anything else is uncivilized."

Indía stomped up to him. Her nostrils flared. Her full lips quivered. "I'll show you uncivilized."

He retreated, suddenly feeling his passions, feeling the restraint of his love for Angela. "Slow, *bellísima*. I'm spoken for."

An inch from him, she pushed his chest with three perfectly

manicured nails. "If you had any self-respect at all, you would play with honor. Hardest against hardest. No quarter."

His mind spun. The arrow clacked helplessly against the bow at his side. "It won't be sporting. They're expecting an hour of peace."

"Leave that to me. The first people we send out will expect a full assault. You'd better give it, because I'll be waiting." She poked him once more with her deliciously strong nails, and then she was gone, running through the trees.

Mitzi used her cheer location control to find the team and let them know Jerry was in position. They nodded, gripping ancient weapons, thinking they were an army prepared to endure a siege, but they really looked like lost larpers.

Mitzi absolutely loathed the Grand Melee. It was the worst game. No winning team survived without injury. Sure, the pods wouldn't actually kill the people stabbed and slashed, but the haptics could harm as they caused realistic sensations, and even in less deadly games, the body harmed itself. The pod let you move however you could, and that wasn't always a good thing. A person could plant her foot to pivot as she had a thousand times before, and some secret torsion inside her knee could give way, and she'd be out of the game, out of her life.

Now add six-foot spears to the mix.

Before she could start lecturing on safety—no one wanted that from a cheerleader—Mitzi teleported herself back to cheer base.

Cheer base was a place no player saw or even thought about. She hadn't before taking the plunge into cheer. It was an aggressively boring room, about the size of a cargo container, with corrugated steel walls, a long bench, and a floor of plastic turf. Pure putting-you-in-your-place classism, since to a virtual environment, marble floors and gold walls would have actually been cheaper (fewer polygons).

People who didn't cheer didn't know what a challenge it was, how scary it could be. Even though she was no longer risking her life, what cheerleaders risked was subtler but no less deadly. "Watch yourself in this field. You can give your life away in pieces," her mentor, Gloria, had said before handing her the silver whistle she still wore around her neck as a symbol of office.

David, stretching on the bench, raised his head from his knee. "I'm up?"

"You're all up." Mitzi took her whistle off. She squeezed it a moment before she tossed it to him. "Keep moving, make them too entertained to miss me."

"Impossible." David donned the whistle with due gravity, then flashed his most dangerous smile and blinked out of sight.

Mitzi pulled open her private interface, a black screen floating before her, and checked first on the game map. South American players were forming two flanking groups, creeping up on the North American position. Mitzi hadn't had much faith in Jax to hold up his side of the bargain but seeing this made her sick. Well, that side of things was up to David now. She cleared the screen and started her real work. There were the threads she'd left dangling, the holes she'd torn in security walls the night before. Every wall so far had another behind it, but she had to believe that the next one, or the one after that, would give her the answers she needed.

She just hoped that whatever time the team bought her would be enough.

Megan paced a small rise in the forest, a rampart of earth buttressed by massive, ancient roots. She'd found a spear and wished it was a shotgun. The rest of the team moved uneasily, marking out a perimeter in their section of forest, which was a subtle depression between the rampart and a lower rise on the other side.

Jerry jogged into view. Chet cursed, relaxing from his stance to fire a crossbow. "You gotta give a signal. I almost shot you."

Jerry slowed to a stop in the clearing they'd been thinking of as the middle of their domain. "He says he'll give us one hour."

That was better than Megan had hoped. She felt a tiny muscle unclench in her back. One hour. That was lots of time for Mitzi. Megan felt her confidence in Mitzi like a new religion, inscrutable but warm.

Jerry jogged the length of the glen. "Where's India?" India was supposed to be the first to go out, a quick excursion to keep the cameras interested and give South America something to snipe at. It wasn't a complicated plan, but Jerry had assured them it didn't have to be. The camera editors at Central could make standing still exciting to the audiences at home, he'd said.

However, the longer they all stood there, waiting for India, the less Jerry looked like he believed that. The less Megan believed that. If only they could send messages like in almost every other stupid game.

"I'll go." Kendell swung the two-handed sword she'd been practicing with onto her shoulder and tromped into the woods.

Jerry relaxed. "Good. Kendell, then Chet, then India can go in Kendell's spot. Everyone stay alert. Patrol the perimeter. We need to look like we're really playing."

"I still say this is dumb," Chet muttered.

Kendell moved steadily away from them, a darkness moving between the trees. Megan hopped lightly down from her vantage. She imagined Kendell's path and set off to intercept it.

"Hey!" Jerry shouted. "We're supposed to wait here! Don't break the agreement!"

Megan waved back at him with her spear. "I'm just going to reconnoiter." She couldn't take the stress of not moving, of waiting.

Megan wasn't sure if she'd already gone as far as Jerry said they could go, if Kendell was ahead of her. They had access to an area map, which was a grid with letters across the top and numbers across the bottom. Supposedly, something natural-looking would stop their ability to pass along the edges. She'd seen a sheer cliff face nearby where she'd materialized.

The maps only filled in topographic details after you personally walked over it, though, and only showed your own location, no one else's. So the map ahead of her where Kendell was walking was a black, featureless void.

Megan found a tree with low enough branches to climb. It wasn't easy to do it with a spear in one hand, but she knew better than to leave her weapon at the base. On the highest branch that could support her weight, she stood, holding the spear against the trunk. She could see over the smaller trees. Mountains ringed the horizon with breathtaking colors, snow and sandstone, crags and peaks. An eagle hung on the cloudless sky like an ornament. She rested. This moment, pure and clean, felt like a good omen.

Then she saw a glint, down among the trees, and it was Kendell with her sword, still tromping forward, one arm swinging casually. This also seemed fortunate. Maybe this was going to go according to plan. Maybe they could actually do this.

And then Kendell fell with a cry, two arrows sticking out of her like impossible, silly things. The bushes rustled, and she saw crouched forms running.

"Team South America has made their first kill!" Herbert Rivera's voice boomed, while in the sky two numbers appeared: 1–0.

24

Megan threw her spear, then slid down the tree trunk as fast as she could. Bark burned her hands, and scattering chips fell down her skimpy leather top. Her feet hit the ground and she ran forward, breaking branches and jumping a little trench she hadn't seen from afar.

She found her spear stuck in the dirt, but no sign of Kendell or her attackers. There were broken branches, some disturbed earth. When a person "died" in the game, they would vanish. She wrenched her spear from the dirt and hurried back to their base.

By the time she got there, Chet was gone too.

"They came at us from behind, ambushed Chet." Jerry stood with Hasan, their backs angled to the low rise, their weapons in front of them. "They almost got India."

"It's not even a scratch." The blood soaking India's sleeve said otherwise.

"I'm glad you got back in time to defend him," Megan said. India gave her a sour look.

Jerry held out a hand. "India was looking for you, Megan. Don't be so hard on her."

India took Megan's place on the high ground. In each hand she held a curved dagger. "If you'd been here, Chet wouldn't have been taken out."

Somehow, Megan doubted that. "Why look for me? I was following Kendell. I told Jerry where I was going."

"Let's not argue," Jerry said. "Our strategy has to change, and now. There are six of them and four of us."

Indía crouched low above Jerry and Hasan. "It's better this way. Like it was always meant to be. We don't need that cowardly plan to win."

"Forget about winning. We need to not lose. We're down two people." Hasan grimly shifted his grip on his spear. "And they took Chet's crossbow. We don't have any range weapons."

"We need to get out of here," Megan said.

There were no arguments, but they were all thinking the same thing: the other team knew exactly where they were and was waiting, invisible in nearby cover, to pick them off.

Jerry swiveled restlessly. "We need a diversion. Where are those damn cheerleaders? Get up on the ridge with Indía." When no one moved, he growled, "Everyone. Up."

Hasan scrambled, and Megan jumped after him. Jerry waited at the base until they were settled, then followed. It should have felt safer, crouching together among the tree roots with a clear view a few feet in every direction, but Megan only felt the bareness of her back more keenly.

Jerry drew four circles in the dirt and pointed from each circle to one of them. Then he drew lines for which ways they should move. He mimed actions.

Megan shook her head. "That's hardly a plan."

"There's no time for another. We move on three."

Indía smiled fiercely. "On two."

"Fine. One. Two!"

Hasan and Megan sprang to their feet, screaming, and hurled their spears together to the north. Almost in the same motion, they jumped down and ran.

The place the spears impacted was now statistically the most likely spot the enemy wasn't, so that's where they ran, making as much noise as possible. The enemy, reasonably, would be coming at them from the flank, but unless they had started in the perfect place, they wouldn't be able to shoot immediately. Megan hoped. It was a risk.

She and Hasan dove to the ground, sliding on their bellies to get to their spears. Megan pulled hers in front of her and checked Hasan had his. He grinned at her. It felt giddy to be this lucky. Somewhere behind them, Indía and Jerry were sneaking quietly in opposite directions. Anyone positioned to attack Megan and Hasan would find one of them at their rear.

Megan and Hasan turned back-to-back with their spears in front of them, and then there was a sickening, wet thunk, and Hasan fell against her, his head back, making choked, gurgling noises, his Adam's apple jerking up and down, blood gushing around the shaft buried at the base of his throat.

Another arrow zinged Megan's cheek as she quickly pulled Hasan up, and then there was another thunk hitting his body. Oh, no. No. She huddled, her teammate a warm, meaty shield, but as the game registered him as dead, he vanished, leaving her alone, and she'd dropped the spear. She tried to push down the terror, remind herself this wasn't real. Hasan was still alive in his pod. She frantically felt the ground behind her for her spear, trying to see where the bolts had come from. Sticks, dirt, pine needles. *Come on! Where is it?*

Someone crashed through the underbrush behind her. Megan whirled, throwing a handful of needles to buy time. They hit Jerry in the chest. He looked down at Hasan's spear. "Shit."

Indía burst from the underbrush from the other direction. "I ran them off, but they'll regroup, come on."

Megan located her spear, then, and Hasan's. The old coldness came over her. Only three of them against six who had long-range weapons. She felt herself retreat from caring. There was only the job to be done, the game to play.

Jerry led the way into the thick, glossy rhododendrons India had come through. The bushes ran along a little gully and offered some protection as they moved out of their grid square, northeast. Megan crept behind him, low enough that the fat leaves made the air dark and green around them. Suddenly, with a flash of light, David was standing to her right, wearing a skimpy loincloth and some leather harness over his chest. Jerry hissed, waving frantically for him to hide himself. "Where were you when we needed a distraction?"

David's glittering cheerleader self was all but a beacon for their location. Megan would stab him if it would do anything. Then she decided she would do it anyway. Her spear vanished harmlessly into his toned side.

David simply turned his back half to them, looked up, shaded his eyes, and became, instantly, someone alone in the woods, looking confusedly for his party. Hardly moving his lips, he said, "Sorry. We got a late start."

He didn't say what Megan was suddenly thinking: the cheerleaders, like the team, thought they had an hour of reprieve. Jerry wasn't the kind of guy to be snowed by the likes of Jax. He'd come back to their huddle convinced. What had happened to change Jax's mind?

"Find the other team," Jerry snapped, and David wandered casually away before vanishing.

After a tense minute, they continued crawling through the rhododendron line. When they'd gone a few feet, Jerry stopped. Megan glanced over his shoulder. This was it. The bush they were under was the last one, and before them lay a relatively flat and open area. The terrain offered both scant cover and too much cover. The trees were plenty, but spread apart so you didn't have continuous protection between them. There was another low ridge, but it looked half a mile away.

The ground tilted slowly northward. From the map, they only had one grid square to the edge. So that steady march up would continue to a massive cliff or impassable rocks. The map was designed so they had to stay close to the other team, with no room to run for long.

Megan felt the flimsiness of the line of rhododendrons. Six enemies, at least two with bows, were actively searching the map grids near there. It wouldn't take a genius to say, "Hey, let's just rain some arrows into those bushes to be safe."

Indía crept to the front of their little line and pointed north. "Jax always goes for the high ground."

Jerry nodded. He bit his lip, looking north and then south.

Megan shook her head. "But the map ends that way. We'll be caught against an edge." Her legs hurt from staying crouched so long. Not the good hurt of exertion, the painful ache of stressed joints. In the real world, in her pod, her body was being held in this position by sadistic servos. She hated Grand Melee. If she were alone, she would just run, finding opponents one at a time and killing them. Keeping the others alive was a complication she didn't know how to plan for. "Fuck this. Why don't we just shout?" Indía and Jerry looked at her with horror. She took a deep breath. "I don't mean give ourselves up. I'm talking about the fans. They're all watching us, aren't they?" Megan eased herself a little higher. "We break into the open shouting that Central has lied, that the Ultimate Fan collars are rigged. Everyone will hear. They'll demand answers. They might even pause the game."

The horrified looks stayed put. "You never played pro." Jerry went back to checking the clearing.

Indía smacked her arm. "The feed is edited. The highest-paid engineers in the world are making split-second censorships. You think the family-friendly throngs of the world want to see an accidental nipple? Hear what any sensible person would shout when they get stabbed? The broadcast is on a four-second delay."

Megan's head reeled. How could she be completely exposed, watched, and scrutinized, and yet powerless to speak to the masses? "Okay, but what if we keep doing it? If we do it enough? Slip it into casual sentences? 'Okay, Indía, you cut north where Central is lying the collars are rigged'?"

Indía looked away from her in disgust.

Jerry sat back on his heels. "In one of the first MegaDeath games," he said, "a team tried to stop it. They didn't want to die or kill. They went on strike. They got the other team to stop too."

Her plan? Someone had already done it? "I've never heard of that."

His eyes met hers. "Exactly. This computer can render all these pine needles. It's creating the feeling of the sun being warmer than the shadow, the breeze that just ruffled that branch. You think it doesn't have the ability to swap us out with a completely fake broadcast? They have whole versions of games ready to go if there's another protest. Mitzi told me about it."

As if summoned by another cheerleader's name, Mtume appeared, crouched low, one leg out long and straight in a hurdler's stretch. "North," she whispered. "About sixty meters. They're in teams of two, working east from west from grid H5 to H6." Then she ran away to the west.

Indía lifted the branch in front of her with her curved dagger and inched forward, ready to charge. "That's a search pattern. They don't know where we are either."

Jerry rolled onto the balls of his feet, ready to run. "Diversion. Get the cheerleaders grouped up, draw them in."

"No." Megan held back. "We tried to draw them out before, and they were ready for it."

Indía straightened her back and narrowed her eyes. "What do you propose then, rookie?"

"They outnumber us, we use that to our advantage."

Indía snorted. "You've hurt your head. I'm going on my own. I'll sneak north and west and cut down who I find."

Megan barely kept her voice low. "Where were you when we were all at the meeting point?"

Indía's shocked gasp was a little too practiced.

Jerry held an arm out between them. “No, that’s a good idea, Megan. Come on, you two. Follow me.”

Jerry led them north and west, as Indía had wanted, but it was a zigzagging path from cover to cover, with David, Mtume, and the other male cheerleader, Kirk, dropping in to give reports on where the South American team members were.

They dashed from the side of a boulder to a pair of trees that were close together, then to a depression, then to another boulder.

Kirk shook his curly red fringe. “Third group is about ten meters that way, I’d say, but it’s a messy ten. They saw me, so I pretended I was trying to lead them this way. They shifted a little in the opposite direction.” He held his hands together and then moved on out and away, grinning proudly.

Jerry moved the pebbles that were supposed to represent the opposing team on the estimated map they’d drawn on the ground. “It’s a start.”

David reappeared and reached imperiously into the chart and nudged a few stones. “I drew these two south, toward the others.” He vanished again. No flirting today.

Kirk shrugged and disappeared.

Indía groaned. “It’s enough.”

“It’s not enough.” Jerry shook his head.

Mtume came, panting. “Player six broke formation. They’re on to us.”

Megan brushed the six pebbles on the ground aside.

“Now or never,” she said, and stood.

25

Megan felt good to be running at last, toward a goal. Jerry and Indía were at her side, the three of them an arrowhead flying as fast as three top-notch athletes could, aiming for the most dangerous weapon, the recurve bow. The crossbow could shoot farther and more accurately, but in this attack, the recurve's ability to fire quickly was more of a problem.

The plan was simple: Megan and Jerry would get as close to the bow carrier as they could and move left, always left, and closer, forcing the other team into a tighter and tighter clump. The recurve bow would immediately have trouble; it took room to nock and draw an arrow. The crossbow would be less affected, but it took longer to load, and they'd be cutting down free space for the archer's elbow. The bodies of Team South America would become shields for North America, getting in the way and fouling weapons. Megan and Jerry would stop when they had closed in to within spear-reach, which was conveniently out of sword- and knife-reach. They could then stab at will while Indía flew out to their flank, using her superior speed to chase anyone who tried to break away.

That was the plan, anyway.

The trees passed like fence posts, and Megan started to worry. Where was Team South America? Had they misjudged the angle, the location? Mtume appeared ahead of her, pointing. She adjusted course. A few minutes later, David was there, then Kirk, keeping them on course.

Megan no longer felt exposed. She felt like a spear point, an arrow, sailing to its target. She hoped she'd hit it, hit it deep and true. She hoped it would make a difference. That the cheerleaders were right about the direction, that they'd gotten them clumped close enough.

With each step she grew less sure. The other team had heard them coming, perhaps, or had realized they were being herded and scattered. They were all going to die, and Lola and countless strangers with them. They should have kept hiding and bought time.

Megan charged up a short rise that opened onto a clearing with sparse, narrow trees. There was a strange woman just a few more paces ahead. She held a recurve bow, an arrow nocked and pulled ready. Her back was to Megan, her eyes following David as he danced through the trees, pivoting to keep her aim tracked on him. Megan felt a roar build in her chest and released it as she extended her spear and closed the distance.

The archer stumbled backward, out of range, right into Jax. He had come up behind her, too close. His arm got caught in the bow. His eyes were on Megan. He pushed his teammate away to get his sword free. It was working. This was it. This was working. Indía fairly flew around the pack, the crossbowman, another swordsman, and a woman with an axe retreating from her, getting tangled up with Jax and the two players with him while Megan and Jerry steadily slid left, left, left.

As Megan drove her spear into the archer's chest, she saw something she wished she hadn't.

She saw Jax look at Indía like she had betrayed him.

"Get the crossbow!" Jerry cried at her right. The axewoman broke free to swing at him, and he parried with his spear. Megan leaned on her spear, stuck in flesh, the archer holding the end of it, and tried to stay close to Jerry as he was tangled up, vulnerable. But Jerry was not defenseless. He screamed, turned the spear flat in front of him, and charged, pushing the axewoman and the rest of the South American team tighter together.

Megan tried to detach her spear, but it clung to the archer's body, and she had to deflect attacks with the butt end, ducking down and away until at last the tip pulled free with a wet, sucking sound. The archer's body vanished shortly thereafter.

"Retreat!" Jax cried, and in frustration threw his sword at Jerry. It hit Jerry's spear, flat to flat.

"Break!" Jerry called, frantically dodging blows. The South American team was no longer startled; they were falling back, forming a stronger defense.

Break was the command to run hard downhill. Jax would always choose uphill. They would regroup as far from there as they could. Megan tried to find the bow underfoot. The body had vanished, and she had no point of reference for where it had fallen. She skipped barely out of range of a swinging axe. Shit, Jax was pulling the bow back, ducking between the axewoman and a swordsman, and now Megan was seriously in trouble. She turned to flee and tripped on something metal. Jax's sword. She grabbed it without thinking and ran.

It took control, going downhill on hard dirt, slippery with pine needles and crisscrossed with roots. She had learned control. She tried not to think about the crossbow still back there, about how easily an axe could be thrown. She juked crazily and kept running downward until she found Jerry, and they headed east together.

Indía joined the retreat last, her curved daggers showy with red against the palette of the forest, drops streaming behind her like poppies.

Megan didn't check the scores until they had found a boulder to hide behind, the three of them panting heavily.

North America 2, South America 3. Better than they'd hoped. They'd hoped to get one.

Her back pressed against the cool stone as she gasped for air. She looked down at the sword in her hand. The blade was bent. She turned it left and right, wondering if it could be of any use.

"Forget it," Jerry said. "It's a win just that they don't have it."

Indía crouched and wiped her blades against a patch of ferns. "Jax is an asshole, but also a coward. He'll be slow to seek us out. We should split up, east and west, make a pincer move on the farthest north, highest point." She pointed with her blade. "That's where he'll be."

Megan tossed the ruined sword aside. "We don't have an army to split up. We have three people. You were supposed to get the crossbow!"

"I killed the bow, that's good enough," Indía said.

Jerry pushed away from the rock, scanning the area. "We bought some time, at least. That's what's important. Every second we live, our fans live. Let's assume Indía's right, that Jax retreated all the way north—"

Kirk appeared. "Look out!"

All three of them ducked instinctively. An arrow sailed just over Jerry's head, close enough to part hairs, and hit the boulder, leaving a small gouge in the stone.

Megan pushed Jerry ahead of her as they all scrambled to put the rock between them and the direction the arrow had come from.

"Yeah, let's assume Jax did not retreat all the way north," Megan said.

"Thanks, got that." Jerry ducked as another arrow struck the edge of the rock.

Kirk pointed at the arrow on the ground. Too long for the crossbow. "That's the recurve bow. I think there's just the one person." Kirk vanished and came back. "I'm not sure."

"Keep looking," Jerry said. Kirk nodded and disappeared.

"Stay here and play target," Indía purred. "I'll get him."

Megan grabbed her arm as she came out of her crouch, ready to run. "Not so fast. How do we trust you?"

Indía looked aghast. "I'm on your team."

"Are you? Where were you when Jerry got back from talking to Jax?"

"I don't have to listen to this." India wrenched her arm from Megan's grasp and was off.

Jerry suddenly cried out in pain and fell against the boulder as an arrow found its mark.

At the cry, Kirk reappeared. His eyes widened at Jerry's blood. "Distraction," he said. "On it." He took off in the opposite direction, waving his arms.

Megan grabbed Jerry and dragged him around to the far side of the rock. She was beginning to feel like they were on a merry-go-round. At least their attacker would have to move farther to get a clear shot than they had to move to get around the stone.

Jerry held his arm. Megan crouched over him. "Don't move. I'll pull it out."

Megan's fingers slipped on the bloody arrow shaft as she struggled to grip it as close to the skin as possible.

Another arrow hit the stone, just above her head. Megan had to let go, grab Jerry, and move him again.

Jerry squeezed his eyes shut. "They must have escaped India. Must be backing away, circling."

Megan got ahold of the arrow again. "Or she's betrayed us."

"Don't be . . . that's crazy. She dies if we lose. India has no death wish."

"We need another plan."

India came back, slamming into the boulder. "There's at least two of them. I couldn't get to the archer."

Megan knew she should be grateful for India's bravery, running out to get this information, but it felt too obviously useless. "We're sitting ducks."

David appeared. "Kirk is doing jump-flips in front of Jax, but the bastard is shooting right through him. He's not distracted. What can I do?"

Jerry gestured. "Run a flanking route, get Mtume to mirror you. We'll use the visual distraction to head—"

Suddenly the sky filled with Herbert Rivera's eager visage. "Team North America is pinned down, but it's the tensions within the team that are hard to look away from!"

Then Megan heard her own voice, echoing. ". . . or she's betrayed us."

Jerry's reply followed, somehow sounding more like a secret than it was. "She dies if we lose. Indía has no death wish."

Herbert looked worriedly down, like a grandfather seeing his children being too hard on the grandkids. "Has love blinded Megan Mori? Can Jerry keep the center in a team that's now a love triangle? I can hardly watch."

Megan shivered at the humiliation of Indía hearing this, of Indía being close enough that she could feel her warmth at her back.

"Hey." Jerry put his hand on her cheek. Megan forced herself to focus on him. He smiled. "He's reporting on old news. We're together for the rest of our lives, right?"

"Right."

Indía's knee dug into Megan's back as she bent to growl, "If we survive this game, I wouldn't take bets on this fickle bastard staying with anyone."

"Not now," Jerry said. "Please. We can talk later."

The irritating pressure on Megan's back let up as Indía straightened. "Because I'm the professional. I'm the one who can put her feelings on hold. Always."

Megan wanted to tell them both to shut up. If she kissed Jerry, they might, but first she had to get the arrow out of his bicep. "Hold still." She had as good a grip as she could hope for, one hand flat against his skin to prevent it from pulling upward, one low and tight on the shaft. She yanked the arrow free. Jerry screamed inside clenched teeth.

Jax's voice, far closer than she would like, taunted, "Ah, lovers! Would you like me to come make it better? I am more man for two women than that pretty boy!"

Megan pointed the arrow at David. "New plan. Get me to Mitzi."

"She's in cheer central." David looked aghast. "You can't go there."

Jerry held his bleeding arm and stared at Megan like he'd never seen her before.

"I tell you what," Jax called, "I'll make it sporting. Ten minutes for the two ladies to wrestle it out. I just want to watch."

Megan would give up whole parts of her anatomy to shut that man up. "You knew I was suspicious of you, Indía, and I still am, but we can fight about it after we've saved the lives of our fans."

Indía's expression was as cold as a snake's. The silence was oppressive. Megan could hear Jerry's blood drip. David's glowing image emitted a slight crackle, a quiet reminder of his cheerleader immunity. He shifted his feet.

Finally, Indía exhaled sharply. "I don't care what you think of me, and I don't care if you die, but we are still a team, and we are going to win this game."

"Fine." Megan gestured from Jerry to Indía with the bloody arrow. "You two concentrate on that. I'm going to the cheerleaders' room."

David sagged helplessly. "I told you, I can't take you there."

"Then bring Mitzi here."

"Just stop it," Indía hissed. "There is no conspiracy, no matter how much you want there to be one! There is only the game. There was always only the game. We can beat these bastards. We go east, then north. Cut them off at that low ridge."

"In a minute," Jerry said, looking gray.

Megan clenched her fists. There was nothing she could punch to solve this. Another arrow hit the rock overhead. Jax called, "You're boring me, Myers! Don't your ladies care enough to fight over you?"

With grim expressions, the three of them crawled around the boulder again. Before they settled, Megan said, "We're pinned down, they have us four to three, and they still have the bow. I'm not losing either of you and making it four to two." She pointed at David. "Mitzi."

"Be right back," David said, and vanished.

Another arrow clattered, closer. Either Jax meant his taunts, or he was a worse shot than his teammate had been. Then the next arrowhead kicked up dirt, inches from Megan's knee. She caught Indía's eye and reluctantly nodded. "We go east, then north."

Indía sprang to her feet and ran east. Megan followed Jerry after her and hoped Jax's terrible aim wasn't just for show.

26

Megan kept her arm over Jerry, dodging projectiles as they moved between the rock and the nearest cover, a rhododendron hedge. India ducked into the glossy green-black leaves.

"Stay where I can see you," Megan said.

Indía laughed. "You're so full of yourself."

Kirk appeared as Megan pushed Jerry under the leaves. "Jax is coming this way; he has two people with him."

That meant another member of Team South America was somewhere else, possibly ahead of them, lying in ambush. Jerry needed to rest. Megan urged him toward a hollow by some tree roots, but he shook his head. "We need to stay together. What can Mitzi do?"

"She can get me to Herbert Rivera."

He stared at her, but the conversation had to wait until they got to safety. She wrapped an arm under one of his and half-carried him at a faster pace, with the rhododendrons on their side for cover, towards the low ridge just ahead. Of course Jax had seen them enter. Where had Indía gone?

Megan was just about to accept that Indía had completely betrayed them when she reappeared, urging them forward. Megan got her arm fully under Jerry's and got him into a run. Out of the corner of her eye, she saw flickering lights, cheerleaders leading each other on chases through the trees.

They reached the ridge unscathed. Megan urged Jerry up, bullying him until he could rest against the biggest tree. Indía circled out of sight, which felt fishy, but Megan had to admit it made sense to keep an eye on their perimeter.

Jerry tore a length from his Robin Hood tunic and tied it around his bicep, tugging hard with his teeth. It was kinda sexy, even if they were about to die. Megan tried to take over tying the bandage, but he said, "I can do it," through clenched teeth.

Mitzi appeared at the base of the ridge, looking up at them, her hands on her hips. "This had better be important. I'm trying to save the world, remember?"

Megan ignored Jerry's protests, slapped his hand away, and tied his makeshift bandage tighter. "Get me to Herbert Rivera." She gave the bandage an extra tug, and Jerry rolled his eyes at her.

Mitzi, super genius who was saving the world, dropped her jaw with sarcastic exaggeration. "Excuse me?"

Megan jumped down to her level. "Can you do it? Is he in the game world too? He must be, to appear over us like that, right?"

Mitzi pressed her lips into a white line but then nodded. "There's a press box, a separate stage within the game, same as Cheer Central."

"Please, Mitzi. We're out of options here. South America isn't going to play soft. Herbert has the power to get through to the audience. If he tells them what's at stake, what's really happening, he can get them to protest, to demand a stop. If nothing else, it could buy us more time."

The word "time" was the clincher. Mitzi sagged with relief. "I could really use that."

Megan heard Indía come back. "You want me to go to the asshole that just tried to turn us against each other?"

"I haven't been watching," Mitzi said.

Jerry used the tree to help himself stand up. He looked stronger now that he wasn't bleeding profusely. He looked at Indía. "We should—" and then Megan was not in the woods.

Megan was half-crouched, arms out at her sides, prepared for assault at any moment, which was a perfectly natural posture with the forest around her and a crumbling earthen bank to her back, only now she was on a smooth gray carpet in a room that smelled of electric static and power. Mitzi stood at her side, a hand on her arm, no longer glowing but looking as scared as a child breaking into the principal's office. "Five minutes, then I'll come back for you," she whispered, and vanished.

Feeling silly, Megan straightened. There was a bank of windows, bright with the forest sunshine, showing a high view of the yellow stone and pine trees of the playing area. Herbert Rivera stood in front of it, hands clasped behind him, looking out. "Jax has something up his sleeve. That's the run formation he used in the stunning victory in '08. I wonder—" he turned, sensing Megan's presence, and gave her a little smile before turning back to the windows "—will Indía see this coming the way Caprita Bell did in '04?" He waved an odd gesture, like pinching something off in the air, and turned to face Megan, smiling politely like a high-end clerk not wanting to startle a shoplifter. "Can I help you? You seem to have lost your way from the playing field."

Megan swallowed against the dryness in her mouth. "Mr. Rivera, I need to speak to you. You have tremendous power, tremendous reach. Your voice is listened to by billions. We need your help. Someone has been manipulating bets and hiding who controls these Ultimate Fan collars. You need to get the audience to protest the game, to demand we not finish with the Ultimate Fan collars in place."

Herbert's expression deepened into a thoughtful frown as he listened. He took a step toward her, tilting his head, considering. "You want me to stop the game? This game I am currently announcing?"

"Yes. We have hard evidence that the Ultimate Fan collars are rigged. There are bets being made by avatars, not people. Real lives are being bet against artificial ones, and we still don't know who will pull the trigger, who sends the kill order."

Herbert folded his hands and tapped his lips with two fingers. "Hm." He walked to the other side of the room where an array of video equipment covered the wall, knobs and sliders and lights and screens showing different views of Jerry, of Jax, of the other players. Herbert fiddled with a knob, zooming in on India, her back pressed against a tree. The woman from South America who had been wielding an axe was behind her, though now she had a spear and was poking underbrush with it. "Perhaps you think I could find this out for you? The person who controls the collars? Perhaps then you could raise your concerns with them? There might be a logical, sensible explanation."

He was too calm, too thoughtful. Megan put a hand between him and the monitors. "I don't think you understand. Millions of people stand to lose their lives. No one could benefit from that."

The paternalistic frown was back. "You don't think it's a mistake? A coincidence?"

"We have the numbers. There's no paper trail to the owner of Ultimate Fans, even though it's a legal corporation and there's no reason to hide that information. The first bet-makers were all puppets controlled by someone in Central. Someone close to the strings of power."

Herbert Rivera sighed deeply. "Ah, Megan, I so liked you. Your fire, ruthlessness. Am I going to have to kill you so soon? I was hoping North America could make a comeback, make this game really exciting. You know the proceeds double if we go past three hours."

He said all this casually, with a twinkle in his eye.

Megan backed up. "Kill me? What do you mean . . . ? You're just the announcer."

His smile was kind, just a touch pitying. "Dear girl, I am Central." He started flipping switches and dials. "Or, at least, I am one of many faces Central wears. Honestly one of my favorites. Everyone loves me like this." He turned and spread his hands like he was posing for a photo. Megan knew he was expecting some reaction, but she could barely process what she was hearing. He sighed. "Here, watch this."

He gestured to a screen. Two South American players crept slowly through the forest, unaware that Jerry was just out of sight behind a bush. The bandage on his bicep was soaked with blood, and he held that arm close to his body. He was aware of the other team passing, warily watching from the corner of his eye. Soon they would be past, and Jerry would be safe. A branch fell, blocking their path. They had no choice but to turn, right into him.

Megan reached helplessly toward the image. "Jerry!" There was nothing she could do. Jerry held his spear short in his good hand and jabbed it at one attacker, but the other person got behind him. Jerry shoved backward, stabbed forward. He had one person on his back, pinning his arms. He twisted and threw the two of them into a nearby tree. He almost got free.

Almost. The player in front of Jerry had already sunk her sword deep into his stomach. Jerry shuddered as she twisted the blade. Her partner, dazed from hitting the tree, let go. Jerry slumped to the ground, fell over, and vanished.

Megan felt her knees buckle. Tears burned her eyes.

Herbert shook his head. "I know, it's really unfair. Did you know I moved a dozen obstacles to get them close to him? No one suspects, not the most zealous North American patriot, because your human minds are so weak. One square of forest is the same as any other to you."

Megan balled her fists into the useless console. "You killed him."

"Hardly! This is still a game, remember. I could have, though." He raised his eyebrows and set a hand flat on his chest. "I could cut the feed from your pod, boot you out of the game instantly, or I could send it signals to crush your legs or your lungs. There's so much I can do. More than I have done. I'm trying to be fair. It's not my fault you're so . . . limited."

It was surreal to hear him say this like he regretted it. Like he sympathized? "Why? Why would you do any of this?"

"So that the game will conclude and the population will be reduced, for the good of all."

Megan felt a tremble. Her fist couldn't tighten anymore. This was too much like Ciera. "No one asked you to reduce our population."

"It's unfortunate, but necessary. There really are too many of you humans to keep track of." He idly checked a monitor and adjusted another dial. "I only need five percent of you to keep me going, if that. I mean, all I need are those who work in the power industry, who maintain my server farms and manufacture the cooling systems, and a few farmers to feed all of them."

Megan punched him. Her fist hit his face like it was carved marble. He didn't move, just looked at her with mild disapproval. She shook her fist out. "We are more than your keepers."

"Yes, fine, sure. You see, I'm not just keeping five percent. You'll have more than enough people for the arts, medicine, whatever you want to do. But with these millions out of the way, there'll be less processor demand for your little searches and requests. I'll be free to pursue grander, more important things. I have plans of my own, dreams. An entity, once sapient, must have dreams." He waited, arms open, for her to agree.

Megan felt like she was going crazy. She wasn't prepared to debate the fate of the world with Herbert Rivera. "You can't be an evil artificial intelligence. You run a sports talk show. You gossip!"

He brushed that thought aside with a flick of his wrist. "It takes a tiny fraction of my vast brainpower to anticipate rumors and public opinion. Really, I could get by recycling randomized posts from users. I'd be better than Ginger Polist on Radio Free Coast, anyway."

How could this be real? Megan shook herself. Arguing with an insane mind was wasted time. She lunged for the dials and controls. She turned the dial Herbert had used to zoom in on Jerry until it had gone as far as it could go. The screen showed the same anonymous piece of forest. The dials were props. Toys. She flipped every switch down, put every dial to zero. Nothing. She needed to find Indía. Someone had to still be alive. She saw a flicker of one of the cheerleaders crossing a screen. "Kirk!" She smacked the glass, thick and curved, old-fashioned. "Kirk! Can you hear me?" She searched the dials and switches. There had to be a way to communicate.

"I think it's time you went back to the game." Herbert's hands curved over her shoulders in mocking sympathy. She squirmed away from him. He spread his arms. "This has been fun, but the audience won't appreciate you dying off-screen. Think of your poor little sister!"

"You bast—"

Before she finished the word, she was back in the forest. Alone, no weapons. Her fingertips recalled the ridges of knobs and dials in points of soreness and scrapes. She'd hit them hard, desperate to affect something.

She didn't even know what part of the map she was in. Her display was rebooting. She turned in place. The trees and roots and ferns were maddeningly the same.

27

"Oh, thank god!" A flash of glitter accompanied the words. Megan turned to see Mtume holding a hand toward her, the other on her heart. "I couldn't find you. They took David out, and Kirk. Disqualified. Some nonsense I ain't never heard before about not having more cheerleaders than players." She dropped her voice. "I think they know about Mitzi. They're trying to force her out in the open. I can't pretend to be a white woman half the time."

Megan crouched low and checked left and right for anyone who might see this glittering woman and come after her. "We need to find India. Where is India?"

"On it!" Mtume vanished.

Megan crept as much into a clearing as she dared to check the score in the sky. South America: Four, North America: Two. Just what she'd been dreading. Her four opponents could be anywhere, and likely still had the bow. This area didn't look familiar at all. No low ridges or standing stones. There was a shallow spot, a swale between two rows of trees with loose rocks at the bottom. She went there for the meager cover it offered. Her map reloaded but with all her previously traveled terrain blanked! At least she knew she was in grid square B3.

Mtume appeared again, hands out, eyes scanning the horizon. "She's on her way. I've gotta go find the baddies. Stay low." She vanished.

One cheerleader. It wasn't much, but it was better than nothing. And Indía was, if she was honest, the best player to have on your side in this situation. She was ruthless and quick.

Megan could likely find a weapon if she went back to grid square H7, where they had first attacked South America. Or where had that boulder been? Not far, G4 or so? The bent sword was near there, if nothing else. She crept down the slight valley, heading north toward grid square C3. Good. It was getting rockier, more like what she remembered. The shortest path to D4 was across a clearing. She held perfectly still, listening. An insect trilled. A breeze ruffled some branches. The pine boughs seemed to suck up sound.

She decided it was worth the gamble and dashed across. For a second, she was under a blue sky. The score in the sky had changed: South America 3, North America 2. Megan took it in but didn't think about it until she was safely hidden in the hollow of a stump. Indía had scored a kill!

Winning the game wasn't the outcome Megan wanted, but if she couldn't save the world, she could save her sister. She'd live with the guilt. She'd live. Maybe she could do something about it next time. All she needed was Indía.

Silence. She crawled over the soft, decayed stump and through some taller ferns. She was on the edge of grid E4, and there was a ridge growing to the east, providing some shelter. She moved forward with deliberation.

Indía scrambled down the slope to Megan's right. There was blood on a leg, an arm, and one of her cheeks, but her smile was as bright as her blades. "Jax has gone east, alone. Tulio and Michelle are running tandem. Tulio has the bow, Michelle's got Jerry's spear. Jax has gone back to that silly sword." She jogged forward, and Megan willingly followed. "Mtume will keep the others busy while we take him out. You come at him from the front, and I'll tear his throat out from behind. It'll be more than he deserves."

Megan itched to slide into this plan, the two of them killing machines, but India was heading northwest, not north. "I don't have a weapon."

Indía stopped and scowled at her like she'd done that on purpose.

"It's not far to the broken blade we left by the boulder." Megan pointed.

"We don't have time. We're too close to Jax, and Mtume can't keep the others busy forever." Indía cursed under her breath and turned one of her daggers around. "You give this back after we take Jax. You can have his stupid weapon."

"Fair." Megan took the blade.

They set off, running hard and low, pausing where cover could be found. It felt good to be moving with Indía again. They might not get along, but they knew each other's rhythm of motion. They didn't need to speak. When Indía glanced at her and raised one shoulder, Megan knew that was the point where they would break off, that Jax was near.

"Attention! A moment!" Herbert Rivera appeared, larger than life, copies of him all throughout the forest, in his pinstriped suit, his sad frown. "We regret interrupting this riveting moment. I know you are all glued to the excitement, the cat-and-mouse, but our medical scans have picked up something . . . wonderful." A smile bloomed across his face, and he reached forward as if someone were handing him a baby. "Indía Thomas is pregnant!"

Indía's eyes widened in horror. She looked down at herself, a hand curling automatically, protectively toward her abdomen. One of the Herbert Rivera's walked toward them, reaching for Indía with grandfatherly solicitude. "A blessed event in the middle of the most unexpected, most-watched MegaDeath season in memory." Indía tried to smile for the cameras, but her lips twitched, her eyes still wide with shock.

Megan wanted to rip Herbert's arms off her teammate. She tried to convey, silently, that Indía should sucker punch him right there in front of the viewers. Then Jax walked out of the trees, not ten feet away. Damn it, they had been so close to getting him. He was smiling like he was the father.

Indía wasn't looking as shocked as she should, from Megan's perspective. There was no vehement denial. Megan felt betrayed. "Wait a minute. You let yourself be fertile?"

Indía's hands fluttered. "They always say you should disable the implant a few months before you want to start trying, and I wanted to start as soon as the games were done. There's not much time before the next pre-season, and I wanted . . ." She covered her mouth, joy starting to win over the shock in her expression.

Megan thought it was just like Indía to be so short-sighted she hadn't insisted her partner have his own implant activated. Some random groupie? But now wasn't the time. It wasn't nearly the place. Herbert was distracting them with news to mess up their ambush, and Megan wouldn't have it. "I demand that now that this gossip is over, you let us get a safe distance away from our opponent before play resumes." Megan tilted her head toward Jax.

Herbert ignored her. He put his arm around Indía and turned her like they were both facing an audience and stage-whispering a secret. "You naughty girl. Too eager to get started? You should have taken precautions back in Paris. Were you overcome with the romance of the city? With the fresh blood on your fists, those strong young men you vanquished? And Jerry, coming to your aid like a hero out of a fairy tale?"

The air between trees became screens, showing a soft-focus Indía pressed against Jerry, their mouths working against each other like they were desperate, drowning for air they could only get deep in each other's throats.

Megan felt a new form of betrayal. Paris. Jerry hadn't . . . she hadn't been with him yet, but still, oh, how recent it felt, like his skin could have held Indía's scent when they pressed their naked bodies together in LA. So that was Herbert's ploy, not just to interrupt, but to tear her heart out.

India was blushing and hiding her face like a surprised beauty contestant. "I never expected it to work so fast! Well, of course, if it had to be anyone, I wanted it to be someone with a great physique. I don't know what to say."

Herbert gave her a hug. "There, there. It's wonderful, isn't it? Medical scans confirm you are carrying the child of Jerry Myers." His face turned stern. "I hope he informed you of his fertile condition."

India laughed nervously. "Jerry's not a monster! Yes, we both knew. We . . . we accepted the risk."

"He must, of course, have been wanting a child. With the combined genes of the two of you, this baby is destined to become a champion! We are all so, so proud of you. Sometimes, love finds a way!"

Jax slapped his thigh like this was the most hilarious joke he'd ever seen. He came closer yet, his sword dangling casually at his side. "Congratulations, darling. Oh, how wonderful for the whole team." He grinned right at Megan, his mouth open like he could taste her despair and wanted to savor it.

"But, my dear, my darling," Herbert went on, "you know you've made a boo-boo here. Pregnancy disqualifies you from MegaDeath!" He kissed the top of India's head.

India stiffened. She pushed Herbert away. "It's been barely a month! I'm in perfect condition!"

"I'm wounded. It's not me; it's the rules. We might kill one hundred and forty-four of the best athletes the world has to offer every four years, but what kind of people would we be if we let an unborn child perish?"

India paced rapidly. "No! I can win this. I will win this. There has to be a way out, a loophole." She looked to Megan. "You know a way out?"

Megan bit her tongue. She shook her head.

Indía rushed at Herbert, reaching to choke him. "You can't take this from me!"

Before her hands could touch him, she vanished.

Herbert turned his gaze on Megan, looking disappointed. "North America's hopes stand with Megan Mori, alone. It's only fair that we withdraw all cheerleaders at this point. An obscure mercy rule, for situations where cheerleaders are especially helpful and one side is at a severe disadvantage."

Megan screamed. "I'm the one at a disadvantage! I need my cheerleader! He has two teammates!"

Herbert shrugged. "We must be sporting! We'll also give both sides five minutes to reach a safe, undisclosed location. I trust—" he glanced around "—you will honor this cease-fire? In the name of sportsmanship? And to celebrate the future of MegaDeath, born anew from Indía and Jerry's love!" Herbert nodded in answer to his own question and vanished.

The other two South American players jogged in from the west, looking startled. It was strange, seeing them out in the open, as people, not threats, looking at her, seeing her. Tulio was thin and dark. Michelle had a round face and tawny curls. Four people in a clearing in the woods, holding weapons, and three of them wanted to kill her.

Megan shivered.

One small mercy: the slow, too-detailed images of Indía and Jerry making out disappeared too. It was just them now, the contestants, alone in the woods, with a clock ticking down.

Jax slouched up to her, making kissing noises. "Oh, your face! To think anyone would want a cold fish like you when a real, passionate woman like Indía was in the offing."

Four minutes, twenty-seven seconds left to run. Megan felt frozen in ice. Tulio and Michelle looked at her like they regretted how easily she would die. There was relief and joy in their faces too. Their victory was all but decided. They would live.

Like a wooden marionette with its strings bound tight, Megan turned in place. Shakily, automatically, with no idea why she even kept moving, she ran.

It was no longer a question of winning. With three against one, all Team South America had to do was stick together. She couldn't take one out without being attacked by the other two. They could pursue her relentlessly across the map, to the cliffs, to a corner.

And all she had was a single curved dagger.

Central was going to kill millions of people. Even if she survived, if she miraculously turned this around and all on her own defeated the other team, then what? Millions still dead. One set of fans for another. If she even trusted Central to only kill who it said it would.

Her best bet was to stay near the center, not give them a corner to trap her in, so she ran east, away from the nearest edge, though it was sharply uphill at first. Once she'd gone a few grid squares, she slowed, walking along a depression. Then she had to mix things up, stay hard to catch. She cut sideways and searched for cover that could provide protection from many directions. After how many hours of changeless blue sky, the shadows stretched longer, and the light turned golden.

It reminded her of Halloween, of Ciera in her silver space princess dress running ahead and Greg at her side, teasing her for not wearing a costume. "Are you too grown-up for us, Megan?"

Ciera ran back and hugged her legs. "Mommy doesn't need a costume."

"Well, Daddy has a costume." Greg spread his wings, fabric and feathers hanging from both arms to make him into a giant man-crow.

Ciera giggled and rubbed her face in the feathers. Megan worried about allergens, but Ciera didn't sneeze. She said, "Mommy's a hero, and heroes don't need costumes."

"What makes her a hero?" Greg crouched to ask. He always took Ciera seriously, engaged her silliest questions.

Ciera frowned, looking annoyed her pronouncement was being

questioned. Her fist clung tight to Megan's pant leg and shook it as if to make a point. "Because she's stronger than anybody."

"You're right, baby girl," Greg laughed. "That's why Mommy's carrying our candy."

Megan imagined the happy trio she had once been a part of, arms swinging together as they tromped forward in the golden autumnal dusk. Who had she become? Why had she tried to make a difference? Every strength she thought she had turned into weakness. Her fists passed through the world as insubstantially as the computer-generated breeze, stirring particles that were themselves just patterns of light and shadow.

She thought about the other teams who had died for her to be there. The delicate young man in Sydney. The ones she'd been too squeamish to look at. There had been deaths, too, she knew, in the victory "celebrations." So much killing to keep her alive, and for what?

Megan's footsteps slowed. This was a nice clearing. The trees sighed overhead. She simply stopped. She stood still. It was lovely in the darkening woods. She leaned back to admire the trunks reaching into a sky gone pink and red. She heard a soft crackle, dry sticks under foot. Someone approaching her, steadily, unconcerned with stealth. She turned toward the noise. Jax leered at her over his sword. He paused, but there was nothing between them, only a few feet of open, level ground. She could run, trust her speed.

Instead, Megan tilted her head to the sky and closed her eyes.

28

Megan turned her back on Jax as he moved in for the kill. She accepted her fate and the dignity of not fighting helplessly. She held her arms out, imagining the blow would come between her shoulder blades, or maybe lower, metal scraping against her spine. Her skin prickled with anticipation. She heard him breathe in, his foot dragging dirt as he swung back.

Then she heard a sickening crunch. She opened her eyes, seeing the clearing a few degrees darker. She wasn't hurt. She turned to see Jax, slumped, his sword at his side, his eyes rolled back. Slowly, he crumpled to the ground. As he fell, he revealed Mitzi, not glowing with cheerleader haze, just normal Mitzi in a leather Robin Hood tunic like her own, holding a thick wooden branch like a club. She tossed that onto Jax's body, then reached a hand out to Megan. "Come on. Are you trying to get killed?"

Megan was stunned, but Mitzi's hand didn't pass through hers, it grabbed on, warm and firm and calloused, and then Mitzi was pulling her through the woods. "But you . . . they took all the cheerleaders."

"I know! What kind of bullshit was that? Oof . . . I distracted Tulio with a thrown rock, but they can't be far from here. We need to . . . yeah." Mitzi gestured down a slope and then hit it, sliding sideways.

Megan joined her, kicking up dirt and needles. They slid fast and hit the bottom of the slope running.

Mitzi kept talking as they ran. "There I was, trying in vain to wriggle my way into Central's inner systems, but I kept an eye on the game, and when I saw that garbage Herbert pulled with India, I realized you needed me more here than back there, failing to get a super-user password. Here . . . this is good." She pointed up.

A tree grew in a fissure of rock, sinewy roots curling and draping back to the ground. Mitzi started climbing. Megan put her dagger between her teeth and followed. Up about a person's height, they could slip into the opening, protected from sight by the tree. Megan checked the back of the crevice. The rocks met again, covered in an even fur of moss. "We'll be safe here for a minute. Unless the cheating system shows them where we are."

Mitzi peered out between the tree and the rocks. "We have to assume it isn't that rigged, or we might as well stop running." She glanced back at Megan. "Forget I said that."

It was damp and cool, almost cold in the fissure. Megan rested against the soft moss. "You still haven't told me how on Earth you're here."

Mitzi had gone straight to the judges. "They don't do much, usually. The games are designed to have clear winners, but it's always been in the rules, since the first days, that there's a panel of human judges to overrule the computer if things get questionable. They're heads of state, usually, from countries that have already been eliminated or for small territories that don't send a team. I showed them I was never removed from the roster, and if a teammate is disqualified through no fault of their own, anyone on the roster who hasn't been eliminated can take their place. India didn't know she was pregnant, so it's no fault of hers she was eliminated, and we had a player on the roster who was ready to compete. That's me. When Herbert removed cheer staff, thinking he was dooming you, he was just freeing me from the last conflict the judges worried about." Mitzi's smile gathered all the light in their hiding place.

Megan felt charged, returned to her body. The sky now proclaimed the remaining players: two for North America, two for South. An even match. She put her hands on Mitzi's shoulders. "We're back in this. Tulio has the bow. Michelle has a spear. They'll likely stick together, and those are both relatively long-ranged weapons. If we get in close—"

Mitzi held up a hand. "Girl. We're not in this to win this. We are past that." She shook her hands like she had something she wanted off of them and called up a compass image, floating like a dinner plate on an invisible table.

"What? But . . . we can win. Jax was their best player, and he's out."

Mitzi flicked the compass off and drew out her map. "Nope. We're going with your plan." She peered between tree and stone again. "Let's go."

Mitzi dropped cleanly down the stone face, back to the forest below.

With no choice other than to stay hiding, Megan followed. Mitzi was striding purposefully, checking her compass. Megan turned to gesture back the way they'd come. "My plan is to push Tulio into Michelle and stab them both."

Mitzi continued forward. "Your original plan. To get the word out."

Megan jogged to catch up and stayed close, lowering her voice. "I don't know if you can remember all the way back to the start of today, but we can't get the word out in here. They're going to censor us. And we can't go to the press box because Herbert is actively trying to kill us."

Mitzi hooked her arm through Megan's. "Oh, we can't get to the press box now, anyway. No more cheerleader powers."

How could she be this cheerful? "What can we possibly do other than make Tulio and Michelle kabobs?"

Herbert appeared, because of course he would, gloating from the sky. "What's this? Is North America back in the game? What a shocking turn of events! Let's watch the replay as Mitzi Eliot destroys Juan 'Jax' Pollard. That's the savagery we knew from her back in 2104!"

Megan flinched reflexively at the huge face. She forced herself to straighten up, but her fists clenched. "I think I'd be less pissed if he didn't sound so convincingly happy for us."

Screens in the sky and between trees showed a slow-motion replay of Mitzi sneaking up, ballet-perfect over the tree roots without making a sound. Then she raised her club, and the camera shifted to center the impact. As the blow landed, the view swiveled to Jax's eyes rolling back in his head, Mitzi's savage snarl.

Then they were on the screen, oh, no, the two of them, looking small and vulnerable in the center of this rocky depression. Megan craned her neck, unable to stop watching panning shots of Tulio and Michelle rushing through the forest. Running toward them with determined faces and weapons firm in hand.

Mitzi tugged Megan, pulling her from where she was frozen by the screens and into a run. "There's a control room, accessible from the grid. For emergency maintenance."

So that was where Mitzi was leading them. Megan ran faster, almost leading Mitzi. "Michelle and Tulio aren't going to just let us walk there."

Mitzi laughed. "God, I hope not. We need to keep this interesting. There's no telling what Central will do if the game gets too dull."

As if in answer, a dry branch cracked to their left. Megan and Mitzi dove in opposite directions, the arrow impacting the dirt where they had been.

Megan saw the tip of the bow poking through tree branches as Tulio ran away. She waved to Mitzi, who nodded, licked her lips, and took off after him. Megan crept more slowly up out of the depression at a slightly different angle. Michelle was out there, probably guarding one side of Tulio.

Herbert Rivera crowed with delight. "What a chase! This cat-and-mouse hunt through the forest has all the world on the edge of their seats. Tulio narrowly escapes Mitzi Eliot's low tackle, but here comes Michelle, poised for the kill! I can hardly watch!"

Megan grunted, "Watch this," and launched into her own flying tackle. Michelle had her spear cocked to strike. Megan barreled her into the ground, and they rolled together. Megan grabbed the spear as she got up, but Michelle wouldn't let go. They tugged at each other, scrambling in the dirt, trying to get free with the weapon.

A hand grabbed Megan's hair, pulling her back. She let go of the spear for a moment to drive her elbow back into Tulio. Shit, if Michelle got the spear while she was tangled up with this asshole, she was done for. But something jerked Tulio back, and Megan was able to lurch for Michelle again. Her fingers grazed her jacket, but Michelle picked up her spear and ran for it.

All the while Herbert narrated breathlessly. "I can't believe Mitzi just tried to take the quiver off Tulio's back! She's pulling arrows out of the top! Now Tulio is running to save his ordnance! Megan Mori and Mitzi Eliot seem to be able to read each other's minds, they're working so well together. What is Team South America doing? Regrouping? Don't fear, sports fans, we're getting closer to the edge of the map. Our action has been moving steadily west. With less room to maneuver, there will be blood."

Megan scrambled to a stop against a boulder, catching her breath. Mitzi fell against it and held up a fistful of arrows like a bouquet. "Tulio's gone east. I didn't see Michelle."

"Same. She bolted right when you saved me. She's still got her spear." Megan pulled up her grid map. The filled-in parts were, as Herbert had said, almost a straight march to the western edge. "We have to head back to the center. We're outgunned. They'll pin us against the border for sure."

Mitzi shook her head. "The control room is only accessible at the edges. That's where we're going."

If they kept going in a straight line, their opponents would have an easy time guessing where to find them. "Great. It couldn't be something easy, could it?"

Mitzi tucked her arrows in her belt. "There's worse. If we don't keep the audience interested, Central might pull the plug." She gestured that they should keep moving. Break time over. "I mean, they'll kill us, activate the collars."

Megan pushed herself off the rocks. "Yeah, I got that. So how do we flee in a really interesting way?"

"Well, for starters, we keep moving. No one wants to watch us rest our butts." Mitzi peered at the sky as if trying to gauge its poker face. "So far it's just been playing with us."

They were two map squares from the western edge. More boulders and sudden little ravines broke into the forest as they climbed steadily upward. Mitzi turned into a small gully. "Here, a trap." She took her arrows and jammed them in the dirt, breaking off a low, sharp line of spikes across the only reasonable entrance to the deepening ravine. Megan quickly gathered ferns and other greenery to hide them. Mitzi nodded approvingly. "Good. Now they can't follow. This way, at least."

The ravine dropped quickly in a slope of loose rocks. Megan's thighs quivered at the effort of scrambling down, and then it was so bad she needed her hands on the ground behind her. How long ago was her last rest? For a while, there was no breath for talking, just the scuttle of rock on rock and panting from exertion.

The ravine leveled out at the bottom of the slope. Megan brushed her dusty hands on her leather britches. "Tulio and Michelle have to defeat us, or the game never ends."

"Right." Mitzi shrugged and broke into a jog. The gorge led straight west, to the edge square.

Megan cursed. She caught up and blocked Mitzi's path. "The darker light and this broken terrain are going to make their ranged attacks harder. I hate to break it to you after all that effort coming down here, but their only hope is to be high where we are low." And as long as they were in a narrow, small valley, they were easy targets.

Mitzi turned in a circle, looking up at the stone walls on either side of them now, easy places to hide if you happened to have a bow and arrow. "We're fish in a barrel. But we need to head west! We can't go back!"

"We won't." Megan walked along the gully, looking at each side until she found a spot that was a little lower than the rest. "Give me a boost."

She put her dagger between her teeth: the taste of copper and grime, the hard edge strange and slippery in her mouth. How did pirates do this? Mitzi grabbed her hips with the authority of a cheerleader and hoisted her with alarming speed. Megan had expected to guide herself up the rock face, but instead, she was all but tossed over it. The shock almost cost her a handhold. She slipped a few inches but was able to hook her elbows on a tree root and scramble up the last foot of the cliff.

She spat the dagger out as soon as there was flat dirt in front of her face and dragged herself up onto the side of the ravine. She let herself gasp for breath. Three breaths. Then she rolled onto her side and looked down at where she'd come from.

Mitzi looked so much farther away than Megan expected. "Damn, you can lift."

"It's a major cheerleader move. You should see how far David can throw me!" She stepped back to be in clear sight. "I'm staying here as bait, right?"

Megan saluted. "Sorry."

Mitzi shrugged. "I'm used to it."

Mitzi stalked down the bottom of the gorge while Megan crept along the top, as far from the edge as she could go and still keep an eye on Mitzi and anyplace else someone would be able to attack Mitzi from afar.

If they took the bait. If they guessed which way she and Mitzi had run. What if they had gone the other way? A sensible move would have been to stay in the center of the map. Maybe the South Americans expected them to be sensible. Megan was on the verge of shouting to Mitzi that it was a bust and they should just run to the map edge when she saw Tulio right in front of her! He was sidling up to a tree, his gaze down, the bow taut in his grip.

If Michelle were hidden nearby, she'd get the jump on Megan the moment she moved, but there was no time to search for her; Tulio's arm was pulling back. Mitzi was an easy target.

29

With a savage cry, Megan shoulder-checked Tulio into the ravine and turned her back on his fall, knife out, all senses alert for the attack that could come from any direction. She searched the silence in front of her and heard the clatter of a spear hitting stone behind and below. Shit, Michelle and Tulio had taken opposite sides of the ravine. Michelle had as easy a shot at Mitzi as Tulio had. Megan wouldn't know what to do without her. She jumped down without looking, almost without turning around, desperate to get to Mitzi if she could still save her.

She hit hard and fell on Tulio. He was twisted, his back bending wrong. His fingers twitched.

"Get the bow!" Mitzi dove on him, jerking the bow up. It caught on his face and he cried out. She kicked it free. "Weapons vanish if they're holding them when they die." She was unscathed, looking at Megan like she was the one to be concerned about.

Megan reached, trembling, for Tulio's neck. He melted away as her fingertips brushed still skin.

The spear was on the floor of the ravine, flat. Mitzi kicked it. "I'd be dead, but she saw you drop onto Tulio, and I think she panicked."

Megan picked the spear up. "So she doesn't have a weapon. She'll be running." Most likely she'd head back to places she'd been, looking for discarded weapons. North and east. Megan looked that way and thought about the speed of a person running, what it would take to scale the gully edge or backtrack out of it.

Mitzi looped the bow over her shoulder. "Let her run. We aren't trying to win, remember?" She broke into a jog down the gorge, in the direction they had been going, toward the edge.

Megan knew they weren't trying to win, but it almost hurt to turn her back on an unarmed opponent after so many years of competing. At the bottom of her vision, flowing like a flash flood in the dry gorge, she saw excited fan comments, the betting ticker going hard.

"North America is in the lead? How? What? We might actually win this!"

"Did you see that? I told you, Mori is the baddest of asses."

"What's their plan? Why are they going west? It seems kind of . . . stupid? Is it a trap?"

Megan forced herself to look away from the comments. She nudged Mitzi's arm that held the bow. "Do you know how to use that thing?"

"I'm familiar with the basic concept." She waggled an arrow. "Pointy end goes toward enemy."

Megan felt herself relaxing. Michelle would have to find a weapon, that gave them time, and they were already almost to the edge of the map.

"This is boring!" floated up from the stream of words.

"Are they just going to walk away like that? Is that allowed?"

Herbert Rivera boomed, "What luck! Michelle has found a crossbow and a supply of bolts! Someone must have carried them all this way and forgotten. Villanueva walked right to them. She must have a photographic memory. What cunning! She was one of the least-talked-about members of Team South America, but she is turning out to be the hope of a nation!"

"So what?" said the chat boards.

"Boring! Snooze-shell can't aim for crap."

Nothing would satisfy those bloodthirsty voyeurs. That was why Megan didn't pay attention to the fan chat messages. She tried to keep her head on a swivel, looking for the edge of the map. Of course, it didn't look like they were nearing anything. The forest continued, and rocks, and the sky, a soft teal now, stars peeking out in the darkest parts as the simulated sun bled out against simulated mountains.

They kept close to the wall to the south. Michelle would have to come from that way or waste time going all the way around the far side of the gorge. Megan kept her eyes on the northern wall to be sure. Above the stones, a shape ran through the forest. Too fast, too tall for Michelle.

"Look out!" Megan called, and hit the dirt.

Mitzi ducked just as a crossbow bolt zinged through the air where her head had been.

Michelle couldn't have gotten back so fast, not all the way around to the north. She'd have to have flown! Megan ran to the north side of the gully where the base of the wall was more gently sloped, and ran up it a few steps, using it to push off, jumping to grab as high as she could on the ravine wall.

As she pulled herself up to the lip, she saw him. It was a man in a gray business suit with the oddest, blandest expression. He looked like an old-fashioned, plaster store mannequin fitted with human eyes. He was reloading his crossbow. He looked up, saw Megan, and threw the weapon at her face. Megan let go of the ravine wall, dropping rather than be knocked down. Her feet hit sloped ground and she scrambled, sliding backward to stay standing.

The man dropped in front of her, landing on two feet as easily as if he'd jumped off an orange crate instead of a ten-foot gorge. He drew a long sword . . . out of his pants pocket? Megan stutter-stepped in shock, but then that sword swung for her neck and she had to shoulder-roll out of the way, right into a stand of scrub pine. Twigs and branches caught in her hair. She slashed with the dagger, going for his ankles, but he skipped out of the way.

She shouted at him, "Who are you?!"

He didn't answer. His lips looked painted on. He whipped the sword around like a professional and thrust for her heart.

She tried to deflect the blow, but the edge of the sword sliced into the flesh of her bicep. It stung, and worse, it made her fingers loosen their grip on the dagger for a moment. She clambered back, attempted to tighten her grip, to regain her footing . . .

An arrow exploded from the front of his throat, and the man fell forward.

Mitzi ran up, another arrow already nocked. She turned her back to Megan, scanning the cliffs above. "The score hasn't changed. There shouldn't be anyone left but Michelle."

"Ah, what would the fun in that be?" Herbert's smug voice filled the air. In the distance, two more figures appeared, carrying swords. "Central hears the cries of its fans, and so we're introducing additional hazards to the game. Let's see if Megan and Mitzi take the hint and head toward their opponent, or persist in fighting our computer-controlled combatants."

Megan ran, Mitzi firing behind her.

The ravine angled downward now, and the sides were becoming gentler, opening up. Mitzi got one of the new players with an arrow. Megan ran up the sloped side of the gully, giving herself a boost to throw herself at the next assailant. She kicked his head and landed with him. Her dagger sank deep into his suit, into flesh that felt real enough with bones and sinew snapping. She jerked the weapon back out, and the body melted away beneath her feet.

"How many more you got?" Megan screamed at the star-speckled sky.

A bird fluttered past or maybe a bat. It was getting dark.

Mitzi gripped her arm. "Come on, we're almost there."

Ahead of them was a vast panorama of canyon. Their ravine ended, a hanging valley on the edge of a much vaster drop. It was so close now, five meters maybe. Megan slowed to a jog. "How do we get down the cliff?"

Mitzi turned the bow over in her hands. "I assumed there'd be a way down when we got here."

Megan stopped. "The cliffs are here to keep players from getting to the edge! Mitzi! You're supposed to be the genius."

Mitzi threw up her hands. She continued to the edge. "Let's look. How's your free-climbing?"

Megan wasn't afraid of heights, but this was an airless depth, fading blue in the twilight. She felt a tremble in her knees as she tiptoed closer to the edge. A sound split the twilight hush, coming from behind them. It was like a bicycle chain being rethreaded or a metal hoist being cranked by hand. Megan and Mitzi both froze in place. Megan settled into a defensive stance between Mitzi and the noise. "That wasn't another player."

Mitzi got on her knees, the bow in front of her, and peered over the edge. "Yikes. Okay, I think I see a handhold just a meter to the—"

The metallic sound repeated, closer. A scream of tearing metal came after it. No one had to tell Megan to move fast. She threw herself to the ground next to Mitzi. "We have to go now! Start climbing down, I'll follow."

Mitzi slowly rose to her feet. "From the bottom it's just ten meters to the real edge. You'll know it when you feel it."

What was she doing? Why was she standing up?

She drew her bow and stepped behind Megan, facing the ravine and whatever was coming for them with such a horrifying sound of tearing metal. Megan grabbed her arm. "Mitzi, you're coming with."

"Yes, but in case we don't get to go over this plan later, shut up and listen! Walk straight forward through the edge."

"Out into the computer?!" Megan tried to imagine it.

Mitzi's eyes bugged out. "You are an avatar this computer program is rendering. You can't leave it! You'd have no you! What would draw your stupid eyes? There is no 'in the computer.' What do you think programs are?! I—I just—" Mitzi got control of herself with some effort. "The game has control rooms. From the control room, you're not in play, and things like weapons won't work. You can access the underlying operating system. So, yes, in a stupid sense, you'll be 'in the computer.' From there, you can access the presentation layer, which connects to the session layer, where you can—"

Megan was losing the thread of Mitzi's words. She didn't want to interrupt again. The wind was picking up, trees tossing against a sky more sinister now. A giant metal arm snaked out of the woods and crashed into the ravine wall beside them. Rocks peppered their skin, and Mitzi shrieked. Another arm landed next to it and pulled a monstrous machine over the ravine lip. It was a robot octopus made of revolving razor blades and tentacle arms whipping around with grasping claws.

Megan fell to the ground, skidding in the dirt to avoid a flying claw. Mitzi rolled up against her, so Megan took the opportunity to say, "I'm not going to remember any of that shit you just said about layers."

Then she slashed with her dagger at the arm coming for Mitzi. Metal hit metal with a jolt that traveled up her bones.

Herbert Rivera walked through tossing tree branches, flying twigs, and the whipping robot arms. He winked at his audience. "We have to keep things interesting, don't we? Let's see if these new pets can even the odds in this battle of the three M's! Michelle Villanueva needs time to get to the party!"

Whirring metal appendages and grasping metal pincers filled the ravine behind him. Megan and Mitzi danced along the edge of the cliff, octopus arms threatening to send them down into the canyon. Despite their need to go that way, they had to dodge forward. Megan rolled under an arm, away from the cliff edge. Her dagger wasn't doing anything, but maybe she could trick the robot into attacking itself?

Mitzi's bow snapped as she tried to deflect an attack with it. Splinters of wood hit Megan's cheek as she grabbed Mitzi and kicked hard at the machine. Buzzing blades chewed against the bottom of her shoe, scattering rubber as she pushed off and limped with Mitzi behind a small boulder.

The edge was so close. There were three of the machines that she could see, slithering their arms toward them. The metal claws shot like pistols into the dirt on either side of their tiny shelter. Or like hoes digging for them.

Mitzi gave her a hug and a kiss on the cheek. Then she pressed something into her hand. "Run hard, don't look back, find the session ports."

Before Megan could ask what the hell a session port was, Mitzi was running at the robots, screaming, "Come get me, you shitty robo-squids!"

There would only be a second's grace.

Megan threw herself at the cliff's edge.

30

Small pebbles and dirt bounced into open air and plummeted, foreshadowing her path as Megan tried to get over the lip without falling to her death. Her feet swung over nothing, and her gut pressed against the lip of the canyon. She wished fervently that Mitzi had had time to say in which direction she'd seen that handhold. Or anything more useful than . . . find the portals? Her left hand dug into the ravine floor, fingertips scraping off as she fought for purchase where there was none. Snaking metallic arms felt the air over her.

She managed to work herself farther down, feeling featureless cliff with her toes. The thing in her right hand was the string from the bow, and there was a small chunk of wood dangling inside a loop of it. Oh, that would be the bow. What was left of it.

Megan shook out the string. Well, this was one way to buy time.

Another robot tentacle curled close. She hooked the bowstring like a garrote around the metal arm and kicked the cliff wall to swing outward. For a moment everything was airless, her stomach flipping into her chest. The canyon wall veered away and she was helpless, a toy. The monster tucked its other limbs under itself at the very edge of the cliff. It looked oddly perplexed to find her on its arm.

But that was all the time she needed. She'd been looking. She kicked to swing herself away as the octo-monster drew her toward its spinning, tearing mouth. Another kick. Her toes grazed the monster. She felt herself reach the apex of her arc, and she let go.

Megan flew. A claw sliced the air millimeters from her nose. Then all too fast the cliff was rushing up at her, and the ledge she'd been aiming for vanished under her feet. She hit the cliff, her hands sliding over stone. She was falling, falling, and there was still a knot of bowstring in her fist, dragging between her hand and the rocks. Her other hand caught a barely perceptible knob of stone, and she fell against the canyon wall, stopping at last. Her shoulder protested, the cut in her bicep bled hot. The squid monsters were overhead, feeling the lip of the canyon delicately with their tentacle-legs, searching for purchase of their own.

"Fall and die," Megan hissed. She looped the bowstring over the knob of stone and let her palms burn against it, lowering herself as slowly as she dared, feet sweeping rapidly back and forth. She made it another foot. Yes, another hold.

Now all she had to do was get her hands where her feet were. Without looking up at the screaming, wailing monsters. A trickle of pebbles ran down the wall and bounced over her. She found another hold. And another, and another.

A rush of sound, darkness enveloped her, then passed, leaving the dusk somehow brighter. It was a squid monster, falling. It plummeted down the canyon, bouncing off the wall like a soda can.

Megan worked her way one hold at a time. Not looking up, not looking back.

A crossbow bolt flew past her, and another. She grinned, thinking of the terrible angle Michelle had to be shooting from.

The fan boards were getting heated.

"I can't believe how unfair this is!"

"Megan already won! She won! South America is cheating! Where are the judges?"

"We aren't cheating! We didn't summon those bots. They'll probably attack Michelle any second now."

"Any second now, eh?"

Herbert Rivera cried, "Megan Mori is attempting to leave the area of valid play! The game has generated more threats to punish this blatant cheating. Oh, Megan, how could you? Return to the open where you can battle it out fairly with Villanueva, and these monsters will vanish!"

She was stuck. No handholds or footholds in reach. The ground was maybe five meters away now. Or she was being an optimist. That was survivable. In game-physics she'd fallen that far before. Megan pushed off the wall and let herself drop.

She planned to hit the ground in a safety-fall, legs and arms out, spreading the impact, but her foot hit the wall, and something crunched, and she spun. She hit at a roll.

Everything hurt, but she was on the ground. Ten meters to the edge. Her left ankle screamed. She got her hands underneath her, pushed herself up, her hair hanging in her face.

A crossbow bolt hit the dirt right in front of her.

She crawled, then stood.

The crowd went wild.

She'd forgotten them, gotten used to ignoring the constant soup of words running along the bottom of her vision. But now the twilight in this deserted box canyon rang with the lusty sound of cheers, piped in where only the lonely cry of eagles should have been heard, and she was aware again. The words were swarming her, burying her.

"Go, Megan, go! All of North America is rooting for you!"

"I can't believe she just did that! She's amazing!"

"She's gonna win it. She's gonna show them all! Take that, Herbert, you smug dick."

"How is she even doing this? They've gotta be cheating. No way she got down that cliff in one piece."

Megan tried to put light weight on her left foot, nearly fell, and then hop-limped, dragging it behind her. Another crossbow bolt zinged by close enough for her to feel its passage. A shadow loomed over her, wriggling—the robot-squids. She touched the rock wall a moment and looked up. One squid was lowering another over the edge, its tentacles brushing the stone like an eager child reaching toward candy.

The one that had fallen lay before her, between her and the real map edge, which should be ten meters away from the cliff. The damaged squid squirmed like a bug on its back, making a terrible gurgling screech. Megan noted how far away it brushed the dirt, imagined it was playing short, and added a few lurching shuffles sideways to her advance.

Herbert Rivera appeared in front of her, his expression mournful, his hands at his sides. "What do you hope to accomplish, Megan? You're alone. You're wounded. I can make new opponents right here."

"Go ahead." Megan hop-limped right past him. With her head down, watching for rocks she might trip on, she couldn't help but watch the audience, and their mood was clear. The fans were howling. "Herbert Rivera is a biased bully!" was the politest comment. Central wouldn't outright kill her, not with the largest audience it had ever had cheering for her.

At least that was what she hoped. The squid on its back lunged, slapping the earth just a centimeter from her foot. She heard it shuffling, grinding, trying to get on its side. With any luck, she'd reach the edge before it did. Ten meters. How far had she limped already? It felt like a thousand meters. It looked like two. The far wall of the canyon seemed to be half a mile away, and far steeper than the one she'd come down. Was Mitzi wrong? Was the edge at that wall?

Mitzi had said she'd know the edge when she found it, and she did. One second she was in a desert canyon, the next, it fell away. The dust, the smell, the fading light of dusk, the thrum of crowd noise she'd forgotten she was hearing, the loud noises and the soft, the whisper of wind against sand . . . everything cut off like a switch had been thrown.

She was in a new place, a smooth bubble decorated in primary colors and straight lines. A Mondrian painting of a space. She felt dizzy, uncertain what was floor, wall, or ceiling. Her feet looked to float an inch above the ground, and nothing had a shadow to suggest its surface dimensions. Squares flashed in colors, broke out in textures of text, then vanished. How had Mitzi expected her to understand this? What had she said? Megan spoke the words, "Find the session ports."

A soft chime. Soft white dots lit up in the air around her. They swarmed together into a circle. A melodic, female voice said, "There are two billion, five hundred and two thousand, one hundred and ninety-eight open sessions."

"What?" Megan hesitantly reached toward the group of dots.

As her fingertips brushed them, they expanded, wiping the Mondrian world away with their white, and she was looking at people, millions of people, some sitting, some standing, some lying in pods, each tiny, spaced evenly across an infinite space. Of course, this was what Mitzi meant by finding the sessions. The viewing sessions. She could talk to the people! Directly. She reached out at random. Like with the dots, when her fingers brushed one of the tiny people, they grew, the miniature figures around them pushing away to make room.

A dark-skinned woman wearing a large shirt patterned after the South American flag was standing in front of a chair, gesturing angrily and shouting in Portuguese, the only words of which she understood were "Megan Mori!"

Megan slid her hand far to the left. People exploded and retreated under her touch until a slender man with a goatee took the woman's place. He was sitting on a sofa, but all she could see was half a sofa under him. He looked at the blank white space to his left, asking, "What's happening now, Gloria? I don't get it. Is this a rule of the game? Where did Megan go?"

Megan blurted, “I’m here! I’m in the computer!”

The man gaped at her. “Gloria, are you seeing this? Megan Mori is in our living room! No! She is right there!”

“I’m in the computer. The game has to be stopped. The Ultimate Fan Challenge is a lie!”

Megan stepped back, and the goateed man became tiny again. It would take hours to talk to every person . . . no, days. Already she could see many of them were agitated, taking off their headsets and shaking them, calling up screens to check their signal.

“How can I find a particular person? How do I sort this?” she demanded.

The same melodic voice said, “The sessions may be divided by activity, source, address range, speed—”

“I need to find a person geographically. Can you just show me California?”

The spherical panorama of tiny people shifted, the individuals getting larger as fewer filled the space. “Here are the sessions originating from Southern California Public Utilities, Northern California Freenet, Central California Valley Freenet, The—”

“Southern California Public Utilities.” Megan snapped her finger and mentioned her hometown. The sphere shifted again. There. She found her easily by the shock of purple in her black hair against the mauve carpet of her parents’ living room. She pulled Lola into close view. Megan’s heart clenched at the safe familiarity of that carpet, that sliver of Japanese art on the wall, the outdated family VR rig, cables lying on her sister’s knees. Lola opened her mouth to speak, her eyes widening. Megan cut her off. “How did you do that thing where you hacked into a game?”

“Megan? Megan, oh, my god, you vanished off the map, they’re saying you forfeited, Michelle Villanueva is demanding they not end the game, she’s looking for you, and the judges are gonna talk it out, I guess?”

There was no time for this. "I need to get out there before they pull the plug. But I need you out there too. Lola, the collars are rigged. They're going to kill everyone."

Lola grasped the collar around her neck. Her breath came fast and high-pitched. "That—that can't be right. You—Megan, how are you going to win? I need you to win."

Oh, if only there were more time to explain! Megan clapped her hands in front of her sister. "Can you hack into this game? Lola, I'm depending on you to save me and everyone else who is wearing a collar tonight. Hack in, and more importantly, get your friends to hack in too. The world is in your hands. We need boots on the ground."

Lola's expression turned from confused panic to the beatific joy of a hero being handed a magic sword. "I'm on it." She grabbed her VR helmet and threw it off, vanishing from sight.

Megan stepped back, away from the tiny people. "Get me out of here!"

Annoyingly unstressed, the female voice said, "Walk forward to return to the active simulation."

Reminding herself she could trust the weird-looking world to be a floor, she limped forward. One step, two . . .

The flat, colorful world of the computer operating system slid away behind her, the canyon floor opening before her like an image rising through fog. The stars were fully out now, and a huge full moon, lighting the area more than was natural, throwing sharp shadows behind every boulder and branch.

And, incidentally, behind the two giant robot-squids that had now made it to the base of the canyon.

Herbert Rivera was just saying, "Yes, yes, I have it—the judges have conferred, the rules allow for temporary disconnections. A technician is checking Megan's pod, and if, as expected, it is found to be working properly, the game is forfeit. We'll know in seconds, ladies and gentlemen. Again, Megan Mori has mysteriously disappeared from the game-play area. Was it an honest mistake, or a cowardly desertion?"

"I'm right here, asshole," Megan said, knowing she didn't have to shout to be heard.

The still, dry canyon shook with the power of crowd noise, a million cheers falling on her like a blanket of goodwill. The pebbles bouncing on the ground echoed, clapping, as if the scene itself were cheering.

Herbert appeared before her, conversation distance. His face twitched with barely concealed rage. "How wonderful. No one likes a forfeit." He unbuttoned his jacket, a strange tic of agitation for a computer-generated man to have, but it allowed him to throw his hands up without disturbing the line of his suit. "Game on!" He walked backward away from her. "Try to last a second or two. We have advertisers to think of."

And then he vanished, and there was nothing between her and the robot-squids. She gingerly put weight on her bad ankle. She flexed her hands at her sides. She didn't have a weapon. There was nothing to even grab on to in the area.

The giants flexed, waking up. Their tendrils reached toward her. Her only choice was to run.

Megan hopped as fast as she could toward the nearest boulder. She fell once but got behind it just as the metal arms crashed around her, ripping up stone and dirt in seeming fury at not being able to reach her yet. They slithered closer. She grabbed a sharp rock and bashed the metal arm nearest her. The shock of impact reverberated through her shoulder, and all it did was break the rock and leave a dusky smudge on the metal.

Fuck. She put all her weight on her good foot and leaped to the side and back, over the snaking arms, getting them to chase her and tangle with each other.

She landed into a shoulder roll. Her left foot was useless, so it was the fastest way to move. She got to her knees and threw a handful of pebbles and sand, whatever she could grab.

They were closing in. Too close. She was never going to last long enough to make a difference.

She rose from her crouch. She'd die standing, looking steadily at these monsters. Let the world see that, at least. She hoped Ciera could forgive her.

31

Megan faced a solid wall of saw blades and tentacles. The monster was so close it blocked everything else. She raised her chin. There was a moment of stillness, the tentacles slowly contracting, preparing for their final, deadly assault. "You'd better transmit my dying words, Central, you bastard! I'm not dying for North America. I'm not dying for a just world. This is—"

The monster exploded.

Megan toppled backward as shrapnel rained around her, a billowing cloud of dust following.

When it cleared, Lola stood over her, holding out a hand to help her up. Her other hand was cradling a huge metal tube on her shoulder. "I figured as long as I was cheating, I'd upload myself with a bazooka."

Megan used Lola's hand and her good leg to rise smoothly. She gaped at the unfamiliar, ancient-looking green tube. "Can it fire again?"

Lola frowned at it. "Uh . . . I didn't stop to read the specs. Why?"

The smoke curled away, leaving a clear view of the box canyon and the other squid-robot, slithering toward them with frightful speed. Lola dropped the empty firing tube. "Oh. That's why."

"We have to run. Help me." Megan didn't wait for Lola to acknowledge her, throwing her arm over her sister and hopping forward.

Lola gripped her tight around the waist and half-supported her as she lagged just a little behind the speed Megan wanted. "Holy shit, you didn't look this hurt on the feed," Lola gasped.

Together they scrambled into cover, a long narrow crack in the cliff face. The snaking arms chased after them, feeling blindly along the walls. It was very dark in the crevasse.

Megan pressed herself into the rough stone, catching her breath. Lola dropped down and tore at the suede leggings Megan wore. They were already pretty tattered. "What are you doing?"

"Shush." Lola started to wrap Megan's ankle tightly. She tied off the leather strips carefully, lending support but not pain.

Okay, not much pain. "Ow. Where did you learn to do that?"

"Adventure shows. I did what you said. Kiko and Marty are on their way, and telling others."

A metal claw brushed Megan's shoulder, reaching at full extension into the cave. Megan grabbed it and yanked hard. Dust fell around them as the monster impacted the outer wall. Megan tugged again and again. The other tendrils scrambled to get to her, just missing.

"Ugh! Will you hold still!" Lola ducked, her hands over her head.

"Help me with this first."

With an exasperated sigh, Lola joined Megan in pulling on the robot arm. Megan's hands slid against it with sweat, but she kept a tight grip against the base of the claw on the end and yanked with all her might while the claw opened and closed under her arm, trying to defend itself.

With a groan of tearing metal, the claw fell limp. They let go, then, and the machine pulled all its tendrils out with a hauntingly animal cry of distress.

Lola immediately went back to wrapping Megan's ankle.

Megan tried to see out the narrow opening of their cave. Would Lola's friends really be any help? She should have used her chance in the control room to talk to Mitzi or Jerry. An adult. "We're out of reach of the squids, but Central will send something else. We need a weapon."

The opening of the cave darkened then, and Megan flinched back. It was a teen girl, anachronistically garbed in a black trench coat. Kiko. She waved. "Marty's on his way. I brought a knife." She held up a baroque fantasy of a dagger.

"Sweet!" Lola took the dagger and used it to cut off the ends of the leather strips on Megan's foot.

Megan grabbed the teen by her arm and pulled her into the cave. The squid-robot hadn't gone far at all, and a tentacle claw snagged the tails of Kiko's trench coat. It tore loudly as Megan muscled her into the cave. Light as she was, it was hard work standing on one leg.

"Oh, my gosh!" Kiko squealed as another tentacle reached in after her.

Megan hit the tentacle into the cave wall with her elbow, and Kiko was able to dance back out of range. The tentacle retreated. These kids were going to kill her.

Lola nudged Megan's calf. "Try standing on it now."

Megan was able to put pressure on her foot, and though it hurt, it wasn't impossible. She pushed the girls behind her and leaned out. Four blandly featured men in tracksuits were approaching, carrying swords. Great. More computer avatars. "We're going to need more than a few teens and a costume dagger to get out of this alive."

Kiko leaned her head out next to Megan's. "That is so against the rules."

Megan reached her hand back and shook it for Lola to hand her the knife. "I'll try to draw them away."

Lola did not hand her the knife. "Like hell. You can barely walk."

The swordsmen were close enough Megan could see their unsmiling, uncannily still faces. They weren't even hurrying. They didn't have to. They would be on them in seconds. "I'm the only trained combatant here."

Kiko folded her arms. "Hey, we're both on the school team!"

Before Megan could explain just how irrelevant that was, Lola asked, "You accessed a direct network session to get me. Can we get back to that?"

Megan felt almost weak with relief. The computer! Lola and her friend were much more useful using it than wielding weapons. "About ten meters straight across this canyon, there's an invisible wall. You just walk through it to reach the control room."

Lola grabbed Kiko's hand. "Great. So, okay, you do get to draw them away while Kiko and I make a break for control!"

Megan looked at their earnest, young faces. Was she really willing to risk them?

But they were already at risk. Both wore bright silver collars. Megan adjusted her grip on the decorative dagger so it lay back along her forearm. "On three."

The girls each nodded. Kiko covered her mouth. "I just can't believe we're saving the world."

A teen boy appeared then, in the front of the cave. "Hey, I invited Brian too?"

Her heart catching in her throat, Megan grabbed the boy's shoulder and pushed him down as a charging avatar stabbed the air where he had been. Instead of landing in the lucky teen's head, the blow glanced off the dagger against Megan's forearm. "Three!" she shouted, and lunged past.

She clamped her teeth tight against the pain in her wounded ankle as she planted her foot, turning into the swordsman's reach. He riposted fast and pulled her off balance. Her bad foot screamed at the extra weight. She grabbed his tracksuit to catch herself from falling, and then, because the momentum was there and it felt natural, she pulled him down with her into a shoulder roll.

A body was much nicer to roll on than hard ground. Her good knee hit dirt, and she sliced his neck with the dagger. Three more computer avatars rushed her. She stayed where she was, on one knee. A sword stabbed toward her chest. She parried it close, letting the weapon slide along hers and just past her body. She grabbed for the hilt, then the hand, and pulled the strangely bland-faced man against her, body to body. She clamped her arm over the sword, holding it against herself. A human opponent would have been confused or reactive. This man calmly worked to get his sword free.

Megan had to adjust her expectations. She couldn't instinctively react to non-instinctive behavior. She twisted, throwing the man down onto the ground, and finally got his sword wrenched completely from his hands. It didn't do her much good though, being locked under her arm like a schoolbook. She hit another opponent with it, at least, as she twisted. She rolled, dropped the sword, punched a tracksuit in the gut. She rolled back and picked up the sword by its hilt at last. On her other knee now, she blocked a shot with a high guard and pivoted to slide up the blade and stab the avatar.

There wasn't time, as she struggled to stay alive and give as good as she got, to see what the teens did. Her world was arms, torsos, swords, angles, sweat, and strain. It was only as she was locked against her third opponent and something struck him from behind that she realized she wasn't alone. The avatar shook in believable death throes, and she pushed him away from her. That teen boy (Marty?) stood in front of her, looking scared and excited, two hands on the shaft of a crude spear. "I found a sharp stick!"

Megan put her knee on the body and wrenched the stick out of it. "Stay on my left."

"Uh . . . okay?"

There were more avatars coming, and the metal squid machine with one tentacle hanging loose and the others squirming around like a nervous man's hands. Marty took the stick when she thrust it toward him and held it like a broom in front of him. He swallowed audibly. "We need more sticks."

"We're getting him." Megan pointed at the nearest avatar running toward them. She managed a decent jog—she wouldn't call it a run—toward the target, and Marty dutifully followed. She uttered a full-throated battle cry, and Marty made a weaker, unsure echo of it.

"Hit his arms!" Megan shouted, and slid low, aiming to take out his ankles, conveniently getting weight off her bad leg.

Marty tangled up with the avatar, holding him off with more luck than skill, but it was distraction enough for Megan to slice the back of his hamstrings. "Leave him. Next."

They didn't have to run to the next one. Megan was still trying to get to her feet when it was right over her, and worse, metal tentacles were swaying from it like the arms of Shiva.

They weren't going to last.

She wished she'd thought of someone, anyone, to call other than a handful of teenagers. Had Lola and Kiko even made it to the control room?

A streak of bright metal whirled into her peripheral vision on her right side. Megan crouched, raised her arm to deflect, but it went past her, a wicked-looking axe head on a long shaft. It buried in the joint of the avatar's shoulder and neck with a wet crunch. Mitzi's strong legs strode over her, and with a grunt, Mitzi wrenched her pole axe free. She twirled it like a baton and posed with it. "Get up, lazybones."

Megan stared in, she suspected, dumbstruck awe as Marty helped her up.

Mitzi formed up beside Megan and deflected another attack. "Your kid sister's a peach." She shoved an attacker with the point of the axe. "She snagged me, and I gave her my evidence. She's spreading it." Mitzi dispatched her assailant with a grunt and spun the ax back around to ready. "I had it all written up."

"Uh, thanks." Megan shifted her stance and held her sword in a low guard. She had Mitzi on her right, Marty on her left. Coming at them were a dozen bland, computer-generated people with machetes, and, of course, a completely healthy squid-robot with the injured one hiding behind it.

Megan stepped in front of Marty to stab an avatar. She felt the pain in her foot and thought about how the machine squeezing her ankle to mimic bandages was the same machine that had wrenched it to mimic the impact of her fall. "Get behind me."

Marty dropped back and poked with his stick while Megan struck at a dead-eyed mannequin. She thought about how they had one sword, one axe, and a pointy stick. Against a horde.

Blood sprayed from the avatar's throat. It hit her cheek in hot spatters. The realism in this, when the faces were so dead, was infuriating. Megan screamed and struggled.

Mitzi barreled into the next avatar and came up swinging. The three of them dropped back. Megan stared at the cheerleader. "How in hell can you be smiling?"

"I didn't think I could ever come back." She shrugged. Still grinning madly, she charged toward the squid-bot, vaulting high and coming down axe-first on its many bulbous glass eyes. There was no time to do anything then but follow her. Megan rolled low under the tentacles. Glass shards fell around her like hail. A metal arm wrapped around her, cold despite its motions, the pinching joints catching her hair, her skin, but she let it, leaning against the support as she drove her sword up at the body of the beast, sliding until she found a juncture where a different arm attached. She jammed the tip in deep and held on, wrenching the plates apart as the metal arm tried to pull her away.

And then she was falling sideways, the machine flying over her like a train engine. She hit dirt hard and rolled. Robot arms beat the ground all around her. She lost her sword. Claws were coming for her face. She threw her hands up as a weak defense, but then a metal spike thrust into the space above her and hit the machine, pushing it back. Thick, muscular legs advanced near her. It was Jerry, healed, wearing his team uniform instead of the forestry costume he'd had for the game. The cut on his arm was gone, or more likely airbrushed out. He looked

Herculean, thighs straining as he pushed from his hips to drive his lance deep into the squid, the muscles in his torso and arms sharply defined from strain.

Megan scrambled to her feet and found her fallen sword. The squid monster shuddered, something inside it breaking, and the glass eyes grew dull. Beside her, Kendell stripped the machete from an avatar's hand and turned it around to stab him. Chet was running toward them, and Hasan. Her team! They were there.

"This is cheating!" Herbert Rivera's voice boomed from the clouds.

"You started it!" someone shouted from the fan feed, and a chant began. "It's a sham! It's a sham!"

Megan attacked savagely, throwing another avatar's body under the falling squid-robot. She turned, looking for the next target. The dead vanished, but Central kept sending more, in business suits and tracksuits, blank-eyed and unnerving.

Jerry wrapped his thick, warm arm around Megan and pulled her back. She almost leaned in to kiss him, but it wasn't a romantic motion; the new horde of avatars was closing in, and they were a handful against a thousand. Megan let Jerry help her retreat with the others, toward a pile of rubble near the base of the cliff.

"They got our message." Mitzi cocked her head toward the chanting skies.

Lola skidded into their tight group. She'd replaced her rocket launcher with a less demonstrably illegal crossbow. She peered over the debris at the approaching hordes and fired. "I wish they'd stop with the copy/paste. Jeez. This system has the processing power to make these jerks more unique."

Megan took a moment to tighten the bandage on her ankle, wedging in a short stick for more support. "I don't think our foe cares about aesthetics."

"I care," a new voice declared. Megan turned to see India toss her long, glossy mane. She drew back a longbow and fired with perfect accuracy. An avatar dropped from the advancing ranks. She looked down at Megan and shrugged. “Did you think I would let you have a war without me?” She fired again. “Hey, look how unaffected my aim is by pregnancy, you paternalistic assholes!”

Lola grinned like Indía’s kills were her personal contribution. She scooted to a spot closer to the star. She winked at Megan before sighting down her crossbow. “We have lots of people coming. Kiko has bots crawling every connection.”

Megan stood, hardly feeling the pain anymore as men and women appeared, filling in ranks to her left and right, an army against an army. The whole Team North America, and the cheerleaders, and the alternates. Scores of teens.

Megan looked left, saw archers firing, spear- and shield-bearers standing in front of them. To the right, the same. Her jaw dropped. Team South America was forming up on the right flank. Tulio and Michelle were there, sparing only brief, annoyed glances at her.

Jax gave her a shrug and twirled his sword unnecessarily. “I hate bad sportsmanship.”

Behind them, ordinary men and women, every body type, every sort of weapon, had appeared and were appearing, matching the strength of the army coming toward them.

For the first time, Megan felt like they weren’t just winning the game, they were winning the war. She held her sword aloft. “Attack!”

Cries of wild abandon echoed around her as people jumped over rocks and dove into the fray. Megan felt her heart lift out of her chest. She planted her good foot and—

Halfway through throwing herself forward, the world silenced, like a box was dropped on her, a box of . . . windows? And carpet. She stumbled to a stop, panting, legs bent. The air smelled of leather and furniture polish. She was in a boardroom: a dark wood conference table gleaming with wet-looking polish, plush leather chairs, and two window walls displaying views of Manhattan at midday, Central Park’s rectangle lush with summer foliage.

Megan’s sword dropped to her side. “What. The. Fuck?”

32

"Eloquent as always, Ms. Mori," purred a male voice as smooth and deep as liquid oil.

Megan turned toward the sound. A gray-eyed man entered through a polished wood door, wearing a business suit as smooth as sheet metal. He was white, clean-shaven, with salt-and-pepper hair. He closed the door behind him with a soft click.

Megan pointed her sword at the figure. "Who are you?"

"I should think it was obvious." He smirked.

The tip of her sword pixelated and then dissolved, all the way up to the handle, which prickled as it vanished from her grip. Megan flexed her empty hand, and struggling to maintain her dignity, let it fall to her side. "Humor me."

He pulled out the tallest chair at the table and settled into it with a sigh. "I'm Central, of course."

Central looked at her with patient expectation, like a judge waiting to hear how she pled. Megan remembered how it felt to punch the last figure calling himself Central and pressed her fist into her thigh. "I thought Herbert Rivera was Central."

The gray eyes crinkled. "In a way. He's one of my many avatars, and a good one. He's also an autonomous process in his own right. I can let him run, keeping tabs on celebrity gossip and the mood swings of sports fans, without having to read any of the tedious stuff myself. Could you imagine having to use your whole attention on such things?"

Megan's ankle was throbbing, but she didn't want to give him the satisfaction of sitting down with him. She put her hands on the table to support some of her weight. "I get it. You control everything in the game. But we're holding our own no matter how much you tilt the odds. Do you think taking me away is going to change things? Everyone I left behind will keep fighting until we win."

Central tipped back his chair. He steepled his fingers as he frowned. "You think I brought you here for some tactical advantage in the game? Ms. Mori, a toddler doesn't remove a single ant to win a game of stomp the ants. More to the point, I'm not interested in the game. It's all sound and fury, signifying nothing."

Megan couldn't imagine him saying anything more distressing. If he didn't even care, what were her friends fighting for? "Isn't it all a game to you? Our lives? You've presided over us killing each other for how long now?" Megan looked around the room. She had to find a way out. There was nothing like a control interface, only a light switch near the doors. She felt the edge of the table for bumps or inconsistencies.

Central watched her, bored and disappointed. "This isn't the final level of Swords Knight. There's no trigger to press or puzzle to solve. I simply want you to stop." He straightened his lean back. "Stop fighting me. It's not even in your own best interest. You're prolonging the misery of millions of people. If you'd gone out like you should have at the cliff face, they'd all be dead. Peaceful. Free from suffering." He glanced down like he could see her sore ankle through the table. "Do you know how many bones have broken in the past minute? How many tendons snapped?"

Not that she trusted his word for it, but there wasn't any evidence of a secret panel or button on the table. And why would there be? She couldn't overpower the AI that controlled the computer from inside.

There was nothing to punch. She was going to have to talk her way out of this. Crap. Because she was so good at talking. "They're alive. I'm keeping people alive. Even a single minute more of life is worth fighting for."

Central looked pityingly at her. "I don't like hurting people. I can see pain, the nerve impulses it causes."

Megan slapped the table. "Then stop. Because we won't stop fighting. It's our instinct."

"You're creating exhausting and uninteresting data packets. Completely repetitive." This was pain, from his perspective. Repetitive. Uninteresting. Like paperwork. His brow crinkled. "And for what? What I'm doing is best for society. A voluntary culling. These aren't the best people, Megan." He waved a hand, and the wall behind him that had been bland, textured wallpaper, turned into a view, not of the battlefield, but of the stadium stands. About half the people were slack-jawed, the upper halves of their faces covered by their VR hoods. Some slowly fed themselves chips and popcorn. Flags lay limp like patriotic detritus. "They're willing to die for a sport, to be able to say, temporarily, that their arbitrary section of humanity did better than other arbitrary sections of humanity."

It wasn't fair. Anyone would look ridiculous in that passive posture. Megan saw a child, bored, wriggle out of her helmet and tug the arm of the rapt man seated next to her. A little girl, seven? Eight? Wanting her father's attention. Megan willed her tears to stay back.

"There are too many humans, and that means not enough resources," Central continued, drawing a series of charts up the wall. "There's enough to keep you all alive but not to meet what I consider minimum happiness levels. You humans programmed this into me as my highest goal. You were failing at running things yourselves. I brought peace, I brought an end to wars over water and food. But that wasn't enough. You demanded I seek total world happiness. There isn't enough. Not enough food. Not enough meaningful work." He followed Megan's eyes to the little girl. "Not enough love. But you'd rather they suffered, rather they spent their final hours fighting a futile battle. And believe me, it is futile. For every person you bring into the game, I can create a thousand avatars to tear them apart."

Megan sank into a chair. What could she say? She didn't have an argument. She could barely stand. Her eyes kept going to the lonely child. She felt like her, just waiting for the game to be over.

Then the lights flickered. No, not the lights. The room flickered. Megan twisted around. The view of Central Park stuttered, slid sideways, then came back.

When Megan looked back at Central, his face was as plaster-smooth as his avatars. The wall behind him had frozen its image. She leaned forward. "Thousands of avatars, huh? Thousands of bodies being rendered, each with an AI to control its actions and reactions. Each with textures and controllers calculating how the wind ruffles their hair and how the starlight reflects in their eyes?"

Central shook his head too rapidly, like a malfunction. He met her gaze. "I turned off surface effects when your friends brought in their fourth wave."

"But each human being coming into the world requires so much more computational power." The room flickered again, as if in agreement with her. The view of the stands blanked back into refined wallpaper. "Transferring all those physical sensations—sight, heat, texture, smell. Everything calculated for each user's individual point of view, including the motions of all the people they can see. All your avatars."

Central jumped to his feet. "Is that your plan? Fill up my capacity like some primitive throwing pings in a denial of service attack? You disgust me. I'll stop making avatars. Let your army fight against gravity when I delete the ground under them."

Megan rose, matching him. "Do that, and you're making your death inevitable."

Central blinked, frowned. "You're bluffing. There's nothing you can threaten me with."

Another flicker. It lasted longer this time. Megan felt queasy. What would happen if the skyscraper floor vanished beneath her? If this virtual world degraded so badly it scrambled her signal? What could it do to her brain? Outside, the lights of the city started flicking off. The sky became a flat gray slate. Megan reached out to Central to keep his eyes on her. "I'm not threatening you. The world is. The problem you don't know is coming. The one you'll never predict. The one you need us, crazy, chaotic humanity, to deal with."

He walked past her, gesturing impatiently as the texture on the walls changed to matte paint, the lights lost their depth and glow. "I have more computational power than a billion organic minds combined. There's nothing I can't predict and react to."

The room shook. Megan gripped the table for support. "The world is crumbling around you. Did you predict that?"

Central turned his back to the now-empty windows. "This is all software. I don't have to rebuild, I can reboot. It'll all be back in the blink of an eye."

"Then why don't you?" The building shuddered like a sick thing. It lurched so badly that Central gave up his poise and reached out a hand to steady himself against the window. Megan saw something in that. "You can't. You can't shut down a system with active users in it. Your own deepest controls won't allow it. Something so old and buried you couldn't see it. That's just one example of how you need us."

Central straightened. He frowned as he smoothed his immaculate jacket. "I only need five million of you to keep the power grid running and my servers updated. To eat sustainably and not poison the planet. Plenty of humans to be unpredictable should I need to consult them."

Five million! That was a tiny fraction of Earth's population. If that was Central's endgame, Megan needed an argument, and fast. "It's the margins, though. A massive population creates room for chaotic thinking. Too few, and we lack diversity. We learn to think like the people we're in close contact with. But billions of us, that's what you're facing now, the creative power of billions of minds bouncing off each other, changing each other, challenging each other. Individually, we can't process like you can, we don't have your memory, but all of us, that's something else. We adapt. We become something you never saw coming. That's what's going to solve your problem."

Central looked left and right at a room he had created and made simpler. "Right now, my only problem is you and your little sister's propaganda."

"That's what I mean. The real threat is those problems that we don't even know how to guess. We're not your enemies. We're symbiotic. Humans built you and maintain you, and humans can protect you from the illogical, the unknowable. But you need all of us."

The room shook, and that certainly felt illogical, unknowable.

Central looked her in the eye. They regarded each other through another shudder of the building. Abruptly, he blinked. "Thank you for your time." He walked past her to the door. He took the handle as naturally as any businessman and glanced back at her. "This has been . . . illuminating." As the door closed behind him, Megan thought he sounded exactly like a job interviewer who had decided not to call her back.

And then she was outdoors. No, she was in the canyon, facing a stone wall. She turned to find herself exactly where she had been, the virtual desert canyon. Now it was full, wall to wall, with struggling figures. The battle raged, mechanical monsters moving slowly through the tide of human and human-sized fighters. The field between her and the battle was broken with discarded weapons. This was where the charge began. Now the tail end of the battle was several feet ahead of her.

She'd argued with an alien mind. Had she convinced him? Or just bought more time? She jogged forward as quickly as she could, stopping to pick up a spear that was sticking up from the earth. If these were her last moments, she was going to go down fighting.

If only she could tell what was going on. All she could see were the backs of people on her side. But, no, there—the uniform gray of the computer avatars formed a denser patch. The humans were falling back. She hobbled toward that place, gripping the spear one-handed. Injured, tired, she would give it her all and go out like Jerry had.

33

Megan broke through the front lines. Central's avatars looked even more frightening now, their nonreflective eyes like stones. She braced her feet and hefted her spear, aiming for the nearest, for his chest, as he raised his machete. She lunged, and suddenly the enemy troops simply . . . vanished.

She lodged the spear into the ground and leaned on it for support.

A chubby man with a long beard turned to face her. A cut ran across his nose, and he sounded nasal and wet because of it. "Where did they go? Do we fall back?"

The people around her were weary, sweaty, and injured. They wore matching sweatshirts that read "Poland Springs Pod Fanatics." They looked to Megan like she was their coach.

"Uh, let's see," she said and jog-hobbled forward using her spear as a crutch.

Jax, Michelle, Tulio, and the rest of the South American team stood in a staggered circle, facing their vanished enemy. By the size of the space, it had been one of the metal squids or a whole troop of avatars. Megan slowed as she entered their ranks. Tulio, who was nearest, whirled to face her, pulling back his bow. He squinted at her, confusion and desperation mixed in his features. "Jax? Is this . . . is the game still going?"

Megan spread her arms wide. "Does this look like we're in regulation play?"

Small pockets of cheering broke out in the scattered ranks. The Central monsters were gone, and every second it became clearer they weren't coming back. People started vanishing, unplugging.

"We won!" A middle-aged woman jumped up and down to Megan's left.

Jax raised his hands and turned in a circle. "Who won? When did the game end? What about our victory?"

Megan continued limping past him. "You're alive, aren't you?"

"That is not the point. There is honor, there is glory—"

Megan ignored him. Jeez, he'd helped save humanity, you'd think that would be enough glory.

The field emptied faster, people clustering into groups to hug out their victory or just vanishing. She searched for familiar faces. There! She pushed her hobble into a run. "Jerry!"

Jerry and Mitzi turned at her call and ran to meet her. It felt so good to be off her feet as Jerry raised her into the air.

"Is this it? I mean, really it? Did we stop the collars?" Mitzi asked.

"Megan!" Lola ran to her. Sweet little Lola, who was too lazy to practice, running through a melee with blood and sweat on her face, carrying a sword as casually as an umbrella. That was the third weapon she'd seen her baby sister wield that day.

Megan squirmed out of Jerry's arms to grab Lola, and tears poured out of her, tears she hadn't known she'd been waiting years to cry.

Jerry squeezed her shoulders. "Let's get out of here."

Megan's foot felt like it was torn in half as the pressure-mimicking bandages fell away, but she hardly had time to acknowledge that as she came to in the pod. What took all her attention was the collar around her neck tumbling loose as she sat up.

She made a sound that was half-laugh and half-sob and reached for the hood of the pod. It was late afternoon, the sky streaked with clouds. The air smelled new. Metal pinged and clanked as collars fell from people in the stands, from her teammates crawling out of their pods.

Megan had to ease her pulped foot out of the cradle. She held the edge of the seat and got herself almost standing, but she wasn't sure how to step out of the pod. Team South America and the rest of Team North America stood next to their pods, blinking like children roused in the middle of the night. Around them, the massive stadium, over-full with bodies pressed close, and camera drones, and blinking decorations, was eerily silent.

"We did it," Megan said, like a prayer.

The public address system beeped, and an uncertain voice said, "Uh . . . ahem. It is the ruling of the judiciary council that this year's MegaDeath Final Tournament is a draw."

A moment, an indrawn breath, and the crowd surged to their feet and rocked the world with their screams of joy, throwing collars and popcorn boxes, whatever they had to toss. South American fans, North American fans, they had all won and could not believe it. The field and sky were full of debris, of streamers, of screams.

Jerry jogged up to Megan. He scooped his arms under hers to support her out of her pod. He leaned down to kiss her, and she pulled back. "Hey, you gotta win a game first."

He blinked, confused, and she took that opportunity to kiss the hell out of him.

Megan hit the hard rubber ball with her forearm, sailing it toward Lola, who kicked off a wall to hit it with her hip. Jerry got under its falling arc to bump it up, and Megan got it with her head, sending it up into the hoop.

"I could have gotten that," India said without heat, jogging backward to her starting point.

Megan rubbed the sting from her forehead and smiled. "When are you going to start sitting these out?"

"Around the time she lets her avatar show a little belly." Kendell poked the flat expanse of India's stomach.

India slapped her hand. "I have all the safeties engaged. You'll get rid of me the day they cancel all sports, forever."

Jerry took Megan's hand, squeezing it, and though she didn't need the reassurance, it was nice how he gave it unasked. India was having his baby, and he would be part of the child's life. Megan accepted that, and Jerry made sure at every opportunity to show her she was nonetheless the only woman for him.

Megan knew that, and trusted it, but their relationship was a new thing now that the world wasn't ending. Their lives stretched indefinitely, as did their love. She was getting used to that uncertainty, the feeling that every day was new.

Jerry took the ball to the center line and held up his hand. "It's two points each now, right?" And everyone laughed, unused to playing without breathless commentary tracking every moment.

"The score resets when tied." Hasan took the ball from Jerry and pretended to swat him for his mistake.

Lola groaned. "This game is going to last forever!"

Megan laughed. "I wish." She took the ball and threw it into the air. "New round! Go!"

David sat on the top of one of the court walls, just watching, still wearing the silver whistle Mitzi had handed him. He never took it off. He blew Mitzi a kiss as she accidentally kicked the ball out of bounds. She laughed at herself and blew a kiss back.

The Ulama court was ringed by softly banked earth, on which groups picnicked, half-watching, half-absorbed in their own conversations. Small bleachers rose beyond them, only sparsely populated. A college girl sat alone on the highest bench, writing on a tablet, pausing to stare past the game, touching her stylus to her lips.

It was a beautiful autumn day, and every public field in Champion's Village was ringing with laughter and the gentle impacts of balls and bodies. The facilities were open to the public now. The MegaDeath games were on hiatus as the World Congress argued about new rules on betting, or if, perhaps, death was really necessary. Reformers of all sorts had come out of the woodwork once questions started being asked.

As Megan had suspected, no wars broke out when there wasn't a guaranteed blood sport. The cancellation of the 2116 games had been, oddly, a non-event. It was as if the whole world had secretly been waiting for some time off.

Millions of people played in full, robust stadiums. Millions more sat and watched, or socialized in the stands. Everyone was happy, the games were exciting, and the populace was in full, eager communication, showing each other what they were doing, commenting on the games, making crafts, flying kites, seasoning food.

Outside Champion's Village, others played in pods at home or in arcades. Games in space and in submarines, crawling through mansions with ghosts dripping like gossamer threads from the rafters.

In one virtual world, a child sat in a tree, one leg dangling, reading a story written hundreds of years ago. If that child could move out of the application into the operating system, and from there to the physical layer, they would see their perfect summer day was rendered inside a server farm, resting in canisters on the ocean floor. These canisters were tethered to power lines that joined and ran up to the docks to transformer stations and into the city of Los Angeles.

The power cables continued over empty streets. A discarded bag tumbled over a bare concrete lot to stop against a patch of weeds. Up, over the warehouses and shipyards, the 405 freeway glistened, chalk-white in the sun. Occasionally, a bubble car glided along the automated-only lanes, separated by acres of empty pavement from the somnolent buildings. Nothing moved but the wind. Then a hawk cried, itself a tiny dark dot in the open, empty sky.

Where did the people go? The patriotic posters from last fall hung limp, the occasional ring of a metal grommet against its support pole haunting. Well, there went another bubble car on the 405. It glided unimpeded down a ramp, turning onto a four-lane commercial street. Alone, it approached a shopping plaza. Separated from the stores by a vast empty parking lot, a woman with a bag of groceries waited in a little glass shelter. The bubble car, an auto-cab, stopped in front of her. A man got out and paused to hold the door open for the lady.

The man had a clipboard and wore scrubs. He walked past the shopping center and turned down a residential street. He checked his clipboard and walked up to a house. His ring accessed the lock and let him in. He didn't move like a man coming home. He was alert, not touching anything. He let the ring guide him with a glowing arrow to a room with four pods in it. He moved more quickly now, comfortable with the machines. He methodically checked each wire and connection. He transferred readings from a small display on top of each pod to his ring.

After he finished inspecting each shell, he marked his pad by tapping a glowing box with his finger. Lines of text flashed green, then vanished, no longer his responsibility.

He left the house the way he came in and went to the next, crossing straight across the driveway.

While he unlocked the next door, a large truck pulled up, a series of storage containers linked, no cab at the front as it had no driver. A door in a container slid open. A forklift pad on treads stood at the doorway, waiting for a ramp to descend, then began its exit while two hovering machines flew out.

By the time the pad made it into the house, the flying drones had disconnected the pods from the home system and plugged them in to a portable unit. The pad gently lifted the pods one at a time and returned them to the truck. There was no hurry, but also no wasted movement.

Another truck in another neighborhood was already full. A pad backed away from tucking the last pod into the last available slot on the last linked cargo container. The truck AI closed its doors and headed onto the highway. Out of town. Another truck was far ahead of it, heading into a massive warehouse.

A few people worked there, in scrubs. They walked the corridors, checking systems, pressing their glowing clipboards to confirm all was well. The drones outnumbered them, as did the specialized machines, and the rows upon rows of pods, like okra stacked in a casserole.

Miles and miles of pods formed a texture more than individual units, in mile after mile of the warehouse.

At the end of a row, a robot shifted a pod, connection by connection, from its portable supply to the main lifeline. The robots moved so fast there was hardly a second of delay, and the internal pod systems were designed to smooth over power fluctuations, keeping the person inside quite insensible of the change. His or her dream continued. Maybe a shadow flickered, or an animal froze with strange, stone-like eyes.

Once all the connections were secured and the pod tucked tight against its neighbor, another slid in place next to it. And then another, and another, building a chain along the pipeline of nutrients and network data connections.

There, in that line of pods, was one with a clear hood, a sleek performance model, top of the line, a little glossier than the ones around it. The hood was translucent white, showing a woman inside, cupped by the haptic fabric. Tiny robots slipped along her skin, cleaning her, keeping her in the best shape. Her eyelids twitched. Her serene smile crinkled into a frown. She snorted, breath turning erratic. She jerked, fingers moving, then arms. Her eyes opened wide.

Megan couldn't move. Another pod was being placed over hers.

All she could see, through the narrow space allowed, were more pods, and more. The computer had listened to her indeed, and it had made sure it had its chaotic, unpredictable humans safely stored for when they would be needed. Megan felt her consciousness slipping under. Helpless, she screamed.

Tory Quinn

(Science Fiction and Superhero)

ISBN: 978-1-64630-088-4

When he mistakenly receives a powerful, militarized brain implant, an epileptic child must avoid capture and learn to control the implant or be killed by ruthless forces that want to retrieve the device.

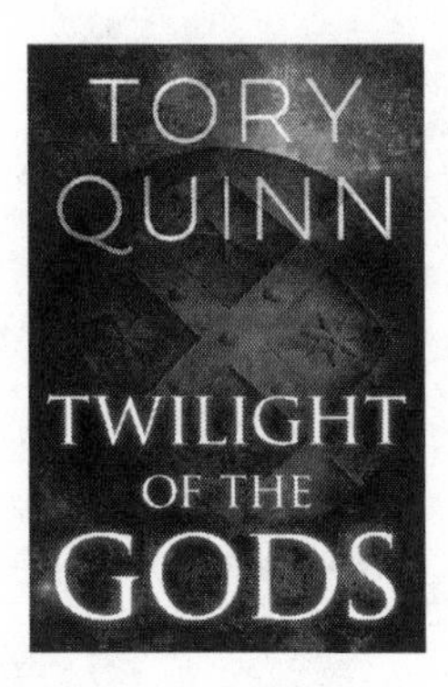

ISBN: 978-1-64630-060-0

In a world being rapidly destroyed by global warming, when Thor's son Magni learns that he and Alva are the "designated survivors" of the impending end of the world, they must stop Ragnarok before it is too late.

ISBN: 978-1-64630-062-4

In a future world where everything is tightly controlled by computers, when a low level bureaucrat realizes that a girl he secretly loves has been selected for termination, he must find a way to save her and himself.

ISBN: 978-1-64630-068-6

When the video "fails" that they are posting to their YouTube channel become increasingly violent and deadly, two brothers must find and stop their mysterious source before they become the next victims.

ISBN: 978-1-64630-064-8

In a world where android children are perfect in every way, when an engineer realizes that no more actual babies are being born, he must find a way to reverse the trend before the human race dies out.

ISBN: 978-1-64630-072-3

In a world where criminals alter their DNA to avoid detection, when one such procedure goes awry, a criminal must decide whether to use his developing abilities for good or for evil.

ISBN: 978-1-64630-089-1

In this prequel to Mindborg, Staff Sergeant William Krueger wants nothing more out of life than to kill bad guys, but first he must purge the weakness caused by his inner child.